Kim stood before his three opponents, totally relaxed.

His adversary lunged, the knife in both hands. Kim pivoted on his left foot, spinning, while his right made solid contact. Before the second knife man could approach to striking distance, Kim was darting forward, one hand closing on the outstretched wrist, his elbow smashing the man's face, once, twice, three times. Kim stepped back to let him fall.

The leader stood alone, a razor in his fist.

Kim circled, amost playfully. He chose his moment and disarmed his quarry with a snap kick. Stepping close, he used a lightning backhand to drop the man in his tracks.

They were still alive...

Bantam Books by Michael Newton
Ask your bookseller for the books you have missed

CHILD OF BLOOD

THE ASIA TRILOGY
Book 1

KOREA
KILL

Michael Newton

BANTAM BOOKS
NEW YORK · TORONTO · LONDON · SYDNEY · AUCKLAND

KOREA KILL
A·Bantam Book / April 1990

ISBN 0-553-28320-0

Published simultaneously in the United States and Canada

Bantam Books are published by Bantam Books, a division of
Bantam Doubleday Dell Publishing Group, Inc. Its trademark,
consisting of the words "Bantam Books" and the portrayal of a
rooster, is Registered in U.S. Patent and Trademark Office and
in other countries. Marca Registrada. Bantam Books, 666 Fifth
Avenue, New York, New York 10103.

PRINTED IN THE UNITED STATES OF AMERICA

OPM   0 9 8 7 6 5 4 3 2 1

To Greg Tobin, for a notion that paid off.

KOREA
KILL

Prologue

Seoul

It made Reese Holland nervous that he couldn't spot the tail.

If he was being followed—and he had no doubt of that—the stalkers should have shown themselves by now. So far, he had not seen a trace of anyone along his track, and that was bad. It told him that the men assigned to hunt him were professionals who knew their job, and that made matters worse.

Still trim and fit at fifty, battle-hardened, showing far less salt than pepper in his hair, Holland could take care of himself in most circumstances. Fear was something to be recognized and quickly put aside in hazardous situations, taken out at leisure when the job was done and analyzed beneath a microscope.

But these were extraordinary circumstances and uncertain times. The old rules did not seem to fit this time.

He had been half an hour early for his scheduled meeting with the new informant, Chon Sohul, a medium-level dealer with yakuza connections. Holland had been courting Chon for weeks, maintaining contact on the sly and haggling to find a price they both could live with. Ninety thousand *won* had been the magic number—something like a thousand dollars—and with all the risks that Chon would have to take securing the vital information, Holland knew he had himself a bargain.

Their scheduled meeting place had been the dealer's home away from home, a small apartment two blocks over from the Weonhyo Bridge, that Chon maintained for sexual liaisons. Seoul had much to offer for a tourist seeking pleasures of the flesh, but upscale mobsters striving for a touch of class risked heavy loss of face among their neighbors if they brought their business—or their pleasure—home.

The rendezvous had suited Holland's needs, as well. If Chon had gotten careless, leaving tracks, he stood a better chance of shaking off a tail on neutral ground. It would not do for Holland to be seen with his informant. The results could be unpleasant for them both.

Arriving early was an inexpensive form of life insurance. Holland killed time window shopping, checking out the neighborhood for indications of an ambush. He had cased the street the day before, checking out approaches and retreats to hedge his bets. He did not like surprises, and he wanted room to run in case the whole thing blew up in his face.

Chon's love nest was a walk-up flat that overlooked a tiny courtyard in a complex catering to bachelors. Women came and went, but there was nothing of the party atmosphere that Holland would have looked for in a stateside singles colony. Discretion was the local password, and the absence of a milling crowd made Holland's stakeout that much easier. If Chon was being watched, it didn't show.

They had agreed on nine o'clock, and Holland made his entrance on the stroke. He moved across the landing with an athlete's easy grace, his jacket open, granting quicker access to the Walther automatic tucked inside his belt, against his spine. He did not catch the smell of death until he stood outside Chon's door.

The hitters had been careless. Holland found the door ajar and palmed the automatic, easing off the safety as he listened for a telltale sound of movement on the other side. They could be waiting for him, but he didn't think so. Killers in a hurry might forget to close the door, but only idiots would make the same mistake when setting up an ambush.

He slipped inside and latched the door behind him, making a mental note to wipe it down for fingerprints before he left. No point in giving the police a clue to work with, if the hitters had not left their own behind.

The small apartment had been trashed, with feeling. In the style of most Korean homes, Chon's furnishings were sparse, but here a love seat had been overturned and disemboweled, its stuffing scattered on the floor. A television set had toppled from its stand, a slender floor lamp still protruding from the center of its shattered picture tube.

The tiny kitchen had exploded, cupboards standing open and their meager contents strewn across formica countertops. The food from Chon's refrigerator had been scrutinized, dissected, dumped together in the sink. A telephone, its insulated guts revealed, had joined the stew for seasoning.

A narrow corridor connected Holland with Chon's bedroom, where the devastation was continued. Here, the central piece had been a king-size bed; its mattress and the box spring stood against opposing walls, eviscerated. Dresser drawers had been removed and emptied, after which they were stacked up in a tidy sculpture that was striking in the midst of so much chaos.

Chon Sohul possessed few secrets, now. His bedroom floor was littered with the props of passion: lingerie (both men's and women's); chrome and rubber sexual devices (with a fair supply of extra batteries); at least three dozen condoms, all unfurled like cast-off snakeskins. In the closet, several leisure outfits and a pair of matching bathrobes had been shredded on their hangers.

Holland found his contact in the shower, kneeling in an awkward kowtow, one ear pressed against the drain. Chon might have been intent on picking up a message from the pipes, but Holland saw the angle of his broken neck, the wide-eyed grimace of surprise that death had frozen on his face.

Stark naked, Chon looked smaller than he had in life. His waxen lips were smeared with blood, more crimson beaded on the porcelain before him, tendrils snaking toward the drain.

A search was pointless, Holland knew. The killers had been thorough to a fault. If Chon were holding solid evidence, it had been lost. If he had stored the information in his mind . . .

A flash of color, from the sink, caught Holland's eye as he prepared to leave the bathroom. Stepping closer, careful with his hands, he read the message loud and clear.

Chon's severed tongue lay in the sink, surrounded by a

scattering of coins. The mark of an informer, executed by his peers.

So much for writing Chon off as the casualty of a drug feud. He was blown and Holland with him. If the killers had not questioned Chon before they clipped his tongue, extracting information on his contact, it was safe for Holland to assume they would be watching the apartment. Waiting.

Cursing bitterly, he backtracked through the claustrophobic war zone, used his handkerchief to wipe the latch and knob before he took a cautious step outside. No sign of life from any of the neighbors, though they must have heard Chon's death throes, his apartment being trashed. Discretion had prevented them from calling the police, and Holland used the lapse in civic consciousness to his advantage, slipping out the way he had arrived, unseen.

He kept the Walther PP automatic in his hand until he reached the street. If they were waiting for him, Chon's assassins might decide to trail him home, where they could work in privacy and toss his flat for any evidence Chon might have passed in other meetings. There was nothing to be found, but the uncertainty was Holland's last, best hope to save himself.

Outside, it was a muggy summer night, the sky threatening rain. Holland took his time on the short walk to Yongsan Station, dawdling past display windows and checking his track. At least two dozen nationals were moving in the same direction, singly and in pairs, but Holland could not spot the tail.

The executioners were either very good, or they had missed their chance and let him go.

He would not gamble on the latter possibility, aware that Chon might very well have spilled his guts before he died. Precautions had been taken—Holland had employed a cover name and lied outrageously about his nonexistent mission for the DEA—but covers could be broken. He would not risk going home, just yet, when uninvited callers might be waiting there.

The embassy, on Sejong-ro, would be his safest bet. A full report to his control, assessing damages, and Holland would be reassigned. His usefulness in Seoul was finished, and the bitter taste of failure was alleviated, to a small degree, by thoughts of going home.

At Yongsan Station, Holland paid his fare and drifted toward the platform, scrutinizing faces with a practiced eye as other passengers arrived. None showed an interest in the tall American, but Holland watched their hands and kept his back protected, just in case.

The train was faster than a four-mile walk through winding streets, and while he could have saved more time by flagging down a taxi, Holland had no way of guaranteeing that he would not find an enemy behind the wheel. With images of Chon Sohul still fresh in mind, he did not care to buy himself a one-way ride.

The train arrived, and Holland found himself a seat adjacent to the double doors. A teenage couple sat beside him, animatedly discussing movies they had seen. Around him, standing as the train began to move, were businessmen and shoppers, tradesmen, students juggling books and loose-leaf folders.

Any of them might be enemies.

At Seoul Station, Holland left the train and bought a subway token for the ride uptown to Sejong-ro. He recognized a dozen passengers with similar intentions, but they seemed oblivious to Holland as they found their seats or took positions in the aisle. Among the unfamiliar faces, a policeman joined the crowd, but Holland took no comfort in the presence of a uniform.

Police in Seoul were probably no more corrupt than any in America, but that would hardly pass for an endorsement. Holland recognized his paranoia and accepted it for what it was, a built-in mechanism for survival that had served him well in other situations where his life was on the line.

The train began to move, accelerating as it left the platform. Two more miles, and he would be beyond the reach of any trackers. Was the young man on the seat directly opposite observing him with more than casual attention? What about the older man who stood on Holland's left, pretending interest in a magazine? Was that a pistol in the pocket of his sport coat, or a gift-wrapped present for his wife?

The sour taste of fear was strong in Holland's mouth. He

shifted in his seat, sat back and felt the Walther digging at his spine, its presence reassuring. Still, if there was trouble on the subway, his assailants would possess the critical advantage of surprise. A silent blade between the ribs would do it, as he rose to disembark. His fellow passengers would think that he had merely stumbled in the crush, until they saw the blood.

The train was slowing for the South Gate platform. Holland left his seat impulsively, was first off when the doors slid open. Other passengers were close behind him, but he did not tip his hand by glancing back. A show of negligence might throw his enemies off-balance, trick them into fatal overconfidence.

The sky made good upon its threat as Holland reached the sidewalk. Raindrops pelted down around him, picking up momentum as he crossed the busy street and started north on Taepyong-ro. Police headquarters stood a short block away, to the east, but he left it behind him, moving with purpose, shoulders hunched against the rain. His back felt vulnerable, tingling in anticipation of a bullet.

Holland took the next street on his right, passing the Plaza Hotel with its empty promise of shelter, brushing past patrons who spilled out of nightclubs and restaurants. Taxis lined up at the curb, but he left them alone. He was changing his course, aiming now for the embassy annex on Eulji-ro, shaving a mile off his journey and throwing the hunters a curve.

When the alley presented itself, Holland took it. The shortcut would save precious moments, depositing him within yards of the embassy annex. He moved through the darkness with confident strides, pausing once as he met a stray dog. The mongrel retreated, lips curled in a snarl.

Fifty yards. Thirty-five.

The young man was waiting as Holland emerged from the alley, his hair plastered down by the rain. He was smiling, a predator's grimace, and Holland thought he had seemed younger before, on the subway.

"You're good," Holland told him, with no trace of flattery, risking a glance to his flank and discovering they were alone. He could still pull it out if he kept his thoughts centered, refrained from all panicky moves.

He was watching for weapons, a hand sliding back

toward his own, when the young man attacked him, greased lightning incarnate. An open hand sliced past his face, snapped his clavicle cleanly in two, and his arm turned to rubber, the impact propelling him into a wall. Holland groped for the Walther left-handed, a sob welling up out of nowhere, and knew he was finished.

He saw the kick coming, a roundhouse that shattered his ribs, driving shards through a lung. There was blood in his throat as he fought to inhale, felt the dull, warm discomfort of hemorrhage deep in his chest.

Moving close, the young man used a backhand to finish it, wielding the edge of his hand like a blade to collapse Holland's larynx. The agent was dead when he fell to the pavement, a straw man abruptly deprived of support.

It required several seconds to roll Holland over and turn out his pockets, but no one was watching; the hunter and prey were alone. Finding nothing of interest, the young man abandoned his victim, retracing his steps toward the traffic on Taepyong-ro. On the sidewalk behind him, a discarded mannequin turned up its face to the rain.

Chapter 1

San Francisco

Driving north on Mason, Barrett Ross was stuck behind a cable car. Competing traffic would not let him pass, and so he crept along, compelled to brake each time the trolley stopped for passengers. The air-conditioner in Ross's rental car put out a stream of lukewarm air for several blocks, and finally gave up the ghost.

Up front, a red-haired boy with freckles and a gap-toothed grin kept leaning forward in his seat to stare at Ross and hoist his middle finger. On his fourth approach, Ross beat him to the punch and flipped the little bastard off. It seemed to satisfy, and he retreated with a beatific smile.

At Filbert, they were treated to the vision of a black man standing in the middle of the street, his head thrown back, one arm extended toward the heavens, index finger aimed accusingly at God. The trolley's brakeman slowed his beast of burden to a crawl, a fat conductor craning out to verify that they had room to spare.

It nauseated Ross, this pandering to human waste. He fought a sudden urge to swerve his car and crush the living statue into pulp.

For Barrett Ross, the freckled brat and posing lunatic epitomized the California Syndrome. San Francisco was a respite from his duty station, but it wasn't home. The product of a Massachusetts shipping family, with blue blood in his veins and old, old money in the bank, Ross thought of San Francisco as a nest of aging hippies, mystic cults, and homosexuals. The city was a breeding ground for dangerous egalitarian ideas, and Ross was constantly on guard against contamination.

Still, his personal aversion to the city paled beside his gut reaction to the new assignment. As a younger man— much younger—Ross had entered the clandestine service of his country in a quest for high adventure, desperately pursuing a diversion from the tedium of family. In place of action, he had found intrigue, the labyrinth of office politics, surrendering himself to the bureaucracy while do-or-die assignments went to others.

Like the man he was about to meet.

No love was lost between them; it was years since they had spoken last. If anyone had asked, Ross would have ventured the opinion that his journey was a waste of time. Adept as they might be at changing history to suit their needs, the Company's commanding officers could not turn back the calendar.

But Ross had not been asked. As usual. His orders were explicit, leaving no room for interpretation or misunderstanding. He would make the offer, catch his eastbound flight on time, submit reports on the success or failure of his mission.

Simple, right.

Except that now, as he approached his destination, Ross could feel his brand-new ulcer working overtime. His palms were moist, his armpits clammy. He began to drum his fingers on the steering wheel, impatient to be finished with his task.

He lost the trolley car at Lombard, making better time without the frequent stops. His freckled nemesis, retreating, raised a solitary finger in salute.

Smart bastard, Holland thought. *You ought to be in school*. But it was June, and California schools were closed for the summer, turning out their rabble for a season in the streets. Bad luck for California. Worse luck, in the long run, for the world at large.

A firm believer in the military school approach to discipline, Ross had no tolerance for the morass of modern education, with its liberal approach to caste and class. The creeping virus had been carried to New England by a crop of "teachers" trained—and brainwashed—in New York, established there by rule or law, and fertilized with federal funds, until the schools that Ross remembered from his childhood were reduced to sideshows, turning out the mediocre and mundane.

There seemed to be no place for excellence at any level of society, these days.

He made a right-hand turn on Jefferson and started looking for an address, Fisherman's Wharf sliding past on his left, in a blur. Location of his target was the easy part; Ross covered three more blocks before he found a parking space, compelled to settle for a lot where jabbering Iranians dispensed the tickets, pocketing the first half-hour's payment in advance. Accepting his receipt, Ross entertained a vision of the rental being held for ransom, facing execution if he failed to bring more tribute back on schedule.

Ross decided he would take his time.

It was a relatively short walk back, on Jefferson. The close proximity of water should have sparked nostalgic memories, but everything was different here. The sights and smells of San Francisco's waterfront bore no resemblance to his recollections of the summers on Cape Cod. Surrounded by a legion of the great unwashed, Ross understood that he did not belong. He was a stranger here, as alien as if he were a visitor from outer space.

The women were enticing, braless under halter tops and golden brown in string bikinis, but for all of their originality, they might have been created by machines. Ross quickly tired of perfect smiles and noses picked from catalogues, the painted eyes that lost their focus when a conversation strayed beyond the symbols of the zodiac. If any dozen of the California girls were carefully dismembered, their component sections mixed and matched, Ross thought the end result would pass inspection by their families and friends.

In California, physical perfection had been packaged, marketed, and sold, on such a scale that abstract standards were a fading memory.

And yet, for all that, there were countless specimens who had not seen the writing on the wall. Ross found himself repulsed by much of what he saw around him. Bikers clad in filthy denim. Homosexuals cavorting in the public eye. An ethnic stew of half-castes who defied description, short of medical analysis. Wild youth, their multicolored hair done up in spikes, dressed out in leather, cartridge belts and handcuffs worn as ornaments.

An honors graduate in history, Ross didn't need a sandwich sign to recognize barbarians on sight. Sometimes, he trembled at the thought of what his country had become.

His destination was an edifice whose aging paint retained the barest hint of its original pastel. A smallish, stenciled sign informed him that the t'ai chi *dojang* could be found upstairs.

Ross mounted the steps like a man on his way to the scaffold, feet dragging, a scowl carving lines in his face. He considered aborting the mission, reporting that Kim had declined without facing the rigors of making the pitch, but discarded the notion at once. Knowing Ramsey, he thought that the Company might make a follow-up call and discover his lie. His objections were noted at Langley, in triplicate. Better to deal with the problem at hand, he decided, and pass on the moves that could put ugly blots on his record.

At the top of the stairs, he was faced with a choice: ballet class on his left, or t'ai chi on his right. As he entered the *dojang*, a strong smell of sweat, long confined, made Ross crinkle his nose.

The studio was roughly fifteen feet across and twice that long, with windows facing water on the east, a little glassed-in office situated at the far end of the room. Perhaps a dozen students, dressed in white karate *gis*, were seated on the floor, around a large athletic mat. Distracted by the entry of a stranger, they examined Ross, but soon returned their full attention to the match in progress.

Kim Sunim was sparring with a brown belt, easily avoiding kicks and blows delivered by his adversary. In his *gi*, the black belt frayed in spots by frequent laundering, Kim seemed diminished, smaller in the flesh than Ross remembered. Still, he had the same old deadly moves.

The brown belt tried a snap kick from the left, and Kim went underneath it, clipped the student's leg from under him and dropped him on his backside. Rolling out of it, the younger man recovered swiftly, scrambling to his feet. He bowed perfunctorily to Kim and struck his posture for another round.

Across the studio, Ross caught Kim's eye. If the instructor was surprised, it did not show, but there was . . . something.

A reaction Ross could not identify by name. He felt a sudden chill and cursed his weakness.

On the mat, the brown belt made his move. A feint, as if to kick, immediately followed by a straight-arm thrust. Kim sidestepped, took the offered wrist and went inside the movement, whipping his opponent through a shoulder roll that left him prostrate. Instantly, before the student could recover, Kim was on him like a panther, kneeling on his chest, delivering a storm of lightning blows to face and throat.

It would have been a lethal move, except that this was practice. Playtime. Still, Ross got the message. Kim had kept his edge. He had the touch.

The student seemed a little flustered, even angry, as Kim helped him to his feet. They bowed to one another, Kim said something, and the brown belt smiled, shook hands. Kim faced the class at large and said, "I think we're finished for this afternoon."

They rose as one and bowed in Kim's direction, peeling off to find their gym bags, sneakers, car keys. Ross stood fast and waited, bearing Kim's appraisal from a distance, confident that curiosity was on his side.

Kim found a towel at ringside, swabbed his face, and draped the towel around his shoulders like a stole. He studied Ross a moment longer, making no attempt to hide the frank suspicion in his eyes.

"My office."

Kim made no attempt to raise his voice, and yet it carried perfectly across the studio. He turned and walked away without a backward glance, secure in the knowledge that his uninvited guest would follow.

Biting off a sharp response, Ross mustered up his finest artificial smile and did as he was told. It would not hurt to play Kim's game a little while. Inevitably, he would learn who made the rules.

Kim Sunim's first glimpse of Barrett Ross upset his concentration, giving Kim's opponent on the mat a momentary edge. The student, Rickey Shadle, was aggressive, skilled, a Berkeley sophomore who approached t'ai chi the same way that he might have tackled student body politics, as one more field to conquer. The method had its weaknesses, but lack of confidence was not among them.

By and large, Kim's students were a different breed, oppressed by fear and doubt before their eyes were opened to a new horizon. They were tired of being pushed around in high school, preyed upon by muggers, terrorized by shadows, and they turned to martial arts as much for therapy as for the relatively simple moves of self-defense. Kim watched them blossom, crawling out of shells they had constructed for themselves through years of self-abasement. None of them might ever use the talents they acquired, but they were changing, growing, all the same.

Rickey Shadle, on the other hand, enjoyed the competition for its own sake, taking less pride in his skill than in the physical defeat of his opponents. Kim suspected that there might be something of the bully in his nature, but the line had not been crossed in class.

Not yet.

Kim brought his full attention back to Shadle just in time, reacting to the feint as his opponent would expect, allowing Rickey to step in close and throw his straight-arm jab. Kim took his wrist and pivoted, allowing Shadle's own momentum to provide the necessary thrust. For something like a heartbeat, Shadle's weight was on his shoulder, then he struck the mat with stunning force.

Kim followed up immediately, pinning his opponent with a knee against his sternum, snapping half a dozen punches toward the brown belt's face. He pulled each blow a millimeter short of impact, watching Shadle flinch. The color in Shadle's cheeks as he rose was equal parts exertion, anger, and embarrassment.

They bowed to one another, Shadle looking sullen. Kim made certain that his voice would not be audible beyond their fighting circle.

"Danger breeds best on too much confidence," he said.

"Confucius, I suppose."

"Corneille. *El Cid.*"

The student shook his head and grinned, despite himself, and Kim dismissed the class. Ross had not moved from his original position, near the door, and while he tried to hold himself with dignity, he came off ill at ease.

Eleven years had scarcely laid a glove on Barrett Ross. There was a trace of silver in his hair, a little extra weight that made him seem more solid, stockier. Beyond the superficial changes, Ross possessed the same cleft chin and heavy brows, the same cold smile that never reached his eyes.

Kim finished toweling off, allowing Ross to wait. The Company had nerve, approaching him at all. Dispatching Barrett Ross to run their errand might have been a calculated insult. No, on second thought, Kim realized the Powers That Be would turn to Ross because of their association in the past. Unhappy as it might have been, it was at least a concrete link.

Kim thought they must be desperate to approach him and was pleased to find he did not care.

"My office," Kim instructed, leaving Ross to follow on his own. He would not make it easy for them. Ross would have to spell it out before Kim turned him down.

The office was a ten-by-fifteen cubicle, its single window facing on the studio. A battered metal desk was shoved against one wall, the cushion of its swivel chair patched up with silver duct tape. Kendo sticks, nunchakus, and a pair of practice swords were mounted on one wall; the other two were bare, but for a calendar above Kim's desk. He took the only chair and left his visitor to stand.

"What do you want?"

"A friendly visit."

"Try again."

Ross flashed the plastic smile. "All right. We have a job that fits your profile."

"I'm retired."

"Oh, yes. What is it, now? Ten years?"

"Eleven."

"Of course. Are you enjoying this?" He scanned the office with a look of thinly veiled contempt. "It can't pay much."

"I'm getting by."

"I see." Ross cleared his throat. "You're missed . . . or, so I'm told."

"No sale. I cut it loose."

"They thought you might be interested in this one."

"No."

"Well, that's all right." He moved to stand before the weapons, studying the swords. "I missed you at the funeral."

"Whose?"

"Reese Holland. He was killed in Seoul, last Tuesday."

Kim absorbed the shock and started counting backward. Tuesday. Six days gone. It seemed impossible that Holland could be dead without his feeling... something.

"How?"

"As far as we can tell, your way."

Kim frowned. "He knew the moves."

Ross's smile was calculated to infuriate. "There's always someone better. Holland found him."

"You could have phoned it in."

Ross shrugged. "Consider it a courtesy. He used to say that you were family."

"That burns you, doesn't it?"

"I'll live." The smile had slipped a notch, before Ross caught himself and saved it. "Ramsey sent me out to offer you a turn at evening the score."

"Is this where I'm supposed to fall down on my knees in gratitude?"

"Your call. I told him that you've been away too long."

Kim recognized the clumsy effort at reverse psychology, and he was not impressed.

"Who made the tag?"

Ross countered with a question of his own. "You in?"

"I didn't say that."

"Well, I need to know. You follow? If you're out..."

"I'll think about it."

He was pleased to see the color bloom in Ross's cheeks.

"I need a yes or no."

"I said, I'll think about it."

"Suit yourself. I'm out of here at oh-eight hundred hours. If I fly alone, we farm the contract out to someone else."

"Where are you staying?"

"At the San Franciscan. Six-eighteen."

"I'll let you know. Now, go away."

"It's been a pleasure, Kim. As always."

Kim sat motionless until the outer door had closed on Barrett Ross. He concentrated on untangling his mixed emotions, grief and anger chief among them, setting each apart to be disposed of in its turn. Above all else, he knew the hunger for revenge could get him killed.

Eleven years and sixteen days had passed since Kim Sunim had stalked another human being to the death. His memories of the event were crystal-clear, but in his heart, Kim wondered whether Ross might be correct about the lapse of time. His skills were all intact—improved, if anything— but he had made a point of weeding out the killer instinct, meditating long and hard.

Until that afternoon, he had believed himself successful. Now, he was no longer sure.

The news of Holland's death had been a shock. Men died, of course. It happened every day, perhaps a thousand times per minute. Some men, though, seemed destined to go on forever and defy the odds.

Reese Holland had been such a man.

Kim pictured Holland in his mind. The athlete's body, kept in fighting trim despite his years, by a routine of exercise that verged on masochism. Square-cut features. Thick, dark hair, cropped close in military style.

It troubled Kim that he could not recall the sound of Holland's voice. If Reese should call him on the telephone, of course . . . but, no.

Kim concentrated on his breathing, waited for the burning in his chest to fade. Emotion bred mistakes, and if he chose to take on Holland's killers—even if he turned the mission down—he knew the price of error in transactions with the Company.

He changed to street clothes, killed the lights, and locked the studio behind him as he left. He spent an hour idling on the wharf and ate clam chowder at an open-air cafe festooned with fishing nets and sharks' jaws. Fishermen were angling from the pier, while seagulls worked the water, eagerly competing for the daily catch. When he had seen enough, he walked back to the *dojang* and retrieved his motorcycle from an alley in the rear.

Home for Kim Sunim was an apartment near St. Mary's Square. At half-past six, he locked himself inside, checked out the answering machine—two salesmen and a hang-up— and proceeded to the bathroom. Stripping off his clothes, he turned the shower on as hot as he could stand and stepped beneath the spray, luxuriating in its heat for several moments, finally reaching for the soap. When he was clean and lobster-red, he switched the temperature to stinging cold, enduring a full five minutes as he purged his mind of conscious thought.

He came out shivering and used a giant bath towel briskly to restore his circulation. Pausing at the sink, Kim studied his reflection in the mirror. He was thirty-seven, but his seamless Asian features could have passed for ten years younger. Barely visible, except to Kim, a crescent scar above one eye had faded over time. Another, more pronounced, ran horizontally across his rib cage, on the left.

The marks of battles, lost and won.

He padded naked through the small apartment, turning on the television set, and dialing past the mindless game shows, finally settling for network news. As always, most of it was bad. A terrorist assassination in the Middle East. An earthquake in Honduras and a bombing in the north of Ireland. Demonstrations to protest the spread of AIDS, as if a virus might be influenced by civil disobedience. The "good" news was a "human interest" item, featuring a matron in her sixties who wore tinfoil hats and preached the imminence of contact with explorers from the stars.

And through it all, no word about the murder of a man called Holland.

Kim turned the television off, retreating to his bedroom. On the bureau stood a single photograph. Its subject was a man decked out in camouflage fatigues, surrounded by a wall of jungle foliage, smiling for the camera. Kim knew the photo had been snapped in Thailand, but it might as easily have been the Congo or the Amazon. As jungles imitated one another, so their wars began to look the same.

He studied Holland's face for several moments, searching for an answer there, and ultimately had to find it in himself. He dialed the San Franciscan, gave the clerk a number, got Ross on the second ring.

"I'm in," he said, and softly cradled the receiver.

Chapter 2

The headquarters of the Central Intelligence Agency—
"the Company" to its employees—stands eight miles and
twenty minutes from the bustling hub of downtown Washington, D.C. Suburban Fairfax County is a different world,
unspoiled, with gently rolling hills and primal forest bordering
the beltway.

Kim Sunim had been to Langley several times, for his
initial training and debriefing after missions, but he had not
seen the place in better than a decade. Riding in an unmarked government sedan, with Barrett Ross behind the
wheel, he was relieved to see that condominiums and shopping malls had not devoured the countryside.

An unobtrusive road sign put them on alert for CIA -
NEXT RIGHT. Until the early 1970s, the sign had borne a
different legend—"B.P.R.," for Bureau of Public Roads—but
the flimsy cover had outlived its usefulness, like Ian Fleming's
"Universal Export," and the Company went public after a
couple of years, during which the access road to Langley had
been totally anonymous.

Ross took the cutoff, slowing on the curve, and soon they
reached a tall gate in the ten-foot chain link fence that
surrounds the CIA's 125 acres of Fairfax County. The fence
was topped with wicked loops of razor wire, and three signs
were appended to the gate. The first read "U.S. Government
Property For Official Business Only." Another warned that
cameras were prohibited. In case a straying tourist missed

the point, the third, and largest sign, was more direct: "No Trespassing."

Unlike the American Nazi headquarters in nearby Arlington, there was no published warning that trespassers would be shot (and the survivors shot again), but Kim would not have cared to test the system. Legend had it that the Langley compound had been penetrated twice in twenty-seven years, by contract agents of the KGB, but neither had returned to file reports. The first had tried to shoot it out with "gardeners," who kept the rolling grounds in shape; the other had been taken in alive, and that was infinitely worse.

Inside the fence, a sentry in the guard house scrutinized their vehicle, made visual I.D. on Ross, and keyed a switch that set the gate in motion, closing it again behind them. Though he wore a military uniform, Kim knew the gate man was a Company employee, armed and ready to defend his post at need. No member of a "rival" service was permitted on the Langley grounds without an escort.

Ross made a sharp left turn past the guard house, and they traveled another hundred yards before Kim had his first glimpse of headquarters, partially hidden behind a thick screen of trees. A tawny doe stood in the middle of the two-lane blacktop, startled by their car. Ross tapped the horn, accelerating, and the graceful animal took flight, escaping toward the forest.

"Ought to hunt the damned things down," Ross growled. "They eat the shrubbery and trip the sensors every time you turn around."

"It sounds like a conspiracy. If I were you, I'd take it up with Special Operations."

Ross shot Kim a baleful glance at the mention of the CIA's clandestine paramilitary arm. "You're well-advised to skip the stand-up comedy routine," he said. "We didn't call you back to entertain the troops."

Kim did not bother meeting Ross's gaze. "You didn't call me back at all," he said. "I volunteered."

The Company's fortress came into full view as they drew abreast of the main entrance. A massive concrete structure, seven stories tall, it offered a forbidding, cold facade to new arrivals. Windows were recessed, like gun ports, those on lower floors secured with screens of heavy mesh. A sole

exception was the seventh floor, with outer walls of deeply
tinted, shock-proof glass.

To the right of the building's main entrance, a separate
domed structure housed the Company's 500-seat auditorium.
Inside the lobby, Kim recalled, a massive reproduction of the
CIA's seal was set into the polished marble floor. On one wall,
to the left as you entered, sculptors with a sense of humor
had inscribed a verse from the Book of John, VIII: 32.

AND YE SHALL KNOW THE TRUTH
AND THE TRUTH SHALL MAKE YOU FREE

"We'll go in black," Ross said.

He bypassed the entrance and visitor's parking, circling
the fortress to reach the executive lot. Langley's parking
facilities sprawled over twenty-one acres, accommodating three
thousand vehicles, but few of their drivers would enter the
building as Ross and his charge were preparing to do.

Stepping from the car, Kim was enveloped in preternatu-
ral silence, broken only by distant snatches of birdsong and
the muffled hum of the facility's air-conditioners. In winter,
even those faint sounds would be suppressed, the grounds as
quiet as a cemetery underneath a layer of snow.

The air-conditioners had posed a problem for a quarter
of a century. When the fortress was constructed, in the latter
1950s, the contractor responsible for installation of heating
and air-conditioning systems inquired as to how many per-
sons the building would accommodate. The Company refused
to answer, citing "national security" in explanation of its
reticence. As a result, the system never functioned adequate-
ly, but the Company's attempts to sue the hapless contractor
were futile, broken on the rocks of bureaucratic secrecy.

Kim clipped a plastic badge to his lapel and followed
Ross inside. The "black" entrance, reserved for VIPs and
agents who could not afford to advertise their presence in the
building, placed them in a spartan lobby where another
guard in uniform sat rigid at his desk. Concealed beneath the
desktop, there would be an Uzi submachine gun and a panic
button, which, if pressed, would bring a dozen backup gunners on the double.

Ross presented his credentials, and the stonefaced sentry

checked their names against a master list, comparing snap-shots with the flesh-and-blood reality. When he was satisfied, he buzzed them through a metal door that stood behind him, following their progress from his swivel chair until they disappeared from sight.

The interior of CIA headquarters is compartmentalized like a submarine, the various wings insulated and isolated from one another in the interest of maximum security. The fortress contains electronics and weapons laboratories; a security nerve center, manning television monitors, alarms, and perimeter sensors; a communications center, sending and receiving from the forest of antennas on the roof; multiple libraries and computer rooms; an "open" cafeteria, for visitors, and a larger "secret" dining room, where Company employees passed armed guards en route to lunch or dinner.

Kim's appointment was with Alexander Ramsey, the deputy director of operations. Formerly Clandestine Services, and later known as Plans, the Directorate of Operations carries full responsibility for gathering intelligence, conducting covert missions, and mounting counterespionage campaigns. It is the heart of the CIA, without which members of the Company's remaining three directorates would cease to function.

A private elevator took them nonstop to the seventh floor. They made the ride in silence, Kim deliberately aloof, Ross straightening his tie and picking fragments of imaginary lint from his lapel.

Another guard was waiting in the corridor, but he had been forewarned of their arrival and dismissed them with a glance. Kim followed Ross along a soundproof corridor to Ramsey's office, entering a spacious anteroom, where they were greeted by a smiling, blond receptionist. Directed to a sofa, he relaxed while Ross was ushered into Ramsey's inner sanctum for his one-on-one report.

Ten minutes passed—Kim paging through an issue of the Company's quarterly trade journal, *Studies in Intelligence*—before Ramsey emerged from his office. With his iron-gray hair and piercing sky-blue eyes, the deputy director of operations looked younger than his fifty-four years. Built like a wrestler, Ramsey seemed uncomfortable in his tailored suit, vaguely out of place in the plush office where he sometimes spent days at a time, without going home.

In Company parlance, Alex Ramsey was a "supergrade," equivalent in rank to members of the military general staff. In concrete terms, he was the fourth man on the totem pole at the CIA, personally responsible to the director of operations, who in turn received his orders from the deputy director of central intelligence, one short step from the throne. The upper ranks of the CIA were an elite fraternity, and those who scaled the pinnacle were men with whom to reckon.

Ramsey shook Kim's hand and offered him a smile that Kim interpreted as genuine. "It's been too long," the big man said, a trace of Texas in his voice. "Come in, sit down."

The carpeting beneath Kim's feet was soft and deep. Three walls were decorated with the work of master artists, while the fourth, all tinted glass, provided Ramsey with a panoramic view of trees and meadows, fading into distant haze.

Kim took a seat in front of Ramsey's massive oaken desk. Ross lingered on the sidelines, finally settled in a captain's chair, against the wall. The deputy director lit a fat cigar and leaned back in his leather chair.

"Retirement suits you, Kim."

"I think so."

Kim felt more at ease with Ramsey than he did with Ross, but he was not prepared to trust the Texan.

"Lots of agents never make the shift up here." The deputy director tapped an index finger on his skull. "The job won't let them go. You ever get that feeling?"

"Once or twice. I took an Alka-Seltzer."

Ramsey blinked, and then his laughter filled the office. Trained to please, Ross forced a chuckle, but it came out sounding like he had a cup of gravel in his throat.

The deputy director spent a moment sucking smoke.

"A sense of humor. That's important to an agent."

"Former agent," Kim reminded him.

"Of course. But, then again, you're here."

"I have my reasons."

"Understood. It was a goddamned shame, the way Reese went. You two were close."

It did not come out sounding like a question, and he

didn't bother with an answer. Ramsey knew the story of his life, no doubt had incidents on file that Kim, himself, had long forgotten. He was not prepared to put his private feelings on display.

Instead, he simply asked, "What happened?"

Ramsey took another draw on his cigar and frowned, considering his answer. "Have you kept in touch with what's been happening in Seoul?"

"I watch the news," Kim said. "I haven't made a point of memorizing details."

"Never mind. Dan Rather doesn't have the shit you'll need." The deputy director seemed all business, now. "For eighteen months, a hard-core leftist cadre has been escalating its campaign against the ROK regime. They've graduated out of strikes and demonstrations into terrorism. Since the first of March, we've logged nine bombings—four with casualties— and two assassination bids against the president, all news of which has been suppressed."

"What's holding back the NSP?"

"Good question. We suspect they've got internal problems, but the story is they're doing all they can, unquote. Which throws it back on us, considering the fact that several targets have been U.S. owned. Big money's talking, and the DCI wants quick results."

"And Holland drew the job?"

The deputy director took a folder, marked EYES ONLY, from his "In" tray, spread it out before him on the desk. Extracting several photographs, he handed them across to Kim.

Three different street scenes, showing men in urgent conversation, casting nervous glances over shoulders as they spoke. Among the several faces, one was constant, mirrored in a blown-up mug shot at the bottom of the pile.

"Meet Chin Kyu Sung. Co-founder of the South Korean People's Army and its sole surviving honcho. He's done time for opposition to the government, but they released him back in '84. Some kind of amnesty, supposed to take the pressure off."

"It didn't work," Ross said.

Kim managed to ignore him.

Ramsey found that his cigar had died; he dropped it in

an ashtray. "Since the heavy action started, Chin's been underground. The NSP can't find him, so they say. Reese had some leads—at least, he thought so—but he never had a chance to run them down."

"And now?"

"We have a green light from the DCI for executive action. Chin iced Holland, or he had it done. We want him rooted out and terminated. With extreme prejudice."

"You must have other wet work specialists on staff. Why come to me?"

"You know the territory."

"*Knew* the territory," Kim corrected. "I'm out of touch."

"You haven't lost your edge. Can I be honest with you? Special Programs doesn't measure up. Their people are a bunch of Cuban thugs and Indiana farm boys. None of them would go the distance."

"So, you need a touch of local color."

"I need someone who can do the job." The deputy director spread his hands. "Besides, there's your relationship with Holland to consider. I believe you're motivated."

"Have you got a line on Chin?"

"We're pretty sure he's still in Seoul. That isn't worth a damn, I know, but Reese was sitting on his information, and he took it with him. You'd be starting more or less from scratch."

"I'd have to freshen up my contacts," Kim reflected. "Some of them may not exist today. It won't be cheap."

"Blank check. We want this business taken care of, soonest."

Kim experienced a sudden urge to scrub the mission, tell the deputy director that his blank check wasn't good enough, but images of Holland lying in a box restrained him.

"I'll do what I can."

"There's one more thing." The Texan cleared his throat. "We have a line on Chin's control, a North Korean agent by the name of Dae Li Chong. No snaps, unfortunately. He's a private kind of guy. The little man who wasn't there. If you run into him, along the way..."

"I understand."

A second writ of execution had been signed, against an individual whose name was probably a pseudonym, his face unknown. Kim felt the old, familiar sense of unreality returning in a rush.

"You'll be reporting to the chief of station, through a buffer," Ramsey told him.

"Who's the chief of station?"

"I am." Barrett Ross had mustered up his most engaging smile, the one that Kim imagined he would wear to executions. "Disappointed?"

"Not at all," Kim told him. "I'm a firm believer in the Peter Principle."

The deputy director intervened before Ross could respond.

"You're back on salary, full benefits, beginning eighteen hundred hours yesterday. There's life insurance, if you want to name a beneficiary."

Kim thought of Marcia, who had shared his bed and life for months, until his own compulsive need for privacy had driven her away. He shook his head.

"There's no one."

"Suit yourself, the offer's open. You'll be out of here tomorrow afternoon, TWA to San Francisco, with connections into Seoul on KAL. Tonight, you're at the Watergate."

"That seems appropriate."

He saw Ross scowling, as the deputy director chuckled, rose, and shook Kim's hand again.

"It's good to have you back on board."

"I'm only passing through."

"Of course. But, hell, who knows? You might remember why you used to like the job."

"I never liked it. It was necessary."

"Still is, son. Still is."

Inside the elevator, Ross screwed up his nerve to challenge Kim. "I don't appreciate the way you tried to make me look back there."

"And how was that?"

"Like some kind of incompetent."

"I'm sorry, Ross. I keep forgetting that you don't need any help."

The South Korean chief of station bit his tongue, a flush of anger rising in his cheeks. "We'll see who needs the help, in Seoul."

Kim's smile was deadly.

"Ramsey promised full cooperation," he reminded the New Englander. "I take that with a grain of salt, considering your limitations, but I won't be jerked around."

"What's that supposed to mean?"

"If I suspect your heart's not in the mission," Kim replied, "I'll have to send it home without you."

The briefing left a sour taste in Alexander Ramsey's mouth, and he was chasing it with smoke, attempting to resuscitate his dead cigar. Considering their history, it might have been an error, bringing Ross and Kim together, but Ramsey did not like surprises, and he feared that Kim might try to scrub the mission if he stumbled over Ross by accident, along the way.

The animosity dividing Kim and Ross had once been legendary in the Far East area division. Memories had faded over time, but Ramsey, as division chief, had viewed the action from a ringside seat. Twelve years, and he could still recall the bungled operation in detail.

And so, he thought, would Kim.

In those days, Ross had been the chief of base in Bangkok, pulling information out of Laos, Cambodia, and Vietnam. The war was over, more or less, and you could talk about your "Peace with Honor" all you wanted to; the fact was that America had been defeated by the communists. If losing Vietnam was not sufficiently traumatic, with its implications for the whole Far East division, Ramsey had been faced with evidence of new guerilla operations shaping up in Thailand. Ross had been specific, picking out the leaders of the movement, naming names. The DCI had managed to secure approval for preemptive action, lopping off the viper's head before it had a chance to coil and strike.

The job had gone to Kim Sunim, with Ross coordinating on-site details. When the smoke cleared, Kim was wounded, running for his life, with Thai security police in close pursuit. The dead included three civilians, a policeman, and a pair of low-life dealers who had stepped on someone's toes by selling heroin without a franchise from the local Triad. Ross, apparently, had let himself be suckered by informants playing both ends off against the middle, using the CIA to execute a contract. Kim had managed to evade and disengage, but he regarded

Ross with frank contempt, and six months later—after one more mission blew up in his face—he pulled the pin.

It had been Ramsey's firm intention to dispose of Barrett Ross, consigning him to some administrative Gulag in the Philippines or Singapore, but Ross was old-line CIA, a lineal descendant of the Yankees who had run the Company from its creation, as a bastard offspring of the wartime OSS, through Dallas and the fall of Camelot. The Johnson-Nixon years had introduced new Western blood, intensifying practical and philosophical disputes between the Yankees and their "Cowboy" opposition, centered in the Far East area division. Ross, meanwhile, had cultivated friends in unexpected places. They agreed that he could scarcely be rewarded for his blunder, but he would not be disposed of, either. Over time, as victories were won to balance out the scale, both Ross and Ramsey had advanced in rank.

If forced to choose, the deputy director would have trusted Kim Sunim above his station chief in Seoul, but he was forced to work within the system, following the designated channels. There were options to be analyzed and exercised, a secret war in progress that the Company could not afford to lose.

He buzzed his secretary, asked her to confirm his luncheon appointment with the director of operations. Ramsey's immediate superior, Francis Bragg, was an old warhorse who had circumvented the sectional Yankee-Cowboy clash by entering the Company through a back door, defecting from Military Intelligence during the Vietnam War. So far, he had outlasted five administrations, rising through the ranks to stand at the DCI's right hand, with some 8,000 agents and staff at his personal disposal.

Bragg was waiting for a rundown on the meet with Kim, and, yes, their luncheon date for two o'clock was on.

Twelve minutes. Time enough for Ramsey to consider his approach and qualify his personal impressions of the briefing. He was not prepared to burden Bragg with his concerns about potential heat between the chief of station and a designated hitter. Cautious optimism was the order of the day.

He found Bragg waiting at his usual table, in the private dining room reserved for supergrades. The Company's executives got better food, at lower prices, than the rank and file were offered in their cafeteria downstairs, served up on fine bone china, spotless linen on the side. The waiters, sworn to secrecy as registered employees of the CIA, were smiling blacks, immaculate in crisp, white dinner jackets.

Francis Bragg was short and slender, five years Ramsey's senior, craggy features topped by thin, receding hair. His flannel suit was gray and nearly matched the color of his eyes. He made a point of glancing at his watch as Ramsey joined him, but the deputy director wasn't worried. He was early, for a change.

The pleasantries disposed of, both men ordered, let their waiter move away before they settled down to business. Bragg plunged in without preliminaries.

"How'd it go?"

"We're set."

"He bought the package?"

"Yes, sir."

Bragg was drinking water, and he sipped it now, a curious expression on his face.

"You're satisfied?"

"I am."

"And when he learns the rest?"

It was the question Ramsey had been hoping to avoid. "It may not come to that," he said. "In any case, by that time, he'll be in the pipeline. Either way he jumps, we ought to get the same result."

"Is that an educated guess?"

"I'd call it a professional assessment."

"Same damned thing. We're gambling on this boy of yours. Eleven years outside can make a difference."

"He's in shape. He's motivated."

"Holland?"

"Yes, sir."

"Well, some good may come of that, at least."

"I'm hopeful."

"Hope's a luxury we can't afford. I put my faith in strategy. Coordination."

"I'm in touch. The chief of station recognizes the importance of the operation."

"Ross?" Bragg frowned. "I seem to recollect bad blood between your players, Alex."

"That's old business. It's contained."

"I hope so. Deviations from the game plan make me nervous."

"And the DCI?"

"He's *always* nervous. I believe it's written in the job description."

"Better him than me."

"Don't tell me that you've reached the height of your ambition?"

"Well..."

"I thought so. Wrap this up to everybody's satisfaction, Alex. It could be a feather in your cap."

Their food arrived, and they began to eat in silence, finally moving on to office gossip and the latest flap from Eastern Europe. Following the conversation out of habit, Ramsey let his thoughts drift back to Kim Sunim, the danger that was waiting for him back in Seoul.

The job would be a feather in his cap if Ramsey pulled it off, a minor setback if he didn't. Either way, he would be safe at Langley, watching from the sidelines.

Ramsey could not shake the grim, persistent thought that he was sending Kim to certain death.

Chapter 3

Seoul

The stewardess's voice woke Kim Sunim at thirty thousand feet, advising him to fasten his seat belt, stow any carry-on luggage, and return his seat to an upright position. Kim removed the plastic earphones, buckling up while the message was repeated for his fellow passengers in Chinese, Korean, Japanese.

The trans-Pacific flight on KAL had taken fourteen hours, overall. Kim traveled tourist class—a stratagem conceived by Ross and Ramsey to divert suspicion—but the flight was underbooked, and he had managed to maintain an empty seat between himself and the anemic-looking Brit who shared his row.

He had been fed three times en route, two TV dinners and a lumpy roll that came with cheese and bore the designation of a snack. Two films were also played in flight—a Whoopi Goldberg double-feature—but he managed to ignore the actress who appeared to wear a spider on her head. Kim tuned his rented earphones to a neutral channel, turned the static down until it barely whispered in his ear, and managed to accumulate nine hours sleep. It was a hedge against the side-effects of jet lag, and, besides, he did not care to think about what might be waiting for him on the ground.

Kim was relieved that Barrett Ross had not been booked aboard his flight, but Ross would be along, he knew, and they would have to work together. Somehow. With a bit of luck, he might be able to complete his mission and evacuate before

31

the chief of station had an opportunity to muck the operation up.

With any luck at all, Kim thought, he might come out of it alive.

Despite the hours of rest, he still felt tired, his muscles stiff from sleeping in unnatural positions, as the 747 circled into its approach. Seoul Airport is located in Yeouido, a suburban district south of the Han River, five miles from downtown. The runway lights were clearly visible in the pitch darkness, reminding Kim of the carvings at Nazca, their shapes discernible only from the air.

He checked his watch on touchdown. They had lifted off from San Francisco shortly after seven o'clock, Tuesday evening; now, through the magic of time zones and the international date line, he was landing in Seoul at 2:15 Tuesday morning. Beyond the plexiglas, a world away, the city sparkled, bright with promise.

Anxious passengers ignored the warnings to remain securely seated while the 747 taxied to the terminal. Kim watched them with detached amusement, jostling one another as they dragged their luggage from the overhead compartments. He had checked his baggage through, and would retrieve it after dealing with the obstacles of Immigration.

Ramsey—or, to be precise, the documents division of Technical Services—had supplied him with a passport in the name of Kim Su Chung. He also carried paperwork revealing him to be a naturalized American citizen (true), who had completed his residency requirement in 1974 (untrue). Theoretically employed by a designing firm, in Denver, he was on vacation, visiting the city of his birth.

Kim waited for the aisles to clear before he left his seat and moved in the direction of the exit. Smiling flight attendants thanked him for his patronage and wished him well in Seoul. When he responded in Korean, no one seemed surprised.

He followed the posted directions in Passport Control, lining up with Americans, Brits, Japanese, an Australian. The uniformed clerks took their time, asking questions and studying documents, peering at faces and photographs, each in the hope of detecting a smuggler or spy. When his turn came, Kim stepped to the counter, presented his papers.

The passport inspector was fat, middle-aged, with the

drab look of someone grown old in his job. Pudgy fingers like sausage links handled Kim's papers, then laid them aside.

"You are not a Korean?"

"American. Naturalized."

"Why?"

Kim ignored the impertinent question, returning the officer's stare without flinching.

"Your business?"

"Vacation."

"With family?"

"Alone."

"Do you have family living in Seoul?"

"I have no family living," Kim answered. And that much, at least, was the truth.

"Length of stay?" His inquisitor seemed to be tired of the game.

"Fourteen days."

Kim had doubled the time he expected to need. If his mission ran over, a visa extension would be the least of his problems.

A stamp was applied to his passport, the folder returned.

"Move along."

She was waiting for Kim on the far side of Passport Control. Kim had not been expecting a woman, but carefully hid his surprise as she offered her hand and addressed him by name.

"Mr. Chung? I do hope that your flight was a pleasant one."

"Yes. And you are?"

"Jamie Constable. I'll be escorting you to your hotel."

Kim placed her somewhere in her early thirties, slim and youthful. Emerald eyes returned his gaze with frank appraisal, and her smile revealed a set of perfect teeth. Her sandy hair was cut short, in a boyish style, but there was nothing masculine about her figure, outlined in a lightweight summer dress. She moved with easy grace as Kim fell into step beside her, making for the baggage carousels.

"We've all been looking forward to your visit."

Small talk. They did not appear to have a shadow, but he played the game.

"I'm happy you could meet me."

"It's my pleasure." She appeared to mean it, and he gave Ross mental points for picking out a decent actress. "You'll be staying at the Metro, if there's no objection."

"No, that's fine."

They talked about the weather, politics, imaginary friends, while Kim stood waiting for his bags. At length, the Oysters surfaced and he plucked them off the carousel, displayed his baggage tickets for a sleepy-looking clerk, and followed Jamie through revolving doors into the chilly, early morning darkness.

"This way."

Jamie led him to a nearby parking lot, where her Toyota sat beneath a streetlamp. Kim deposited his baggage in the trunk and took the shotgun seat, while Jamie slid behind the wheel. They cleared the lot before she dropped her smile and got around to business.

"Mr. Ross is flying in this afternoon. They hung him up at Langley."

"Ah." Kim saw no point to feigning interest in the chief of station's movements.

"I'm your handler, by the way." She glanced at Kim and caught the bare suggestion of a frown. "Is that a problem?"

"No." *I hope not.*

"Good." Relief was audible in Jamie's voice, but she remained defensive. "I can do my job, as long as macho types don't try to second-guess."

"I'm not a macho type."

"Let's hope not." Then, as if some further comment was required, she added, "I was handling Domino."

Kim felt a chill as she pronounced the code name Holland had been using when he died.

"That isn't much of an endorsement."

Startled by his tone, the handler concentrated on her driving. Satisfied with silence for the moment, Kim relaxed and closed his eyes.

They left Yeouido via Weonhyo Bridge, passed Hyochang Stadium, and caught the major artery to downtown Seoul below Seoul Station. Traffic did not pose a problem at that hour, but police cars were in evidence, and Jamie took her time, examining her passenger with surreptitious glances.

Stung by his remark, she wrote it off to traveler's fatigue and anger at the passing of a friend. She felt a measure of responsibility for Holland's death, misplaced perhaps, but there it was. Each time a handler lost an agent, there were questions to be answered and procedures to be analyzed. The toughest questions, Jamie realized, were those she asked herself.

Now, it was payback time. Kim's mission in the city would be life and death—his specialty, according to the file she had received last night, in preparation for his visit. Jamie knew the dossier was sanitized at Langley, prior to its transmission, but enough remained intact to make her handle Kim Sunim with caution. As a Special Forces sergeant, he had served a double tour in Vietnam, chalking up forty-seven registered kills with the Phoenix program. Recruited by the Company on discharge, Kim had turned his special talents to the "wet" assignments CIA was theoretically prohibited from mounting. Operations—minus any culpatory details—were recorded from Korea, Thailand, Tokyo, Cambodia and Laos, Taiwan, the Chinese mainland. Dates and places, coinciding with a rash of sudden deaths that proved untraceable, despite the allegations and suspicions of survivors.

Kim did not resemble other killers she had known. In Jamie's limited experience, professional assassins normally put on a face of stone, or overcompensated for their occupation with a show of artificial joviality. The man who sat beside her now was . . . different. Reserved, without seeming defensive. Casual, rather than paranoid.

She wondered how he handled it, what made him leave. Above all else, she wondered how the Company had wooed him back. What kind of friendship caused a man to leave the safety of retirement, risk his life and take the lives of others?

It seemed incredible, but Kim had left the Company two years before her own recruitment. At thirty-two, Jamie had nine years in service, and sometimes she still wondered how it had all come about. A political science major at UCLA, she had been apprehensive about graduation, uncertain of what she should do with her life. She had forestalled the decision by enrolling in a graduate assistant program, the position evolving into a short-run romance with her professor while Jamie scanned dead-end clerical jobs on the side. One afternoon, her lover had suggested that she try the CIA for "something different." It had been a joke, at first, but she had filed the application, tolerated background checks and polygraph exams, surprised to find herself accepted as a new "career trainee."

It took a month for Jamie to decide she had been actively recruited by the man who used her body, and it startled her to realize she didn't care. By that time, her relationship with the professor had been severed, amiably, and she had a new career in hand. She liked the new direction that her life had taken, and she had no thought of turning back.

Initial courses for trainees were taught by Company instructors at the Broyhill Institute, in Arlington, Virginia. Jamie had been drilled on various security procedures, structure of the CIA and various competing agencies, along with the tactics and goals of world communism. From Broyhill, she went on to more intensive schooling at Camp Peary, outside Williamsburg. "The Farm," as it was known to Company insiders, bore a strong resemblance to a military installation, sprawling over 480 wooded acres, complete with weapons ranges, jump towers, obstacle courses, and a simulated closed border, patroled by scowling "Soviets."

Instructors at the Farm had checked her out on weapons, cryptography, rudimentary demolitions and electronics, surveillance, escape and evasion. It had been exciting, but to date, her only brush with death had come through handling Reese Holland, known as Domino.

And that had blown up in her face.

She still had no precise idea why Domino was killed, or who had done the job. Presumably, her passenger would find the answers, pay back blood for blood. If he survived that long.

Kim's friendship with the murdered agent was a problem. Jamie knew that close emotional attachments altered judgment, skewed perception, sometimes prompting rash— or even suicidal—actions. Kim Sunim did not strike her as the impulsive sort, but she was worried, all the same.

A second loss would definitely mar her record as a handler; never mind what it would do to her inside.

The South Gate loomed before them, and she passed beneath it, bearing north and east through spotty traffic. Beside her, Kim might have been sleeping as they passed the Bank of Korea and Seoul's central post office. His silence, the casual air of dismissal, struck sparks. She swerved her Toyota into the KAL Building's half-empty lot and slammed on the brakes.

"I'll say this once," she snapped, as Kim came instantly alert. "I know my job. I'm good at what I do, all right? I didn't blow the game for Domino."

"What happened, then?"

His tone deflated some of Jamie's anger.

"God, I wish I knew. We followed Company procedure down the line, used cut-outs, blind drops. It was textbook, all the way."

"Except?"

"About three weeks ago, he stopped reporting. Missed his scheduled contacts. Christ, we even tried an open line, but he was never home."

"You should have pulled him in."

"We did. I mean, we *tried*. Sent chasers out to run him down. He lost them once, and when they picked him up again, he put them in the hospital. By that time—"

"You began to wonder if he hadn't turned?"

"What *could* I think?"

"Who tagged him, Jamie?"

"I don't know." Her voice was firm, despite the fact that she was trembling inside. "It wasn't us, if that's what's on your mind. You know the Company. We work through channels, and there simply wasn't time."

"A free-lance?"

"No." She shook her head. "I'm sure I would have seen the tracks."

"I hope you're right."

She held his gaze, and felt herself beneath a microscope. "I don't know why he chose to break the chain and isolate himself. I can't say what was going on inside his mind. Whatever brought him down, it's not my fault."

"You're not on trial," he told her.

"No? I feel as if I am."

"Paranoia is an occupational hazard."

"Maybe so, but just because you're paranoid—"

"It doesn't mean that no one's out to get you?"

"Right."

"I'm counting on your full cooperation."

"Certainly. Just tell me what you need."

"A shower would be nice. That is, if we're all finished, here."

"Of course."

She put the car in gear and headed for the Metro, one block south of Eulji-ro. Relief was tempered by the fact that Kim did not entirely trust her, yet. His life was on the line, a friend was dead, and Jamie knew that trust would be in short supply until the killers were identified, their sponsors singled out and marked for Company reprisal.

In the meantime, she would help Kim all she could, as per her orders, and she would refrain from crossing him unless the mission clearly called for handler intervention. Jamie meant to follow her instructions, play it safe, and come out on the other side alive.

She parked in front of the hotel, unlocked the trunk for Kim to get his bags. Her offer of assistance with the check-in was declined.

"I make it three-oh-five," she said, after a consultation with her watch. "You'll need some rest, I know, but we should really put our heads together on some kind of strategy."

"Agreed."

"How's dinner sound?"

"I'm free."

Kim offered her a cautious smile, which she returned with interest.

"Six o'clock all right?" She caught herself. "I should say eighteen-hundred hours."

"Six is fine."

"I'll make some reservations. Anything off-limits?"

"Airline food."

"Okay, I'll see you then."

She watched him disappear inside before she drove away. There were reports to type and file before she slept, but Fitz would have to cope with routine traffic. She was handling, and that demanded concentration.

Having fumbled once, already, Jamie prayed that she was equal to the task.

The Metro's lobby seemed deserted, but a second glance revealed the concierge. Kim dropped his bags and showed his passport to confirm the reservation held for Kim Su Chung. The concierge ran off a charge slip on his Visa card, provided by the Company, and tapped a bell to conjure up the porter.

"Seven twenty-one." The bellboy nodded, palmed a key, and double-checked the number. Then, to Kim, "Enjoy your time in Seoul."

"I will."

He trailed the porter to a bank of elevators, where they found one standing ready. On the seventh floor, Kim waited while his door was opened, lights turned on, his bags deposited beside the bed. He tipped the porter twenty *won* and got his room key in return.

Examining the room for bugs was probably a waste of time, but Kim went through the motions, checking picture frames and lamp shades, peering under furniture, dismantling the telephone to look for an infinity device that could, upon command, transform the phone itself into a bug. He knew there were a hundred ways to wire the room, beyond the reach of any normal hands-on search, but he did not intend to transact business there, in any case.

The flight had left him feeling sweaty, soiled. He stripped and headed for the bathroom, thinking of Jamie Constable as he turned on the shower, adjusted its spray, stepped inside. Kim ignored the faint stirrings of animal attraction, concentrating on a rough analysis of Jamie's character, her capabilities.

A fair judge of people, he suspected that her show of anger and frustration over Holland's death had been sincere. Within the limits of her job, she seemed straightforward, open—though such naive terms as "honest" would be out of place. Jamie might be an excellent actress, but Kim didn't think so. There was an equal possibility that she, herself, had been deceived.

Which brought him back to Holland. Reaching for a towel, he sifted through the reasons why a seasoned agent might decide to isolate himself from his control. The obvious

solution was a leak. At some point, Holland had suspected
that communications with his handler were not secure. He
feared a leak, somewhere along the line, that would have
jeopardized his mission—or his life.

It might be worse than that, but Kim was not prepared
to shadowbox with adversaries of his own imagination. He
had enemies enough in Seoul, without inventing more.

He slipped a robe on as he headed for the balcony. His
room faced westward, toward the high-rise heart of Seoul,
where office buildings, banks, hotels, and shopping centers
etched their outlines on a velvet sky. Examining the city that
was once his home, Kim noted striking changes, milestones
on the march of progress, but he also saw that much remained
the same, evoking memories. He shuffled them aside and
concentrated on his job.

Three hours, yet, to dawn, and twice that long before he
could begin to make connections in the city. Many of his
former contacts would be obsolete, Kim reasoned. Death,
retirement, relocation would have thinned the ranks, but one
or two should be enough, if he selected them judiciously.

No need to trouble Jamie Constable with the arrangements. She would ask for details, explanations he was not
prepared to offer, and despite his first impressions of the
woman, he was not prepared to trust her with his life.

Not yet.

She *was* attractive, undeniably. Her green eyes hinted at
a mystery behind the cool facade, and Kim suspected that it
bore no correlation to her duties with the Company.

He felt the first, faint stirrings of a biological response
and pushed them out of mind. Retreating from the balcony,
Kim shed his robe and took up a position in the center of the
room. Expelling conscious thought, ignoring the persistent
tingling in his groin, Kim focused full attention on his feet,
imagining that they had taken root. His concentrated force
responded to the pull of gravity, like iron compelled to seek a
magnet, feeding on an elemental force of nature, growing
stronger through the mutual exchange.

When he was satisfied with his foundation, Kim began
the solitary t'ai chi exercise, meticulously executing each of
sixty-five distinctive postures. Alternately swift and slow, his
movements were designed to concentrate attention on the

body, its immediate environment, subjugating flesh to will. Kim kept his eyes closed, screening out distractions, finding everything he longed to see within himself.

The *kata*, executed properly, consumes a quarter-hour. Kim ran through it twice, enjoyed a second shower, and slipped naked in between the crisp sheets of his queen-sized bed. Another fleeting thought of Jamie crossed his mind and vanished, as he focused on the corridor of sleep.

Kim hoped he would not dream.

Chapter 4

In the beginning, there was war.

Incredibly, despite the countless warnings, months of saber-rattling on both sides of the parallel dividing North and South Korea, the eruption of overt hostilities took South Korea's thin line of defenders by complete surprise. The twenty-fifth of June had been a rainy Sunday morning, storm clouds massing low on the horizon. Sentries, huddled in their ponchos, first mistook the rumble of artillery for thunder peeling in the north. The proof of their mistake arrived with fire and steel, as long-range shells exploded in their midst.

Across the parallel streamed 90,000 North Korean troops, preceded by an armored column consisting of several hundred tanks. The tanks, to no one's great surprise, were Soviet-designed and manufactured—the monster T-34s, with their impenetrable hides and roaring 85-mm cannon. Stunned by the ferocity of the assault, stood garrisons of ROK militiamen at half their normal strength; commanders had released the other half for weekend leave in Seoul, some fifty miles below the parallel. Equipped with puny 37-mm anti-tank guns and a few 2.36-inch rocket launchers, the ROKs were helpless against Soviet armor, dismayed as their projectiles detonated harmlessly or ricocheted off sturdy armor plate.

The desperate defense became a rout as Russian tanks and North Korean infantry rolled south, invulnerable, sweeping everything before them. Terrified, ROK soldiers dropped their weapons where they stood and raced for safety, to the rear.

In Seoul, PoSun Sunim was not surprised by the invasion of his homeland. He had listened carefully to speeches, news reports, as Syngman Rhee, the South Korean president, had vowed to liberate his northern kinsman from the yoke of Russian bondage. From Pyongyang, the outlawed voice of Kim Il Sung had promised to relieve the southern populace of their oppression by Americans and fascist lackeys. Recently, however, North Korea's voice had called for peace, a laying down of arms, and so PoSun Sunim prepared himself for war.

His preparations had been gradual and unobtrusive, nothing to disrupt the flow of business or his daily life in Seoul. A merchant trading gold and jade, he carried choicer items from his inventory home at night, prepared to save his stock in the event of an attack. His wife, Mai Kwan, was not aware of any change in his demeanor—or, if so, she wisely kept it to herself.

PoSun Sunim went into work as usual on Monday morning, after the invasion. There were preparations to be made, in case they had to flee the city, but he cherished hope that ROK defenders might recoup their losses, halt the communist advance at Uijongbu, twenty miles due north of Seoul.

The town of Uijongbu is a hub of transportation, dominating all roads south. It was the natural selection for a last-ditch stand, and there two ROK divisions gathered on the twenty-sixth of June, determined to repulse their enemy.

Two highways enter Uijongbu from the north, and on the morning of the twenty-sixth, invaders held them both, advancing swiftly toward the final obstacle that blocked their march on South Korea's capital. A ROK division on the western fork attacked in strength, surprising the invader with the sheer ferocity of its assault, and drove the North Koreans back. Despite their heavy losses, the defenders got a fleeting taste of victory.

Behind them, on the eastern road to Uijongbu, a commander whose contempt for the defense plan had been overruled by his superiors sat sulking in his tent, refusing to deploy his troops. An armored column crushed him, put his men to flight, and flanked the bold defenders on the west, compelling them to scatter through the countryside.

The road to Seoul lay open. Waiting.

Saddened by the news, PoSun Sunim made ready to evacuate his home. That afternoon, before he closed his shop, he filled a leather satchel up with gold, the finer bits of jade, and left the rest behind. At home, he told Mai Kwan they would be leaving Seoul tomorrow, for the south. She asked no questions, made no protest. Lying at her husband's side that night, immune to sleep, she heard the grumble of artillery, like giants bickering among themselves in language that she could not understand.

They packed the next morning, sorting through the items they had managed to collect in seven years of marriage. Much of it would have to stay behind, but Mai Kwan made a point of holding out her cooking implements, supplies, sufficient clothing for them both. PoSun Sunim did not believe in banks, and as his trade had been successful, so he had accumulated a substantial cache of currency. They might be hounded into exile, but with gold and ready *won* in hand, they would not go as peasants, driven by the wind.

Despite his relative prosperity, PoSun Sunim maintained a modest home. In the Korean style, it was a single-story box, divided into smallish rooms within. A Western visitor would likely have remarked upon the small, infrequent windows, but Korean homes are built to shelter their inhabitants from cold and rain. A man who wants to see the sky need only step outside.

Inside the house, there was a minimum of furniture, with seating on the floor. In winter, heat was radiated through the *ondol* floors from sub-floor-level flues. The central living room served double duty as a dining room and sleeping area for guests. As master of the house, PoSun Sunim maintained the front room for himself, a male preserve that Mai Kwan was prohibited from entering. An educated man, he furnished his retreat with cushions on the floor, shelves stocked with books, an ornate desk, the dwelling's single chair. Mai Kwan's room, at the rear, held bedding, wardrobes, sewing articles, her art supplies.

PoSun had never squandered money on a car, but they were fortunate in owning two small carts that could be pushed or pulled by hand. When both were heaped with articles they could not bring themselves to leave behind, their fortune cleverly concealed, Mai Kwan prepared a final meal at home and they sat down to eat, refusing to be hurried. It was after one o'clock before they left the house and plunged into the chaos that was Seoul in flight.

It seemed that every one of Seoul's four million people

had been simultaneously set adrift. They crowded streets and alleyways, brought motor traffic to a standstill, giving way reluctantly before the military convoys pushing north, to meet the enemy. In the jeeps and trucks, young soldiers scanned the throng with haunted eyes, as if aware that they were riding to their death.

Mai Kwan stayed close behind her husband as he navigated through the crowd, occasionally making progress, sometimes forced to stand and wait for what seemed hours, while policemen fought to clear the intersection just ahead. Around them, mothers clung to screaming children, cradling infants in their arms. Old men and ancient crones were jostled to and fro like cattle in a holding pen, until a few of them gave up and squatted in the middle of the street, defying anyone to make them move. The stronger refugees bore A-frames on their backs, their worldly goods bound up in rope and rags, while others held the reins on ox-drawn carts.

The few policemen they encountered on their way were powerless to stem the tide. Most huddled in the doorways of abandoned shops; a few attempted to control the human tide and keep it moving, swinging truncheons at the slower refugees. As Mai Kwan watched, three officers surrounded a suspected looter, trapping him against a lamp post, flailing with their clubs in helpless rage until the man was scarcely recognizable.

The broad Han River forms a barrier to traffic south of Seoul. Three railway bridges and a single highway bridge had been erected or repaired with the expulsion of the Japanese invaders, after World War II, and all of them were crowded now. Pedestrians and oxen, bicycles and handcarts jammed together so that trains were forced to stand and wait, while cars and trucks were fortunate to creep along at a walking pace.

By twelve o'clock that night, PoSun Sunim had reached the highway bridge, his wife in tow. A walk that normally required four hours had consumed eleven; crossing over would require another hour and a quarter, by itself. Behind them, red artillery had found its range and high-explosive shells were falling on the northern outskirts of the city, churning homes to dust, incinerating dreams.

If Seoul was chaos, then the south bank of the Han was pandemonium. It seemed that, having once escaped the city, many refugees had no idea of what to do or where to go.

They milled about like termites, jabbering excitedly, their tension and frustration flaring into shoving matches, fistfights. Pushing past the aimless and abandoned, Mai Kwan trailed her husband as he made his slow way south.

An army jeep was rolling toward them, struggling against the tide, its driver leaning on the horn. The driver was Korean, but his passenger was an American, broad-shouldered, flushed with anger as he cursed the refugees and motioned them aside.

The bridge was still a hundred yards away when sudden thunder rippled through the soil. Before PoSun Sunim could turn and face the Han, a second thunderclap erupted, followed swiftly by a third and fourth. His mouth fell open as he caught a glimpse of hell on earth.

The bridges had been wired for detonation in the face of an advancing enemy, but someone in the ROK command had issued orders for their premature destruction. Battered by the shock waves, watching men and women fall on every side, PoSun saw girders, slabs of concrete, oxen, human bodies, airborne in a roiling storm of smoke and dust. His ears were numb and ringing; when he called out to Mai Kwan, he could not hear himself above the din of the explosions.

The tall American had left his jeep and stood beside it, pounding on the hood with angry fists and weeping openly. His driver slumped behind the wheel, eyes closed, as if he had been stricken lifeless where he sat.

The Han was momentarily obscured by drifting smoke. As it began to clear, Mai Kwan beheld the swirling water jammed with rubble, mutilated bodies, shattered railroad ties. In places, blackened rails thrust up like pylons from the current, snagging corpses, holding them in place, pale faces upturned toward the smoky sky.

She gave up counting, knew there must be hundreds from the highway bridge alone. A hand upon her shoulder startled Mai Kwan, made her jump. She turned to face her husband, hardly recognized him in his dusty clothes, a smudge of grime across his forehead.

"Come."

She nodded silently, took up her cart and followed. Southward.

*   *   *

It took two weeks to walk the hundred miles from Seoul to Pusan, in the south, along a dusty highway clogged with refugees. PoSun Sunim would not attempt to count the lifeless bodies he had passed, their clothing and belongings stripped away by relatives or strangers who believed that they could carry just a little more. At other points, where strength and will had snapped before the heart gave out, he saw the scattered vestiges of someone's worldly goods, discarded in their flight, fair game for human scavengers.

The one thing he saw little of was uniforms. It would be weeks before a final tabulation was completed, and the wartime censors would "revise" initial estimates, but more than 40,000 soldiers of the South Korean army had been trapped, abandoned to the tender mercies of their enemy, when bridges south of Seoul were detonated prematurely. Those who managed to escape were more concerned with fleeing for their lives than mounting a defense against the communists.

Upon arrival in Pusan, they were directed to a teeming settlement of refugees beside the Nakdong River, west of town. Construction crews were busy round the clock, erecting plywood shanties on a barren stretch of ground already crowded, growing more so by the day. PoSun Sunim surveyed the camp in all its squalor, recognized it as another test of will, and vowed that he would not allow himself to be defeated.

With the gold and *won* he carried, better quarters were available, but nothing could persuade PoSun to touch the money yet. Two weeks of marching in the sun had left him thinner, filthy, and exhausted like the rest. There was no reason any of them should suspect he was a man of property and means.

The lessons of the highway had impressed themselves upon PoSun Sunim. He had observed the way catastrophe demolished social mores, scourging filial respect, until the young felt free to loot their elders, even strip their bodies as they lay beside the road. The message had been clear; he must refrain from tempting any of the thieves around him with a show of wealth. In any case, he thought, the gold and money would be needed when they got back home, to Seoul.

Their lodging in the compound was a one-room hovel,

walls of plywood and a roof of corrugated metal. In the rain, PoSun imagined, the interior would echo like a kettle drum. A single door provided entry to the shack, and windows were a luxury the builders managed to avoid. Their absence was a blessing in disguise, PoSun decided, since their neighbors had been crowded in at four-foot intervals, another row of shanties at their back. The simple layout had delineated dusty streets throughout the compound, gritty under foot, that would be churned to mud the moment it began to rain.

For purposes of sanitation, a communal shower was erected at the center of the compound, with the water strictly rationed, men and women granted time to wash themselves on alternating days. Latrines had been constructed at the north end of the camp, but new arrivals outstripped hasty plans, and soon shacks sprouted up around the reeking trenches, marching north as if to meet the enemy, in carbon-copy rows.

Mai Kwan did what she could to make the plywood box a home. She put down salvaged rugs to hide the rough-hewn floorboards, decorated homely walls with swatches of material that she had carried south with the intent of sewing dresses for herself. As summer crept toward fall, PoSun spent several *won* on oilcloth, and they did their best to insulate the tiny house against the winter yet to come.

Close quarters and a total lack of privacy placed heavy strain upon the husband-wife relationship. Like most Koreans of their generation, PoSun and Mai Kwan had been selected for each other by their parents, at a tender age, the bargain signed and sealed without a pretense of consent from would-be bride and groom. They had been strangers at their wedding, stepping into roles ordained by national tradition. Females were subordinate to males in the Korean family, expected to maintain a home, obey their husbands, and refrain from any major contact with society at large. So rigid were the guidelines of familial behavior, that the rooms within a house were sexually segregated; trespass in her husband's study was forbidden to a wife, while men, except at bedtime, were excluded from their spouses' sitting rooms.

Inevitably, the traditional arrangements produced mutual alienation between husband and wife. They came together over meals and after dark, for sleep or sex, but otherwise their lives were largely separate, with only incidental points of contact. Family life might not be passionate, but it was ordered and secure—until the shells began to fall on Seoul.

At one rude stroke, tradition and the social fabric of the family had been ripped away, discarded in a flight for life that ended in the camps outside Pusan. It was impossible for man and wife to go their separate ways inside a one-room shack, and while PoSun Sunim was not averse to sharing Mai Kwan's company, per se, the situation struck him as unnatural. In time, it grated on his nerves and he became resentful, punishing his wife for something that was not her fault, inflicting stony silences that lasted hours at a time. He could not bring himself to touch her, when they lay together in the darkness, and PoSun consoled himself with the belief that touching would have been a fruitless exercise.

The primary function of a Korean family is the propagation of children, specifically sons, to carry on the name. In seven years of marriage, Mai Kwan had produced a single child—a daughter—but the gods had frowned and taken back their gift a few days later. Doctors stolidly assured PoSun Sunim that having other children should not be a problem. None of them could readily explain Mai Kwan's continued failure to conceive.

In the tenth week of their exile at Pusan, American Marines surprised the communist invaders with an amphibious landing at Inchon, storming enemy defenses, racing inland toward the capital. Seoul's liberation from the godless North Koreans was proclaimed on September 26th, producing a carnival atmosphere among refugees in the south.

PoSun Sunim observed the celebration, smiling with his neighbors, sharing in the homemade wine that passed from hand to hand. The reservation in his manner passed unnoticed by the others, and he spoke no word to dampen their enthusiasm for the victory.

Mai Kwan did not imbibe—no wine was offered to the wives and daughters of the compound—but she felt rejuvenated, all the same. They would be going home soon, picking up their normal lives as if the interruption had been fantasy, a waking dream. God willing, she would find their home intact, and if repairs were necessary, she would gladly undertake the task herself.

The celebration started losing steam near midnight, and Mai Kwan was waiting when PoSun returned. He smelled of wine and fireworks, and she thought he might have been a little drunk, but he was steady on his feet, carrying himself with familiar dignity.

The spark in PoSun's eyes, however, had been less familiar in the weeks since they were driven from their home. Mai Kwan immediately recognized his need, before he took her hand and led her to their sleeping pallet in a corner of the room. She felt a quickening within herself and followed him with downcast eyes, afraid that he might recognize her own excitement.

Before her marriage, Mai Kwan had received instruction in the duties of a wife. Her mother had explained that, while the marriage bed might be repulsive, it was necessary to the survival of the family in future generations. If she kept her wits about her, offered no resistance and produced the sons her husband needed to fulfill himself, she would discover that male ardor faded over time. Cessation of the appetite with age was nature's gift to women, a reward for all the suffering of youth.

Mai Kwan had been surprised, therefore, to find that she enjoyed the act of sex. PoSun, for all his clumsy inexperience, lit unexpected fires inside her, and they learned together, through experience. The perfect wife in every way, Mai Kwan was careful to conceal her pleasure, never venturing to act as the aggressor. Fulfillment in their coupling was Mai Kwan's own sweet secret, and she kept it to herself.

This night, PoSun undressed her with an urgency that made her heart beat faster, dropped his clothing in a pile, and pulled her down beside him on the pallet. Smothering her throat and breasts with hungry kisses, teasing at her rigid nipples with his tongue, PoSun aroused her to a state of trembling desire. His fingers grazed the flat plain of her stomach, rummaging between her thighs, and Mai Kwan spread her legs in welcome. Delicacy lost the race to zeal, but she was too excited now to care.

When she was wet and ready, PoSun moved between her knees and entered her by slow degrees, prolonging the exquisite agony of penetration. As he filled her, Mai Kwan arched her back, unable to contain herself, responding automatically to PoSun's driving rhythm. She surprised him, and he missed a stroke, recovering at once to match her tempo. In her near delirium, Mai Kwan was certain he had never delved so deep before. When he exploded, going rigid as a dead man, she was filled with scalding seed.

She lay awake long afterward, knees drawn up tight against her chest, and cherished the sensation of his warmth, his strength, within her body. As she drifted off to sleep, near dawn, her drowsy mind was swimming with the images of new life sparking in her loins.

Next morning, many of their neighbors in the camp were packing up to leave for home, encouraged by reports of the United Nations forces rolling north through scattered opposition, driving battered communists before them. Soon, a full-scale exodus was under way, reversing the traumatic flight from Seoul. Each day, Mai Kwan expected to be told that they must pack their things and take the road, and every night she watched PoSun, aware that he was struggling within himself.

It would have been a simple thing to leave the camp behind and travel north with all the others, trusting the Americans to hold their enemies at bay. In spite of optimistic news from Seoul, PoSun Sunim was hesitant to move, expecting treachery and further disappointment if his calculated moves were premature. He followed the American advance by means of radio, and heard the warning rumbles out of China as MacArthur's troops approached the Yalu River. If the Chinese giant was aroused to fight, the war might take a very different turn. Until the matter had been settled, it was best to watch and wait.

In late October, Mai Kwan broke the news that she was pregnant. PoSun put a solemn face on his elation, kissed her once, and set about the task of finding better quarters for his wife and child-to-be. Until the baby was delivered, there could be no thought of going home to Seoul.

With vacancies throughout the camp, he found a two-room bungalow constructed in the early days of war, to house a larger family, before the trend had run to tiny shoebox dwellings. For a modest fee, he managed to convince the compound supervisor that his altered situation warranted a change, and so the move was made. Mai Kwan experienced a certain sadness at the thought of being kept away from Seoul, but it was not her place to interfere.

On November 29, 850,000 Chinese "volunteers" attacked across the Yalu, scattering their ROK opponents, cutting off American Marines at Chosin reservoir. By early January, they were in the streets of Seoul, and PoSun's private doubts were realized as South Korea's capital became the fulcrum of a lethal seesaw. United Nations troops recaptured Seoul in March, were driven out again in May, returned to stake their claim in June.

Mai Kwan, for all her eagerness to see their home again, was thankful for her husband's wisdom as she listened to the grim reports of tragedy from Seoul. PoSun saw fit to pamper her, in violation of traditions that required a woman to maintain her active role as housewife through the final stages of a pregnancy, and Mai Kwan understood his fear that something might go wrong, some damage might be suffered by their child.

For once, his premonitions were unfounded. In the third hot week of June, a few days after U.N. troops began their final push through Seoul, she was delivered of a healthy son.

An hour after giving birth, Mai Kwan consumed a meal of rice and seaweed soup, the only food considered healthy for new mothers. While PoSun Sunim was not a superstitious man, he took no chances with his son. A table was erected in the corner of his wife's delivery room, bowls of rice and clear, cool water left upon it as an offering to *Samshin Halmoni*, the spirit charged with standing guard at childbirth. Across the entrance to their bungalow, PoSun tacked up a length of twine—the *inchul*—strung with bits of charcoal and red peppers to denote a man-child's birth. No visitors, including relatives, would cross that boundary line for twenty-one days, insulating the child from contagion during his first three weeks of life.

Korean children are not named, officially, until they come of age. In keeping with tradition, "birth names" are affixed to boys, while girls remain anonymous throughout their early years. PoSun Sunim did not consult Mai Kwan before he chose a birth name for their son. It was a woman's task to bear the child, to bathe him, keep him clothed and fed, but she would have no voice in the decisions that determined how his life was spent. Selection of a name, a mate, and a career would be the father's sole prerogative.

PoSun Sunim spent four days pondering the problem of a birth name, finally settling on "Kim" because it was his father's name, a gesture of respect. In truth, he had no great affection for his father—who was dead, in any case—but the selection of a simple birth name gave him years in which to find his son a perfect name.

Emerging from his quarantine, PoSun informed the compound supervisor that his family would be leaving soon, for Seoul. Mai Kwan was both excited and unsettled by the news, delighted to be going home, afraid of what she might find waiting for her, there.

PoSun acquired an ox and cart, with ample room for their belongings and a rough wood seat for them to ride on. Four weeks after Kim was born, they left the Pusan camp forever, moving north toward what had been their home.

With decent transportation and a highway relatively clear of refugees, the trek to Seoul took seven days. They found the city ravaged by artillery and house-to-house combat, the streets still heaped with rubble where construction crews were taking stock and measuring the task of reconstruction. Animated scarecrows drifted through the wreckage, feeding out of trash bins, scattering at the approach of soldiers or police.

PoSun's first destination was his shop. Surprisingly, the street had suffered little damage, save for broken windows, doors pried open by invaders or the looters who had followed in their wake. The pavement glittered with a layer of broken glass, but window panes and doors could be replaced.

Across the street, a bank had been demolished by the point-blank cannon fire of Russian tanks, its gutted hulk a monument to PoSun's private skepticism of financial institutions. Money would be needed, to repair his shop, but cash was not the problem. With the resurrection of official buildings underway throughout the capital, he worried most about a shortage of proficient carpenters.

No matter. If it came to that, PoSun would renovate the shop himself, work day and night to see it finished. With another mouth to feed, a son to carry on his name and trade, the merchant could afford to spare no effort.

Mai Kwan had a premonition of disaster as they left the shop and clattered through the streets of Seoul, toward home. PoSun seemed pleased that nothing worse had happened to his shop; it was presumptuous to think they should be doubly blessed and find their house intact.

Approaching the familiar neighborhood, they trespassed on a field of desolation, jolting over pavement gouged and furrowed by the treads of armored vehicles. The shelling had been brutal here, and nothing recognizable as human habitation had survived. Mai Kwan wept silently as they approached their home—a crater now—and tiny Kim observed her tears, reached out to dab them from her cheeks with childish curiosity.

They spent a week in makeshift quarters, hastily designed for homeless refugees, before PoSun's connections in the war-torn city brought him word of other housing. Certain wealthy neighborhoods had managed to escape with only superficial damage, homes deserted by their occupants when the invaders entered Seoul. There had been looting, vandalism by the communists, but many of the houses were intact. A number were available at bargain prices, now that families decimated by the war could not afford their upkeep.

PoSun visited a dozen empty homes before deciding, on his own, which one to purchase. Mai Kwan was permitted to approve his choice, a gesture she found touching, though she entertained no thought of argument. With twice the floor space of their former home, the structure seemed a palace. Mai Kwan was delighted, but her joy was tempered with a sadness for the loss of others.

The repairs on PoSun's shop proceeded swiftly, once he found a team of workmen equal to the task. By August, he was back in business, joined by other merchants in the neighborhood, their patrons drawn primarily from government and Seoul's prevailing upper class, survivors who had managed to escape the city with their fortunes more or less intact. Attempting to rebuild their lives, restore their station in society, the wealthy spent their cash compulsively on clothing, trinkets, household decorations. PoSun's gold and jade attracted customers in record numbers, and he made important friends while raking in their money. It seemed to matter little that the war dragged on, along the parallel, no more than fifty miles from Seoul. Reports of casualties brought more business to the shop, from patrons anxious to forget the fighting.

On October 2, the hundredth day of life for Kim Sunim, his parents paid their homage to tradition by inviting friends and family to an elaborate feast, in honor of their first-born son. Mai Kwan prepared large quantities of food, and the invited guests brought rings of gold as presents for the child, receiving rice cakes in return. In days to come, PoSun would sort the rings and save a dozen of the finest for his son; the others would be melted down, refashioned into jewelry for his shop.

PoSun Sunim was proud of Kim, but their relationship was necessarily reserved, its boundaries predicated on tradition. Filial piety is the cornerstone of the Korean family, dictating absolute subservience of child to parent, with the father-son relationship exalted over any other bond—including man and wife. Mai Kwan accepted the inevitable, doting on her son, and there were times when she believed the child had actually brought her closer to her husband. Having once fulfilled her function as a woman, she found greater favor in his eyes, and he rewarded her with gifts, increased attention, more affection in the marriage bed.

On Kim's first birthday, yet another banquet was convened. The *tol* feast is a ceremonial occasion, theoretically designed to chart an infant's course in life, and while PoSun Sunim dismissed the superstitious aspect of the ritual, he realized that an observance of the *tol* would be expected from a man in his position.

Kim was dressed resplendently for the occasion, in a pointed cap and tiny silken robes that whispered when he moved his arms. He felt uncomfortable as the center of attention, seated at a special table, but his childish curiosity soon focused on the objects there arranged. A hank of yarn, a writing brush, a book, some coins and other common items were displayed before him, and he studied each in turn, directing frequent glances at his parents in an effort to discover how he was expected to perform.

Tradition indicated that selection of specific objects by a

child at *tol* was useful in determining his future. Thus, a twist of yarn became the symbol of longevity; selection of the coins meant future wealth; the writing brush implied a bent toward scholarship, and so on. It was a game the grown-ups played for their amusement, only half believing, while the star performer sat bewildered in a crowd of strangers.

Lacking any guidance from his parents, Kim Sunim began to stir the brightly colored items aimlessly around the table, pushing some away, retrieving them a moment later, fondling others. Once, he struck the center of the table with a tiny fist and watched the objects jump. Amused by the reaction of his audience, he kept it up until the coins were hopping. One of them fell off the table, landed on its edge, and rolled between his father's feet.

"A fighter," someone in the crowd proclaimed.

"A soldier," one of his companions added. "Probably a famous general."

There was laughter all around, and Kim joined in, his small face lighting up. He struck the table once again, for emphasis, and looked around for something he could eat.

PoSun Sunim accepted the congratulations and the gifts of his invited guests, but he was not amused. No son of his would be a soldier, squandering his life in uniform while there was money to be made. The *tol* was peasant superstition, nothing more. He was prepared to offer living proof that men of strength controlled the destiny of those who bore their names.

The formalized cessation of hostilities with North Korea, in July of 1953, did little to alleviate the siege mentality in Seoul. Obsessed with the pursuit of "traitors," acting on authority from Syngman Rhee, Korea's CIA began a concentrated purge of dissidents and malcontents at every level of society. Suspected communists were clapped in prison by the thousands; hundreds, charged with sabotage or spying for the North, were shot by military firing squads. Suppression of dissent extended to the press, where censors were installed by government decree, and labor unions were unmercifully harassed, their every movement undermined by state *provocateurs*.

At first, PoSun Sunim ignored the purges, concentrating

on his family and business. As a solid anticommunist, he felt
no sympathy for radicals and revolutionaries; unions, for the
most part, were a nuisance, seeking higher wages for their
members who, in many cases, were already overpaid. If
certain items were deleted from the daily news before it went
to press, what of it? Syngman Rhee's regime had saved the
nation—with some help from the Americans—and the economy was on its way to full recovery.

The change occurred by slow degrees, beginning with a
whispered word from this or that respected customer, accelerated by the news that an acquaintance had been taken for
interrogation in the middle of the night. Reports of torture at
Remonclo, where the CIA maintained its base of operations,
led PoSun to wonder if the war had done some lethal damage
to the fabric of society.

One August afternoon, he was approached by Sung Lo
Chi, a merchant in the neighborhood, requesting signatures
on a petition for release of prisoners detained without a trial.
PoSun declined, requesting time to think about it, reading
disappointment in Sung's eyes, but still unwilling to commit
himself, risk everything for strangers.

Walking home from work that day, he passed Sung's
shop—a haberdashery—in time to see a black sedan pull up
outside. Four men, disguised as laborers in brand-new khaki
shirts and trousers, left the car and went inside. PoSun was
watching through the window as they greeted Sung with
smiles, then set upon him with their fists and boots, continu-
ing to kick him as he lay unconscious, helpless, on the floor.

Ashamed, PoSun Sunim retreated, dizzy with the feeling
that he should have intervened—done something, *anything*—
to help Sung Lo Chi. He did not burden Mai Kwan with his
thoughts, but in the morning, bright and early, he sought out
another copy of the dissident petition, signing with a flourish
for the world to see.

A smiling stranger called upon him three days later,
carrying a copy of the document, suggesting that PoSun had
been deceived by faithless friends, enticed to lend his name
and reputation to a cause he did not fully understand. In-
censed, the jeweler told his grinning visitor that there was no
mistake; he understood the plight of prisoners condemned to
jail without a trial and wished to see them freed. Suggestions

that he reconsider his position prompted him to terminate the interview.

Next morning, he arrived to find his windows smeared with paint, the sidewalk scrawled with epithets attacking both his politics and parentage. PoSun recruited urchins from the street to scrape his windows clean and scrub the pavement, trying to dismiss the incident from his mind, but he had kicked a hornet's nest.

Within a week, his business fell away by half; the next week, half again. His neighbors on the street seemed nervous in his presence, anxious to avoid him, and his telephone rang periodically throughout the day, with only silence or malignant laughter on the line.

One evening, in the third week of his ordeal, he received a cautious visitor at home. His caller was a longtime friend and customer, employed by the police department as a clerk. For friendship's sake, he was endangering his own career—perhaps his life—to see PoSun at home.

An order had been issued from Remonclo, to police in Seoul. PoSun Sunim, suspected of affiliation with the enemy, was now the subject of a state security investigation. The municipal police were cautioned to avoid all interference with the CIA.

PoSun immediately recognized his danger. In the future, if he was assaulted on the street or in his shop, police would find a reason not to intervene. He could be robbed and beaten, like Sung Lo Chi—or worse—and no protection from the law would be forthcoming.

Still, his visitor suggested, there might be a way to solve the problem. If his wife and child were safe...

That night, as they prepared for bed, he gave Mai Kwan an edited account of his predicament, aware from the expression on her face that she was not deceived.

"What shall become of us?" she asked, when he was finished.

"In the morning," he informed her, "I must take our son to Songgwang Sa."

Chapter 5

Songgwang Sa

Kim Sunim last saw his mother on the doorstep of their home, in Seoul. Delivery of their son to strangers was a father's task, and as a woman she would not be welcome at their destination, so Mai Kwan prepared a meal for traveling and tried to put a brave face on her sorrow.

Kim, initially, was more intrigued by preparations for the trip than worried, but he sensed his mother's grief, and at their parting he began to cry. His father's stern demand for strength dried up the tears, but Kim was left with new anxiety about their journey, frightened that his mother might not be there when they both returned.

A rickshaw had been summoned and was waiting in the street outside. Kim's bag was loaded and he sat beside his father, turning for a last glimpse of Mai Kwan as they set off.

His fear was quickly overpowered by the sights and sounds of Seoul. The streets were crowded, merchants making for their shops and peasant farmers bringing goods to market, early shoppers waiting to be first in line for bargains. Kim absorbed it all, the colors and aromas of the city, thinking that his father was a very lucky man, to work in such a place. This morning, though, he seemed distracted, almost angry, as they clattered through the early morning traffic, bound for Yongsan Station.

PoSun Sunim had not been absolutely honest with his wife. It was a man's responsibility to shield his family from the harsh realities of life, and so he had deleted certain details in his explanation to Mai Kwan. She knew there was a

problem with the government, and she was vaguely conscious
of the risks involved, but he allowed her to believe the
situation could be swiftly rectified. Removing Kim to Songgwang
Sa was a precaution, nothing more. A few short weeks, and
they would all be reunited in their home.

In fact, PoSun had no intention of placating the KCIA.
Respect for authority was ingrained in his nature, a natural
adjunct of filial piety, but his respect for this particular
authority had been irreparably damaged by experience. He
might debase himself sufficiently to pacify his enemies, but
he could not abide the thought of losing face to that extent.

Whatever happened, he did not believe Mai Kwan would
be at risk. Their son, however, was a different matter. As the
product of his father's loins and bearer of his name, Kim
stood to suffer when the government began exacting retribution for PoSun's imagined crimes.

But Kim would be secure at Songgwang Sa.

At Yongsan Station, PoSun paid their fares and took his
son aboard the waiting train. His early fears forgotten now,
Kim gazed about him with a look of wonder on his face,
delighted when his father let him have the window seat. He
would have been content to sit and watch the crowds all day,
but he was thrilled when they began to move.

Kim still had no idea where they were going, but he
stared with rapt attention at the landscape scrolling past his
window. First, more crowded streets, immediately followed
by the dizzy crossing of a railroad bridge across the Han.
They hurtled through the city outskirts, rolling south past
farms and paddies, rural tracks with carts and livestock
raising dust, between the hills where forests stood, un-
touched by man. For Kim, it was a voyage of adventure, with
its destination hidden from his sight.

They left the train at Suncheon, 120 miles southwest of
Seoul, in Chulla Namdo province. The depot was smaller
than Yongsan Station, its people more rustic in dress and
manner. After pausing on an outdoor bench to eat their
midday meal, they hired a donkey cart, PoSun dictating
orders to the driver. Moments later, they had left Suncheon
behind.

The monastery at Songgwang Sa was established in the
early thirteenth century, by the Zen master Chinul. It lies

midway between the towns of Suncheon and Kwangju, accessible by transit of a narrow, unpaved road that winds through rising, wooded hills. Songgwang Sa sits nestled in a natural circle of steep, forested peaks, insulated by nature from disturbances of the outside world. Its isolation served a double purpose in those days, providing the serenity required for meditation by its monks in residence, occasionally granting sanctuary to selected refugees from persecution.

Kim was spellbound by the forest as they wound along the narrow, climbing track. At one point, they passed close beside a waterfall, and Kim stretched out a hand to catch the spray. Birds welcomed them with song, and several times he was alerted to the rustling of furry bodies in the undergrowth beside the road.

Their first view of the monastery was imposing. It appeared to be a fortress, ringed with steep, forbidding walls, but Kim immediately saw that there were no guards on the parapets. The massive wooden gates were opening at their approach. Kim caught his breath and waited for a dragon or a troop of swordsmen to emerge, unable to disguise his disappointment when a solitary man appeared.

PoSun requested that their driver wait, and Kim surmised their visit to the fortress would be brief, since carts cost precious *won*. He walked one pace behind his father, moving toward the gate, his full attention focused on the stranger who was waiting to receive them.

Kim could see the man was old, although he had no frame of reference for estimating age. The stranger's head was shaved, but he wore sideburns and a long mustache, both snowy white. His face was deeply lined, and he appeared to be as slender as a reed inside his spotless linen robes. His feet were shod in leather sandals, with the toes exposed.

Despite his years, the old man held himself erect as they approached. He radiated silent strength, and if he feared the new arrivals it was hidden well beneath a stoic facade.

PoSun Sunim was first to bow, and Kim was quick to emulate the gesture of respect. The old men took his turn, though he did not bow quite so deeply.

"Welcome. I am Kaesong Rhee."

Kim had expected something like the sound of parchment, but the old man's voice was firm and strong. When all the introductions were complete, he led them through the gate, and Kim was treated to his first full view of Songgwang Sa.

A spacious courtyard stood before them, flanked on every side by structures that, when viewed from outside, offered the appearance of a plain, unbroken wall. Within, the square was dominated by the monastery's Buddha hall, an impressive wooden edifice topped by a slate roof, constructed in the Chinese style. The walls of this and other buildings were decorated with colorful figures from the Buddhist pantheon, sweeping landscapes, and scenes from the lives of famous monks. Smaller temples ringed the courtyard, smaller copies of the Buddha hall, each dedicated to a different Bodhisattva—saintly individuals who had achieved enlightenment but willingly postponed Nirvana to assist their brethren. Rounding out the circuit were the kitchen, dining hall, and spartan quarters kept for guests.

Behind the Buddha hall, and elevated fifty feet above it on the hillside, Kim made out another clutch of buildings, isolated from the rest. Despite his curiosity, he dared not interrupt his father to inquire about their purpose. It was wrong to eavesdrop on an adult conversation—which he did not understand, in any case—and so Kim concentrated on his new surroundings, studying the painted walls and silent doorways, startled to discover they were not alone.

Across the courtyard, several boys were sweeping off the paving stones with brooms of straw. They ranged in age from five or six years old to roughly twice that age, and all of them were dressed alike, in plain white shirts and trousers, sandals on their feet. The older boys had shaven heads, except for plaited scalp locks. None of them appeared to notice Kim, but rather bent industriously to their sweeping, moving in a line across the square.

PoSun Sunim had struck some bargain with the old man, finishing their business, and he turned to face his son, depositing Kim's bundle on the ground.

"You must remain when I have gone," he said. "Show Master Rhee the same respect you give to me."

Kim blinked at the instructions, nodding, though he did not understand. His father turned to go, and Kim picked up his bag, prepared to follow, but the old man stopped him with a firm hand on his shoulder.

"No."

Kim glanced at Master Rhee and felt a sudden tightness in his chest. His eyes were burning as his father disappeared beyond the gates, but he recalled an order to be strong and kept the tears at bay.

He felt a strange sensation, like the fleeting touch of spider's legs, that told him he was being watched. Half turning, he discovered that one boy had interrupted sweeping to observe the little drama by the gates. Kim's senior by perhaps four years, the boy had straight, dark hair and darker eyes, like chips of flat obsidian. He stared at Kim without a trace of pity or compassion in his face.

And slowly smiled.

Kim was delivered to the hands of Brother Chin for introduction to the cloistered world of Songgwang Sa. A postulant considerably younger than the master—younger even than PoSun Sunim—Chin worked at putting on a solemn face, but Kim saw through the mask instinctively, detecting smiles and laughter just beneath the surface. Coping with his loneliness, confusion, and the strange surroundings, Kim was grateful for the opportunity to deal with Brother Chin, instead of the forbidding Master Rhee.

His newfound home consisted of a tiny cell, devoid of windows, with a door that had no latch. A simple sleeping pallet filled one corner of the room; the other furnishings consisted of a table and a row of wooden pegs inserted in one wall for hanging clothes. Upon discovering that Kim was much too short to reach the pegs, Chin fetched a stool to add the necessary height.

Kim was provided with a uniform that matched the other boys', the sandals oversized and floppy on his feet. He caught Chin smiling as he tried them on, and nearly giggled at the slapping sound they made with every step. His shoes and clothing he had worn from Seoul would stay inside his room until the day his father came to take him home again.

A guest of Songgwang Sa without the privileges of membership, Kim was assigned to work within the limits of his age and capability. He rose at five o'clock—two hours later than the postulants—and joined the others for their morning meal. Each tenant of the monastery had his place inside the dining hall, before a shelf that held four bowls bound up in cloth. The phases of each meal were signaled with a wooden clapper. First, the bowls were carefully unwrapped, then three were filled with water, soup, and rice, respectively. The fourth held pickled vegetables and soy cakes, chosen from a side tray. After eating, on the given signal, every diner rinsed and cleaned his bowls, securely wrapped them, and returned them to his designated shelf.

Once daily, following the evening meal, Kim joined the monks for worship in the Buddha hall. Inside, he marveled at the ceiling, with its multicolored patterns and motifs. It made him dizzy, kneeling with his head thrown back to study every detail, and he blushed when Brother Chin surprised him at it, rapping on his skull to focus Kim's attention on the service.

Brother Chin observed his small charge with a mixture of amusement and concern, at meals and as Kim went about his chores. Too young for heavy work, he was assigned to sweep the courtyard on occasion, sometimes weeding in the garden, learning from the older boys. On alternating days, his work was supervised by Brother Kee, an older monk who had forgotten how to smile.

Aside from Kim Sunim, six boys resided at the monastery. By the end of his first week at Songgwang Sa, Kim was on speaking terms with five of them, and counted two as friends. The eldest, Jonsun Chee and Sun Il Kwan, were twelve years old and had been dedicated by their families to the priesthood. Daisong Chiun was also training as a monk, but he was only nine years old and would not wear a scalp lock, like the older boys, for three more years. All three regarded Kim with a benevolent detachment, offering advice on simple jobs he was expected to perform, but they spent hours every day in meditation, and he saw them only in the afternoons, or during meals.

Kim's special friends at Songgwang Sa were Monsin Dok, an eight-year-old, and Jung Kaesong, age five. An orphan from Kwangju, Dok was related—distantly—to Brother Kee, but the connection spared him neither work nor discipline. If anything, it seemed that Brother Kee expected more of Dok, as if to prove he played no favorites among the boys. Kaesong was small for five, the son of dissidents imprisoned by the government. He had been living at the monastery for a year, without a word from either of his parents in that time. His story troubled Kim the most, although if pressed, Kim probably could not have vocalized his fears.

The sixth boy, Tonsung Yun, spoke rarely to his fellows and ignored Kim absolutely, looking past him, *through* him, with the eyes that had arrested Kim's attention on the day of his arrival at the monastery. When he did speak, it was frequently to snap at Jung Kaesong, denouncing him for some imagined failure at his chores, and Yun would sulk when reprimanded by the older boys or Brother Kee. The monastery's youngest monk-in-training, it appeared—at least to Kim—that Tonsung Yun had far to go before he reached enlightenment.

Each afternoon, an hour past the midday meal, the postulants forsook their meditations for a trek to the restricted portion of the compound, on the slope behind the Buddha hall. As simple guests, Kaesong and Kim were not permitted to attend these sessions, but they watched the older boys on their return, observed them practicing their solo exercises like a troupe of dancers, sometimes pairing off to spar with one another. Of the lot, Kim saw that Tonsung Yun worked hardest at his lessons, interrupting each new exercise to start from the beginning if he made the slightest error.

"That's t'ai chi," Kaesong informed him on the first occasion of their spying. "Master Rhee is *go-jang* for the province. Maybe for the country, I don't know."

"*Go-jang?*"

"Grand master. He has never been defeated."

Fascinated, Kim began to memorize the students' moves and tried to practice in his tiny room, at night, but there was obviously something missing. Several times, he failed to pull a punch and struck the wall, inventing stories to explain the scrapes and bruises on his knuckles. He began to wish that he could join the others in their lessons, studying with Master Rhee.

By his eleventh day at Songgwang Sa, adventure had begun to lose its novelty for Kim Sunim. He wondered if his parents had forgotten him or found a better child to take his place. If he could only have a second chance, Kim knew that he could please them, make them change their minds and take him back. It seemed unfair that they should cast him out, when he had done no wrong to warrant punishment.

Or had he?

Was he, somehow, guilty by the very fact of his existence? Was there something evil in his flesh and blood that made his parents give him up, as all his new-found friends had been delivered by their families to Songgwang Sa?

That afternoon, the keeper of the gate announced a visitor's approach. Kim's heart began to pound, and he forgot his broom, exhilarated at the prospect of his father coming back to claim him. Master Rhee swept past him, moving toward the gates, and Brother Kee, though frowning, did not scold Kim for his sloth.

The gates were opened, and he froze. The visitor was not his father, but Kim recognized the face. This man had called upon his father, at their home in Seoul, the night before they came to Songgwang Sa. Perhaps, he thought, his father was detained by business at the shop; he might have sent this friend to fetch his son.

Across the courtyard, Kim imagined that the new arrival spotted him and cringed, as if with shame or guilt. He bowed to Master Rhee, and they began to speak in whispered tones, too far away for Kim to catch their words. From time to time, he thought the man glanced back in his direction, careful not to meet Kim's eyes.

A few more moments, and he realized the man was leaving. Had he known the stranger's name, Kim would have called to him, ignoring the proprieties to seek an explanation. As it was, the stranger turned away without a backward glance, the gates closed tight behind him.

Shaken, Kim was barely cognizant of Master Rhee's approach. The old man stood before him, gazing down at Kim with eyes that had seen everything, forgotten nothing.

"Come with me," he said.

"My work . . ."

"The dust will wait."

He followed Master Rhee into the Buddha hall, depositing his sandals on the threshold. Once inside, the old man led him to a corner, sat beside him on the floor.

"You know the man who spoke with me just now?"

"No, Master. I have seen him once before."

"In Seoul."

It had not been a question, but Kim nodded, all the same.

"He is your father's friend."

"I think so, Master Rhee."

"He brings us news, about your parents."

Kim could think of no appropriate response, and so kept silent. Master Rhee continued, couching his report in terms a child might comprehend.

"They have been called away," he said. "A journey lies before them which is theirs alone. You understand?"

"No, Master."

"Every life is filled with partings, separations. Sometimes, those we care for most are chosen by the fates for other duties."

"I should join them," Kim responded hopefully, excited by the prospect of another journey.

"It is not your time. Each man is called according to his karma. Some are called to lead, and others follow."

"When will they return?"

"No man can say. In time, you may discover answers of your own. For now, your home is here, at Songgwang Sa."

"Am I a brother, now?"

Rhee smiled. "A student only. There is much that you must learn."

Kim had no grasp of death, but he had grown familiar with a sense of loss. He felt tears burning in his eyes but held them back, remembering his father's adjuration to be strong.

Upon acceptance as a student, Kim was led by Brother Chin to stow his few possessions in a locker at the meditation hall. He was assigned a cushion in the double row along one wall, his place—the last in line—determined on the basis of seniority. The walls and ceiling of the meditation hall were painted white; its floor was covered by a layer of varnished yellow-ocher paper, heated by a wood fire from below. Distractions had been minimized by the removal of external objects, but an altar stood against the long back wall; above it hung a mirror, symbolizing the exalted mind monks sought to realize. The doors were sliding paper screens that also filtered sunlight during daytime. After dark, a dull electric lamp suffused the meditation hall with a pervasive aura of simplicity and peace.

For Kim, admission as a postulant meant access to the formerly restricted area, above the Buddha hall. Here stood the meditation hall, a spacious lecture room, two smaller temples, and the private quarters of the *go-jang*. Elevated as it was, the compound offered Kim a bird's-eye view of Songgwang Sa, complete with panoramic view of the surrounding hills. Kim spent less time with Jung Kaesong these days—and saw a great deal more of silent Tonsung Yun—but chores and classes brought them back together in the afternoons.

The day began for postulants at three o'clock, with a short service consisting of three bows before the altar. Students then took their place on the cushions, facing the wall, for their first period of meditation, concentrating on selected *koans*—mysteries for which the answer grows more distant and complex as logic is applied. Throughout each session, students were compelled to deal with drowsiness and boredom, personal distracted thoughts and fantasies, the pain of immobility that racked their shoulders, backs, and legs. Unlike the Japanese approach to Zen, there was no disciplinarian, armed with a switch, to enforce correct posture. Each student was left to himself, with the knowledge that failure or final success was his own responsibility.

For Kim Sunim, the worst distractions—after thoughts of home and family—were visions of the forest that surrounded Songgwang Sa. He had not stepped outside the compound's wall since his arrival, and he longed to go exploring in the trees, discovering the plants and animals so alien to any he had known in Seoul. So far, his life at Songgwang Sa had been defined by work and study; no time had been set aside for play.

The monastery's hours were divided into fifty-minute meditation sessions, broken up by brisk ten-minute walks around the hall. The adult postulants spent twelve to fifteen hours every day in meditation, pausing only for their meals, but younger students were compelled to study other subjects on the side. They learned to speak and read Chinese, promoting comprehension of the classic Buddhist scriptures. Japanese was also taught, at Master Rhee's command, since decades of invasion, interaction, and eventual cooperation had conspired to mix their separate cultures. Brother Chin conducted classes in arithmetic, while Brother Kee made history a plodding, lifeless subject.

Every fortnight, coinciding with the phases of the moon, all postulants assembled in the lecture hall to hear a discourse by the *go-jang*. After chanting several prayers, the postulants would wait for Master Rhee to mount the elevated Dharma seat, bowing three times in his direction before they settled in rows, on the floor. In front of Master Rhee, a wooden lectern bore his written text, with candles burning at each corner. Clad in formal robes, a gnarled staff in his hand, the master scrutinized his audience for several moments, making certain that he had their full attention.

In his discourse, Rhee began by reading from the text of Chinese characters, the lecture interspersed with verses chanted in an undulating rhythm. Periodically, the formal presentation would be interrupted by a shout from Rhee, the striking of his staff against the floor, or stony silence as he scanned the ranks of postulants, in search of answers to a question. On occasion, monks would venture to engage the *go-jang* in a dialogue, attempting to win plaudits for their understanding, but the master normally rebuffed them with an even more obscure remark or cryptic references to scripture. Kim enjoyed the show, but often questioned whether he was making any progress toward enlightenment.

The monastery's year was broken into three-month phases, roughly coinciding with the seasons. Summer and winter were devoted to intensive study in the ways of Zen, with meditation lasting hours at a time. In spring and autumn, schedules were relaxed a bit, and Kim discovered that a number of the postulants moved on to other monasteries, new arrivals turning up to take their place. Kim's second spring at Songgwang Sa, he said good-bye to Brother Chin, uncertain whether they would ever meet again.

This time, his loss was tempered by experience—and by a brand-new sense of purpose. Kim had not forgotten home and family. But he had found t'ai chi.

Three days after their discussion of his parents, Master Rhee called Kim away from sweeping in the afternoon. At

first, Kim feared he was in trouble for the violation of some
unknown rule, but he recalled that normal discipline was left
to Brother Kee. In spite of that, he felt uneasy as he followed
Master Rhee up winding steps of stone. Their destination was
a private garden, near the *go-jang*'s solitary quarters.

"I have seen you watch the other boys at practice," Rhee
informed him.

So, he *was* in trouble, for evading chores and spying on
the others.

"Master—"

"Do you know the purpose of their exercises?"

Puzzled by the question, Kim put on a frown. "They
learn t'ai chi."

"And what does that mean?"

Kim thought of several answers, none of them appropriate, and hung his head, embarrassed by his ignorance.

"I do not know."

Instead of scolding him, the master ordered him to sit.
Kim waited for the old man to be seated on a mossy stone,
then settled on the grass. When they were comfortable, Rhee
began to speak.

"The name 't'ai chi' is drawn from the Chinese philoso-
phers. Its best translation, although imprecise, is 'supreme
ultimate'—the perfect balance of nature."

Pausing, Rhee observed the boy's confusion and remembered he was speaking to a child. The master raised his left
arm, drew his sleeve down to the elbow, and revealed a small
tattoo inside his forearm.

"Do you recognize this symbol?"

"Yin and yang," Kim answered instantly, eyes focused on
the mark with rapt attention.

Master Rhee seemed pleased and dropped his arm, his
sleeve obscuring the circle subdivided into teardrops, black
and white.

"It is the symbol of t'ai chi, adopted to remind us
of the balance that must be our goal. All things in life
are male or female, light or dark, firm or soft, positive or
negative, active or passive. From the interaction of these
qualities spring the five basic elements—fire, water, earth,
wood, and metal."

Kim nodded, pretending to understand all that the *go-*

jang was saying. In fact, while he grasped at the heart of the concept, the details continued to slip through his fingers like sand.

"Your *chi* is the intrinsic energy that you must learn to channel and control if you would have success in life. It comes from here"—Rhee pressed a finger to his temple, slowly moved it downward, toward his heart—"and here."

Kim nodded, pointing at his head and heart in imitation, trying hard to understand.

"Three basic elements of t'ai chi are correct instruction, perseverance, and natural talent. I will supply the instruction; your task shall be to persevere and practice diligently."

"And the talent, Master?"

Rhee dismissed the question with an airy gesture. "Talent is the least important factor. Thus, Confucius has described the superior man: He will not interrupt his labor. If another succeeds by one effort, he will use ten; if yet another succeeds through ten efforts, he will use a thousand. Should a man proceed in this manner, though dull, he will surely become intelligent; though weak, he will surely become strong."

"I understand."

"Not yet, perhaps, but soon. Stand up."

When they were facing one another on the grass, Rhee demonstrated *Yu-pei Shih*, the stance of preparation. Kim noted that the master's feet were slightly parted, arms held loosely, fingers slightly curled.

"To properly begin, you must relax. In t'ai chi, every move proceeds from a relaxed body, a calm but concentrated mind. Throw every bone and muscle open, and allow your *chi* to travel unobstructed. First, relax your chest and lungs. Allow your *chi* to sink and settle here." Rhee drew a hand across his waist, below the navel. "Given time, you will experience the feeling of your *chi* as it begins to circulate throughout your body."

Kim felt nothing yet, but he assumed his emulation of the master's stance was inexact.

"Imagine that your head is held suspended from a ceiling by the scalp. This posture will immobilize your head and spine, allowing neither to move independently of your body as a whole. Thus, your spine is strengthened, and your *chi* is

set at liberty to circulate. Your limbs should only move by the
accumulated force of *chi*, their movements circular, preserving energy, negating tension, and enhancing relaxation. The
beginning move is called *ch'i shih.*"

As he spoke, the master slowly raised his arms to shoulder height, palms down, and drew his hands back toward his
chest before he lowered them again. Kim noted that the old
man's arms appeared to rise and fall as if controlled by some
external force.

"Grasp sparrow's tail and ward-off, left," Rhee named his
next intended move. Shifting his weight to the left leg,
lowering his body as he swiveled from the hips. His right arm
rose to armpit level, left arm tucked across his waist, the
palms opposed as if he held a globe against his chest. A
forward step, and Rhee appeared to block the thrust of an
imagined adversary on his left.

"Grasp sparrow's tail and ward-off, right."

His former movements were repeated now, in mirror-
image, pivoting and blocking to the right, while Kim tried
clumsily to imitate the move.

Rhee led his newest pupil through the thirty-seven
postures of the t'ai chi solo exercise, with names for each.
When they had run the gamut twice, consuming half an hour,
Rhee stood back to watch Kim exercise alone.

"Slow down!" he chided, when the boy's impatience
made him rush. "Relax. No postures should be executed
swiftly in the solo exercise. Slow practice makes each movement separate and distinct. Imagine that the air is water,
offering resistance. Learn to be a graceful fish that swims in
air."

They spent another hour on the exercise, Rhee pointing
out mistakes, reminding Kim to regulate his breathing, shift
his weight on cue, keep one knee or the other bent until the
final posture brought him back to full attention, with his arms
against his sides. In truth, Rhee thought the boy learned
quickly for his age—perhaps an indication of the talent he
had denigrated earlier—but praise was best reserved for
more remarkable achievements.

"Perseverance," he reminded Kim before the boy went
back to sweeping. "Only practice brings perfection. Concentration is the sure path to enlightenment."

Kim bowed and took himself away. Once out of sight, as he believed, he struck a fighting stance and whipped through several of the postures, fending off imaginary enemies. Remembering the *go-jang*'s words, he stopped, backed up, and tried the moves again, more slowly, striving to become a fish that swims in air.

Behind Kim, watching from the shadows, Master Rhee allowed himself the small indulgence of a smile.

Next day, Kim joined the t'ai chi class that Master Rhee conducted three times weekly, for an hour before the midday meal. Except for Jung Kaesong—who, as a refugee, was still prohibited from joining in—the other boys were present, with a number of the older postulants. For purposes of sparring, Kim was paired with Tonsung Yun, who came the nearest to his size and age.

Some four years older and a full head taller, Yun accepted the assignment grudgingly. He dared not argue with the master, but he would not speak to Kim and only met the new boy's eyes directly when they faced each other for a practice match.

Their first such confrontation came on Kim's third day of class, and set the tone for what would follow. Tonsung Yun approached the sparring session with aggressive confidence, "forgot" to pull his punches, bruising Kim before he used a squatting kick to bring his small opponent down. Kim landed on his backside, heard Yun laughing as he scrambled to his feet, the color flaming in his cheeks.

Embarrassed, angry, Kim ignored his timing, circled close to Yun and tried to land a body blow. His adversary used the twenty-seventh posture—*yu fen chiao*—to hook one foot behind his forward leg and drop him on his back again. This time, Yun followed his advantage, closing with his arm cocked for a blow that might have blacked Kim's eye.

It never fell.

As smoke in human form, the master stepped between them, caught Yun's wrist between his thumb and finger, and restrained the boy without apparent effort. Reaching backward with his other hand, Rhee helped Kim to his feet.

"We find the evidence of courage in restraint," Rhee said, and while his words were offered to the class at large, they seemed to shrivel Tonsung Yun. His face was frozen, blanched by anger, as he bowed to Master Rhee and took a short step backward, disengaging from the match.

To Kim, the *go-jang* said, "Your anger at defeat reveals a fundamental error. Concentrate on the perfection of technique. Defeat will cease to be a problem."

Kim bowed deeply, but his childish skepticism was apparent. Frowning, Rhee bent down to draw a line between them, in the dirt.

"How can this line be shortened?"

Kim examined it for several moments, pondering, and finally used his toe to draw an intersecting line. "We break it here."

Rhee shook his head and scratched a longer line beside the first. "How does the first line look?" he asked.

"It is the shorter of the two."

"Correct. A wise man will improve his own line, strengthen his technique, instead of struggling to cut an adversary's line. Consider this. Proficiency comes only through rehearsal."

In the weeks and months ahead, Kim kept the *go-jang*'s words in mind and practiced diligently, stealing time from sleep to hone his skills in solitude. In six months time, he found that he could hold his own with Tonsung Yun, their matches winding up most often in a draw. Yun recognized the change in Kim, and it appeared to put a new edge on his private animosity. Outside of class, he turned his back whenever Kim approached and broke off conversations when the younger boy appeared.

For his part, Kim had tried to puzzle out the older boy's instinctive hatred. Failing to divine its source, he put the problem out of mind, accepting Yun's behavior almost as an elemental force that he was powerless to change. Still close with Jung Kaesong, and growing closer to the others day by day, Kim had enough friends that Yun would not be missed.

On the occasion of his anniversary at Songgwang Sa, an autumn day, Kim felt that he was ready to defeat Yun in a practice bout. He recognized the danger posed by overconfidence, but Master Rhee had noted his improvement in the class, and Kim was certain now that he possessed at least some measure of the talent Rhee had mentioned in his introduction to the art. If nothing else, his hours of secret practice should be good for something.

When the matches were arranged that afternoon, Kim faced his adversary squarely, noting Yun's habitual pugnacious frown. Their bows were empty ritual, devoid of mutual respect. Kim did not wish to share his enemy's contempt, but grim experience had taught him there was nothing to be gained from courtesy.

He circled warily around the older boy, allowing Yun to make the first aggressive move, commit himself to action. Feinting to the right, Yun sidestepped, striking on the left, but Kim applied the thirty-second posture—*yu nu ch'uan-so*—and deflected his attack.

Yun took the move in stride and followed up his slim advantage, alternating fists and feet to drive Kim back across the grass. Around them, other sparring partners stepped aside to watch the show, and Master Rhee, for once, did not rebuke the slackers. From his ringside vantage point, the *go-jang* studied both combatants with a look of mingled disappointment and expectancy.

Yun saw his opening as Kim stepped backward, nearly lost his footing on a stone, and faltered in his stride. Attacking with a flourish, he was totally committed to the move when Kim—who had, in fact, maintained his balance perfectly—reacted with a sweeping kick and cut Yun's legs from under him.

Yun tasted grass, immediately scrambled to his feet, and pressed home the attack. His fury made him careless, let Kim step inside a roundhouse swing, and take his sleeve before Yun recognized the danger of his move. An instant later he was airborne, gasping as he struck the earth with force enough to empty out his lungs.

This time, when Tonsung Yun regained his feet, the master stood before him, cutting off his access to the enemy. He felt the others staring at him, some of them amused by his humiliation, and he could not meet their eyes.

"An angry man defeats himself in battle, as in life," said Master Rhee. "Control your emotion, or it will control you."

The *go-jang* turned to Kim and was relieved to find him solemn in his victory. Humility was better learned in youth, while most of life's embarrassments still lay ahead.

"You have improved your line," he said, "but you have far to go."

Kim bowed before the master, satisfied, while Tonsung Yun stood back and nursed his wounded ego, concentrating on revenge.

That evening, as they left the dining hall, Yun idled by the open door to wait for Kim. It was the first time they had spoken, and he wasted no time on preliminaries, stepping out to block Kim's path as he approached with Jung Kaesong in tow.

"Your parents didn't go on any trip," Yun said, enjoying the expression on his adversary's face. "They're dead. Both dead."

The story was confirmed, in private conference, by the *go-jang*. There were no hard facts available: the deaths had been reported as a traffic accident, although PoSun Sunim had never owned a car. In troubled times, the master told him, certain questions had no answers.

Rhee took pains to help Kim understand the Zen philosophy of death as a progression in the karmic cycle of the soul, but Kim was young and frightened, unprepared to grapple with the concept. Still, he kept the tears at bay, impressing Rhee with his reserve of inner strength. In fact, the shock had numbed him, insulating him from pain, and Kim was not prepared to share his grief.

The master offered him an afternoon of leisure, to accommodate his loss, but Kim insisted on returning to his work. He saw the monastery in a different light, as home. The brothers were his family now. His only friends were there, at Songgwang Sa.

And there, Kim knew, he had at least one enemy.

That night, before he slept, Kim spent three hours working on his t'ai chi exercises, waiting for fatigue to purge his mind of faces, images from an abruptly severed childhood. Kim was not a man, by any means, but neither could he be a little boy. He had responsibilities—to Master Rhee, the brothers, to himself—and there were dangers he might have to cope with, soon.

Like every child of tender years, Kim had invested both his parents with a kind of hopeful immortality, regarding them as elemental forces placed on Earth to shelter and protect him. Their abrupt removal shattered his conception of the world, drove home the lesson that no man—no *child*— was absolutely safe. If death could touch his parents, then it followed that their son was not immune.

Alone in darkness, Kim wept for his parents and himself. It was the last time he would give himself to tears.

The days began to pass more quickly, running into weeks and months as if through sleight of hand. Kim studied diligently in his classes, put in extra hours of practice at t'ai chi, and was occasionally singled out for cautious praise by Master Rhee. He had no fear of Tonsung Yun, although the older boy increased his practice likewise, working hard to show Kim up in class. A surge of growth between his sixth and seventh years put Kim on nearly equal footing with his adversary, and their sparring matches typically resolved themselves as draws, with neither boy a clear-cut winner. Kim was satisfied to take the standoff in his stride, but Yun was so embittered that the *go-jang* finally split them up as partners, pairing Kim with Monsin Dok, while Yun was matched with Daisong Chiun.

Outside of class, Yun had retreated into stony silence, but he aired his festering dislike for Kim in other ways. When Kim was given duties in the garden, unseen hands attacked his crop by night, uprooting tender plants and leaving them to die. If Kim had been assigned to sweep a portion of the monastery, piles of excess rubbish surfaced on the spot. When Tonsung Yun was serving in the kitchen, he would sometimes spill Kim's food, emerging from his silence with profuse apologies before he felt the hand of Brother Kee.

For his part, Kim was not prepared to hand the problem off by speaking to the monks or Master Rhee. He had no proof of Yun's vendetta, and preferred to deal with it himself, in any case. One day, his enemy would slip, and Kim would catch him at his games. On that day, he resolved that Yun would be repaid in kind.

Exasperated by frustration, Tonsung Yun considered different angles of attack. If Kim could not be personally goaded, there were other ways. Yun concentrated on the outcast, Jung Kaesong, whom Kim had chosen for his special friend. His new approach was more direct, involving overt confrontations

with the younger boy. He badgered Jung at work, chastising
him for carelessness and threatening to summon Brother Kee
if this or that unpleasant task was not redone. Sometimes, in
his darker moods, he speculated on the fate of Jung's imprisoned
parents, rambling on at length about the agonies inflicted on
political detainees by their keepers.

Kim had marked a change in Jung's demeanor over time,
but Jung was steadfast in refusing to discuss the reasons for
his new solemnity. In place of the accustomed laughter, Jung
was frequently distracted now, his features often twisted in a
frown. Though younger, Kim could see through Jung's attempts to shrug the problem off, and he made up his mind to
solve the riddle on his own.

He found the answer, quite by accident, one summer
afternoon. Assigned to work the garden plot with Daisong
Chiun, Kim went to fetch the tools and was returning by a
different route when he encountered Tonsung Yun and Jung
Kaesong. He did not overhear their words, but Jung was
obviously on the verge of tears. Kim thought he saw a flash of
guilt—or was it triumph?—in Yun's eyes.

Kim dropped his tools and closed the gap with measured
strides, ignoring Jung and concentrating on his enemy. He
met Yun's gaze, aware of hands and feet without dividing his
attention.

"I believe your quarrel is with me," he said.

Yun took a short step backward, shuffling his feet. "There
is no quarrel. We were just discussing prison life. Your friend
seems interested."

Kim concentrated on his breathing, centering his *chi*. If
Yun attacked, he was prepared to counter; if he ran, Kim
would pursue.

"From now on, anything you say to Jung is said to me."

His adversary flushed with anger, seemed about to strike,
and then thought better of it.

"As you say. Another time, perhaps."

Kim made no effort to return the mocking smile.

"Another time."

Chapter 6

Some afternoons, they played the game of stones. Kim sat before the *go-jang*, with a simple lacquered box between them. In the box were colored stones—some red, some blue, some green, with a preponderance of black. Kim would be given time to count the stones before Rhee closed the box, and then, from memory, he would recite their numbers. Seven red. Four blue. Six green. Eleven black.

The numbers changed, but there was never any variation in the game.

From time to time, the master questioned Kim or prompted him, suggesting that there might be seven green, instead of six, three blue, instead of four. He sometimes told the truth, and sometimes lied.

The first time Master Rhee deceived him, Kim was stunned, reluctant to believe the *go-jang* might be capable of trickery. The old man recognized his hurt expression and responded with a frown.

"There is a lesson in the game," he said. "Rely upon yourself in observation of the world around you. Recognize that other men—or women—may attempt to sway your mind for reasons of their own. Trust no one absolutely, with the sole exception of yourself."

In time, as Kim developed and displayed a talent far outstripping others in his class, the master offered private sessions, touching on the hidden intricacies of t'ai chi. Among those was the concept of *mushin*.

"*Mushin*," Rhee said, "is a state of consciousness the Japanese *sensei* call 'no-mind.' It is present when the actor stands apart and separate from the act. No conscious thought disrupts the movement. In *mushin*, the mind flows like a stream of water, never stagnant."

"How may I achieve *mushin*?"

"Through practice, diligence, and concentration. When your movements have become as second nature, you are almost there."

On occasion, Master Rhee would wear a padded leather mitt, and Kim would try to strike it, on command, with fist or foot. It seemed a simple exercise, but Rhee would never hold the target still. Each time Kim primed himself to strike, his punch or kick would miss the gliding mitt by inches. Once, he tried to fool the master, feinting with a punch, then pulling back to throw a kick that missed the target by a foot and very nearly dumped him on his backside.

Winded and embarrassed, Kim stepped back and bowed, to signal a cessation in the drill.

He asked, "How is it, Master, that you seem to know each move before I make it?"

Smiling through his long mustache, the *go-jang* said, "I read it in your face, and in your body. Through your very concentration on a move, you signal an opponent what that move will be."

"But, you have said that concentration is essential."

"So it is, in complement to relaxation. Too much concentration will defeat itself."

Kim bowed his head. "I do not understand."

Rhee answered with a parable. "Some years ago, a young man traveled far, from Pyongyang to Pusan, in search of a superior t'ai chi instructor. Finally, he reached the dojang of a master recognized throughout Korea. He approached the master with respect.

"'What is it that you wish from me?' the *go-jang* asked.

"'I would become the finest student in your school,' the boy replied. 'In fact, I would become the finest in Korea. How long must I study?'

"Pondering his words, the master said, 'Ten years, at least.'

"The young man was dismayed. 'Ten years is such a long time,' he responded. 'I will study twice as hard as any of your other students.'

"'Ah,' the master said, 'in that case, it will take you twenty years.'

"Dismayed, the young man cried, 'What if I practice every day and night, with all my effort?'

"'Then it will take you thirty years,' the master said.

"'Why is it, sir,' the young man asked, 'that every time I say I will increase my effort, you respond that it will take a longer time?'

"The master smiled and said, 'The answer should be obvious. With one eye fixed upon your destination, you have only one eye left with which to find your way.'"

"I understand," Kim said.

They tried the exercise again, and still he could not seem to strike the mitt. At last, Kim realized that he was concentrating all his energy upon *not* concentrating, thus allowing Rhee to read his thoughts as if his forehead were a pane of glass.

Disgusted with himself, Kim scowled and threw a swift, unthinking punch.

His knuckles made a loud, resounding *slap* on contact with the mitt.

"At last!" the *go-jang* said. "You ceased to care, and thus succeeded. Pure, instinctive action is the trademark of a master. When your mind is calm, detached, regardless of the threat confronting you, then you have grasped the central principle of all t'ai chi."

In demonstrations, Kim observed the master smashing bricks and breaking boards with naked hands and feet. Though fragile in appearance, Rhee was capable of feats that obviously did not stem from strength alone. At something over sixty years of age, he did not have the muscles of a man who spends his free time lifting weights.

Kim posed the question to his teacher in a private lesson. Rhee considered his response for several moments prior to answering.

"Each move is visualized," he said at last, "before I set my body free to act. In this way, I direct my *chi* to best effect. If I must break a board or brick, for purposes of demonstration, I will *see* it break before I strike."

"And if you were attacked?"

"The same. *Mushin* permits my mind to flow ahead and chart my course before I move."

"And still, your enemy is unaware of what you plan to do?"

"If I am calm enough and swift enough."

"Forgive me, Master but I would not have believed you strong enough to shatter bricks bare handed."

"Strength is secondary to the proper application of your *chi*," the master told him. "With proper application, the practitioner becomes an elemental force of nature. As a breath, nothing is softer than air; as a droplet, nothing is more pliable than water. Yet, consider: as a hurricane or tidal wave, the air and water carry all before them. Nothing built by man has greater strength."

In early lessons, matched against a larger sparring partner, Kim displayed a tendency to shy away from contact, going tense in preparation for his adversary's moves. A period of observation led the master to instruct him in the technique of determining a threat.

On Master Rhee's instruction, Kim stood still, extending one leg to its limit, pivoting while Rhee inscribed a circle on the ground with chalk. Kim's body was the midpoint of the circle, with its radius the distance of his outstretched leg.

When he was finished, Master Rhee took up a fighting posture, facing Kim, perhaps six feet outside the circle. Kim immediately tensed, his own hands rising in a gesture of defense.

"Why are you frightened?" asked the *go-jang*. "Can I reach you from this distance?"

Kim considered it, relaxing as he shook his head. "No, sir."

"Correct."

Rhee took a long step forward, pausing when his toes were just across the line of chalk. Again, Kim felt his muscles tightening, but he resisted the temptation to assume a fighting stance.

"You see that I am still not close enough to harm you. There has been no threat."

So saying, Rhee advanced once more, approaching Kim so swiftly that the boy instinctively retreated, stopping only when the gap between them was restored.

"Your choice was proper." Master Rhee allowed himself a smile. "You moved your circle to maintain a fitting distance from your adversary. Thus, a threat is neutralized without the use of force."

"And if I cannot move my circle, Master?"

"If the circumstances—or your heart—forbid retreat, then you must fight. Until such time, maintain control and keep your distance."

Later, in their private sessions, Master Rhee would sometimes have Kim stand immobile, arms against his sides, while Rhee snapped kicks and punches past his face from different angles, missing him by fractions of an inch. Although he felt the breath of each potentially destructive blow, Kim learned to keep his eyes wide open and resist the primal urge to flinch away. In time, he learned that fear could be controlled and used against his adversary in a match.

"Imagine that which frightens you the most," the *go-jang* said one afternoon. "Perhaps a tiger from the forest, or a serpent coiled to strike. Make this your adversary when you exercise, and take it with you into dreams at night. Examine what you fear, to learn its strengths and any weakness that work to your advantage. You may not emerge victorious each time, but neither will you always lose. Surrender fear, and let its place be taken by respect."

In spite of Master Rhee's instruction, inadvertent contact with his sparring partners—or deliberate pounding of the *makawara* board, designed to toughen hands and feet—inevitably left Kim bruised and hurting. After one particularly jarring session, which had seen him thrown four times by Sun Il Kwan, he sought the *go-jang* out, soliciting advice on the control of pain.

"Your pain is here," Rhee said, and tapped a bony index finger on his skull, "as much as in your ribs or hands. Control your mind, and you become the master of your pain."

Rhee taught Kim how to regulate his breathing, while his eyes and mind were fixed on something else—a knothole in the wall, a creeping insect, anything at all. With practice, concentration, and control, Kim gradually learned to banish pain, and used the same technique to rid himself of headaches, stiffness in his muscles after practice, the discomfort caused by blisters, cuts, or bruises. It was a useful trick, but he surmised there must be limits, and one day expressed his doubts to Master Rhee.

"The limitations lie within," Rhee answered, rapping on his skull again for emphasis. "If you believe a certain pain cannot be tolerated, it will certainly defeat you. Rather, I should say you will defeat yourself. With ultimate control, you leave the pain behind and take yourself beyond its grasp."

"But surely, Master, even you are not immune to injury."

"I bleed," the *go-jang* willingly acknowledged, "but I do not choose for pain to be my master. Given time and practice, as your *chi* is cultivated in the marrow of your bones, they shall become as steel. Let *mushin* guide your thoughts, while *chi* protects your Earthly shell."

By slow degrees, in practice bouts, Kim noticed that the pain of accidental kicks and punches faded, leaving him aware of contact, but without the incapacitating side effects. One night, he worked the *makawara* board for better than an hour, finally called away by Jung Kaesong, who pointed out his split and bleeding knuckles. Only at the sight of blood did Kim experience a flash of pain, and he was able to suppress it while his hands were bathed and wrapped in linen bandages.

I am discovering a new side of myself, he thought, and with the wonder of it came a fleeting pang of fear.

Kim was discovering a brand-new side of Songgwang Sa, as well. The monastery, once accepted as his home, no longer seemed confining; rather, it provided him with shelter from a world both fearsome and alluring. Sent to work outside from time to time, in company with others, Kim enjoyed the freedom of the forest, and he sometimes stood upon the road that, years before, had brought him to his mountain hideaway. At day's end, though, he always found security within the walls and sought his quarters with a measure of relief.

He wondered, on occasion, how the other postulants survived their treks between one monastery and another. Was their *chi* so strong that they could face the dangers and temptations of the world outside? And what of those who never came again to Songgwang Sa? What proof did he possess that they had not been swallowed up alive?

Kim's strained relationship with Tonsung Yun had stabilized into something like a truce, the boys ignoring one another absolutely. Yun no longer taunted Kim or any of his friends, and there were no more "accidents" as Kim attended to his chores. Aware that Tonsung Yun could never bend enough to be his friend, Kim satisfied himself with being left alone.

And on the side, as a precaution, he began instructing Jung Kaesong in certain basic t'ai chi moves. Though older, Jung was not as tall as Kim, nor did he have the same coordination. In their early lessons, Kim suspected that his teaching was deficient, but he ultimately realized the problem lay with Jung. For all his joviality and energy, Jung did not possess determination or the will to win.

One afternoon, when they had worked together for perhaps three weeks, Kim was surprised to find the *go-jang* watching from the shadow of a doorway. Kim had taken pains to keep their sessions private, fearing the derision of his peers and conscious of the fact that he was still unqualified to teach. At the sight of Master Rhee, he braced himself to bear a stinging reprimand in silence, but the *go-jang* merely turned away and vanished in the shadows.

It had been a trick of lighting, Kim supposed, that made the old man seem to smile.

At twelve years old, each student destined for the priesthood lost his hair, except for the distinctive scalp lock signifying his position in the monastery. On attaining manhood, that would go as well, a clean scalp signifying full acceptance in the order. Sideburns, whiskers, even a mustache would be permitted as the monk matured in years and strove to reach enlightenment.

When Tonsung Yun was shaved, he wore his scalp lock like a badge of natural superiority, his selfish pride so evident that Brother Kee was forced to reprimand him several times. Kim took a secret pleasure in the pained expression that his adversary wore on those occasions, instantly repenting as he realized the feelings were unworthy of a man.

Sometimes, in gatherings or over meals, Kim felt his flesh begin to crawl and knew that he was being watched. Invariably, when it happened, he would find Yun staring at him from across the room, the dark eyes curious and hostile, all at once. Kim shrugged it off, and once or twice returned the stare until his evident distraction brought a warning growl from Brother Kee.

As he approached his own twelfth year, Kim knew he was not destined for the priesthood. Knowing was a matter of the heart, beyond the scope of words, but Kim was certain that his calling should have made itself apparent long before. He had discussed the problem with his *go-jang*, at some length, and Rhee had finally conceded—with a trace of visible reluctance—that monastic life was not the course for every man. If Kim was certain that he lacked the calling, he should carefully consider the alternatives. Of course, he would be free to study at the monastery while he made his choice, and to return for visits after he had gone.

It was the act of leaving that disturbed Kim. He had watched the older monks depart in spring and autumn, others moving in to take their places, and he experienced no sense of loss at their departure. It was not the same with Brother Chin, who took his leave of Songgwang Sa in Kim's sixth autumn at the monastery. He was missed, but Kim had learned to live without his ready smile and cherish memories instead. And, while he would have gladly bid farewell to Brother Kee, the scowling ogre showed no signs of going anywhere at all.

When Kim departed Songgwang Sa at last, he knew that he would not be moving to the safety of another monastery. That was *all* he knew, however, and the future was a dark, intimidating void. Outside those cloistered walls, the world was fraught with peril, and he drew no comfort from the rising tide of refugees.

By early 1961, Kim's eighth year at the monastery, South Korea's government was hamstrung by corruption, crushing debts and runaway inflation, rising unemployment and increasing disaffection from the people. Waste and frank mismanagement of foreign aid had strained relations with America, while national hostility against Japan prevented South Korea from participating in the rise of Asian industry. Unknown to Kim, the stage was set for revolution when the military moved to take a hand in politics.

On May 16, an army loyal to Major General Park Chung Hee surrounded the administrative heart of Seoul, usurping power in an almost bloodless coup. That afternoon, the ancient radio at Songgwang Sa rasped out a message from the Military Revolution Committee in Seoul, proclaiming the seizure of all three government branches. Kim listened spellbound, as the junta's spokesman pledged himself to anticommunism, the eradication of corruption, and a closer bond with the United States. The army would endeavor to reunify Korea, while respecting the provisions of a document that Kim had never heard of, called the UN charter. Once the military's revolutionary mission was accomplished, government would be returned to capable civilian hands.

Despite his general ignorance of politics, Kim understood that he was witnessing a fateful change of course for South Korea. Master Rhee was silent as the tinny voice droned on with platitudes and promises, but the expression on his face spoke volumes. As the *go-jang,* Rhee would never be afraid of anything, but he appeared uncomfortable now, as if forseeing problems in the days ahead.

On May 18, Prime Minister Chang Myon convened his final cabinet meeting, publicly acknowledging responsibility for the conditions leading to a military coup. His resignation was accepted, and the cabinet members cast their final ballots for a resolution placing South Korea under martial law.

The refugees began to trickle in next morning, claiming sanctuary as the army launched its purge of "communists" and "traitors." Some were necessarily rejected—girls and women were prohibited from setting foot inside the monastery, thereby cutting off escape for men who would not leave their wives and daughters—but in six months' time, two hundred extra souls were crowded into Songgwang Sa. Kim wondered what their crimes had been and thought about the hundreds—maybe thousands—crowding into other monasteries, seeking refuge from the army and the CIA.

Unlike his parents, these would have a chance.

The refugees were given work assignments and applied themselves industriously, showing Master Rhee and other normal residents of Songgwang Sa the courtesy of those who stay by sufferance. In fact, except for females and the perpetrators of specific heinous crimes, the *go-jang's* code did not permit him to reject a refugee. If space or food ran short, they would be forced to cope as best they could.

Kim mingled with the refugees whenever possible, absorbing stories of the world outside, its marvels, and the dangers the refugees had faced en route to Songgwang Sa. If they were truthful—and it seemed to Kim that very few were lying—some of them had done no more than criticize the state in public, where their words had flown to hostile ears. A few had tried recruiting workers into labor unions; others had been friends of those who spoke against the government or published editorials demanding change. Kim listened to their stories, and he learned that careless words could lead to grief. Not even private thoughts, it seemed, were safe in Seoul.

For his part, Tonsung Yun contrived to hold himself aloof, avoiding contact with the new arrivals. He would sneer at the sight of Kim, the discussion of politics or simple daily life with any of the refugees, expressing his superiority through gestures of disdain. Kim left him to it, unintimidated by his adversary's ignorance.

In Seoul, meanwhile, the Military Revolution Committee had renamed itself the Supreme Council for National Reconstruction. A new constitution was accepted in a national referendum and promulgated in December 1962, thus inaugurating the Third Republic. Major General Park, retired from military service, was elected president the following October, his administration taking steps to shore up the economy and normalize relations with Japan. New economic growth of nine percent per year was testimony to the Park regime's success.

Concealed from residents of Songgwang Sa, except through stories told by refugees, there was a dark side to the miracle of reconstruction. The improvement of relations with Japan brought members of the *yakuza* to South Korea in the guise of honest businessmen, their luggage fat with yen acquired through gambling, extortion, prostitution, drugs. In time, corruption under Park Chung Hee would rival and surpass the indiscretions of his predecessors.

Pledged to national redemption from the threat of creeping socialism, Park's regime launched random witch hunts, jailed suspected enemies, and muzzled the dissenting voices of the press. Unleashed to hunt "subversives" on its own, Korea's CIA conducted private inquisitions at Remonclo, holding thousands in detention, making dozens disappear.

ABOUT THE AUTHOR

MICHAEL NEWTON was born in Bakersfield, California, and has worked at various trades and professions including schoolteacher, security guard (for country-music artist Merle Haggard), and professional writer. Since 1977 he has produced 90 books, most of them novels in the action-adventure genre. He has been a full-time author for the past four years.

At present, Newton lives with his wife in a log cabin in Nashville, Indiana. He is at work on a new novel for Bantam Books.

"Guess not. The way it looks, somebody made you working Tommy Ma and set you up. Decided what the hell, let's waste him too, in case he's playing footsie with the narcs."

"A leak?"

Ray frowned. "I hate to think so."

"Still...."

"Time's up." Nurse Reilly in the doorway, giving Ray the evil eye.

"Okay. Stay frosty, kid." He cut a glance at Reilly, looking back to wink at Joe. "Not bad, at all."

It was amazing, how a simple conversation, lying on his back, could sap a grown man's strength. Before he drifted off again, Lee thought about the setup that had taken Eddie's life. His partner, three months' work, and One-nut Ma, all shot to hell in ten or fifteen seconds.

Christy didn't want to think about an inside leak, okay. That didn't mean there wasn't one.

It was an angle, anyway, and something for his mind to work on when he finished counting holes in the acoustic ceiling tiles. It pissed him off, and that was fine. The anger gave him focus, and he nursed it, like a precious candle in the dark.

Right now, he needed light to find his way.

working on the streets whenever possible. He wore an old, familiar hound's-tooth jacket with a tie that didn't match.

"The man came by?"

"I caught a glimpse."

"That guy, I tell you." But instead, he asked, "How are you, Joe?"

"Fucked up, I guess."

"I came to see you two, three times before, but you were always out on something."

"Lots of dope around this place. You want to raid it?"

Christy smiled. "The doctor wouldn't tell me much of anything, you know their bullshit, but he said you ought to get around okay, you do some work and all."

"That's what I hear."

"At least you've got insurance, huh? No raise this year, but anyway, you're covered if the fuckers blow you up."

"It could be worse."

That brought them back to Eddie, Ray about to light a cigarette before he flashed on where he was and put the pack away.

"The funeral was Saturday," he said.

Two days ago, while Lee was drifting in the fog.

"You talk to Chan?"

"I called his mouthpiece for an interview, he tells me when I get a warrant we can ask him anything we want."

"So, get one."

"Based on what?"

"The bastard set up us."

"*You* say. The judge, he's not so sure."

"And what do you think, Ray?"

"I think you're right, but what the hell do I know? Take a hunch to federal court, they have themselves a laugh and point you toward the street."

"So, what, that's it?"

"Not quite. We found the shooters' car—one of them—in McLaren Park. Reported stolen when the owner got off work, that afternoon. I'm pretty sure he's clean. No prints or pieces, but they left all kinds of brass inside. Nine-millimeter. We can match the firing pins and the ejectors through ballistics, if we ever find the guns."

"Don't hold your breath."

pin in his lapel. His tie was silk, wine-colored, with a perfect Windsor knot. Dark, wavy hair combed back without a part. Lee could not see his shoes, but knew they would be polished to a mirror shine.

"How are you, Joseph?"

"Better, sir." What could he say?

"You had them worried for a while."

Not *us*. The Northern California regional director of the DEA did not allow himself to worry over trivia like dead and wounded men.

"I must've missed it, sir."

"Good man." The politician's smile clicked on and off. "I wanted you to know we're working overtime to clear this up. It's top priority. No stone unturned, you have my word."

"Yes, sir."

Kephart already moving toward the door, his duty done.

"If you need anything at all—"

"I'll let you know."

"You do that, Joseph. Take your time and follow doctor's orders, now. We've got your case load covered."

Thanking empty air as Kephart disappeared, a man in motion. Ten or fifteen seconds for the air-conditioning to deal with his cologne, and there would be no proof that he was ever there.

Lee scowled and muttered to the ceiling, "Cover this."

Ray Christy wandered in about an hour later, while the nurse was checking out Lee's vital signs. She didn't seem tremendously impressed with his credentials, and she let him know that it would be ten minutes, max, before he got the boot. A little smile for Lee, before she left the two of them alone.

"Not bad." Ray cocked a thumb in the direction of the door.

"I guess."

At forty-five, Ray Christy could have passed for ten years older, maybe fifteen in a pinch. His craggy face was topped by salt-and-pepper hair run wild around the ears and collar, looking vaguely scruffy even on the rare occasions when he had it trimmed and styled. The half-moon scar beneath one eye stood out in pale relief against a tan that came from slipped one arm around his neck, her body weighing next to nothing as she locked her thighs around his hips and guided him inside.

Warm velvet.

Pressing Nancy back against the tile, he gave himself to the sensation, rutting desperately. He found it hard to breathe, with all the steam, but Joey didn't care. It didn't matter if he suffocated there and fell down dead, as long as he could finish first.

"You ready, yet?"

The voice behind him, Eddie Hovis standing in the shower with his clothes on, dripping. Rusty swirls of blood around the drain. He had a pistol in his hand, extending it to Joey Lee.

"Let's go."

"Hold on a second."

Turning back to Nancy, and she wasn't there.

"C'mon, we're late."

Lee recognized the street as part of Chinatown, bright neon signs imparting colors to the fog. It must be eight or nine o'clock, with all the people on the street, and none of them the least bit interested in the gun he carried or the fact that he was naked. Eddie steered him toward an alley where the street lights did not penetrate, rough gravel underneath his feet.

"We're almost there."

Above them, searchlights blazed and swept the alley with their blinding beams. One of them overshot the mark and came right back, the others burning down on Joe and Eddie like a multitude of suns. Hot needles in his eyes, but he could still see well enough to note the blood that soaked through Eddie's shirt and jeans. His partner turning with a shuffling zombie walk to shout, "Surprise!"

His eyes snapped open in the darkness, spilling tears across his cheeks. The pain was coming back, but he refused to buzz the nurse. It was the least that he deserved. Instead, he lay there staring at the ceiling, still awake when day's first light came slanting through the blinds.

That morning, Leland Kephart paid a token visit, stopping in before his driver took him to the federal building. He wore gray for the occasion, custom-tailored wool, with a masonic brought a visitor. He welcomed Eddie Hovis with the logic of a dreamer, not at all surprised to see a dead man more than twenty years his senior in the room.

"You look like shit," his partner said. "What happened?"

Joey had to blush as he explained about his bicycle, the pothole that had jogged him out in front of traffic.

"Barely clipped me, anyway. I'm going back to school on Monday."

"Never mind all that. I got a lead on Bobby Chan."

Lee felt his stomach tighten with excitement.

"Really?"

"It's the big one, man. You'll have to skip that test in algebra."

He was considering his grades when Eddie lit a cigarette.

"You smoke too much."

"What can I say? It's something oral." Wolfing down a handful of the oyster crackers. "Have you got your piece?"

"It's in the bathroom."

Crawling out of bed, he gimped across the carpet in his walker cast, a five-foot Frankenstein. His mother would have worried if he left the pistol lying out, so Joey kept it in a plastic bag, inside the toilet tank.

Before he crossed the threshold, he could hear the shower running. Steam inside the bathroom, warmer than the mist that formed the borders of his dream. A pale, familiar shape behind the plastic shower curtain.

"Nancy?"

"Joe, I couldn't wait." She drew the curtain halfway back, to let him in, and he could see the water glisten on her shoulders, on her breasts. One perfect drop suspended from her nipple, like a jewel. "Do you forgive me?"

Glancing down his naked body, toward the swelling he could not disguise.

"I take that as a yes."

He pulled the curtain shut behind him, stepping into Nancy's arms. The steam enveloped them, her body molded tight against him, muscles rippling beneath his hands. She tasted good enough to eat.

"I felt that."

Reaching down between their bodies, Nancy found him, stroking. Joey wasn't sure if he could take it, but she knew just when to stop. A squeeze to break the rhythm, and she

"The best thing you can do, right now, is rest."

His chest and shoulder had begun to throb, three wounds in close proximity. Lee thought his hip was waking up, on top of everything, but he determined not to let it show while Dr. Beck was in the room. Alone, he simply didn't care enough.

It should have hurt more, lying there, instead of feeling faraway and dulled by the residual effect of local anesthetics. If it hurt him more—enough to make him cry, let's say—then maybe he could shake the guilt that came with being a survivor. Eddie Hovis cooling in a drawer somewhere, or stretched out in a box, and he was lying there with tidy bandages, an I.V. tube and plastic hip.

Alive.

It was the feeling of relief, immediate and undeniable, that made him doubt his own humanity. Instead of being racked by grief at Eddie's loss, he felt like cheering for himself. And might have, if his wounds had not prevented it.

"Goddamn it."

"Sorry?"

He had missed the door, Nurse Reilly coming back with something in her hand. A plastic throwaway syringe.

"I don't need that."

"A sedative," she told him. "Right now, sleep's exactly what you *do* need."

Searching for a vein and giving him the mickey with an angel's touch. He hardly felt the needle, alcohol before and after, cool against his skin.

"I ask you something?"

And the mist was coming back, but he could see her face and hear her say, "Sure thing."

"You ever feel like cheering, when you know you should have died?"

He floated through an endless fever dream, where time and space were stripped of any concrete meaning. Still in bed, he saw himself at twelve years old, the summer that he broke his leg. His mother brought him tea and egg drop soup with oyster crackers. All the television news breaks, in between the innings of the Dodgers game, were Nixon politics and Vietnam. They seemed impossibly remote to Joey Lee.

Like death.

His mother came again, to fetch the dishes, and she

downward, into contact with the joint itself. Are you familiar with anatomy?"

"I took biology in college."

"Fair enough. The hip joint is a ball-and-socket type." Beck demonstrated with a fist and the opposing palm. "It rotates, so. Intrusion of a foreign object limits that mobility, of course, and violent impact is potentially destructive to the mechanism."

"Can you spell it out?" The left side of his body still felt numb, between the waist and knee.

Beck frowned, considering his words. "The femur's head was shattered, with corresponding secondary damage to the innominate bone—that is, the socket. In the circumstances, there was no alternative to total hip replacement."

"Jesus."

"On the up side, with some healing time and therapy, a bit of coaching, you should be as good as new. In fact, considering the quality of our materials, you may be better."

"Stainless steel?"

"A brand-new polymer. Less weight and nearly zero friction. Any difficulties you encounter will be caused by muscle damage to the gluteus."

"How long until I'm mobile?"

"We should have you on your feet in three, four days. Then, therapy. The pace depends entirely on your stamina and personal determination. Right?"

"I hear you."

"Excellent. I'll check on you again, tomorrow. In the meantime—"

"One more thing."

He caught Beck turning toward the door. The doctor hesitated.

"Yes?"

"My partner."

It took everything Lee had to speak the words, and he could see the answer written on Beck's face.

"I'm sorry, Mr. Lee, there wasn't anything—"

"Okay."

"I know how difficult this is, but you should really try—"

"The funeral?"

Beck drew a blank. "I'll check that, if you like."

"Yes, please."

wound beneath the nipple. You could say the fractures saved you. Give or take a centimeter, and it would have passed between your ribs. All kinds of nasty things, in there."

Lee cataloged the dull, insistent ache beneath his arm, the wad of bandage like a sagging breast.

"Another bullet struck you in the left side of the upper back. It chipped the scapula—no problem, there—and pierced your lung. We had to reinflate, but you've been breathing on your own since Friday noon. You should expect discomfort for a while, but it'll pass."

His groggy brain identified the pad of gauze and tape below his shoulder blade. More pain, though still remote. A stuffy pins-and-needles feeling on the left side of his chest when he inhaled.

"Okay." His voice was stronger now. He almost sounded like himself.

"The other wounds are more complex. You took a bullet in your shoulder, here." Beck's finger tapped his lab coat, on the left. "The movies tell you shoulder wounds are no big deal. Clint Eastwood stops a bullet, and it barely slows him down. The truth is something else. A shoulder is among the human skeleton's most delicate and complex moving parts. You've got the clavicle and scapula to deal with, plus the joint itself, the deltoid muscle and trapezius. Cut the subclavian artery, and you're talking lethal hemorrhage in four, five minutes, tops."

Lee got the picture. "What's the verdict?"

"Bottom line, we had some luck. The wound was through and through. It missed the bones—don't ask me how—but there was major damage to the muscle tissue. Once the sutures are removed, you'll have to work on learning how to use that arm again."

"That still leaves one."

"Left hip," Beck said, an index finger demonstrating on himself. "This bullet struck the illium—your hip bone—and disintegrated. Part of it came out in back, above the buttock, and a smaller fragment pierced the bowel. We cleaned that up, and you're receiving antibiotics as a hedge against peritonitis. It shouldn't be a problem."

"But?"

"Exactly. The projectile split three ways on impact, and the biggest piece—we estimated forty grains—was driven

In and out of mist that smelled flowers.
In and out of pain.

The first two he could clearly focus on were strangers dressed in white. The woman—nurse—was pretty, fair complexion with the barest hint of freckles, sandy curls beneath a starched white cap, her smile encouraging. The nameplate on her breast was black and read "L. Reilly."

The man was tall and thin, his long face thickened by a beard that came in white around his chin. It made a striking contrast to the darker foliage on his cheeks, and neither matched the chestnut hair above, meticulously styled. His wire-rimmed spectacles reflected the fluorescent ceiling lights. A stethoscope, protruding from his pocket, was the only badge of office he required.

"Good morning, Mr. Lee. I'm Dr. Beck." Still fuzzy, but at least the words made sense. A radio announcer's voice. Lee wondered if he practiced with a mirror. "We've been hoping you might join us."

"Long."

His throat was parched, and it felt bruised inside. The question came out sounding like a feeble belch.

"How long?" Beck seemed to give the weighty matter deep consideration. "This is Sunday morning; you arrived on Wednesday night. Let's say three days."

He tried to swallow, lubricating rusty vocal cords, before he asked, "Where am I?"

"San Francisco General. It's a private room. We moved you out of ICU last night."

Lee knew the question he should ask but could not bring himself to face it, so compromised. "How bad?"

A signal passed, unseen, between the doctor and his nurse. She flashed Joe Lee another smile and left the room. Beck waited for the door to close before he spoke.

"You were in critical condition on arrival, but we've scaled that back to serious and stable. Major blood loss was a problem, but we've got no shortage on Type O. You want the gory details?"

"Please."

"Okay. In essence, you were shot four times, producing seven wounds. One bullet entered on the left side of the thorax, just below the armpit, broke two ribs and left an exit

Chapter 2

The pain came later.

First, he was aware of drifting in state of semi-consciousness, his body weightless, blessedly anesthetized. Around him there was mist, but it was not the gray, polluted fog of Mission Street. He would have said it was a *friendly* mist, if that were possible. It had a fragrance he could not identify, a sweet relief from car exhaust and cordite. The uncompromising, gritty pavement was replaced by something soft but firm, supporting him without abrading skin or bruising muscle.

There were disembodied voices in the mist, a few of them familiar, but he could not concentrate enough to pick out Eddie's as the babble faded in and out. He tried to listen with an ear for Mandarin or English, but the words were gibberish, a language he had never taken time to learn.

From time to time, the mist retreated and his body felt like molten lead. The pain intruded then, but it was never bad enough to make him scream. Not yet. He recognized the bed, with metal railings on the sides and stiff white sheets drawn up around his chest. An I.V. rig above him, the transparent hose attached to something in his arm.

There always seemed to be a face above him when the mist pulled back. He understood that some of them were people he should know, but names eluded him. They spoke to him and smiled, but there was cotton in his ears, a side effect of the sedation. Others came to study him and ask him questions he could not interpret, much less answer. He ignored them.

Drifting.

Within a few short weeks, the spoor of human prey led hunters south, to Songgwang Sa.

Initially, the CIA was courteous, approaching Master Rhee with all the dignity befitting his position. Certain desperate criminals were sought by the authorities, and evidence had traced them to the gates of Songgwang Sa. No doubt, these traitors had deceived the *go-jang*, playing on his generosity and kindness as they begged for sanctuary. Rhee should understand that some of them were communists, the mortal enemies of all religion, and as such were not entitled to his aid.

Rhee listened with respect and thanked his visitors for their most generous advice. Of course, as master of the temple, he could not expect the government to share his moral burden in regard to refugees. He hoped his guests would have a pleasant journey back to Seoul.

Rhee's obstinacy angered leaders of the CIA, accustomed as they were to groveling subservience. If not for his position, Master Rhee might have suffered an "accident," but planners at Remonclo were not ready for an all-out confrontation. Instead, they opted for surveillance and subversion, planting agents in the neighborhood of Suncheon, with orders to report on any new arrivals at the monastery. If the gates were barred, there might be other ways to see inside.

One afternoon, as Kim and Jung Kaesong were working in a field outside the walls, they saw a man approaching on the road from Suncheon. His clothing marked him as a peasant laborer, but Kim immediately noticed that his face seemed pale for one who earns his living in the sun. At second glance, his hands were soft, with none of the expected calluses a workman should have earned through honest toil.

"Hello," the new arrival hailed them from a distance, putting on an artificial smile as he approached. "Are you from Songgwang Sa?"

"We are," Kim answered, leaning on his hoe. "And you, sir?"

"From the town of Suncheon, just there."

"We know Suncheon. What brings you here?"

"I come in search of men who love their country."

"Ah, then you must speak to Master Rhee."

The stranger shook his head. "Another time, perhaps. Today, I seek a man—or boy—who would be master of himself."

"How so?"

"By helping to discover enemies of the republic."

"Enemies?"

"Subversive traitors."

"What have they to do with Songgwang Sa?"

"Your master shelters refugees."

"In strict accordance with our faith."

"Of course." There was a trace of condescension in the stranger's smile. "Some of his guests may not be what they seem."

Kim thought he knew, already, what the stranger wanted, but he played along. "How may the traitors be discovered?" he inquired.

"Through watchfulness. Their every move must be examined for the evidence of treason."

"I would not know what to look for," Kim responded.

"That is why you must report. Let others bear the burden of analysis."

"Report to whom?"

The stranger's grin was cunning as he threw his shoulders back and tapped his chest. "To me. Of course, you would be compensated for your efforts."

"Compensated?"

"Paid."

Kim stalled for time, pretending to consider the proposal, glancing over at his friend. Jung glowered at him, half-believing Kim had fallen for the stranger's line. The stormy frown evaporated with a wink from Kim.

"I will discuss the matter with my *go-jang*," he declared, "and give my answer in the morning."

"No!" A sudden flash of panic wiped the stranger's smile away. "It would be best if no one knew about our conversation."

"Why?"

"Because the traitors may have friends inside. For all we know, your master may embrace their cause."

"Enough!" Despite his years, Kim matched their visitor in height, and now his voice had turned to stone. "It is forbidden to insult the master of the temple."

A trace of angry color blossomed in the stranger's cheeks. "I mean no disrespect."

"Your words are disrespectful, and your lies transparent. You are not from Suncheon, where honest workmen labor with their hands."

The stranger's grin was cold, reptilian. "Your tongue is sharp. Be careful that it does not cut your throat."

Kim straightened, shifted to a fighting stance, one hand still resting on the hoe. He visualized a circle, with the stranger safely out of reach. Beside him, Jung Kaesong stood ready with a spade.

"Our business is concluded."

Glancing back and forth between the boys, the stranger nodded. "So it seems. Until we meet again."

They watched him go, relaxing only when the slouching figure disappeared from sight.

"We should inform the master," Jung suggested.

"Yes. Tonight."

In fact, Kim was distracted from his mission hours later, when the monastery gates were opened to a smiling Brother Chin. That night, there would be stories of the world outside, and as the days slid past, their meeting with the stranger faded in importance, soon became too trivial to waste the *go-jang's* time.

Kim listened to the tales of Brother Chin with rapt attention, fascinated by the details of his journey to another monastery, in the north. Kim's childhood memories of Seoul were fractured bits and pieces now, almost devoid of detail, and he relished Chin's account of passage through the city.

On his second visit to the capital, en route to Songgwang Sa, Chin had observed the military on patrol with weapons drawn. There had been demonstrations, fighting, but the demonstrators had been driven from the streets by gas and water cannons. Twice, the soldiers had been moved to question Brother Chin about his destination, his political affiliations. While his answers did not seem to satisfy their curiosity, he was released each time, unharmed.

"And so I came here," he finished with the old, familiar smile. "To see my brothers once again."

Kim had a thousand questions, but he knew that it was

time to sleep. There would be days ahead, for coaxing every detail of his journey out of Chin, revisiting the parts that proved most interesting.

For a time, Kim was content with stories of the world outside the monastery, storing information that, he hoped, might help him choose a path when it was time for him to leave. That day was coming, slowly but inexorably, and he realized that he must be prepared for anything if he intended to survive.

A fortnight after his encounter with the stranger, Kim was wakened in the middle of the night by an insistent call of nature. Clouds were shifting restlessly above the mountains as he left his quarters, threatening a rainy day tomorrow that would cancel any plans for working in the fields. Erratic beams of moonlight pierced the cover, sriking here and there at random, picking out small details for illumination. Finished with the toilet, Kim was moving toward his quarters when a quiet shuffling sound across the courtyard banished any thought of sleep.

He froze, concealed by shadows, certain that the sound had been a careless footstep. A moment passed before his eyes picked out a human silhouette, now frozen, waiting to discover if the sound had made its presence known.

Kim held his breath, afraid to make the slightest sound in case it might betray him. He was feeling dizzy—and a little foolish—when the silhouette began to move. He gave the shadow-man a fair head start and fell in step behind.

It was ridiculous, of course, to act as if there was some mystery afoot. A postulant or refugee had been aroused from sleep, as Kim himself, and he was going... where?

The toilets were behind them, on the far side of the compound. Nothing lay ahead, except the inner gardens and a small gate leading to the fields outside.

His quarry would be making for the gate; Kim knew that much instinctively. Suspicion darkened what had been a game, and now the stalk became more serious.

What business would a student have outside the monastery at that hour? Why would any refugee risk setting foot outside? Kim's mind searched diligently for alternatives, but all of them were dark with treachery.

His prey had reached the gate, drew back the inner latch

and left it open, as the outside bore no means of access.
Pausing in a shaft of moonlight, hesitating in the knowledge
of his guilt, the prowler turned to cast a glance across his
shoulder.

Kim beheld the face of Tonsung Yun.

His adversary disappeared and left the gate ajar behind
him. Kim slipped forward, cautiously, a portion of his mind
suspecting that the whole charade might be a trap. It was
ridiculous, and yet...

He huddled by the gate and watched Yun cross the field.
A flashlight winked beneath the dark trees opposite, a signal,
and a moment later Kim made out the figure of a man
emerging from the woods. Approaching Yun, the new arrival
briefly lit his face for purposes of recognition.

Even at a distance, Kim made out the features of the
stranger who had questioned him the day of Brother Chin's
return.

The spy had plainly found himself a pair of eyes inside
the monastery.

Though he could not overhear their conversation, Kim
was confident that it would deal with the identity of refugees,
remarks they made about the government, the attitude of
monks like Brother Chin, who had observed the state of siege
firsthand.

They spoke for several moments, Yun directing frequent
backward glances toward the monastery. Parting, Yun received some object from the stranger—payment, Kim surmised—
and tucked it in a pocket of his trousers.

Kim retreated at the older boy's approach, but he made
no attempt to hide himself. Around him, thunder growled its
warning of the storm to come. He watched Yun close the
gate, secure its latch and turn, immediately frozen on discovering
that he was not alone.

Kim felt an urge to lunge at Tonsung Yun and strike him,
but he held his ground. Yun circled warily, eyes locked on
Kim, until his back was to the courtyard, twenty paces from
the gate.

"You have no proof," he said at last.

"I know what I have seen."

"Who will believe you?"

"Master Rhee, perhaps."

Yun's laughter sounded forced and brittle.

"Tell him, then. Let us discover whom he chooses to believe—a postulant devoted to the priesthood, or a son of traitors."

Furious, Kim held himself in check with grim determination, calling up the master's own advice against permitting rage to guide his actions. Heavy raindrops pattered on the paving stones around him.

"You may wish that you had stayed in bed this night," Yun said, and then the heavens opened, drenching both boys to the skin.

His adversary used the cover of the rain to make a swift retreat, while Kim stood rooted in his tracks. It seemed a long walk to his quarters, where he changed his sodden clothes and lay down on his pallet, knowing that he would not sleep.

Next morning, Kim did not approach the master with his story. Long reflection had convinced him Yun was right; he had no proof, and with the well-known animosity between them, any accusation would be treated as a gesture made from spite.

He picked at breakfast, answered Jung Kaesong in monosyllables, and set about his task of sweeping out the lecture hall. Kim had completed roughly half the task when he was called away by Brother Kee.

"The master wishes to discuss a matter of importance with you, in your quarters."

Hiding his confusion, Kim laid down his broom and followed Brother Kee down winding steps, across the courtyard, to his tiny corner room. The door stood open. Waiting on the threshold, he saw Master Rhee . . . and Tonsung Yun.

Kim felt a dead weight settle in his stomach, knowing Yun had beaten him before the *go-jang* spoke.

"There have been certain accusations," Rhee informed him, when the ritual of bowing was completed. "Did you leave your quarters in the night?"

"I did."

"And visited the western gate?"

"Yes, Master."

"This was found beneath your pallet."

In the master's outstretched palm, a crumpled wad of bills. No more than fifty *won* in all.

Kim understood at once, and marveled at his own stupidity. He should have known that Yun could never let the matter rest between them. Seizing the initiative, he had already branded Kim a traitor, planting evidence to prove his case, thereby negating any countercharges Kim might raise in self-defense.

Before Kim realized that he was moving, he had closed the gap with Tonsung Yun, one fist exploding in the startled face. Yun staggered, falling, dark blood spurting from his nose as Kim was physically restrained by Brother Kee.

The master stepped between them, stonefaced, but there was a hint of sadness in his ancient eyes.

"Your actions leave me no alternative," Rhee said. "You must depart from Songgwang Sa today."

"As you command."

Behind the *go-jang*, huddled on the ground, Yun flashed a bloody grin of triumph. At a signal from the master, Brother Kee led Yun away to clean his face and change his bloodied clothes.

"I will be gone within the hour." Desolate, Kim thought he did a decent job of covering his shock.

The master searched his eyes, found something there that made him pause and frown.

"Before you go," Rhee said, "there may be time to play another game of stones."

Chapter 7

Seoul 1966

Kim recognized his target from a block away and moved to close the gap between them, quickening his pace. The small man seemed oblivious to danger, taking no security precautions as he moved along the sidewalk, pausing here and there to window shop. A casual observer would have thought he did not have a care on Earth.

The small man's name was Lee Cheong Mok. A gambler who had never learned to judge the cards or dice, he was perpetually in debt—most recently to Kam Chun Il, a local operator with a reputation for collecting overdue accounts at any cost. Kam Il was anxious for his money; Kim Sunim had been dispatched to bring it home.

He overtook Lee Mok on Donhwa-ro, before they reached Pagoda Park, and jostled him off stride, propelling him in the direction of a nearby alley. Mok did not resist, nor did he seem surprised, although Kim's youth appeared to give him pause. He was accustomed to collectors with a few more years beneath their belts.

Kim saw no point in wasting time. "You owe Kam Il eight hundred *won*," he said.

Mok seemed to wither. "Yes, it's true."

"I want the money."

"If I had it . . ."

Kim was perfectly familiar with the drill. He slapped Lee Mok, but put no force behind the blow.

"The money."

Digging in his pockets, Mok produced 300 *won* and change. "I swear that this is all I have."

Kim palmed the bills, ignored the several coins.

"Kam Il will not be happy."

"Please, present my most sincere apologies. Next week, I should be able to repay the full amount."

"With interest," Kim reminded him.

"Of course."

Kim slapped Lee Mok again, with force enough to split a lip this time, because it was expected of him—both by his employer and by Mok himself. Collection of a partial debt to demanded some retaliation. Kam Il had a reputation to protect, and evidence of injury, however slight, would help Lee Mok preserve his fading self-respect.

Emerging from the alley, Kim felt soiled, unclean. He often felt that way when he was working for Kam Il, but there was cash involved and money meant survival on the streets of Seoul.

In nineteen months, since his expulsion from the monastery, Kim had learned to face the harsh realities of city life. He had endured the long trek north by living hand to mouth, surviving off the countryside and begging rides where transport was available. Pusan was closer, but he had been drawn to Seoul by fragmentary childhood memories, a homing instinct he could not explain.

In Seoul, Kim learned that hunger was not bound to mountain roads and paddy fields. It stalked the city streets as well, and preyed on those who had not strength or nerve to make their way. Kim slept in doorways, parks, abandoned buildings—or in one of several crowded "men's hotels," when he obtained the cash required to rent a bed. He learned to scavenge from the garbage bins of restaurants and markets, making do with scraps of food that had been deemed unfit to serve or sell.

For money, Kim began to work odd jobs. He was adept at running errands, bearing messages or burdens, watching shiny cars to guarantee that they were not molested. Aided by his fluency in Japanese and Chinese dialects, he charmed the Asian tourists, working hard at English for the benefit of rich Americans. With others like himself, he loitered near the great hotels—the Lotte or the President, in Eulji-ro; the

Grand on Taepyong-ro—in search of tourists who required a guide, until the doormen ran him off. Sometimes policemen joined the chase, but they were slow and apathetic, giving up when Kim poured on the speed.

If things were slow at the hotels, he tried Seoul Station, toting baggage in return for coins. (On principle, he stayed away from Yongsan Station, with its memories of Songgwang Sa, the last trip he had taken with his father.) Other days, Kim worked the South Gate Market, helping shoppers with their parcels, sometimes stealing fruit when he could not afford to buy. If that proved unrewarding, there were always the department stores—the Saerona, the Shinsegye, the Arirang—with shoppers so tired out from spending money that they could not lift their packages.

The street gangs were a problem early on. At first, they picked on Kim and tried to steal his meager earnings. Through experience, they learned that he would not submit without a fight; it took six larger boys to beat him down, and none of them emerged unscathed. In time, the local gangs developed a respect for Kim, accepted his decision not to join their ranks, and left him to his own devices. They did not molest him on the street, and Kim avoided any moves that might have been interpreted as trespass on protected turf.

He knew it would have made life easier to join a gang, but his acceptance into any given clique would make the others automatically his enemies. While he was not afraid to fight, the prospect of an endless war for "territory" struck Kim as ridiculous. Above all else, he scorned their thievery, the crude protection rackets that extorted tribute from the smaller shops. Reduced to theft of food on various occasions, Kim was never proud of stealing and he could not share the obvious delight gang members took in terrorizing merchants.

As the word of his combat skills began to circulate, Kim was solicited for other jobs. Despite his tender age, he was employed part time to keep the peace in different taverns, earning the respect of older patrons after he had beaten several drunks in stand-up brawls. Kam Il had witnessed one such bout, recruiting Kim as a "protector" for his string of prostitutes, eventually broadening the scope of Kim's employment to include collections from reluctant debtors. With a small but steady income, Kim obtained a small hotel room and began to eat with something close to regularity.

Despite his personal reaction to the work he did for Kam Chun Il, Kim drew a line between his own behavior and the predatory action of the gangs. Kam's patrons paid their money, took their chances, and they knew the rules. If someone tried to injure one of Kam Il's girls, the punishment was swift and sure. If gamblers chose to welsh on debts, they understood that there were certain penalties involved. Kim's work did not involve extorting cash from honest working men or terrorizing families as they tried to earn a living. Kam Il's enterprises were illegal, but they seemed to have no victims—no *unwilling* victims—and to Kim it made a difference.

If only he could shake the vague sensation of complicity in something dark and dirty.

Kim was walking west on Jong-ro when he noticed the American. An average tourist in his early thirties, dressed for comfort, lightweight clothing to accommodate the weather. He was absolutely unremarkable—except that he was being followed.

Trailing him by half a block, three street toughs paced their quarry, hanging in without alerting him to danger. Just ahead, on Kim's side of the street, two more were moving parallel to the American, prepared to intercept him if he saw their brothers and attempted to escape. It was a classic stalk, invariably ending in an alleyway or narrow side street, where the tourist would surrender cash, his watch, and any other valuables upon command. If he was lucky, and the take was adequate, the hoodlums might decide to let him go without a beating.

Kim had seen the method used before. He did not recognize the boys, but knew their type, accustomed to the casual violence of the streets. He knew enough to let them go, and yet he fell in step behind them, adding one more entry to the small parade.

The money in his pocket was forgotten. Kam Chun Il could wait another hour for his pay. Against his own best judgment, driven by an urge he did not fully understand, Kim trailed the tourist and his shadow entourage toward Chonggye-ro.

*   *   *

At thirty-one, Reese Holland sometimes felt that he had been a soldier all his life. The part of it that mattered, anyhow. By grit and nerve and sheer persistence, he had risen to the rank of captain in the U.S. Special Forces, but it did not show that afternoon in Seoul. Decked out in civvies—a button-down sports shirt, casual slacks, and loafers—Holland made the perfect, stereotypical tourist. There was nothing he could do about the military haircut, on short notice, and he could not bring himself to slouch, but otherwise, he thought the cover would withstand at least a casual inspection.

Eleven years in service, Holland sometimes felt diminished, less than whole, without his uniform, but he had jumped at the Korean gig without a second thought. It was a change of pace, a variation in routine, and Holland thought he just might do some good along the way.

Unlike most tourists in a foreign capital, Reese Holland did not wear a camera around his neck. He did not need a snapshot to remind him of the city's beauty—or its peril. He had seen both sides, already, in his walking tours by day and night, examining the shrines and works of Eastern art, declining offers from the prostitutes of both sexes who surfaced at dusk, emerging from their burrows to reclaim the streets.

There might be time for some diversion of a carnal nature when his job was done. Until that time, his mind was focused on the mission with a singleness of purpose that had always been a Holland trademark.

His assignment, simply stated, was to pave the way for South Korean military aid to Vietnam. The war was heating up in what had once been Indochina, and while Holland was inclined to wish the French had stuck it out, instead of running with their tails between their legs, he was accustomed to obeying orders, dealing with reality.

The captain had been training South Vietnamese in August 1964, when communist torpedo boats attacked the *Turner Joy*, in the Gulf of Tonkin. Senate resolutions and retaliatory air strikes had followed in swift succession, raising the ante. A Viet Cong rocket attack on the American base at Pleiku, in early February 1965, brought more reprisals in the air and on the ground. American troops launched their first full-scale combat offensive on June 28. By the end of July, it was announced that the United States had something like 130,000 men in Vietnam, with more to come.

It was a touchy situation. As a soldier and a patriot, Reese Holland was committed to containment of the communists at any cost, but things were seldom quite so cut and dried. It would be crucial to avoid the semblance of an occupation, thereby offering the enemy a propaganda weapon. If the South Vietnamese could make a decent show of standing on their own, with more support from other Asian anticommunist regimes, it would deflate Hanoi's predictable assertions of American imperial expansion.

Holland had been meeting quietly with officers of the ROK army and the KCIA, trying to sell his program with some help from the Domino Theory. South Korean leaders still remembered 1950, and they knew the price a nation paid for weakness in the face of communist aggression. Holland's arguments were bolstered by the detonation of a Chinese A-bomb in October 1964, an incident that raised the paranoia level in Seoul's presidential palace to an all-time high.

If Vietnam was gobbled up, he told the South Koreans, Laos and Cambodia were sure to fall. The communists would naturally be emboldened by their victories. In Pyongyang, Kim Il Sung would doubtless cast a hungry eye across the parallel. With Russian tanks and Chinese nukes behind him, who knew what the North Korean bandit might attempt—or what he might achieve?

It was a hard sell, granted, but sincerity was on Reese Holland's side. He honestly believed that creeping communism was a menace to the world, to peace. If history proved anything, it demonstrated that the reds were ravenous—for power, land, prestige. Specific leaders might—or might not— be committed to the party line about exporting revolution, but they did their best to make the nightmare real.

In Seoul, Reese Holland thought that maybe he could slow them down a bit. Of course, his conversations with the South Koreans had been strictly off the record, laying groundwork for a team of diplomats and higher-ranking officers to follow. They would clinch the deal and ultimately claim the credit, but for Holland, there would still be satisfaction in a job completed to the best of his ability.

And there was Seoul.

So caught up was he in the wonders of the city, that it took a while for him to realize that he was being followed. Clumsy, that. He made a casual confirmation, spotting three behind him, two more on the far side of the boulevard. They looked like street punks, teenage muggers, and he said a silent prayer of thanks that no one more efficient had decided to surprise him while his mind was out to lunch.

Five kids. If they were like the gangs in Saigon, they would probably be armed with knives or razors. He could handle five-on-one, if they were dumb enough and slow enough, but Holland wished he had not left his .45 in the hotel room. Even with a gang of street punks, five-on-one could get a little dicey.

He would have to get them off the street, for openers. Whatever happened, it would not look good to his superiors or contacts if he got picked up by the police for public brawling. If the play went sour and he had to waste somebody, Holland damn sure did not want patrolmen breathing down his neck before he had a chance to clear the scene.

He chose a narrow side street, turned off Chonggye-ro, aware of his pursuers from the right flank crossing over, mobbing up behind him. On his left, an alley offered something in the way of privacy and Holland took it, conscious of the fact that there had been no time for adequate reconnaissance.

The alley looked like any other, gritty pavement underfoot and garbage dumpsters, scattered refuse that had overflowed the bins or never made it in the first place, mangy cats that fled for cover at the sound of his approach. He glanced around for weapons, came up empty, and his eyes were momentarily distracted by a movement at the far end of the alley, half a block down range.

Where three more punks stood waiting for him.

Damn it!

They had suckered him, and eight-on-one was killer odds without a piece, unless your opposition was extremely slow, supremely stupid. From the way these kids had boxed him in, Reese figured he could kiss that hope goodby.

He halted halfway down, beside a garbage bin. He was not in a corner, and the dumpster would protect his back—at least until the action started. After that...

The young men formed a fighting ring around their prey, and Holland cursed himself for making it so easy. There were several ways that it could go, all bad, and Holland could not see a decent option short of giving up his wallet, hoping that the meager wad of bills would satisfy them, let him slip away without a beating. On the other hand, if they were out for sport with an American, he could be looking at intensive care.

"Your money," one of them demanded.

Right. So far, so good.

The captain's hand was on his wallet when a soft voice broke the silence. Holland did not speak Korean, but he recognized a challenge in the tone.

Beyond the circle of his adversaries stood another boy, a trifle younger than the others, dressed without the same self-conscious flash. Too frail to constitute salvation, there was still a chance that he might have diversionary value. If a few of Holland's adversaries were distracted long enough, he just might have a chance.

The captain stood his ground and waited for an opening.

Kim had not counted on another three opponents. Five were bad enough, but easily divided if the tall American had nerve enough to fight, instead of cowering or running for his life. With eight, Kim felt a pang of apprehension. Evenly divided, they were still long odds. If he was left to face the gang alone, he would be killed.

They did not hear him coming. That was something, granting him a small advantage of surprise. When one of them demanded money from the tourist, Kim was nearly close enough to strike. Impulsively, he answered in Korean while the chosen target slipped a hand inside his pocket, hoping to exchange a billfold for his life.

"No money," Kim declared.

He had their full attention now, and several of them turned to face him, others watching the American in case he tried to make a break. The nearest of them drew a knife and flicked it open with a practiced gesture, scowling as another circled to his left, intent on flanking Kim.

They wanted him between them, pinned, without a chance to run or pick his targets. Kim defeated them by stepping toward the knife-bearer, surprising him into a backstep as Kim altered course without warning, one foot snapping out toward the boy on his flank.

It connected with ribs, and his target went down. The knife-bearer muttered a curse and attacked, lashing out with his blade in a thrust toward Kim's face. Fading back, Kim accepted the wrist that was offered, brought pressure to bear on the elbow. He struck with the flat of his hand, putting force in the blow, and the sound of a twig snapping clean lost itself in the older boy's bellow of pain.

On his left, moving warily, half in a crouch, came a heavyset boy with a long, livid scar on his cheek. From his posture, the sounds that he made, Kim surmised he had studied a little karate and thought himself dangerous.

Weighing the distance between them, aware that his circle was safe for the moment, Kim checked out his flank and saw two more opponents advancing, one armed with a brick and the other a chain. By the dumpster, the tall man had chosen his moment, a sharp backhand dropping one boy out of line, putting two others on the offensive.

Kim waited, his mind counting heartbeats, rehearsing the moves in advance. As the brick hurtled toward him, he sidestepped and heard it rebound from the wall at his back. Ducking under the chain, he put all of his strength in a fast double-punch to the older boy's abdomen, driving the wind from his lungs.

He rolled back, came erect with a snap-kick that flattened the brick-thrower's nose, spraying blood from his nostrils. The boy with the chain had gone down on one knee, doubled over and retching. His lunch looked like noodles, but Kim had no time for inspection. He struck from behind, rigid hand to the base of the skull, and his target went down in a heap.

He was vaguely aware of the tall man, still grappling with someone, but Kim's full attention was focused on Scarface. The heavyset boy moved with short, hopping steps, one hand poised overhead like a scorpion's tail, while the other extended in front of him, sweeping the air like a scythe.

Kim allowed him to close within six feet, alert for the signal he knew would proceed an attack. When it came, with a grimace and growl denoting an amateur, he was prepared.

Sliding under a high kick, Kim hooked his left foot on the other boy's ankle and toppled him onto his back. Sparrow-quick, Kim was after him, dropping a knee on his rib cage and hammering piston-like blows in his face.

From behind him, a scuffle of feet, and he turned, one arm raised to deflect a blow aimed at his head. Rolling back with the impact, Kim scuttled away, coming up to confront the first boy he had kicked. Pale with anger and pain, the young hoodlum was swinging a short length of pipe he had found in the rubbish. Kim's forearm and shoulder were throbbing, but pain was an enemy now, and he pushed it away.

The attack, when it came, was both awkward and slow. Moving close to avoid the boy's swing, Kim drove elbows and fists into ribs that were already bruised. As the pipe fell behind him, he finished the bout with a knee to the genitals, leaving his foe on the ground in a tight fetal curl.

On the battlefield, three boys lay where they had fallen; the rest were in flight or its limping equivalent, beating a hasty retreat. The American faced Kim Sunim with a smile on his face, and Kim noticed the blood on his sleeve.

"You are injured."

A razor had passed through the fabric, drawn blood, but the wound was not deep, and the boy who inflicted it lay near the trash bin, unconscious.

"It's nothing," the tall man replied. "Hey, I owe you one, kid. They were serious."

Nodding, Kim called on a phrase that he had picked up from servicemen.

"Bad motherfuckers."

The tall man blinked once, then exploded in laughter. Kim smiled in response, pleased to note that the fight, although tiring, had not left him feeling unclean, like his work for Kam Il. It was different, somehow.

"My name's Reese," the American told him, extending a hand.

"I am Kim."

"Kicking ass makes me hungry, Kim. How about you?"

Kim considered the proper response.

"Fucking ay."

Chapter 8

Seoul 1988

Kim woke promptly on the stroke of eight o'clock. He felt refreshed, despite his journey of the day before, the relatively small amount of sleep. Aware that jet lag was primarily a problem of the mind, he had refused to let it bother him.

As always, he began the day with half an hour of t'ai chi exercises, concentrating on his moves and timing rather than the coming day's activities. Kim found it helped to clear his mind and sharpen his perception, ultimately granting him the power to cope with problems more efficiently. Above all else, it kept his body fit and limber, primed for action, and he knew that he might need that edge in Seoul.

When he was done, Kim made two phone calls. First, he asked the Metro's concierge to make arrangements for a rental car and add the charges to his bill. Next, he placed an order with room service, indulging himself, and headed for the shower while he waited for his breakfast to arrive.

Kim had finished toweling off and had a robe on when the porter brought his food. He signed the ticket, added on a tip, and double-locked the door behind the porter. Sitting down to eat, he was surprised to find that he was ravenous.

His order was the Metro's "Western Breakfast": three eggs, over easy, bacon, toast and coffee. Smiling, he discovered that the meal had come with steaming rice, although it was not listed on the menu and he had not ordered any. Some things, he decided, never change.

As he devoured the food with relish, Kim reviewed the

mental list of tasks he needed to complete before he kept his dinner date with Jamie Constable at six o'clock. Securing a safe house was his first priority, a fall-back option, just in case the job went sour. That accomplished, he was looking forward to renewing old acquaintances, reopening his channels of communication on the street. He counted on a fairly high attrition rate among his former contacts—many things could happen in eleven years—but one or two would be sufficient for his needs, if they were properly selected.

Finished with his meal, Kim dressed himself in casual clothes of Western style, aware that he would not seem out of place in modern Seoul. He did not carry firearms. They were difficult to transport, too much trouble if discovered, and—he hoped—unnecessary for the job at hand. The buckle of his belt concealed a three-inch blade, but he was otherwise unarmed. If other weapons were required, he could obtain them locally.

Downstairs, he signed a standard rental contract for the waiting Hyundai sedan, refreshed his memory by checking out a street map of the city, and left the Metro, driving west. Three blocks away, he found a public parking lot and spent ten minutes scouring the car for listening devices, emptying the glove compartment, peering underneath the seats and dashboard, checking the upholstery for stitches that seemed new or out of place. A brief examination of the trunk, and Kim felt reasonably satisfied the car was clean as he proceeded on his way.

New shops and office buildings, some refurbished store fronts, gave the streets of Seoul a fresh appearance, but the streets themselves had undergone no fundamental change. He still found people going on about their daily lives, pursuing livelihoods identifiable by clothing, mannerisms. Leaving downtown Seoul behind, with its prestigious banks, hotels, and shopping plazas, Kim examined people on the street, including some who made the streets their home. Twice the size of San Francisco, housing twenty times the California city's population, Seoul exhibited a multiplicity of faces to her visitors, and some of them were grim.

Kim found a rental agency and paid a hundred *won* for Xeroxed listings of available apartments. He might be forced

to visit several, but he had all day, and patience was a trait he
had acquired at Songgwang Sa.

In fact, Kim found his safe house on the second try. It
was a small apartment—what the Californian's would have
called a "studio"—located in the northwest quadrant of the
city. Within an easy walk of Yonsei University, the neighborhood was student-oriented, but the summer months created
many vacancies.

Kim toured the layout with the manager, remarking on
the bathroom—large enough to be mistaken for a walk-in
closet—and the kitchen nook. The place came "furnished,"
with a stove, refrigerator, and a double bed that filled one
corner of the central room, its box spring resting on the floor,
without a frame. A telephone had been installed, and Kim
was told that service could be instantly connected, for a
price.

He signed a three-month lease and laid out 27,000 *won*
to cover two months in advance. Nine hundred more secured
a promise that his telephone would be in operation by that
afternoon. Kim memorized the number, palmed a set of keys
and thanked the landlord for his time.

The rent was largely wasted, as he did not plan to spend
a month in Seoul—much less the summer—but a safe retreat
was vital to his plans. As for the lease, it had been signed by
"Kim Su Chung," who likewise would receive the monthly
bill for telephone expenses. When his job in Seoul was
finished, Kim would leave no traces of himself behind.

His next intended stop would be the pawn shop run by
Syngman Chiul, and Kim took extra time to guarantee that
he had not acquired a tail since leaving the hotel. There was
an outside chance the Hyundai had come with a directional
transmitter tucked away somewhere, invisible to naked eyes,
but he would have to take the chance. If he was being
followed through the streets of Seoul, it didn't show.

He passed the shop on Sinmum-ro and parked his rental
three doors down. Before he left the car, Kim scanned the
crowded sidewalk, marking faces. Anyone who showed unusual interest in his movements, any passerby who seemed at
once *too* casual, might be an enemy. When he was satisfied,
Kim locked the car and went to meet his contact.

Syngman Chiul had been conducting business at the

same address for twenty years. The shop was more or less as Kim remembered it, still cluttered, cramped, in need of cleaning. Dusty warehouse merchandise was on display with items unredeemed by owners strapped for cash. The windows featured mandolins, a saxophone, and a display of wicked-looking knives; inside, the stock ran more to jewelry and appliances.

Chiul made a living from the business, but his true vocation lay in dealing contraband. A man of many contacts and connections, he could offer weapons and explosives, documents and information, stolen vehicles with faultless registration—anything, in short, except for drugs. Chiul left that trade to younger men who valued money more than self-respect.

A jangling bell announced Kim's entry, and a moment later Syngman Chiul emerged from his small office in the back. Eleven years had scarcely touched the ageless face. Chiul might have been an ancient fifty, or a youthful sixty-five, but Kim had never felt the need to ask. It seemed that dating Syngman Chiul would somehow have diminished him. He was content to leave the mystery unsolved.

In other days, when Kim was working for the CIA full time, he had relied on Chiul for contacts, information that the Company could not—or would not—place at his disposal. In addition to his stand on drugs, the broker was a dedicated anticommunist whose politics, along with well-placed bribes, had offered a degree of insulation from police harassment through the years.

"You have returned," Chiul said.

"A visit."

"I have been expecting you."

It was the closest Chiul would come to mentioning Reese Holland. Kim did not regard himself as overly predictable, but Syngman Chiul was wise, and they had known each other for a long, long time.

"I felt the urge to see old friends."

"Of course. How may I be of service?"

"I require a sweeper."

"And?"

"Perhaps some information."

"Come with me."

Kim fell in step behind the broker, through a narrow doorway, pausing long enough to draw the curtain that divided office space and storage from the public section of the shop. The clutter here was indescribable, but Syngman Chiul knew every piece of merchandise by heart. Kim scanned the shelves and waited while his host retrieved a small transistor radio.

"Effective to a range of fifty feet, in line of sight," Chiul said. He handed Kim the radio.

"The setting?"

"Seven-fifty kilohertz."

"How much?"

"For you, nine thousand *won*."

"A bargain."

"It is last year's model. Tea?"

Chiul brewed a pot of strong ginseng and cleared a stack of catalogues and papers from his desk. They sat together, sipping tea and reminiscing over trifles. Kim found out which sources had retired—or died—and which were still available for consultation. When their cups were empty, the demands of hospitality fulfilled, Chiul brought the conversation back to business.

"You require some information?"

"I am looking for a man."

"His name?"

"Chin Sung."

The broker did not look surprised. "A man in much demand," he said. "He makes himself deliberately difficult to find."

"I realize that it will not be easy. Nor should it be inexpensive."

"Price is not the question." Syngman Chiul dismissed the notion with an airy gesture. "Chin Kyu Sung must realize his life is forfeit if he shows his face in Seoul. The NSP officially desires to question him, but unofficially. . . ."

He smiled and spread his hands. The Korean CIA had changed its name to the Agency for National Security Planning (NSP) in January 1981, as a result of bad publicity concerning torture and the scandal dubbed "Koreagate" by certain journalists, but any alterations in the agency were strictly superficial. Agents of the NSP were charged with all the duties of the "former" CIA, and they were said to exercise their powers with a classic disregard for human life. Chin Sung might not be shot on sight, but neither was he likely to survive incarceration.

"I am interested in meeting Chin," Kim told the broker. "Privately, at a location and a time which satisfy his need for privacy. If such a message could be passed along, somehow..."

"All things are possible. And if the answer was affirmative?"

"I'm at the Metro, in Room 721." He did not write the name or number down, aware that Syngman Chiul would not forget. "Our friend should ask for Kim Su Chung."

"A friend of yours?" The broker smiled.

"We're practically inseparable." Kim thought about it for a moment, finally said, "There is another address where I may be reached, in cases of emergency."

He rattled off the address of his safe house, once again without resort to pen and paper. Chiul repeated it, to fix the address in his memory, and then did likewise with the number of Kim's telephone.

"A last resort," Kim said.

"Of course."

He rose to leave, his business finished. Syngman Chiul would pass the message if he could; if he should fail, the effort would be free of charge.

"My friend," the broker said, when they were standing on the threshold of his shop, "I hope we meet again."

"I hope so, too."

Returning to his car, Kim slid behind the wheel and spent a moment fiddling with his newly purchased radio before he started the ignition. Raising the antenna to its full extension, he dialed the tuner to 750 KHz and swiveled in his seat, listening to soft static as he scanned the Hyundai's interior for listening devices. Kim was smiling as he stowed the sweeper underneath his seat and put the rental car in motion.

He had three more stops to make, reminding old associates of debts unpaid, promoting distribution of his message. None of those remaining on his list possessed the reach of Syngman Chiul, but some had different contacts, varied methods of collecting or disseminating information. Kim was groping in the dark, so far, and he could not afford to overlook potential sources of illumination.

When he was finished, in perhaps two hours, he would double back to the hotel, inspect his suite for bugs, and rest awhile before he had to dress for dinner with his contact. Thinking now of Jamie Constable, Kim was surprised to realize that he was looking forward to it.

"You up for lunch?"

The sound of Ray Fitzpatrick's voice distracted Jamie from her reading, but she masked her irritation with a rueful smile. "Can't make it. Sorry, Fitz," she gestured to the folders spread across her desk, "I'm up to here."

"I'll bring you something."

"Thanks, but no. I'm fasting. Have to watch my figure."

"I can watch it for you, if you like." Embarrassed by his own impulsive words, Fitzpatrick blushed behind his horn-rims. "Sorry, James. Just kidding."

"Later, Fitz."

"Okay."

He wasn't kidding, though, and that was more than half the problem. Jamie did not think that Ray Fitzpatrick was in love with her, but he was working on a king-sized crush, and given any vague encouragement at all the situation could be damned uncomfortable. Fitz was nice enough—too nice, perhaps—but he would never pass for the elusive Mr. Right. An office interlude was something Jamie definitely did not need.

She rose and moved to stand before her window, working out the kinks with both hands raised above her head. From Jamie's office, on the third floor of the U.S. Embassy, she had a clear view of the Sejong Cultural Center, across Sejong-ro. Considering her cover—as the first assistant to the cultural attaché—Jamie found the setting perfectly appropriate.

Downstairs, Fitzpatrick paused in conversation with the uniformed Marines on duty at the gate. They passed him through, and Jamie watched him for a moment, weaving through the crowd with his peculiar slouching walk, until she lost him in the traffic.

"Sorry, Fitz," she said again, and went back to her reading.

On her desk lay four EYES ONLY files, the folders edged in red denoting their top secret status. The subject of the open file was Kim Sunim; the others Chin Kyu Sung, Reese Holland—code named "Domino"—and North Korean agent Dae Li Chong. The latter file was disappointingly, embarrassingly slim, consisting of a few reports that added up to hearsay, speculation, and some educated guesswork. In the place of non-existent photographs, a poor Identi-Kit composite sketch had been prepared, depicting someone who appeared to be a cross between Bruce Lee and Charlie Chan.

The other files were more substantial, though she knew they had been sanitized at Langley, limiting her information on the grounds of need-to-know. The essence was intact, but much of what she hoped to learn—especially in regard to Kim—had been deleted from the copy in her hands.

She was determined not to let the mission slip away from her again. The loss of Domino was bad enough, but it had been an aberration, something no one could foresee. The dead man had been negligent, avoiding contact at the designated times, attempting to play cowboy on his own initiative. She blamed his death on attitudinal malfunction, and her Company superiors did not appear to blame her for the setback.

Yet.

It would be something else, entirely, if she dropped the ball with Kim Sunim. His independence, verging on hostility, had set her nerves on edge.

The personal connection was a problem, Jamie thought. It was the key to bringing Kim around, inducing him to take another mission, but it also made him dangerously unpredictable. In order to control him, or at least anticipate his actions, Jamie knew that she would have to gain a deeper understanding of the man.

His file would be of little help in that regard. The standard psychiatric profiles had been excised, leaving Jamie with a stock biography composed of names and dates, statistics— all the bureaucratic stock components of a life reduced to paper. Orphaned in the early 1950s, sheltered in a Buddhist monastery through his early adolescence, cut adrift in Seoul two years before he met Reese Holland on the street. From there, Kim had been taken stateside—Holland pulling strings, apparently—and tutored to the point where he could function in a military school. Enlistment in the Special Forces was a natural progression, whether emulating Holland or attempting to learn more about himself. A double tour in Vietnam, immediate acceptance by the Company on discharge, and a string of missions that were classified so heavily she could not trust the sketchy information in his file.

She knew the facts by heart, but they were not enough. To do her job correctly, competently, Jamie had to know why Kim had walked away at twenty-six, forsaking his career, the pension—everything—to open up a school for would-be martial artists. Burn-out was a possibility, but in their single brief encounter, Kim had not displayed a quitter's nerves. He seemed so goddamned *confident*. Not arrogant, exactly, but infuriating all the same.

She caught herself. Emotional involvement was the kiss of death on field assignments; Jamie knew that much without referring to the service manual. If Kim Sunim could make her angry, he might also make her care in other ways, and then, if something happened to him . . .

No!

Deliberately, she closed Kim's file and pushed it to the side. Their target, Chin Kyu Sung, required an equal measure of attention. If they missed him, let him slip away, then Kim was wasting time in Seoul. And there was no way Jamie could explain a second failure. Not this soon.

Despite the urgency of Chin Sung's file, she found her mind returning irresistibly, to Kim. Perhaps at dinner, if she used a little charm, she might secure a handle on this man who walked away from Agency involvement and returned, a decade later, to conduct a private war. With any luck, she might develop deeper insight into his relationship with Domino, his motives for emerging from retirement—anything at all to help her keep the lid on a potentially explosive situation.

Perhaps.

It was a challenge, Jamie thought, but she would rise to the occasion.

If she failed, there could be hell to pay.

Chapter 9

The elevator brought Kim to the Metro's lobby at precisely six o'clock. Punctuality was a habit learned in childhood, nurtured in the military until it became second nature. He was pleasantly surprised to find Jamie waiting.

Rising from her chair, she took him by surprise. She had seemed smaller, less well-rounded, at the airport. Kim ascribed the difference to a change from normal street clothes to the clinging dress she had selected for their evening out. Its fabric was a deep, cool green that complemented Jamie's eyes. She had not made a special point of altering her hair, and Kim was glad.

"All set?"

"If you are."

Jamie made a subtle point of checking out his suit, prepared to deal with any obvious display of weaponry. She seemed relieved to find he wasn't packing.

"Seafood?"

"Fine."

"Okay. I know a place."

He followed her outside and waited, making small talk, while the valet fetched her car. There was no obvious surveillance, and a sweep that afternoon had found no listening devices in his suite. Kim idly wondered if the NSP had really missed him, or if they had simply found another way to monitor his progress. Seeing Jamie smile, he hoped that she would not betray him as a favor to her South Korean counterparts.

Kim had no wish to kill her.

Driving west along Jong-ro, then north on Sejong-ro, she

let him have a running commentary of the recent changes wrought in Seoul. New shops and office buildings, renovations, changing ownership on major plots of real estate. She neglected to point out the American Embassy, but Kim recognized it well enough. Their destination was nearby, within sight of the domed capitol building.

Jamie had selected a diplomatic restaurant, convenient to the several seats of power; its decor was simple elegance, without a rigid standard of formality. The maitre d' and waiters dressed in tails, while the visible female employees wore traditional Korean costumes. It was a blend of East and West that fairly epitomized modern Seoul.

The place would be convenient for surveillance, Kim decided. Tables could be wired and surreptitious photographs collected; agents could be dressed as waiters to complete the package. In a pinch, an order might be spiked with chemicals designed to free the tongue or fog the mind.

Kim realized that he was being paranoid. The Company, per se, was not his enemy. If Barrett Ross decided to inform the NSP of Kim's assignment, there should be no problem. Everyone was banking on the same result, and Seoul's best interest would be served by letting Kim proceed, unhindered. Still, Remonclo's memory was long, and retribution came in many forms.

They were conducted to a quiet corner table, drifting in and out of contact with subdued conversations en route, picking up fragments of diplomatic gossip. The maitre d' seated Jamie and left Kim to fend for himself. The wine steward and waiter arrived in swift succession, offering menus, suggestions, compliments on their final selections.

Jamie ordered a Korean dish, with shrimp and shellfish in a fiery pepper sauce, while Kim chose the broiled lobster tails.

"You've lost your taste for native food," she said, when they were finally alone.

"Perhaps. I never think about it when I'm home."

"You think of the United States as home?"

He shrugged. "It's over twenty years. I'm getting comfortable."

"It must have been a drastic change."

"In the beginning? I suppose it's never easy for the new

kid on the block. Things happen. There were rough spots. Nothing terribly traumatic."

"Holland took you?"

"Sent me," Kim corrected. "He was still assigned to Vietnam."

"You made the trip alone?"

"By that time, I was used to traveling. Besides, I had a welcoming committee."

"Still, it must have been a shock."

"I didn't mind."

Reese Holland had arranged for Kim to stay with friends in West Virginia, while a tutor ironed the rough spots out of subjects he would need to hold his own in military school. His years at the academy, outside of Wheeling, had been geared toward preparation for an Army life, but Kim had always known that he was free to choose another path. The ultimate decision was his own. By 1969, when he enlisted in the Special Forces, there was nowhere else he cared to be.

"You volunteered for Vietnam?"

"A soldier's trained to fight. It seemed the thing to do."

"And now?"

"I teach t'ai chi."

"I meant—"

He raised a hand to interrupt her. "I'm aware of what you meant. Do I regret the choice? Did my experience in uniform affect my life? Am I a walking casualty of Vietnam? The answers would be 'sometimes,' 'yes,' and 'no.'"

"I didn't mean to pry."

"You haven't. It's predictable, that's all." He smiled to let her know he was not angry. "Notice how we've gone through phases in our attitudes about the war. While we were fighting, hawks and doves felt honor bound to pick a side. When it was over, everybody wanted to pretend it never happened. Fifteen years go by, and now the war's back 'in,' with movies, television shows, and novels. Everybody wants to know a vet and talk about how rough it must have been."

"I never thought about it that way."

"You were still a child. For you, the war is history."

"You make it sound like ancient Rome."

"It feels that way, sometimes."

"What made you choose the Company?"

"You have my file."

It had not come out sounding like a question, and she didn't bother with an answer. "I'd be interested in hearing it from you," she said.

"All right. I was recruited for the Phoenix program when I got to Vietnam. Are you familiar with the background?"

Jamie nodded. Phoenix was the CIA's contribution to domestic pacification in South Vietnam. Its nominal umbrella covered many operations, but the heart of Phoenix had been wet work, termination of suspected traitors, infiltrators, and collaborators with the Viet Cong. Occasionally, probes of Laos, Cambodia, or the north country were ordered for elimination of "special" targets. Forty-seven kills had made Kim something of a legend in his unit, and she wondered how this slim, soft-spoken man had worn the mantle of assassin.

"Someone must have liked my work," he told her simply. "After Vietnam, I got an offer and I took it."

"With the Asian section?"

"I suppose they thought I might stand out in Liechtenstein."

Her laughter sparkled, and he offered her an unaffected smile. They ate in silence for a moment, Jamie finally coming back to what was really on her mind.

"What made you leave?"

"Korea?"

"No. The Company."

"I had enough."

"From out of nowhere? Just like that?"

"It happens."

There was skepticism in her eyes, but she was clearly hesitant to push it. Kim decided that it couldn't hurt and let her have an opening.

"Your boss and I had different views on how to do the job," he said.

"You worked with Mr. Ross before?"

"In Bangkok. He was farther down the ladder then, of course."

"Was there—" She caught herself and frowned. "I shouldn't ask. I'm sorry."

"Don't be. I'd say it was fifty-fifty, personal and business."

"But you're back."

"A one-shot deal. No encores, no extensions."

"You relate to San Francisco?"

"I enjoy it, and I take what comes. Relating burns up too much energy."

"Touché."

He stepped into the momentary silence. "What about yourself? When I was at the Farm, the female CTs looked like spinsters from Peoria."

"Thanks...I think." A trace of color darkened Jamie's cheeks. "The gloomy, sheltered look is out."

"I'm glad to hear it."

"Anyway, I thought the job might offer something different from the normal nine-to-five," she said. "It has."

"How long?"

"Nine years."

"You're satisfied?"

"So far."

"No urge to run away and start a family?"

She surprised him by not taking offense. "I don't have a maternal bone in my body."

"A liberated woman?"

"Damn right." She shifted gears. "Your teaching. Does it meet your needs?"

"So far."

"You haven't missed the job at all?"

He shook his head. "I'm working off a debt."

"To Domino?"

"Myself."

She seemed to understand and let it drop. "How was your day?"

Kim kept his face impassive. If the Company was trailing him, a lie might register on Jamie's face. If not, they could survive without a blow-by-blow account of his activities.

"I took it easy, I'm afraid. A little tour to get my bearings. Nothing heavy."

She smiled. If there was a reaction, she concealed it well. "We don't expect a tag your first day on the ground."

"Chin Sung won't make it easy."

"No. If it was easy—"

"Ross could handle it himself."

"I won't touch that one. How will you approach him?"

"It's impossible."

"I beg your pardon?" Jamie seemed confused.

"I can't approach Chin Sung. I don't know where he is, how many men he has on hand. It's hopeless."

"So?"

"I let him come to me."

"And then?"

"We see what happens."

They had finished, more or less together, and a waiter cleared their plates away. They declined dessert and settled for coffee.

"How do you like Korea?"

"I love it," she answered. "Everything goes to extremes— the weather, the landscape. Nothing seems average."

"A Western perspective." Kim smiled. "Most Koreans regard those traits as hardships, to be overcome. You make them sound like tourist attractions."

Jamie blushed again. "I'm sorry. I've offended you."

"By no means. I chose San Francisco for similar reasons. You can be anyone there, as extravagant or laid back as you like, and no one really gives a damn."

"Are you laid back?" Her interest, or, at least, her curiosity, appeared sincere.

"I'm satisfied with what I have."

"And where you're going?"

"I resist the urge to plan ahead."

"Sometimes it's necessary."

"That depends on what you want. I have no schedule, no agenda. If I don't earn X amount of cash this year, the world keeps right on turning. Guaranteed."

"I'm not sure what I'd do without the job," she said.

"You have my sympathy."

The check arrived and Jamie claimed it. "Courtesy of Uncle," she informed him. "Shall we go?"

Outside, the night seemed cooler. Jamie looked for stars, but they were lost, as always, in the ruddy afterglow of neon. Feeling Kim beside her, she was worried for a moment that she might have probed too deeply, gone too far, but he had not appeared to take offense. If anything, he seemed amused by her attempts to draw him out.

His animosity for Barrett Ross had captured her imagination, but a follow-up would have to be discreet. Kim did not seem the type to nurse a petty grudge, but Jamie had perused the dossier on Ross two years ago, when he became the chief of station. There was passing mention of his time in Bangkok, nothing to excite suspicion.

But, of course, the files were sanitized.

The sound of chanting voices brought her mind back to the streets. A hundred yards away, proceeding north on Sejong-ro, she saw a crowd approaching, six or eight abreast. Well-dressed, as demonstrators always seemed to be in Seoul, the men wore sports shirts—mostly white—with slacks or jeans; the women, few in number, wore crisp blouses over skirts that hid their knees. They carried placards—both in English and Korean—calling for American withdrawal, government reforms, an end to censorship. There might have been five hundred or a thousand marchers; Jamie could not tell.

Beside her, Kim was also watching the procession. "I appreciate the gesture," he informed her, smiling, "but it really wasn't necessary."

Jamie felt a tightness in her stomach. "We should go now."

"In a moment."

Uniformed police were following the march, prepared for trouble, but their main force would be waiting at the capitol with gas and riot gear. The crowd had not turned violent yet, but it made Jamie nervous, all the same. When demonstrators took the streets these days, round eyes could be the ticket to an unprovoked assault.

"It really isn't safe," she said. "We ought to leave."

"Hold on."

Outside the U.S. Embassy, some members of the march had broken free and rushed the gates, surprising the Marines on night watch. Rocks and little jars of paint were thrown with greater zeal than accuracy, many falling short. The guards stood fast inside, and helmeted police cut off the rock-throwers' retreat, arresting several, beating others to the ground with their batons.

The column forged ahead, abandoning its stragglers to the law, and Jamie felt a momentary surge of panic as the crowd—a living thing—approached. She felt exposed and vulnerable, like an insect on a drainboard when the lights come on, but she suppressed the urge to run.

"Let's go," Kim said. "I've seen enough."

Her car was parked behind the restaurant and hidden from the street. She turned her back to the procession as it drew abreast, retreating toward the parking lot with Kim beside her. Jamie had her key in the lock of the passenger's door when she felt Kim's tension, realized they had been followed.

Glancing up, she saw three young Koreans, dressed as members of the demonstration. None of them held placards, and they were not chanting now. She wondered how they managed to evade police, why they had followed her.

"Get in the car," Kim told her, speaking softly. "Be prepared to drive away."

There seemed to be no time for a debate, and Jamie did as she was told. Kim moved around the car to meet the new arrivals, and she caught a flash of steel as one produced a razor, flicked it open with a practiced motion of his wrist. The men on either side of him were armed with knives.

Jamie's stomach twisted into a tight knot of fear. Unarmed, she wondered whether it would help to lean on the Toyota's horn and draw attention to their plight. On second thought, perhaps she ought to gun the engine, try to mow their adversaries down. Unable to decide, she settled for a passive role and waited, hands white-knuckled on the steering wheel.

Kim stood before his three opponents, seeming totally relaxed. His lips were moving, but she could not hear him and she dared not roll her window down. As Jamie watched, the leader swung his razor with a flourish, answered Kim, and spat between them, on the pavement.

Concentrating on the razor and its owner, Jamie missed the move on Kim's left flank. His adversary lunged, the knife secure in both hands, thrusting, but its blade pierced empty air. She saw Kim pivot on his left foot, spinning, while his right made solid contact with the target. Knife forgotten, Kim's assailant staggered, fell, blood pumping through the fingers pressed against his face.

The two survivors moved as one, relying on numerical

superiority. Ashamed of her inaction, Jamie was afraid to watch, afraid to look away. She sat, transfixed, as Kim absorbed the brunt of their attack.

The razor missed his face by fractions of an inch, and Kim moved in beneath the swing, a swift blow hammering his adversary's ribs. Before the second knife man could approach to striking distance, Kim was darting forward, countering the enemy's momentum, one hand closing on the outstretched wrist and hauling him off-balance. Like a piston stroke, his elbow smashed the knife man's face, once, twice. The third blow was superfluous, and Kim stepped back to let him fall.

The leader stood alone, his free hand clasping injured ribs; the razor in his fist had lost its gleam. Kim circled, almost playfully, and Jamie saw that he was smiling now. He chose his moment, feinted to the left and easily disarmed his quarry with a snap kick from the opposite direction. Stepping close, he used a lightning backhand stroke to drop the young man in his tracks.

It took a moment to decide all three of them were still alive, and Jamie let her pent-up breath escape. As they were driving south on Sejong-ro, she found her voice.

"I told you it was dangerous to hang around a protest march."

"Those men weren't demonstrators."

"What?"

He answered with a question of his own. "Who knows I'm here, in Seoul?"

"From our end? Mr. Ross. Myself."

"Your counterpart with NSP?"

"They might have been informed. That isn't my department."

"Check it out. I need to know their target."

Jamie's flesh was crawling. "I don't follow."

"They were pros," he said. "Assassins. Bargain basement, maybe, but they've done this kind of work before."

"There must be some mistake."

"Agreed. They made it. Next time, their employer may invest in quality."

"Next time?" She did not like the sound of that.

"I can't imagine getting off this easy."

"What you said before, about their target . . ."

"I don't know if they were after you or me."

She was surprised to find her hands were trembling. "Me?"

"It's possible. You've been here long enough to step on toes."

"And if it isn't me?"

"Then I've made contact."

"Chin?"

"When I can answer that, we're halfway home."

She parked outside the Metro, feeling suddenly conspicuous beneath the lights. At any moment, she imagined, someone might step up and smash her window, reach inside—

"I'm going for a drive tomorrow," Kim said. His smile was hesitant. "You're welcome, if you care to come along."

"I have a lot of work to do."

"Will any of it wait?"

"It might. Where are we going?"

"It's a secret."

"Honestly, I think you ought to wait for Chin—"

"He'll find me when he's ready," Kim assured her. "If tonight's snafu was his idea, he'll need some time to lick his wounds."

"And if it wasn't?"

"Then," he said, "I've got a whole new problem on my hands."

Chapter 10

Barrett Ross was waiting in his office, at the embassy, when Jamie Constable arrived. The demonstrators had retreated, and Marines were cleaning up their mess, but it was early yet. A recent bachelor after thirteen years of marriage, Ross had no engagements for the evening and was not expected anywhere. The paperwork and waiting helped him fill his time.

When he reflected on his marriage—seldom, now—Ross thought of the relationship as a belated Cold War casualty. Too many days and nights away from home, too many secrets, had eroded the foundations of a loving partnership designed to last forever. Slick divorce attorneys were the beneficiaries of his domestic trauma, but the Company had saved him in the end. He had been able to conceal sufficient assets, covering his tracks with "national security," to keep Lucille—the bitch—from getting everything.

The vehemence of his reaction to a memory was troubling for Ross. Initially, the revelation of Lucille's affair had made him sick with rage and jealousy. Upon discovering that it was not her first, he passed through all the classic phases—guilt, denial, ultimate acceptance—but in record time. Conditioned to respond in crisis situations, Ross had put his wounded pride on hold and set about the business of survival.

It was difficult, at first, because he had been scrupulously faithful to Lucille. No fun and games in Washington or Bangkok, no long weekends with the boys on "diplomatic business." He had listened to Lucille's complaints about the Agency as mistress and dismissed them as the drivel that they were. His job was critical to the security of the United States.

Lucille was smart enough to know that, if she ever started thinking with her head, instead of with her hormones.

Single living, as he found, was nothing to write home about. The sexual revolution had come and gone without him, leaving paranoia and AIDS in its wake. Ross had emerged from the marital cocoon into an emotional demilitarized zone, where strangers circled warily around each other, demanding sexual histories and health certificates. Put off by the idea of dating, he avoided prostitutes as well, afraid of being somehow compromised.

A man in his position had responsibilities, commitments he must honor. Private pleasures had a low priority, when Ross considered them at all.

He was expecting Jamie's knock, responded automatically. "Come in."

She seemed a little flushed, but Ross ignored it, wrote it off to his imagination. Still, she made a fetching picture with the color in her cheeks. That dress...

He caught himself and waved her to a chair, determined to ignore the way her skirt rode up on creamy thighs.

"How did it go?"

"We were attacked outside the restaurant," she said.

"Explain."

He felt a knot of apprehension tighten in his stomach.

"They were dressed as student demonstrators, but they left the march and came for us. For Nemesis, I think."

The code name had been Ramsey's choice, a touch of cowboy melodrama.

"And?"

"They're neutralized. Non-lethally."

Ross did not know if that was good or bad. Three bodies could be trouble, but if Kim was turning gun-shy, backing off...

"Your bottom-line assessment?"

Jamie thought about it for a moment, prior to speaking. "Someone has a line on Nemesis. It may be Chin, but it's too early for a solid reading."

"Vibes?"

"Not yet."

"Has Nemesis decided on a strategy?"

"He's playing watch and wait, right now."

Ross frowned. He favored an aggressive attitude, the better to dispose of Chin Kyu Sung and get Kim out of South Korea in the minimum amount of time. He didn't like the bastard, and the risks involved in long-term penetration were an aggravating factor. Still, the rules of play would have to be Kim's call—at least until he demonstrated inability to cope.

"I'd like to get this over with," Ross said.

"He seems to know his business."

"I should hope so. He's been at it long enough."

"I'd like to know a little more about him," Jamie said. "It could be helpful, handling his case."

"You've got his file."

"Yes, sir...what's left of it."

"That's Langley. They decide what's fit for publication."

"I just thought, if you knew anything..."

Ross thought he saw where they were headed, and he did not like the view.

"I'll make it short and sweet," he said. "Your man's a wet work specialist. A weapon. Point him, pull the trigger, let him go. And pray you don't get any on you while you're at it."

It was Jamie's turn to frown. "He doesn't strike me as a cowboy, sir."

"I've seen him work," the station chief reminded her. "Don't get me wrong, he does the job. Sometimes he does it too damned well."

"If I could have some background on his other operations..."

"Send it up through channels," Ross advised her, "but don't hold your breath. He shouldn't be around that long."

"You've worked with Nemesis before?"

"In Bangkok." Ross could feel his stomach going sour as the memories returned. "It was...unusual."

He said no more, and Jamie let it go. "He's asked me to go out with him tomorrow."

"Out where?"

"He wouldn't say."

The frown became a scowl. "We don't have time for fun and games," he snapped. "A handler needs to keep his distance."

Bristling, Jamie held her voice in check as she replied.

"If Nemesis is right about this evening's play, the opposition has him marked. That means they've marked me, too."

"Not necessarily."

"It's even money. I'd appreciate a chance to see it through."

"You're losing objectivity."

"No, sir. I've dropped one agent—"

"No one's blaming you for that."

"—and if I drop another one, I mean to know the reason why."

"He should have iced the bastards."

Jamie shrugged. "It wasn't necessary."

"Watch your step with this one," Ross instructed. "It could blow up in your face."

"I've got it covered."

"I sincerely hope so. Anything on tap that Fitz can't handle while you're gone?"

"I'm clear. It's just the afternoon."

"Remember that. You're not assigned to Nemesis as any kind of backup."

"No, sir."

"He works solo, all the way."

"I understand."

"All right, then. If we're finished . . ."

Jamie rose to leave. Ross tracked her with his eyes, embarrassed when she turned and caught him at it.

"Bangkok."

"Yes?"

"I'm curious, that's all."

Ross thought about his answer for a moment, knowing Jamie was not ready for the truth.

"I lost my distance. People died."

"And Nemesis?"

"He walked away from it. He always walks away."

"Good night, sir."

" 'Night."

The door swung shut behind her, leaving him alone.

He always walks away, Ross thought. *But maybe not this time*.

Jamie Constable's apartment building stood on Yulgog-ro, a short walk from the zoo, on Seoul's northside. She seldom went to see the animals, disheartened by their pacing in the pits and cages, but she sometimes left her windows open when the nights were warm and listened to their sounds, competing with the noise of traffic. In the crowded heart of Seoul, it helped her stand apart and find some distance from a world of concrete, glass, and steel.

Tonight, she thought the big cats sounded restless, apprehensive. It was nonsense, Jamie knew; she was projecting, playing mind games, but she could not shake the premonition of impending violence.

What had she expected? They were sending out a killer to avenge the loss of Domino, indulging in a game of payback with the opposition. Violence had been guaranteed from the beginning.

Old hands called it wet work, executive action, or termination with extreme prejudice, but they normally spoke in the past tense. Killing assignments had been rare in Jamie's time. When someone bought the farm these days, they went like Domino, devoured by a mission run amok. Deliberate assassination was passé, the Senate watchdogs pouncing eagerly on any scent of blood.

It made her nervous, taking part in a deliberate murder plan, but Jamie knew it came with the territory. If the opposition was allowed to move at will, secure against reprisals, no one would be truly safe.

She only hoped that Kim would do his job efficiently and swiftly. Every day he spent in Seoul increased the likelihood of broader violence, multiplied the odds of injury to Kim, himself.

She hesitated, analyzing her concern. He was an agent in her charge, but was there more? Had she unwittingly allowed herself to care about the stranger known as Nemesis? Not yet, although he did possess a quality that simultaneously frightened and attracted Jamie. There was danger in his eyes . . . and something else.

The red light on her answering machine informed her there had been a call while she was out. She ran the tape back, listened with a frown to Ray Fitzpatrick's voice.

"Hey, James," he said, and she could almost see him grinning with embarrassment, his eyes averted as he spoke, afraid of contact. "I just thought I'd call and see if you were doing anything tonight. Too late, I guess. I'll see you at the office. 'Bye."

He had not asked her out before, except to lunch, and Jamie understood that she would have to rain more forcefully on his parade. She did not need the kind of subterfuge and tension that surrounded office romance, failed or otherwise. Above all else, she did not need the extra headaches now.

Undressing for the shower, Jamie caught herself comparing Kim Sunim and Ray Fitzpatrick. Both were quiet men, but there the similarity evaporated. Fitz was muzzled by a lack of confidence that doubtless had its roots in childhood. Jamie would have bet that Ray had few, if any, dates in high school. Painfully repressed, he would have sublimated his desires in "safe" activities like band and campus journalism. Jamie pegged him as a virgin—or at least a novice—and she had no interest in providing his remedial instruction.

On the other hand, Kim's silence seemed to emanate from strength, a confidence that rendered words superfluous. She had no means of gauging his experience with sex, but Kim impressed her as a man who stood in awe of no one. He was obviously capable of self-defense, but there was more than physical assurance in his manner. Jamie sensed a deep reserve of power—over his emotions, his environment—that enabled Kim to stand apart and view his fellow men as a detached observer.

Moving naked toward the bathroom, Jamie pictured Kim in combat, and a chill raised goose flesh on her arms. It might be incorrect to say he had enjoyed their brief encounter with the hoodlums, but he had disposed of them with cool efficiency, a master practicing his craft. In memory, she saw him circling the razor man, a tiger playing with a rabbit, working up an appetite.

And yet, he had not killed. Her explanation to the station chief had been a private reading. She preferred to think that Kim had voluntarily restrained himself because a death—three deaths—would not have served his mission. Living adversaries, properly chastised, would become de facto messengers for Kim, delivering the word that he could not be shoved aside so easily. If they were sent by Chin Kyu

Sung, the beating might provoke a personal reaction from their boss. If not...

She stepped into the shower, standing with her head thrown back as water drummed against her face and breasts. Its warmth began to melt the tension she had carried from her conference with Ross, and Jamie blanked her mind deliberately, avoiding conscious thought. She found the soap by touch and turned her back against the spray as she began to wash herself.

Unbidden images of Kim returned to haunt her as she raised a lather on her tingling skin. She saw his lethal hands in motion, lightning fast, and wondered how they might apply themselves to a more leisurely caress. Her nipples puckered at a touch and Jamie shivered, passing off her sudden dizziness to the accumulated steam inside the shower.

In Asia, it was widely held that expert martial artists were possessed of corresponding skill in other areas, including sexual performance. Focusing on Kim, the warm illusion of his touch, she wondered whether there was any truth in old wives' tales. If so...

She caught herself as soapy fingers slid between her thighs. A blush of mingled passion and embarrassment brought color to her cheeks as Jamie turned to face the shower nozzle, groping for the temperature controls. A heartbeat later, icy needles pierced her mental fog and she was shivering from cold, relying on the arctic spray to smother her libido.

Jamie was humiliated by her weakness, startled by the yearning that had taken her off-guard. She heard the voice of Barrett Ross inside her skull: *A handler needs to keep his distance.*

Right.

She knew that, recognized the wisdom of a rule that strictly separated work from recreation. Personal involvement lead to careless errors, and a careless handler could be lethal to the agents under his—or her—control. If Jamie could not hold her objectivity intact, she had no business in the game.

Kim was a soldier, nothing more. Upon completion of his task, he would depart, and they would never meet again. It would not do for Jamie to project emotion into their relationship, attaching some ulterior significance to their respective roles.

She turned the shower off and snared a bath towel from the rack. Examining her own reflection in the full-length mirror, Jamie found a stranger staring back at her, eyes shining with the heat of her illusory encounter with a stranger.

Jamie knew that she was skating on thin ice, endangering her job—perhaps her life—but there were questions still unanswered in her mind. She would not rest until she understood Kim's stake in picking up the tab for Domino. And through that understanding, she might come to grips with Nemesis, himself.

Returning to his room, Kim left the sweeper on its shelf. A film of talcum powder, dusted lightly on the outer doorknob's underside, was undisturbed. The room had not been penetrated in his absence.

Shrugging off his jacket, working on the tie, he pondered the attempt upon his life. Initially, he had considered Jamie a potential target, but the notion did not play. She lived in Seoul, was readily accessible at any time, and there would be no point in striking when she had an escort, in a public place. Despite their obvious inadequacies, Kim's assailants would have known enough to wait for her at home, where they could work in privacy.

A move this early in the game meant Kim had touched a nerve. But whose? Ideally, given time and opportunity, he would have questioned the attackers, picked their brains for any useful bits of information. Jamie's presence and the public setting had prevented him from following his instincts. He had done the next best thing, permitting them to live and thus delivering a message to their master. Better men—and better planning—would be needed to complete the job.

Kim was not ready, yet, to blame Chin Sung for the attack. The close proximity of student demonstrators proved precisely nothing, since the NSP was known for infiltrating every major group of dissidents in South Korea. Anyone could stage an incident to coincide with turmoil in the streets, though fabrication of a protest on short notice would require affluence and skill. Again, the blame might lie with Chin—or with the men who wished to see him dead.

In his employment with the Company, Kim had been forced to work with the Korean CIA on various occasions, childhood animosity evolving into a mature contempt as he observed their work firsthand. The "accident" that claimed his parents was an ancient scar, and Kim had early recognized the blind futility of trying to identify their killers. Even so, he viewed the KCIA—and its "new" successor—with suspicion, stopping short of full cooperation when assignments brought him home to Seoul. Their last encounter, eight months prior to Kim's retirement, had erupted into violence that put a covert strain on U.S.–ROK relations, landing Kim in Bangkok, where he was assigned to work for Barrett Ross.

His mission had revolved around the fresh discovery of infiltration tunnels, excavated by the North Koreans from Kaesong, beneath the parallel, to Munsan in the south. Assigned to hunt the architects and punish them as an example to the communists, Kim had established a relationship with certain Munsan natives, gleaning information from their conversations as they came to trust him over time.

The masters of Remonclo had grown anxious, waiting for results, and they dispatched a team of heavy-handed thugs to speed things up. Abducting one of Kim's informants—a young woman—the interrogators worked all night to shake loose information she did not possess. Kim tracked them down in time to save her life, and spent his wrath on her inquisitors. One drew a pistol; his unarmed companions survived, in altered forms, and murder charges were reluctantly abandoned after spokesmen for the Company insisted Kim had honestly mistaken South Korean patriots for northern reds.

Old memories died hard, and Kim knew there were veterans within the NSP who would be pleased to see him dead. If word of his arrival had been leaked—by Ross or someone else—Chin Sung might have to wait in line to take his shot.

Of course, there was an equal possibility that Chin, or one of his associates, had opted for a swift preemptive strike. If so, they would be smarting from defeat; the failure of their bid might be enough to help Kim win the audience he sought with Chin Kyu Sung. And once his target had been lured into striking range . . .

He dropped the train of thought, refusing to pursue it further. Kim had promised to eliminate Reese Holland's killer, but his acquiescence in the game did not encompass blind presumption of responsibility by any given individual. The Company had fingered Chin, and the assessment might be accurate, but Kim would have to be convinced before he made the tag.

He owed that much to Holland's memory.

He owed it to himself.

If Ross and Ramsey were mistaken, somehow, he would have to make adjustments in the game plan, follow through on instinct, and to hell with Langley's expectations. Once a target was confirmed, he would be ready to proceed, and he would live—or die—with any consequences of his action.

First, however, he had business in the south. A brief diversion from the deadly mission that had brought him back to Seoul. It pleased him that he would not have to make the pilgrimage alone, but he did not allow his thoughts to linger long on Jamie Constable. Tomorrow, on the road, there would be ample time for learning more about his handler, sorting out her personality from the persona artificially imposed by her established duty to the Company.

Kim thought there might be something worth discovering, beneath the cool, professional facade. He hoped that she would not turn out to be an enemy.

Chapter 11

They met at half-past nine, outside the Metro. Jamie was prepared to drive, but Kim surprised her with the rented Hyundai, insisting that she let him do the work, since the excursion had been his idea.

"I ought to leave some word of where we're going," Jamie said, "in case they need to call me from the office."

"Sorry, but we won't be near a telephone."

"I've never been a great one for surprises."

"So, it's time you learned."

He kept her guessing on the long drive south, through Pyongtaek, Taejon, Chongju, and a dozen smaller towns. After an hour or so, she stopped referring to her watch and let herself relax a little, concentrating on the scenery.

"You haven't told me why you left the Company," she said at last.

"It should be in my file."

"I got the *Reader's Digest* version."

"Let's just say it had to do with Bangkok."

"Ross?"

"What happened to the 'Mister'?"

"I'm off duty here, remember?"

"Right."

"So, *was* it Ross?"

"In part."

"You know, I could have gone to dental school if I was interested in pulling teeth."

He smiled. "Okay. It's been a long time, anyway. Ross got approval for an executive action. Chicom terrorists, he said. The operation went to hell, there were civilian casualties. An absolute snafu. The punchline was that neither of the targets had a thing to do with terrorism."

"I don't understand."

"They were a pair of dealers, moving China white without a franchise from the local Triad. Someone found a tidy way to put them out of business."

"Someone?"

"I could never point a finger. Everyone involved pled ignorance. They're good at that."

"And so you quit."

"I had a choice to make. It worked out, all around."

"Was there resistance to your leaving?"

"Some, but they got over it. I wasn't going public, and the brass knew that. It hasn't been a problem."

She was silent for a moment, screwing up her nerve to ask the question she had been avoiding.

"Was it difficult? I mean . . ."

"The sanctions?"

Jamie could not meet his eyes. "I'm sorry. That's a stupid question, and I'm out of line."

"You'd be surprised how many people are afraid to ask. Inside the Company, I mean. They want to know exactly what it feels like, so they watch you from the corner of their eyes and try to read it on your face, but they can never find the words."

"I'm really—"

"Nothing."

"What?"

"It feels like nothing. All the novelty wore off in Vietnam. You have a job to do, like stamping envelopes or taking out the trash. It doesn't make you feel superior or sad. Sometimes, if there's a problem and you beat the odds, it just feels good to be alive."

They rode in silence for a time. Kim sensed her reticence, a fear of inadvertently offending him, and knew that he would have to break the ice.

"I'm taking you to Songgwang Sa," he said.

"The monastery?"

"You're familiar with it?"

"There's a reference to it, in . . ."

"My file," he finished for her, watching color tinge her cheeks.

"Are they expecting us?"

"I doubt it. No one's lived at Songgwang Sa for twenty years."

She frowned. "I don't believe I've ever heard of a Korean monastery going out of business."

"There were 'special circumstances.' Government informers— *one* informer—charged the leadership with giving aid and comfort to the communists. It was alleged that infiltrators from the north had friends at Songgwang Sa."

"And did they?"

"Monasteries aren't political. Of course, they sometimes shelter refugees, without regard to ideology. In 1968, that added up to treason."

"Were there prosecutions?"

"Nothing that dramatic. Innuendo, for the most part, building up hostility among the peasants. Warnings to the leaders of the faith, that Songgwang Sa might be a liability. A couple of the monks had 'accidents' while traveling; the rest moved on."

"The refugees?"

"A few were smuggled out. The rest wound up in prison, where they saw the error of their ways."

"You put all that together by yourself?"

"My first time back, on business for the Company, I paid a visit to the monastery. It was empty, and I started asking questions, pulling strings. It took a little time."

"You mentioned an informer."

"Tongsung Yun." The name lay bitter on Kim's tongue.

"A personal acquaintance?"

"Once, I had a chance to stop him and I let it pass. A serious mistake."

"I've made a few of those myself."

"Did yours cost lives?"

"My point is that you're not responsible for someone else's actions. You weren't even in the country during 1968."

"The file again."

"I wouldn't be much use if I was ignorant, now, would I?"

"No." He saw the highway sign for Sunchon and was relieved to change the subject. "Lunch?"

"I'm starved."

They found a little family-run cafe that featured wholesome food without the "atmosphere" demanded of a tourist stop, and Kim picked up the tab in spite of Jamie's protest. She was working hard to keep the conversation light, apparently regretting her attempt to draw Kim out, but he did not regard the effort as a cover-up. Instead, she seemed to genuinely care about his feelings, and he wondered how she would survive in her position as a handler. Caring—any real emotion—could be detrimental where a life-and-death decision was involved.

"You must be looking forward to a posting in the States," he said when they were nearly finished.

Jamie seemed surprised by his remark. "I'm happy here," she said. "Well, ninety-five percent. No Langley desk jobs, thank-you all the same."

"There can't be much in terms of social life."

"You'd be surprised. They throw some awesome parties at the embassy."

"And that's enough?"

"I manage," Jamie told him, "if it's any of your business."

Kim decided not to press his luck with an apology. Instead, he checked his watch and said, "We'd better go. It's still another half an hour."

"Lead on."

The narrow track from Sunchon to Songgwang Sa had not been kept in good repair. Kim held the Hyundai to thirty miles per hour, dodging pot holes, slowing to a crawl at points where mountain streams had overflowed in rainy months and swept debris across the road. Around them, pressing close, the virgin forest was alive with calling birds and brilliant foliage.

"Someone should have warned me we were going on safari." Jamie's tone betrayed a blend of wonder and suppressed anxiety.

"You're safe," he told her, grinning. "It's been years since anyone reported tigers in the neighborhood."

"Terrific."

Climbing past the waterfall, Kim thought about his first

trip up the mountain, in a donkey cart. It was the last time he had seen his father, and he was surprised to feel a sudden emptiness. Caught up in private thoughts, he recognized the sound of Jamie's voice but missed her words.

"I beg your pardon?"

"This is beautiful," she said again.

"I used to think so."

"Used to?"

"Now it just seems... alien."

He shifted into low and crawled along the final hundred yards of winding track. Beside him, Jamie gave a small, involuntary gasp as she beheld her first glimpse of the monastery.

Vines had overgrown the outer walls in places, making Songgwang Sa resemble something from a jungle travelogue. An ancient ruin on the Amazon, perhaps. The stones were blotched with moss, and geckos scuttled into fissures as the car approached, disturbing their routine of basking in the sun.

"It's fabulous," said Jamie, but Kim marked a tremor in her voice. "You're sure it isn't haunted?"

"Friendly spirits," Kim assured her, pocketing his keys and moving toward the gates. They stood ajar, perhaps the mark of prowlers, but the lichen growing on the threshold had not been disturbed for years. He gave one side a shove and listened to the hinges groan.

"Be careful."

"There's no danger here," he said. And thought: *Not now*. Whatever good—or evil—had been hatched within those walls, its power had been neutralized by time.

A flock of brightly colored birds erupted from the court-yard, wheeling overhead and screeching as their sanctuary was invaded. Jamie caught her breath, then laughed, embarrassed by her own reaction.

"Guess I'm not your average hearty pioneer."

"You'll do."

He scanned the courtyard, noting all the changes wrought by time and nature. Weeds had sprouted here and there, between the paving stones, and creepers from the outer wall had found their way inside. The leaves deposited by over-hanging trees, swept daily under Brother Kee's command, had taken full advantage of his absence, gathering in drifts against the temple walls.

Kim stood before the Buddha hall and saw that doves had nested underneath the ornamental roofing tiles. They shifted restlessly at his approach but did not fly away.

The doors at Songgwang Sa were not equipped with locks. Kim stepped inside the narthex of the Buddha hall, with Jamie on his heels, pausing long enough for his eyes to adjust in the semi-darkness. Lamps and candles had provided most of the illumination in the temple proper; shadows held dominion now, and Kim moved warily, alert to any sign of wild inhabitants. A scuttling sound behind the altar marked the passage of a rat, and Jamie moved a little closer to him, studying the floor around her feet.

"The brothers worshipped here," he told her. "It was brighter then, and always warm."

In winter, he remembered, temple services had been a welcome respite from the cold outside, the heat from open flames and human bodies trapped inside the Buddha hall a cure for hands and faces numbed by biting winds. In summer, though, the hall became an oven; prayers and lectures were a trial to be endured.

A rustling in the rafters captured Kim's attention. Squinting, he could make out several dozen fruit bats, hanging upside down with folded wings, like fruit gone brown and withered on the vine.

Beside him, Jamie saw them too, and made a face. "If you don't mind," she said, "I'll wait outside."

"I'm right behind you."

Reemerging into sunshine, Kim led Jamie on a tour of the quarters where his nights were spent at Songgwang Sa. She poked her head inside one spartan cell and came out frowning.

"It reminds me of a prison."

"Minimal distractions are the key to meditation."

"I suppose. Did you enjoy it here?"

"At first," he said, "I thought it was a great adventure. Later, I was scared and homesick. Time went by, and it was all I knew."

"No women?"

` "Strictly out of bounds. As far as I know, you're the first inside these walls."

"I should feel honored."

"Absolutely."

"Still, it must be strange."

"No stranger than a female raised in convent school."

"At least she'd see a priest from time to time."

"That doesn't count."

"You'd be surprised."

He led her through the inner garden, overrun with weeds and creepers now, the vegetables and flowers run amok and gone to seed. Kim hesitated by the gate where he had stood one night, in darkness, watching Tonsung Yun betray them all.

"A penny for your thoughts."

"You wouldn't get your money's worth."

On impulse, Kim directed Jamie toward the stairs that served the inner compound, drawn to stand once more inside the heart of Songgwang Sa. The gate, unlatched, swung gently in a mountain breeze, revealing glimpses of the meditation hall and master's quarters as they climbed the hillside. Kim felt his heartbeat quicken briefly—apprehension or excitement, he could not have said precisely which—and brought it back to normal with his mind.

No ghosts, he thought, and yet he could not climb those stairs without imagining the face of Master Rhee, impassive as he supervised the lesson of the day. Unbidden memories recalled their hour together, when they played the game of stones. Kim heard the master's voice, as if Rhee stood beside him even now.

"Remember to be always honest with yourself," the old man whispered, leaning close. "You may not always speak the truth to others, but a spirit fed on secret lies must starve."

Before the memories could stop him, Kim pushed through the swinging gate and stepped into the compound.

Fascinated by her strange surroundings, Jamie followed Kim inside. The upper level of the monastery had been clearly separated from the common ground below, a sanctuary for the chosen, and it still retained a certain air of mystery. The Catholic training of her youth had been discarded years before, but Jamie still recalled the feel of hallowed ground. She almost thought it might be sacrilegious, here, to raise her voice above a whisper.

Sudden movement at the corner of her vision captured Jamie's full attention, and she turned in time to glimpse the form of a retreating fox, jaws clasped around the flaccid body of a snake. Unable to suppress a shudder, Jamie turned away and found Kim watching her.

"The practice field," he said, and pointed toward an open space at one end of the compound. Trampled bare and hard, the soil had thus far managed to resist encroachment by the creeping undergrowth.

She played a hunch. "T'ai chi?"

He nodded.

"Isn't that a paradox? I mean, a church devoted to enlightenment and peace, instructing young men how to fight? That has to be a contradiction."

"Not at all. T'ai chi has less to do with combat than it does with self-control and personal development—the very heart of Zen. By mastering the body, placing self in harmony with nature and the elements, a student learns his limitations and potential. Only through discovery of self may one achieve enlightenment and inner peace."

Afraid of pushing Kim too far, she still could not resist the urge to pick his brain and find out how he functioned.

"Still," she said, "there must have been some radical adjustments in the military, Vietnam, and later with the Company."

Kim answered her obliquely, moving gradually across the compound while she fell in step.

"Zen has no ideology, no dogma for the masses," he replied. "In place of your commandments from the mountain top, practitioners of Zen attempt to find the truth within themselves. And, having found it, each endeavors to fulfill his private destiny."

"Through violence?"

"Warriors have their place. In ancient times, they were exalted, even deified. Today, we keep them out of sight and pray they won't be needed, but we can't afford to let them go."

"And you felt called to be a warrior?"

"Not called. The choice was mine. I didn't talk to any burning bushes."

Jamie felt the color rising in her cheeks. "I'm sorry. No offense."

"None taken." The amusement in his smile seemed genuine. "My talents coincided with a given need. There was a clear and present danger from the enemy."

"Those enemies are still around," she said.

"I'm sure they are. The trouble was, they started looking too much like my friends. I couldn't tell the difference any more."

"You still came back."

"I had no choice."

"Because of Holland?" She was careful not to use the dead man's code name.

"Partly."

"Were you very close?"

"We understood each other."

Jamie didn't want to dance around the problem any longer. "I've been going over every move we made," she said. "I can't find any holes or violations of procedure to the point where Holland terminated contact."

"Fair enough."

"I honestly don't think we blew it."

"No one said you did. Things happen. People die."

"So, why do I feel guilty?"

"It's instinctive. Give it time. You haven't learned to shut your feelings off."

"I'm not so sure I want to."

"It's the only way to go. The job will drive you crazy, otherwise."

"Is that your secret?"

"One of them. Remember, I'm inscrutable."

They stood before the meditation hall, its thin walls eaten through in places by exposure to the elements. She followed Kim through sliding doors, into a spacious room where filtered sunlight swam with motes of dust, describing abstract patterns on the floor.

"What's that?"

She pointed to a series of Korean characters, inscribed in fading paint above an altar, on the opposite wall.

"*Ban-yok*," he read aloud. "That's 'treason.' A memento from the witch-hunt."

"Things have changed," she told him.

"Some things."

Passing through a different exit, they emerged onto a terrace with a panoramic view of Songgwang Sa and the surrounding forest. Flanked by temples that were smaller versions of the Buddha hall, cut off from any view of modern dwellings, Jamie felt herself transported to an alien, archaic world. Her gaze was drawn to a discreetly isolated bungalow that occupied a nearby corner of the compound.

Kim anticipated her unspoken question. "*Go-jang's* quarters," he informed her.

"What's a *go-jang?*"

"In t'ai chi, a master of the art. In Zen, a venerable priest and counselor."

"Your parents brought you here?"

"My father."

"For protection from the purges?"

"Yes."

She took a chance. "What made you leave?"

"Times change."

His frown showed concentration, rather than resentment of her question. Crouching by a long-neglected flower bed, Kim filled his palm with sandy soil and made a fist, the dark grains trickling through his fingers.

"Holding on too tightly," he continued, "we may lose the object of desire." His fingers clenched, sand spilling out in greater quantities, then opened to reveal a clump of earth still nestled in his palm. "The greater wisdom sometimes lies in letting go."

"It isn't always easy."

"No." He dusted off his palm and smiled. "I don't suppose it is."

"When you've completed your assignment..."

"I'll be going back to San Francisco. I'm retired, remember?"

"You have friends there? Family?"

"No family," he said, confirming dated information from his file. "I'm not so sure about the friends. I have my students."

"No one special?"

"Special?" Kim regarded her with interest. "You mean like a great romance?"

A blush warmed Jamie's cheeks. She found she could not meet his gaze.

"I'm prying. I apologize."

"For what? A handler ought to know her agents inside-out." His smile was obviously meant to make her feel at ease. "In answer to your question, I've been told that I'm impossible to live with."

"Please—"

"The truth is, I suspect I'm just too dull."

"I doubt that very much."

"You'd be surprised. I can't remember when I had to fight my way out of a restaurant, before last night."

She laughed, her tension broken. "I suppose we should have left a bigger tip."

"I'll make a note of that, for next time."

"Kim—"

She could not find the words, felt foolish as he watched and waited for her to continue.

"Yes?"

"It's getting late," she said at last. "We have a long drive back."

"And dinner?"

"Well . . ."

"You have to eat. A hungry handler makes mistakes."

She read no accusation in his tone, allowed herself to smile. "All right."

"I know a little place in Taejon, on our way, if it's still open after all these years."

"We could go back to my apartment."

Jamie had not planned to speak; the words came out impulsively, surprising her as much as Kim. Unable to withdraw the invitation gracefully, she stammered through an ad-lib explanation.

"You were nice enough to show me all of this," she said, "and I've got lots of food at home. I'm not too shabby in the kitchen, if I do say so myself. But if you'd rather—"

"I accept."

"You do?"

"I do."

So much for distance, Jamie thought, but she experienced a certain feeling of accomplishment, despite her own misgivings. As they left the upper compound, crossed the open courtyard of the monastery proper, she examined Kim discreetly, studying his profile. In a way, she thought he seemed at home in those surroundings. Modern clothes and spoken English not withstanding, part of him belonged.

She saw him as a man divided, torn between the modern and traditional, between the East and West, but Jamie thought she might be oversimplifying. Kim, in jest, had called himself inscrutable, and that seemed closer to the truth. For the duration of his mission, part of Kim belonged to her, and Jamie was determined that he should not come to harm through any fault or oversight of hers.

The sun was dipping lower as they cleared the outer gate, and Jamie paused for one last look at Songgwang Sa, before she turned and raced her shadow to the car.

Chapter 12

It was dark when they returned to Seoul. Kim drove directly to the Metro, pulling up behind the space where Jamie's car was parked and waiting while she found her keys.

"I'll lead. It isn't far."

He gave her one more out. "You've still got time to change your mind."

The flash of disappointment in her eyes did not strike Kim as feigned. "Don't tell me that you're backing out."

"And miss home cooking? Not a chance."

"That's better."

Jamie's fragrance lingered in the car, and Kim rolled down his window, welcoming the city's warm, polluted breath. He was disturbed by the attraction that he felt toward Jamie, her ability to draw him out. Emotion had no place in covert operations, least of all emotional involvement with his handler. Feelings made an agent vulnerable, and he had enough to cope with as it was, in terms of Holland's murder.

Following the small Toyota north on Donhwa-ro, past the Pagoda Park and Royal Shrine, Kim told himself that he was being foolish. Jamie had invited him to dinner, nothing more. His ego might elaborate upon a simple invitation, but he had no reason to suspect ulterior designs. Despite his dossier, she hardly knew him, and a casual liaison—worse, involvement with an agent in her charge—did not strike Kim as part of Jamie's style.

With any luck, he might be wrong.

Above all else, it irritated Kim that he was *hoping* she might want him. It was bad enough to flaunt established discipline, but he had more immediate concerns. Distraction from the focus of his mission could be lethal. He had not come home to die.

Kim concentrated on his driving, traffic thinning as they passed the zoo, and Jamie led him into residential streets, with tall apartment houses pressing close on either side. The neighborhood was limited by price to members of the upper-middle-income bracket, though the flats themselves were not luxurious. An American like Jamie would make do with an apartment here; a native would aspire to residency in the district as a symbol of achievement.

Jamie's building had a subterranean garage for tenants, with a smaller, open lot for visitors in back. Acknowledging her pantomime directions, Kim went on to park his car and doubled back to meet her on the street. She joined him shortly, wearing an apologetic smile.

"Security. I pay an extra hundred-fifty *won* a month for parking underground, and then I have to come back out if I have company."

"That's progress."

"That's a crock."

They entered through a well-kept lobby, paused for Jamie to collect her mail, and caught the elevator to the seventh floor.

"Ignore the mess, okay?"

"It can't be any worse than home."

Kim half expected meager furnishings, in the Korean style, but Jamie had contrived to make the place her own. There was no mess, but she spent several moments straightening a cushion here, a picture there, before she laid her purse aside and waited for his verdict.

"Very nice," Kim said. "It suits you."

"Thanks . . . I think. Would you like anything to drink? Some wine? A beer?"

"Beer's fine."

She poured herself a glass of wine and left it in the kitchen. "Make yourself at home," she said. "I need to get things started."

"Can I help?"

"I don't believe in putting guests to work."

Drifting toward the sliding windows fronting on her tiny

balcony, he scanned the lights of Seoul and thought how easy it would be to make himself at home.

Too easy.

Seoul had not been home to Kim Sunim for over twenty years, and he was not entranced by the idea of turning back the clock. Whenever Kim imagined "home," his memories of Songgwang Sa and San Francisco ran together, intercut with fragmentary scenes of training at Fort Benning, Vietnam, the places where his duties for the Company had taken him to war. He rarely thought of Seoul, and never as a place where he was comfortable, safe, and warm.

Outside, the city lights seemed cold, remote, like something from a distant galaxy. They offered no security, no real illumination in the darkness; rather, they would rob you of perspective, blind you if you stared too long.

Tonight, they helped conceal the target he had traveled half way around the world to kill.

Ray Fitzpatrick sat and brooded for a quarter-hour after Jamie and her date had gone inside. Surveillance of her building was a bad idea, he understood that now, but she had not returned his call and he was worried when she didn't show for work that morning. Never mind the word that she was "absent on official business." Ray knew Jamie did not handle field work on her own, and he had been concerned.

Not jealous.

That came later.

He had spent the morning in a dither, frightened that she might have stepped outside the bounds of her assignment. Jamie was a stickler for procedure, but she also had ambition. Sitting at a desk in Seoul for years on end was not the ticket to promotion. Jamie seemed to like her duty station well enough, but Fitz knew she was waiting for a handle, anything at all, to give herself a long boost up the ladder.

Recently, instead of boosts, there had been setbacks. He was not conversant with the details of her work—such things were strictly "need to know"—but it was rumored she had dropped an agent in the field. The pressure would be on for her to save the play. He worried that she might go overboard and place herself at risk to make it right.

Her answering machine had greeted him with counterfeit sincerity throughout the day, until he tired of leaving messages. She would not call him back, in any case. She never called, preferring casual interrogations at the office. Was there something that he needed? Information on a case? A certain file, perhaps? Deliberately avoiding any personal connection, she emasculated Ray Fitzpatrick with a smile.

And he forgave her everything.

She did not mean to hurt him; he knew that instinctively. Her first commitment was The Job, and nothing else would be allowed to interfere. She would reject the notion of an office romance for the stigma that it carried. If she made it up the ladder—*when* she made it—Jamie Constable would leave no ready ammunition for detractors.

Still, Fitzpatrick waited, stubbornly refusing to abandon hope. He knew that people and perspectives changed with time. If Jamie understood his feelings, realized that he would never compromise her game plan, her resistance might begin to weaken. If he only had a chance to tell her once, without the interruption of an oh-so-urgent meeting or a phone call from the chief of station.

Thus, the stakeout.

It was meant as a surprise, complete with flowers—wilted, now—and candy, which he would be forced to eat himself. She would be startled, possibly annoyed, when he turned up without an invitation, but his charm would win her over in the end, convince her she had been mistaken all along. Fitzpatrick had rehearsed his speech before a mirror, in the men's room, and again at home. It was not poetry, not even close, but he was concentrating on sincerity. If Jamie heard him out, he knew she would be moved.

It angered Ray Fitzpatrick now, to realize that he had been deceived. He had imagined Jamie working overtime to compensate for her mistakes, perhaps exceeding her instructions, risking everything. Instead, he found that she had stolen time for some diversion on the side, permitting him to worry while she played her dirty little games.

Fitzpatrick did not recognize the man, was not con-

cerned about his name or background. It was obvious that
Jamie had enjoyed her day enough to ask for more. Emerging
from the underground garage, she smiled with an expression
Ray had never seen before—complicity incarnate—and the
stranger followed her inside. Upstairs, she would erase
Fitzpatrick's messages, forget him in the time it took to
punch a button on the answering machine, and then she
would be free to spend the evening as she chose.

She owed him nothing, but Fitzpatrick's anger did not
have its roots in obligation. Rather, the sensation of betrayal
sprang from his imagination, feeding on his fantasies. As
Jamie sidestepped his pathetic overtures, Fitzpatrick's mind
had cloaked her in the attributes of sainthood, chastity
included. She was pure in flesh and spirit, scorning the
entanglements of love and sex because they interfered with
her pursuit of a career. As she rejected Ray Fitzpatrick, so
she would deny all men the pleasures of her company, her
body.

He had been a fool.

How many others had she entertained behind his back,
while he was mustering his courage to suggest a movie,
dinner, anything at all? How many men had used her while
Fitzpatrick sat at home, rehearsing speeches for an audience
of one?

He scooped the wilted flowers up and tossed them out
the window. It would serve her right if he went up to face her
now, demanding an apology, but he was rooted to his seat.
Fitzpatrick hated confrontations, shied away from situations
where he might be called upon to make a stand, and he was
not prepared for Jamie now. Her anger—worse, her laughter—
would destroy him, shatter any vestige of the dignity he
struggled to maintain.

Tomorrow at work, he would pretend that everything
was normal, greet her in the usual way, without alluding to
her absence. If the subject should be raised, let her initiate
the conversation. He would listen to her lies and smile, the
same deluded idiot to whom she was accustomed. Nothing
would induce him to betray the fact that he could smell the
stranger's taint upon her skin.

In time, when he had laid his strategy and Jamie least
expected it, his wounded pride would be avenged. Fitzpatrick

could not visualize the proper form of retribution, yet. His wounds were still too fresh. But when the time came, he would know it, and he would not be afraid.

A block from Jamie's flat, he pitched the candy out and saw the box explode, dark chocolates rolling in the gutter.

"Eat that," he muttered, unaware that he was weeping.

And the darkness saw him safely home.

"More coffee?"

"Not for me, thanks."

Jamie poured another half cup for herself and sat back on the couch. The meal had been a qualified success—her salad was a masterpiece, the steaks a trifle overdone—but Kim had complimented everything and cleaned his plate. He seemed contented now, but still on guard, and Jamie wondered if he ever truly let himself relax.

"I want to thank you for this afternoon," she said.

"No need."

"I think there is. You took the time to show me something very special."

"Ruins."

"More than that. Another side of life. A different side of you."

His smile was hesitant, self-conscious. "So, the mystery's unraveled?"

"Not entirely, but I'm working on it."

"Save your energy. There's no solution."

"I enjoy a complex problem."

"A persistent sleuth."

"I can be."

"Do you handle disappointment well?"

"I'm never disappointed. Some things take more time than others, but they work out in the end."

"I'm happy for you."

"How about yourself?"

"I've learned to modify my expectations."

"That's too bad. I would have said you have unlimited potential."

"Don't confuse potential with ambition."

"Are they very different?"

"A world apart," he told her.

"So you really don't regret retirement? Giving up the game?"

"I found another game. It's more my speed."

"I've seen your speed. You haven't lost the edge."

"I've lost the need."

"Which need is that?"

"To prove myself at the expense of others."

"Now you're sounding like a pacifist."

"I don't trust labels," he replied. "Let's say I had enough of hunting men for money."

Jamie frowned. "I don't believe you ever did the job for money."

"No?"

She shook her head. "It doesn't fit. I see you more as an idealist."

"Maybe, once upon a time. No more."

"You're here."

"We've covered that. I'm paying dues."

He checked his watch, and Jamie knew that she had pushed too hard.

"It's getting late," he said. "I'd better let you get some rest."

"I'm wide awake," she told him. "Too much coffee."

Kim was on his feet, and Jamie went to fetch his jacket, startled by her own reluctance for the evening to end. She met him at the door, the jacket folded in her arms, uncomfortably aware of his aroma on the fabric.

"Dinner was delicious, Jamie."

"Thanks." Impulsively she added, "Sorry there was no dessert."

"I'll take a rain check."

"Are you sure?" Her cheeks were suddenly on fire, but Kim pretended not to notice her discomfiture. "I mean, you still could have it . . . now."

The room was spinning now, and Jamie knew that she would die from sheer embarrassment as Kim reached out to claim his jacket. She was startled, nearly lost her balance, as his strong hands slid around her waist instead and pulled close.

Their lips met, softly, slowly warming to the kiss as passion flared. Kim's jacket, caught between them, was an irritation now and Jamie let it fall. Pressing close against him, she could feel the strength of his arousal, rivaling her own.

She opened her lips under Kim's gentle pressure, tongues dueling as his hands slid down to cup her buttocks through the fabric of her slacks. He pulled her tight against his loins and let her feel his power, making Jamie tremble with excitement. Dizzy from the maelstrom of emotion raging through her body, conscious of the fact that she had well and truly lost her "distance," Jamie moved against him, gasping as he found and matched her rhythm.

Jamie broke the kiss, reluctantly, her legs unsteady as she took a short step backward. Capturing one hand in both of hers, she drew him toward the bedroom, letting action take the place of words.

Kim hesitated. "Jamie—"

Knowing everything he was about to say, she smothered his objections with a burning kiss, the contact of their bodies telling Kim that she had weighed the risks against her need and found the danger trifling by comparison.

In fact, a portion of her conscious mind was screaming at her, hell-bent on asserting its control before she violated every regulation in the book. *Too late*, she thought, and this time Kim did not resist her lead.

They clung together in the bedroom, standing, while he bathed her face and throat in kisses, nimble fingers busy with the buttons of her blouse. A tremor rippled through her body as he slid the garment off her shoulders, down her arms. He found the clasp of her brassiere, released it, and her breasts swung free, the nipples stiffening in sweet anticipation of his touch.

He cupped her breasts in gentle hands and bent to tease her nipples with his tongue. Impulsively, she locked her fingers in his hair and pulled him closer, suckling Kim as if he were a child. He worked his way from one breast to the other, back again, until her knees felt weak. So close that she could taste it now, she was afraid of falling if she lost her grip on Kim's dark hair.

A world away, his fingers were unbuckling her belt, unfastening the snap and zipper of her slacks. He knelt before her, peeling slacks and panties from her hips together, dropping them around her ankles. Hobbled, she became his willing prisoner.

The first intrusion of his darting tongue stole Jamie's breath away. She might have fallen, but he grasped the firm globes of her buttocks, fingers probing deep along the cleft, and held her upright. Jamie threw her head back, thrust her hips against his face, inviting him to taste her essence.

Startled by the sudden violence of her climax, Jamie wept with pleasure, fingers interlocked behind Kim's head to force his lips and tongue against her burning flesh. Afraid that he might suffocate, not caring in the moment's fierce intensity, she held him as a drowning man would clutch a life preserver.

Moments later, when he broke her hold and pressed her gently backward, toward the bed, she gratefully surrendered to the draw of gravity. Kim stood before her, framed by light that spilled in through the open doorway, stripping off his clothes. Her thighs, already spread in invitation, trembled with the aftershocks of her release.

Kim joined her on the bed, caressing her, and they were locked together, eager hands and mouths exploring, seeking points of maximum response. He seemed to read her body like a pleasure map, eliciting sensations she had long forgotten, sparking others that were new and unexpected.

Jamie found his shaft, caressed its length, was bent on guiding it inside her when he gently disengaged her hands. Bewildered, breathing heavily, she offered no resistance as he turned her over, lifted and positioned her, distributing her weight on knees and elbows. Kneeling at her back, Kim stroked her sex with educated fingers, finally satisfied that she was ready.

Entering, he gripped her shoulder with his left hand, slid the right across her stomach to the juncture of her thighs to find her clitoris. The juxtaposed sensations brought her off a second time before she had an opportunity to catch her breath.

She found the strength to match his rhythm, thrusting backward with her hips and taking every inch of him inside. Kim's free hand left her shoulder, slipped around to stroke her breasts. Incredibly, she felt another climax building in her loins, the cyclone gathering momentum. Jamie gasped and clenched the rumpled sheet between her teeth to keep from crying out.

This time, as she was trembling on the edge, Kim started pumping furiously, working toward his own release. The altered tempo was enough for Jamie, touching off another round of deep orgasmic tremors. Kim was right behind her this time, stiffening in freeze-frame as he filled her with his seed.

They lay together, afterward, and she could feel his heartbeat, slow and steady. Fascinated by his level of control, the magic in his hands, she was reminded of the rumors circulated in regard to martial artists and their prowess in the bedroom. Helpless to contain herself, she started giggling.

"What's funny?"

"Nothing, really." Jamie lied to save the moment. "I was thinking this is better than aerobics."

"Maybe you should make a video."

"I'd need a partner."

"Are you taking applications?"

Jamie wriggled back against him. "Sorry, the position's filled."

"It may be, if you keep that up."

"Big talk." She stirred reluctantly. "I need a shower."

"I could scrub your back, or something."

"Don't make promises unless you can deliver."

"I enjoy a challenge."

Sliding one strong arm around her waist, Kim pulled her close. Impossibly, she felt him stirring, rising in response.

"Oh, my." She found him with her hand, confirmed his readiness. "I'll race you for the soap."

"You're on," he answered.

"Hold that thought."

Kim left her sleeping, curled beneath the rumpled sheets with knees drawn up against her chest, as peaceful as a child. He dressed in Jamie's living room, to keep from waking her, and left a simple note beside the telephone, where she would find it in the morning. It was one o'clock before he reached the street, retrieved his rental car, and started back for his hotel.

The interlude with Jamie left disturbing questions in his

mind, but Kim was not prepared to deal with them tonight. He would assess their new relationship objectively, in daylight, after time and sleep had doused the fire inside. He was afraid that Jamie might feel compromised, but she had taken the initiative, and Kim suspected she was strong enough to live with her decision. If she woke to second thoughts, a sense of guilt, they could pretend the night had been a dream, removed from cold reality.

Objectively, he saw no reason why their brief encounter should affect his personal performance. Sex and duty were, in Kim's mind, mutually exclusive. Nothing that he felt for Jamie would prevent him eliminating Holland's killer, if and when the target was identified.

It troubled him to think that Jamie might have used her body as a tool, to keep him pliable, but Kim dismissed the notion. She was a professional, but that did not equate with prostitution, and he doubted whether she possessed the callousness required of women who perform on cue, without regard to their emotions.

Kim parked the car himself, avoiding the valet, and caught the elevator up to number seven. Jamie on his mind, he slipped his key inside the lock and almost grasped the knob without examining the layer of talcum underneath.

Almost.

The powder had been wiped away.

He paused outside the door, considering the implications. He had left an early call for service, and the maid had done her work before he went downstairs to Jamie. No one else had any business in his room, but someone had come calling in his absence, stood where he was now, their fingers wrapped around the doorknob.

Kim dismissed the various implausible solutions. An unnecessary second visit by a different maid. A gift of fruit, delivered by the management. A clumsy guest mistaking Kim's room for his own and trying out the key. All possible, but he could *feel* the presence of an enemy.

Kim knew the prowler might be waiting for him, just inside, but he was not prepared to call the desk—or worse, the Seoul police—and ask for help. Forewarned, he had an edge, and that made all the difference in the world.

He fumbled with his keys, deliberately making noise and

giving any adversaries time to find their places. If a trap was waiting for him, he improved his own survival odds by following the script.

A twist and shove, with all his strength. The door swung open, slammed against the wall with force enough to cold-cock any lurking foe. Kim cleared the threshold in a diving shoulder roll and came up in a fighting stance.

The empty room regarded his performance with disdain.

He toured the bedroom, balcony and bath, reminded of a scene from *Psycho* as he checked the shower. No one in the closet. Nothing underneath the bed.

When he was satisfied, Kim closed and double-locked the door. He fetched the sweeper from its shelf, examined it for signs of tampering, and scoured the suite for listening devices.

Nothing.

Acting on his instincts, in defensive mode, he nearly missed the note beside the telephone. There was no message, only numbers, printed with a felt-tipped pen.

He lifted the receiver, dialed, and waited.

"Yes."

The voice was ageless, perfectly asexual.

"My name is Kim Su Chung." His cover might be blown, but he would not assume the worst.

"One moment."

Silence on the line, protracted by his own impatience.

"You received my message."

It was not a question. This time, he immediately pegged the voice as male.

"It was concise."

"You wish to meet Chin Sung?"

"I do."

"Your business?"

"Life and death. I will explain the details when we meet."

"Why should he trust you?"

"He should not. Let him decide the time and place."

The word came back without a heartbeat's hesitation. "Noon tomorrow, at the Independence Arch. A student rally has been organized. You are invited to attend. Alone."

"Will I be recognized?"

"We know your face, Kim Chung."

The information came as no surprise.

"Until tomorrow, then."

The line went dead before Kim finished speaking, and he cradled the receiver, frowning.

Much could happen in a crowd, but he had been in no position to reject the terms. If Chin Sung showed himself, Kim would be forced to mold his strategy around the moment, calling on his instinct and experience.

With any luck at all, they just might see him through the afternoon alive.

Chapter 13

Jamie called as Kim was sitting down to breakfast.

"Hey," she said, "what happened?"

"Well, as I recall—"

"Not *that*." He felt her hesitation, as she sought the perfect words. "I thought you might still be here."

"Jamie—"

"No," she cut him off, "don't say it. Dumb idea. I'm sorry."

"Don't be."

"Are you eating lunch today?"

Her voice was light, too casual, and Kim knew he had hurt her feelings.

"Doubtful. I've got people I should see, to move this thing along."

He had considered telling her about the phone call, his prospective meeting with their target, but decided it was not a good idea. Her first responsibility was to the Company, and Jamie might insist on sending "help" in spite of anything he said. A fumble would destroy his chance of meeting Chin Kyu Sung and could result in loss of lives, his own included.

"I'll be looking forward to your next report," she said.

"I should have something by this afternoon."

"Be careful, will you?"

"Always."

Breaking the connection, Kim felt no regrets about his lie to Jamie. He was reasonably sure that she wouldn't deliberately betray him; still, an overzealous bid to wrap the mission up would have the same effect. He wanted time to speak with Chin, confirm the target for himself, before he made the kill.

With time to spare, he drove out Euiji-ro, past the Italian Embassy, and circled Independence Arch. The crowds had not begun to gather yet, but Kim picked out a scattering of undercover types from NSP, already staking out their vantage points for observation of the rally. They were simple watchdogs, not assassins, but he noted their positions all the same.

Kim worked the side streets, found a parking space three blocks away and left his rental there. If anything went wrong, the car was readily accessible, and it would not be trapped by crowds of demonstrators from the rally. In the worst scenario, a total foul-up, he could slip away on foot and find a place to hide, returning later for the car.

He moved along the sidewalk aimlessly, examining the wares displayed in windows, killing time. Seoul looked like any other city in the world, and Kim was vaguely disappointed that he felt no sense of personal belonging. He imagined that there should be something, a sensation of discovering his roots, but nothing moved him.

Thoughts of Jamie Constable intruded on his consciousness, and Kim dismissed them out of hand. This afternoon was business, and he had no time for sentiment. Distractions— sweet or otherwise—could get him killed.

Around eleven, crowds of students and their varied hangers-on began arriving for the rally. Kim saw buses, cars, and motorcycles bound for Independence Arch, unloading bright-eyed boys and girls along with scruffy rabble-rousers, priests and nuns, a Buddhist monk or two, obligatory teams of Western journalists. The veteran demonstrators wore bandannas tied around their necks, to screen the tear gas if police elected to disrupt the rally. Motorcycle helmets—useful in protecting skulls from nightsticks—were in vogue among the seasoned dissidents.

The rally, publicized for days, had drawn its share of gawkers on the sidelines. Mostly Europeans and Americans on holiday, they were distinguished from the press by gaudy shirts and cheaper cameras. They reminded Kim of children in a schoolyard, hoping for a fight to liven up their afternoon.

Police were also on the scene by now, dressed up for war.

Their body armor, shields, and helmets lent a curious medieval tone to the affair, invoking images of knights arrayed against a peasant army. Kim knew other officers, in street clothes, would be circling the crowd and seeking vantage points for the erection of their movie cameras, anxious to collect as many photographs as possible for their "subversive" files.

He passed a small cafe, considered lunch, and instantly rejected the idea. If there was trouble in the next three-quarters of an hour, he would function better on an empty stomach. Settling for tea, he drank it slowly, checked his watch when he was done, and drifted back toward Independence Arch.

A two-block stretch of Euiji-ro was closed to vehicles by now, with officers directing traffic east and west through side streets. Speakers for the rally were assembling on their makeshift stage, a flat-bed truck, and checking out their P.A. system. Shops surrounding Independence Arch were closing down for the duration, writing off potential loss of revenue against the greater risk of theft.

Kim mingled with the demonstrators, moving aimlessly across the plaza, south to north. He had been told that Chin Sung knew his face, and he was not about to make things easy for the NSP by acting as a stationary target. Let them capture him on film, for all the good that it would do. A dozen years had passed since Kim set foot in Seoul, and photo analysts would be hard pressed to recognize him now.

The speeches were beginning, with an introduction from a strident beanpole of a man, all head and Adam's apple, warming up the audience with verbal brickbats aimed at the police. A murmur of approval rippled through the crowd, a scattering of weak applause, increasing as the speaker broadened his attack to cover Tokyo and the United States. The present South Korean government was pictured as a puppet state, subservient to Japanese and Yankee businessmen, oppressive toward the native working class. The answer lay in protest, barricades, and brickbats, ultimately forcing recognition of a "new agenda" written by The People, with some help from "liberated" neighbors.

Kim was too familiar with the rhetoric to be impressed. He turned the speaker off, paid no attention to a dumpy woman who replaced him at the microphone, expounding variations on the central theme. He understood the politics of revolution, recognized the various techniques through which manipulative leaders won themselves a following. There *was* corruption in the present government, and agents of the NSP *were* guilty of brutality against some prisoners. Despite all that, his mind was not prepared to make the quantum leap to blind acceptance of the North Korean system as a viable alternative.

It made him smile to think of demonstrators gathering in Pyongyang's streets. Machine guns would have sprayed their ranks, instead of water cannons, and the press would come down solidly behind the state. Kim thought it might be educational to air-lift several hundred demonstrators into North Korea, stripped of their identity as favored "Southern comrades," and examine how much progress they achieved toward liberation.

Seconds later, he was conscious of a man behind him, on his right. Surrounded by the crowd, hemmed in on every side, Kim felt the new arrival's subtle difference. This one was intent on watching *him*, instead of following the speakers.

Turning smoothly, in anticipation of a touch, he took the new arrival by surprise. The hair was longer, Ray-Bans and a thin mustache completed the disguise, but Chin Kyu Sung still bore a strong resemblance to his photographs on file at Langley.

"Twelve-fifteen," Kim told the man he was assigned to kill. "You're late."

Chin smiled and said, "I had to satisfy myself that you were not accompanied by an escort from the CIA."

Chin Sung's reluctance to arrange a meeting had been overcome, at last, by simple curiosity. The first reports, from his informers on the street, said simply that a stranger, Kim Su Chung, was looking for a rendezvous. The name meant nothing and was probably an alias, but Chin had been intrigued, despite the risk. He had established casual surveillance at the Metro, and the stranger had obliged by meeting with a woman from the U.S. Embassy. A careless amateur had lost them half a mile from the hotel, but Chin identified the woman as a "cultural attache" at the embassy, which virtually guaranteed that she was working for the CIA.

Reese Holland came to mind immediately.

The Americans were doubtless looking for his killer, hampered by the breakdown of communications during Holland's final days in Seoul. Chin knew he was a suspect—probably the *only* suspect—and the Agency might have him marked for termination, even now. There was a fearful risk in breaking cover, making contact with the enemy, but there was also much to gain.

Chin Sung was not afraid of risks. In seven years, since his enforced departure from the university, he had become adept at spinning out his life on borrowed time. The NSP might take him yet, but he would not go quietly or make it easy for his executioners. Before they traced his movements and arranged a lethal "accident," he meant to strike a telling blow against their rotten house of cards.

There was an outside chance the stranger could assist him, if they managed not to kill each other first.

Chin had regarded Holland as an enemy, in the beginning. Hard-core CIA, committed to a counter-revolutionary doctrine that was decades out of style, the gruff American had been a most unlikely ally. Still...

A penetration of the stranger's room had turned no weapons, but their absence simply meant that he was cautious, a professional. Chin waited for the phone call to decide, and there was something in the other's voice that finally persuaded him to fix a meeting, under more-or-less controlled conditions. He would speak with Kim Su Chung, evaluate the opposition, and proceed from there.

The scheduled rally was a natural. Chin moved among the students in disguise, unrecognized, and felt the same attraction that had drawn him years before. There was an elemental power in the movement that excited him, despite the suffering and disillusionment he had endured, the violence that had gone before. With its polemics and obligatory buzzwords stripped away, the message still rang true for Chin Kyu Sung.

A child of affluence, he had been called to revolution by degrees. At first, he viewed the student demonstrations as a casual observer, marking time between his classes, joking with his friends and keeping score as boys and girls his age were gassed and beaten to the ground. He felt no more involvement with their struggle than an entomologist would feel while studying a colony of termites.

Li Nampo made all the difference. Soft as velvet on the outside, tempered steel within, her beauty lured him at first. Chin wasted days before he found the courage to approach her, certain she would laugh at him and send him on his way. Amazed when Li accepted him without a second thought, he played a perfect fool until she urged him to relax and be himself. Within a week, she took him to her bed, and Chin knew he had found the focus of his life.

Li seldom mentioned politics at first, preferring not to waste their stolen time, but Chin was bent on knowing everything about her. It had startled him to learn that she was active in the student protest movement, twice arrested in her freshman year for throwing rocks and bottles at police. She spoke with such conviction of her righteous cause that Chin was moved, despite deep-seated doubts.

Li never asked him to participate in demonstrations; Chin, for his part, gave up watching from the sidelines. He was auditing a tiresome seminar on business management the afternoon Li's skull was fractured by a tear gas canister outside the National Assembly. She was dead before the ambulance arrived, and breathless classmates brought the news to Chin as he was idling in the campus cafeteria.

Li's other friends, among the radicals, were quick to seize upon Chin's grief and use it to promote their cause. Transcending ideology in his obsession for revenge, he wasted no time pondering their motives. As a public speaker, Chin was startled to discover he possessed charisma, the ability to sway a crowd of strangers, bring them to their feet. He played on raw emotion in the early days, disguising ignorance with venom, the enormity of loss. By night, he studied tracts and pamphlets, poring over dusty speeches, hearing Li's voice all the while. He learned to think as well as feel, and thus became more dangerous to the establishment.

From speeches, he had moved to demonstrations, challenging the state to steal his life as it had stolen Li's. Renowned for his ferocity in combat with police, he was arrested seven times in one semester, beaten twice in custody. Inevitably, burdened with a private war, Chin Sung had little time for study. In the second quarter of his senior year, he was expelled.

Intended as a stinging reprimand, Chin's severance from the university had come as a relief. Fed up with lectures, stale debates of meaningless hypotheses, he concentrated all of his attention on the struggle, losing sight of personal vendettas over time. As Li Nampo had been his life, too briefly, so the movement took her place. He recognized its faults and weaknesses, made changes where he could, and kept his eyes fixed firmly on the common goal.

In recent years, the struggle had attracted individuals who worried Chin. The anarchists and nihilists were manageable through appeals to vanity, if nothing else. A more disturbing element was lured by the smell of blood, the prospect of a violent confrontation. Action was its own reward, and never mind the cause.

Chin weeded out the psychopaths whenever possible, but it was difficult, these days, to make a case against selective use of terrorism. Prisons filled with dissidents bore testimony to the failure of the old approach. The new breed answered calls for moderation with reminders that a single well-placed bomb accomplished more than weeks of demonstrations, thousands of arrests. Chin had begun to feel the movement slip beyond his grasp, and he would need a major coup to save it now.

If fate was smiling on him, the Americans might save him yet. It would be perfect irony. Poetic justice.

Kim Su Chung was spotted quickly in the crowd, identified from snapshots taken at the Metro. Chin spent several moments trailing him across the plaza, making sure the CIA had not supplied him with a shadow, finally approaching as the second speaker launched her diatribe against Japan and the United States.

As he approached, the stranger turned to face him, warned by some sixth sense of Chin Sung's presence. "Twelve-fifteen," he said. "You're late."

Chin smiled. "I had to satisfy myself that you were not accompanied by an escort from the CIA."

If Kim Su Chung was startled by the penetration of his

cover, he concealed it well. "You know my mission, then?" he asked.

"Of course. You wish to know if I'm responsible for the elimination of your agent."

"We were friends," Kim answered.

"Ah, a personal involvement."

Moving through the crowd, Kim felt as if he had a bull's-eye painted on his back. Chin had him pegged; his cover was a shambles. On the plus side, he was still alive, which meant the target felt like talking. There was still a chance, however slim, that Chin Sung might not realize he had been marked for termination.

On the other hand, Kim thought, he might be used to it by now.

"Will you believe me if I say I did not kill your friend?"

"I have no preconceptions."

"And your sponsors?"

"They inform me he was sent to look for you in Seoul."

"He found me. We had several meetings, spoke of many things. In time, we found it beneficial to cooperate."

"On what?"

"An issue of concern to both our nations."

"I require specifics."

Chin was silent for a moment, staring toward the dais, frowning as another speaker took the microphone.

"You are familiar with the yakuza?"

Kim nodded. A generic term for gangsters in Japan—like "Mafia" or "Syndicate" in the United States—the label covered eight distinctive "families" and countless small, affiliated gangs. With better than 100,000 members overall, the yakuza outnumbered Yankee mobsters five to one.

"The Western press regards the yakuza as an amusing curiosity. The members wear tattoos and practice *yubitsume*—amputation of the little finger—as a gesture of humility. They are 'a local problem' for the Japanese police."

Kim waited, letting Chin Sung set the pace.

"In fact, our own society and all of Southeast Asia is corrupted by syndicates. They buy our women, our police, and politicians. Many in the new republic have been quick to sell their souls."

"Corruption is a fact of life."

"Perhaps, but silence only nurtures the disease. Since 1965, when South Korea normalized relations with Japan, our cities have been overrun each year by 700,000 Japanese."

"You hate the tourist industry?"

"I hate the fact that ninety-four percent of them are businessmen who leave their families behind and visit us in search of whores. We have a quarter-million prostitutes, according to the last official tally. Peasant girls are bought and sold like livestock in the countryside. Not long ago, the Japanese ambassador's official residence in Seoul was flanked on either side by *kisaeng* houses, each one capable of servicing eight hundred men at once. They operated under full protection from the NSP."

"We were discussing Holland's death."

"And so we are. Before he came to Seoul, I was collecting evidence of state corruption, focused on the trade in drugs and women."

"Drugs?" A loud alarm was going off inside Kim's mind. "You mean narcotics?"

"Methamphetamine, specifically. In the United States, I think you call it speed. In Tokyo, it is *shabu*—'white diamonds.' The yakuza depend upon *shabu* for half their income every year, and seventy percent of their supply is manufactured here, in South Korea."

"What has this to do with Holland?"

"As you may already know, the yakuza are rapidly expanding. In the past five years, they have established outposts in Brazil, Colombia, and Paraguay. They launder money in Australia, purchase drugs in Germany, sell weapons to the terrorists in Italy and France. Hawaii is infested, and the syndicates have footholds in New York, Los Angeles, Las Vegas, San Francisco."

"Holland," Kim repeated, sharpening his tone until it showed a razor's edge.

"He was concerned about the yakuza proliferation in America. The night before his death, he spoke of information linking the intelligence community to sale of arms and drugs."

"The NSP?"

"Of course, but he was more concerned about American

intelligence. Why else would he have broken off communications with his contact?"

"Names?"

Chin frowned and shook his head. "There was a source, but Holland kept it to himself."

"And you suggest that he was silenced by the CIA?"

"I'm not prepared to point a finger at his killers. Yakuza or NSP or CIA—they all had means and motive."

"So you say."

"But you are not prepared to trust me. I admire a prudent man," Chin said. "Consider this: the single largest manufacturer of methamphetamine in South Korea is a man named Su Min Wha. Coincidentally, he is the richest pimp in Seoul. His contributions to the ruling party may be found in public records. Other contributions, which protect him from arrest and prosecution, have been traced with greater effort. He has good friends in the NSP, the national assembly... some say higher yet."

"Was Holland on his case?"

"All roads lead back to Su Min Wha. He is a spider, crouching in the center of a web that spans the hemisphere. Unwary insects brush against the strands and die."

"There is another possibility," Kim said.

"Of course."

He knew the risks and forged ahead, regardless.

"Holland was assigned to chart your operation. He discovered your connection with the North Koreans, through their agent Dae Li Chong, and you were forced to silence him before exposure of your treason cost the movement several thousand members. Not to mention life imprisonment for you, upon conviction."

"Life?" Chin smiled. "I'm dead already. Never mind the courts. The NSP has reason to be frightened of the testimony I would offer on my own behalf. The leadership has promised I will never come to trial. As for the North Koreans, they were useful at a time when more enlightened nations branded me a communist and turned their backs. A self-fulfilling prophecy, perhaps. In any case, those ties were severed long ago. I have not seen or spoken to Dae Chong in fourteen months."

He studied Chin Kyu Sung in silence for a moment,

conscious of the fact that everything depended on his own acceptance or rejection of the target's story. Lies would mean that Chin had orchestrated—or at least participated in—Reese Holland's murder. If he spoke the truth . . .

Behind Chin Sung, Kim spied a pair of carbon-copy thugs approaching through the crowd. They both wore jackets in defiance of the noonday heat, dark glasses rendering their eyes invisible. He did not know if they belonged to Chin or someone else, but they were trouble on the hoof and they had found their target now.

Chin marked the shift in his attention, glanced across his shoulder, turning back to Kim with hatred in his eyes.

"You bastard!"

"Guess again. They're not with me."

The fugitive ignored him, searching for a rapid exit from the plaza. Kim was faster, having planned it out beforehand.

"This way, quickly!"

"Go to hell!"

"Your choice."

He turned away, saw one of the pursuers draw an automatic pistol fitted with a silencer, the second man a trifle slower as he reached inside his jacket. Deprived of options, Chin Sung spat a bitter curse and followed.

Thirty feet away, the gunner raised his weapon, aimed, and fired.

Chapter 14

The first shot passed between them and exploded in the face of an anemic-looking college student, knocking him off-balance. Blood was splattered over those around him, but it took a moment for their minds to grasp what they were seeing. Kim and Chin were past them by the time a pair of girls began to scream.

A second round hummed past Kim's ear, an angry hornet seeking prey. He could not hear the muffled shot, but its effect was obvious. In front of him, a slender co-ed turned to check out the commotion, stopped the bullet with her breast and sat down hard, her face reflecting pure bewilderment.

Kim vaulted over her, with Chin a step behind. If they were separated, it would be too bad, but Kim did not intend to sacrifice himself on Chin's behalf.

Reaction to the shooting had begun to spread like ripples in a pond. Both gunners held their weapons in the open now, and demonstrators in their path were scrambling desperately to save themselves. It was a vain attempt, surrounded as they were, and shoving matches escalated rapidly toward brawling pandemonium. A solitary student tackled one of the assassins, trying to disarm him, but the other doubled back and shot his partner's adversary in the ear.

Around the fringes of the crowd, police in riot gear were sluggishly responding, taking stock before they waded in with nightsticks flailing. One more student riot to suppress, another tantrum by the pampered children of the upper crust. If nothing else, it gave the officers a chance to teach these whining brats a lesson.

Kim took full advantage of the spreading chaos, weaving

through the crush like smoke in human form. He risked a backward glance from time to time, found Chin within arm's reach, the gunners falling farther back. If they were lucky and avoided the police . . .

He felt the presence of an enemy before the man took shape in front of him, emerging from the crowd to block his path. Like those behind, the shooter wore a plain dark suit and shades, a uniform adopted by the NSP along with countless other plain-clothes officers and low-rent thugs. This one was strictly backup, and the automatic pistol in his hand had not been fitted out with a suppressor.

Kim responded to the threat at once, his instinct over-riding conscious thought. Without a break in stride, he ducked inside the shooter's firing radius and slapped his gun arm to the side. The piece discharged, producing an immediate cacophony of screams as Kim drove stiffened fingers underneath his adversary's rib cage. Twisting, feeling muscles separate and tear, he followed with a sharp blow to the larynx, cutting off the gunner's wind.

Kim left him gasping on the pavement, demonstrators stumbling over him like lemmings in their flight, and reassured himself that Chin was still in touch before he forged ahead. Police were battling to close the box on three sides now, but they had not sealed off the Independence Arch itself. Kim joined the rush in that direction, trusting Chin to follow as the human river carried them along.

The first report of gunfire galvanized police around the plaza, putting them in fear of snipers. Tear gas canisters were fired at random, bursting overhead in choking clouds that settled, wraithlike, on the milling crowd of demonstrators. On the dais, a professor seized the microphone, demanding calm before a pair of riot cops descended on him, swinging truncheons.

They were nearly through the arch before a flying squad of helmeted police arrived to cut off the retreat. The front ranks wavered underneath a rain of blows, some demonstrators falling, others falling back. If they were pinned here, with the gunners closing from behind, they were as good as dead.

A fresh barrage of tear gas saved them, bursting just inside the arch and driving hundreds back in the direction of the street. The dozen officers on guard were overrun and swept aside, their nightsticks wrested free and broken over helmets as the demonstrators turned from flight to sweet revenge.

Kim made the sidewalk, doubled back for Chin and dragged him through to daylight. The fugitive had lost his shades and he was bleeding from a gash above one eye, but he was also smiling, flushed with the excitement of the chase.

"These bastards think that they have an easy target," he declared. "I don't lie down and die for any man."

"You will, unless we get away from here. Come on!"

Chin caught his arm. "I still don't trust you."

Kim glanced down at the restraining hand, then back at Chin.

"Trust this," he said. "A clumsy firing squad is not my style."

Behind them, reinforcements were arriving at the arch, too late. The street was filled with shouting, milling demonstrators, some intent on venting rage against the most convenient targets. Stones and bottles smashed the windows of a nearby shop, immediately followed by a second and a third. Young vandals toppled mannequins, hurled merchandise across the sidewalk, while proprietors fought hopelessly to save their stock.

"Time's up." Kim twisted free of Chin Sung's grasp and turned away. He felt the other's hesitation and refused to waste another backward glance. An instant later, Chin was at his side.

"My life is in your hands," he muttered.

"I'll remember that."

They left the sidewalk, giving the shops a wide berth as police rushed past them, abandoning positions on the barricades to catch the looters by surprise. Another crash of glass, the shrilling sound of whistles, and they put the combat zone behind them, picking up their pace.

Kim led his reticent companion up a narrow side street, moving south from Euiji-ro. Pedestrians and merchants were collected on the sidewalks here, exchanging dire predictions as the sounds of combat moved inexorably closer. Kim had estimated there were twelve thousand to fifteen thousand people gathered at the arch, corralled by four hundred officers. Without dramatic reinforcements in the next few moments, the police would have to be content with mopping up once the explosion ran its course.

They reached the Hyundai and Kim slid behind the wheel, unlocking Chin's door from the inside. He had his key in the ignition when a man emerged from the confectionary, two doors down. Immaculate in suit and tie, the shopper held a paper bag in one hand, labeled with the name of the establishment.

A sweet tooth. Why else would he have his right hand tucked inside the bag, unless—

"Look out!"

Kim gunned the rental's motor, swung out from the curb without examining his rearview mirror. Down range, Sweet Tooth mouthed a silent curse and broke in the direction of the street, the sack discarded to reveal a pistol in his hand. He dodged between parked cars, emerging in a classic shooter's stance, his weapon steady in a double-handed grip.

Kim aimed the Hyundai like a projectile, hunching lower in his seat. Beside him, Chin identified the enemy too late, reached out to brace one hand against the dashboard as the gunner opened fire.

His first round drilled the windshield cleanly, while the second punched a hole six inches in diameter. There was no third, as Kim accelerated into crushing impact, scooping up his target on the hood. The gunner lost his weapon, cracked his skull against the glass, and left a crimson smear behind him as he slithered off the starboard fender.

Somehow, they had followed Kim in spite of his precautions. Either that, or they had known his destination in advance. Regardless, if a gunman had been left to watch the car, he might have backup on the street.

The rearview mirror instantly confirmed his fear. Pedestrians were gathering around the fallen gunman as a dark sedan swept past them, kissing close, the driver leaning on his horn. Kim drifted toward the center line, ensuring that the chase car would not draw abreast until they reached a wider street.

"We've got a tail!" he snapped at Chin, and then glanced over when his passenger did not respond.

Chin slumped against the door, his shirt already drenched

in blood. A shoulder wound, perhaps a lung; Kim had no time to make a clinical evaluation. He could not be certain whether both the gunner's rounds had found their mark.

My life is in your hands.

So much for the illusion of security.

Before he thought of helping Chin, Kim had to shake the hunters who were closing on them, even now. The dark sedan hung close behind him, taking full advantage of its larger engine to reduce Kim's lead. He caught a vague, reflected hint of movement in the front seat, thought he saw the shotgun rider holding up a microphone.

Terrific. If the hounds were radio equipped, with other cars at their disposal, he was flirting with a no-win situation. Kim would have to lose them soon, before the backup teams arrived to box him in. Surrounded, they would simply have no chance at all.

The chase car had an edge on speed, but Kim possessed a slim advantage in maneuverability. They were approaching Sinmum-ro, the traffic signals flashing out a warning. Several cars were slowing down in front of Kim, the chase car gaining rapidly. The shotgun rider had his window down, his gun arm braced against the sideview mirror as he aimed.

Kim saw his opening and took it, swerving to the left, accelerating in the empty lane reserved for oncoming traffic. The driver of a Honda Civic, turning in from Sinmum-ro, was suddenly confronted by a madman, but he saved himself by taking to the sidewalk, scattering pedestrians and shearing off a hydrant at its base.

Behind Kim, his pursuers loosed a burst of automatic fire that shattered half the windows in a compact Subaru. Kim veered around four waiting cars and blasted through the intersection, narrowly avoiding impact with a charter bus. His rearview mirror showed him several other drivers, turning off of Sinmum-ro, all slowing in confusion now and blocking off pursuit.

Before he could congratulate himself, a second dark sedan appeared beside them, suddenly emerging from an alleyway. The driver cut his wheel hard right, and this time it was Kim's turn on the sidewalk, toppling a mailbox, whipping up a paper blizzard as he passed a corner newsstand.

They were closing on another intersection, thick with

traffic, when the chase car opened fire. A bullet cracked the window just behind him, others punching craters on the driver's side. Kim locked his brakes and gave the steering wheel a mighty left-hand twist, whipping the rental through a sharp 180-degree turn.

They finished the skid with two wheels on the sidewalk and two on the street, the Hyundai's nose pointing back toward Sinmum-ro. The chase car's driver, slower to react, rolled on for half a block before he hit the brakes and threw it in reverse. By that time, Kim was headed west and gaining speed.

Directly toward a makeshift roadblock, formed by two more black sedans.

He coasted to a halt and let the engine idle, counting half a dozen weapons aimed directly at his face. Behind him, swinging wide across both lanes, his recent adversary closed the box. More guns emerging, taking up positions for a cross fire.

Deprived of viable alternatives, he killed the engine, waiting for the signal that would loose a storm of high-velocity projectiles. He was surprised when one of the pursuers laid his pistol down and cupped both hands around his mouth.

"Step clear," the gunner barked, "and raise your hands."

Chin wasn't going anywhere, but Kim obeyed. Experience had taught him that survival was the first priority in combat. Blind defiance of a firing squad would gain him nothing but a quick trip to the cemetery.

Standing ten feet from the car, hands raised above his head, he waited for instructions. Nervous gunners trained their weapons on the Hyundai, covering Chin Sung.

"Step clear, or we will open fire."

"He's wounded," Kim informed the leader. "Probably unconscious."

At a signal from their chief, two gunmen cautiously approached the car. One kept his distance, ready with an Uzi submachine gun as his partner took a closer look. Confirming Chin's condition, he stepped back and flashed a high sign to the man in charge.

The others closed at once, two roughly dragging Chin out of his seat as Kim was covered, frisked for weapons. He considered putting up a fight and instantly dismissed the thought as suicidal.

Firm hands on his shoulders held him still as one of the commandos pulled Kim's hands behind him, snapping handcuffs into place, the ratchets tightened painfully. He saw Chin carried to a waiting car and dumped inside, his captors piling in behind the wounded man. Kim was directed to a second vehicle, positioned in the back seat with a guard on either side. The leader sat up front but turned to face him, scowling as he thrust an automatic pistol in Kim's face.

"If you resist in any way," he said, "I will be pleased to kill you instantly."

Jamie spent a restless morning at the embassy, attempting to regain some semblance of routine. She started off by scanning new communiques from street informants, typed by Ray Fitzpatrick, but she lost her place repeatedly and found that nothing seemed to make much sense. Her mind was in a turmoil, and at last she pushed the file aside.

Fitzpatrick had been cool to her that morning, even distant, though his attitude made no significant impression at the time. Now Jamie checked her watch and found that it was half-past twelve. Her stomach growled in confirmation of the fact that she was missing lunch. Ray had not made his usual, obligatory stop to ask her out, and Jamie wondered what was wrong. Was there a chance that he had finally given up?

Too much to hope for, she decided. And she had more urgent problems on her mind, in any case.

Like guilt, for openers.

Remembering her interlude with Kim, she felt a rush of contradictory emotions. Lust was represented, loud and clear, evoking warm sensations even now and making Jamie's heart beat faster. Thinking of his hands, so swift and sure, she pressed her thighs together, trembling.

Love was not at issue. Neither of them sought commitment, a relationship beyond the here and now. It would be madness, a deliberate sacrifice of her career—and all for what? Kim offered nothing, made no promises. Outside the present job, their lives were mutually exclusive.

Guilt, above all else, kept Jamie's nerves on edge. Advised by Ross to keep her distance, she had violated regulations with a vengeance, jeopardizing her career, the mission, and—perhaps—Kim's life. Impulsively, without regard to consequence, she had indulged her flesh at the expense of duty and responsibility. For passion's sake, she had ignored her training, nine years of experience. But why?

Kim was prepared to leave—indeed, he had been at the door—when Jamie made her move, discarding caution and propriety. It was not rape, of course, nor truly a seduction. Kim's response was energetic, his enthusiasm obvious, but Jamie had initiated the encounter, stepping out of character to put her hunger on display.

Worse yet, she had been disappointed, even angry, when she found his note that morning, realizing he was gone. It was strategically correct, she realized, for Kim to spend the night at his hotel. He had a cover to protect, already jeopardized by public contact with his handler, their excursion to the monastery. Still, as the alarm woke Jamie she had reached for him, disturbed to find herself alone.

The call to Kim's hotel had been another serious mistake. She had been weak and peevish, sounding like The Woman Scorned. It was humiliating, and she knew it would be difficult to deal with Kim in future, dogged by memories of her ridiculous performance.

How could she command respect from Kim, much less obedience, when she had taken him inside her body, trading every vestige of control for the intoxication of his touch?

She told herself that it was possible to save the mission, yet. If she had flaunted regulations, Kim was no less culpable. Regardless of her momentary lapse, she still spoke on behalf of Langley and the Company. If necessary, she could recommend they pull the plug and ship Kim back to San Francisco.

All it would require from Jamie was an absolute admission of defeat.

Uncompromising in her self-evaluation, Jamie knew the mission had been slipping from her grasp before she went to bed with Kim Sunim. The loss of Domino had been an omen. Choosing Kim Sunim to balance out the books was Langley's brainstorm, but the buck would stop with Jamie if he failed. No matter that his personal involvement and aggressive independence should have been sufficient grounds for using someone else to make the tag. His failure, if it came to that, would settle squarely on the shoulders of his handler.

And failure, in this instance, would equate with death.

She felt a sudden rush of panic at the thought of filling out a KIA report on Kim. Reese Holland's death had been the first time she was forced to cope with details of an agent killed in action, and she sidestepped issues of responsibility with reference to his unilateral disruption of communications. This time, if their private interlude made Kim decide to freeze her out, she would be forced to answer for her own mistakes.

And yet, she recognized that fear of possible disgrace was secondary to her fear of losing Kim. It made no sense, defied all logic, but the thought of going in to view his body at the morgue left Jamie weak with terror. If she lost him now, before—

She dropped the train of thought and concentrated on her job. Chin Sung had murdered Holland. He was still at large, and Kim Sunim had taken on the contract, under Jamie's supervision. Anything outside the operation was superfluous, a dangerous distraction.

Jamie had allowed herself to be distracted once, but she was now determined to assert herself, regain control at any cost. If only she could make herself forget his touch, the way it felt when he—

"*Goddamn* it!"

Scowling, she retrieved the file of raw intelligence reports and started over on page one. Fitzpatrick's prose was crisp and clinical, the Langley style, devoid of color and interpretation. Everything he gleaned from street informants was recorded, summarized in black and white. Evaluation would be Jamie's task, with help from Ross if something clearly fell outside her field of expertise.

The bulk of Ray's material concerned the rising tide of student demonstrations, marked by violence toward police and other symbols of authority. Chin Sung was mentioned here and there, a shadow lacking any substance. It was rumored that he authorized a bombing in Pusan. Another source suggested his connection with the strike at Dongguk University. Chin's personal involvement in the Taejon rioting was vouched for by "a source of known reliability in ROK intelligence"—that is to say, the NSP.

She memorized the salient details, realizing as she did that the various reports proved nothing. None of them contained a reference to Domino, his mission, or his death. The very silence was peculiar, in itself. It might suggest that Chin employed extraordinary care in setting up the kill. Conversely, silence on the streets could be interpreted to mean that he was not involved.

She filed the latter notion, unprepared to rock the boat by searching for another suspect. Domino had been assigned to find Chin Sung; his execution indicated he had done his job. A hunted man, Chin had the most to gain—and nothing more to lose—by covering his tracks with blood.

She checked the time again, decided she should eat before a headache added to her problems. Over lunch, she would decide how best to deal with Kim, defuse the situation that her own pathetic weakness had created. She was not prepared to play the tyrant; neither would she crawl. Somewhere between the two extremes, there had to be a middle ground where they could function as a team.

The only problem was that Jamie wanted him again. Inside her, filling her. She wanted to experience his strength, surrender to his intimate caress, explore his body and submit to exploration in return. Her hunger was a living thing, distinct and separate from reason.

Sudden anger focused on herself, her negligence and irresponsibility. If anything went wrong now, anything at all, the fault would be her own.

She stood behind her desk, sat down again, forgot about the cafeteria. Her appetite was gone, and Jamie felt the headache coming now, like distant thunder in her skull.

She glowered at the telephone.

"Just call me, damn it."

And she passed the afternoon in silence.

Waiting.

Chapter 15

The NSP's command post at Remonclo, situated half a mile outside of Seoul, was built with maximum security in mind. Externally, the complex passes for a block of office buildings, slightly out of date, their architecture drab and uninspired. Within, there are administrative offices and class-rooms, a communications center and a weapons lab, deten-tion cells, a block of small, soundproof interrogation rooms.

No prisoner has ever managed to escape, though some have disappeared from custody, a circumstance their captors are unable to explain. If pressed, which happens rarely, they may shrug and smile, suggesting that perhaps detainees were released without completion of the proper forms. Of course, it is beyond the scope of NSP's authority to guarantee that former prisoners go home or contact waiting relatives upon release.

Kim wore a blindfold on the fifteen-minute drive but knew where he was going. Prisoners from Seoul invariably found their way to the Remonclo lockup, whence interroga-tion could proceed without unnecessary interruptions from defense attorneys, magistrates, or civil libertarians. If the inquisitors went overboard in their enthusiasm to protect the state from communists and radicals, disposal was a relatively simple matter.

Kim had been inside the complex once before, a guest that time, on business for the Company. Conducted on a tour of the detention wing, he still recalled the smell of disinfec-tant lavishly applied, as if the tenants sought to purge their guilt with Lysol.

From the car, he was conveyed through automatic sliding

doors, held fast by guards on either side. His escort moved
along a corridor that echoed with their footsteps, pausing
twice at checkpoints, covering perhaps a hundred yards
before they reached their destination. In his memory, Kim
saw a double line of metal doors, all painted beige to match
the walls. One of them opened, closed behind him with a
sound of grim finality.

Acoustics placed him in a smallish room, no more than
ten by twelve. His keepers led him to a straight-backed chair
and sat him down. Kim offered no resistance as his ankles
were secured; a gentle shifting informed him that the chair
was bolted to the floor.

His blindfold was removed, and Kim blinked twice, his
eyes adjusting to the bright fluorescent lights. Before him,
perched upon one corner of a metal desk, the officer assigned
to break his spirit studied Kim with an ingratiating smile. His
shirt and slacks were neatly pressed, the tie immaculate, his
hair trimmed close enough to let the scalp show through on
top.

"Good afternoon." The voice was pleasant, artificial in its
tone of camaraderie. "I am Lieutenant Colonel Park Han Yee.
And you are . . . ?"

"Kim Su Chung."

"Of course." Yee lit a cigarette and blew the smoke in
Kim's direction, casually. "Your true name, please."

"I told you, Kim—"

Behind him, one of his interrogators swung an open
hand, connecting with Kim's cheek, resounding impact cutting off the lie.

"Your *true* name."

"Kim Su Chung."

The slugger used both hands, a brisk half-dozen blows
that left a distant ringing in Kim's ears. His vision blurred for
several seconds, came back into focus on Yee's face, distorted
by a drifting pall of smoke.

"Your name?"

Kim braced himself for more, anticipating application of
"the telephone"—palms clapped together over both ears
simultaneously, perforating eardrums—but the lead interrogator shook his head, delaying further punishment.

"Perhaps it would be simpler if I told you what we know,

already. You are Kim Sunim, a native of Korea, born in 1951. Your parents were subversive enemies of the republic. In your fifteenth year, you emigrated to America with the assistance of an Army officer from the United States. Your education was completed there, you spent four years in military service and became a U.S. citizen at twenty years of age. A short time later, you enlisted as an agent for the CIA. Have I forgotten anything?"

Kim shrugged. "I wouldn't know. My name—"

"Is Kim Sunim," the colonel cut him off, unsmiling now. "Twelve years ago, you meddled in an operation crucial to the national security of the republic. Lives were lost as a result, but you were spared in deference to our friendship with the CIA. Your presence in Korea violates a sacred promise."

Kim made no reply, considering his options. He was blown, his cover trashed, but there was still a chance the NSP had not divined his mission. While uncertainty remained, survival was at least a possibility.

The colonel crushed his cigarette butt in a metal ashtray and immediately lit another, studying Kim's face.

"You've cost me two more officers this afternoon."

"When strangers try to kill me, I react."

"What business have you with Chin Sung?"

"My own."

A flicker of the eyes, and Kim was hammered from behind with force enough to make his nostrils bleed. The fourth blow hurled him sideways to the floor, his ankles twisted painfully in shackles as he fell. A moment later, he was lifted by his armpits, dropped back in the chair. A crimson mist of pain had settled in the space behind his eyes.

"Chin Sung is a fanatic communist and a traitor to his country. Anyone assisting him in his subversive schemes will be regarded as an enemy of the republic."

Kim ignored the colonel's voice and concentrated on his breathing, taking care to fill the lower portion of his lungs, imagining each breath as lightly scented mist. He visualized it circulating through his abdomen and limbs, escaping through his nostrils, and the throbbing in his skull began to fade.

"I know your reputation as a martial artist and assassin." Circling the desk, Yee interposed its bulk between them.

"You believe yourself immune to suffering, the perfect superman. A critical mistake."

Kim licked his lips and tasted blood, eyes focused on his enemy. The colonel reached inside a drawer, withdrew a pistol, leveled it at Kim.

"Release him."

First, the shackles. Kim sat motionless until a rigid finger prodded him between the shoulder blades.

"Stand up."

He rose, ignoring protests from his ankles, watching Yee, the pistol in his hand. He could expect another gun, somewhere behind him, to insure against a sudden lunge.

The handcuffs were removed, and Kim began to flex his fingers, normalizing circulation. Could he vault the desk, rip out the colonel's throat, before a bullet brought him down?

"Remove your clothes."

There are divergent schools of thought on torture. Some practitioners maintain that subjects must be forcibly disrobed, to demonstrate that they are helpless; others counter that a victim, forced to strip before his captors, suffers guilty feelings of participation in his own debasement, thereby hastening collapse. A few are known to vary their approach, depending on their captive's sex or age.

Kim had no feelings on the subject, either way, and took his time about undressing. Glancing underneath one arm as he removed his slacks, he counted two more goons behind him, both with guns in hand. He thought he might reach one, with luck, but it would take a miracle for him to kill all three.

One of the sentries caught a signal from his chief and moved to stand beside a door positioned on Kim's left. He knew the entrance from the corridor was on his right; this second door could only serve a more secure interrogation room.

The door swung open on command, confirming his suspicions. Soundproof walls, a concrete floor that sloped to feed a central drain. Above the grate, a stainless steel trapeze affixed to chains had been suspended from the ceiling.

"Step inside."

Kim crossed the threshold, tasting musty air inside the claustrophobic chamber. There could be no air-conditioning for this room, since the ducts might carry screams. The drain was immaterial, as only sewer rats would hear him down below.

He turned to face his captors, noting that they kept their distance, pistols tracking him from different angles.

"On your knees."

Kim thought about resisting, forcing them to kill him quickly, but he could not bring himself to throw his life away. The floor was smooth and cool.

One of the gunners passed his automatic to the colonel, circling Kim, approaching from his flank.

"Face down," the colonel ordered. "Hands behind your back and bend your knees."

He knew the drill. Handcuffs secured his left wrist to his right ankle, another pair completing the cross from right to left. His spine was slightly arched, his shoulders cramped, but he could live with it. So far.

Above him, rattling chains marked the descent of the trapeze. Yee's goon released one end and slid the metal bar between Kim's calves and buttocks, taking care to wedge it tight behind his knees. The anchor chain was reattached, and Kim watched patent leather shoes retreat in the direction of the door.

He braced himself, was ready when the winch began to lift him, putting awkward pressure on his neck and spine at first, then hoisting him completely off the floor. He hung inverted, like a bat, immediately conscious of the pressure in his skull.

Remembering his training, Kim picked out an arbitrary point of focus on the concrete floor below. A rough, discolored spot, perhaps an inch across. His concentration sharpened, he could almost hear the voice of Master Rhee. *Control your breathing. Fix your eyes and mind outside the pain. Savor your point of focus, its taste and smell. Invest it with color and dimension.*

Kim barely noticed Yee, the three-foot shock baton he carried as he moved to stand in front of Kim. The colonel's voice seemed faint with distance.

"It is time for your instruction to begin," he said, and pressed the shock baton against Kim's chest.

* * *

The afternoon had been a waste for Jamie Constable. She felt a mixture of relief and irritation as she left her office on the stroke of five o'clock. If Kim would only keep in touch . . .

She knew it was ridiculous, expecting him to drop whatever he was doing and report on schedule like a rookie covering his first assignment. He was busy, touching base with contacts, chasing leads. The last thing on Kim's mind would be a chat with his control.

But she was worried, damn it. Holland's death had taught her anything could happen; everyone was vulnerable all the time. It did not help to know that Kim had done this kind of thing a hundred times before. He had been out of service for eleven years, and that meant he was rusty. One mistake, and she could have another body on her hands.

She pushed the grisly image out of mind and slid behind the wheel of her Toyota, mustering a smile for the Marine on duty at the gate. He waved her through and Jamie caught an opening in traffic, making half a block before the snarl reduced her progress to a crawl.

She found an English-speaking station on the radio and caught the news in progress. Wall Street had begun to rally from a slide the week before, and White House sources saw no cause for panic in the fluctuation. Arab refugees were raising hell outside Jerusalem again, and the authorities in Vietnam had suddenly "discovered" the remains of two more MIAs. In Seoul, a leftist demonstration at the Independence Arch had turned to violence, with reports of sniper fire and looting, several deaths.

Disgusted, Jamie turned it off. She understood the media approach—good news was no news—but her daily tolerance for mayhem was exhausted. As she made her slow way home in silence, Jamie thought about the hours she had spent with Kim, just yesterday, and cursed herself for being such a fool. She could have spared herself an untold measure of anxiety by following the book, maintaining proper distance from an agent she might never see again.

Too late.

Her objectivity was blown, and she could not erase her memory like data from a floppy disk. If Kim was damaged . . .

Jamie wore a sour expression as she turned off Yulgog-ro.

Her vanity was showing, and the thought did not improve her mood. By any definition, she had thrown herself at Kim; his own reaction was instinctive, automatic. Jamie had no reason to believe he felt a thing for her above the waist, much less that he would jeopardize his mission on account of the distraction.

Kim was a professional assassin, trained to kill without emotion. Jamie realized that she was flattering herself, imagining that sex on any level would divert him from the task at hand.

Projection and transference, she decided, falling back on a semester of psychology. She had allowed herself to feel for Kim, assuming the emotion was reciprocated. Feeling angry and embarrassed, Jamie almost passed her building, braking hard to make the ramp in time.

The underground garage was cool inside, a man-made cavern sheltered from the summer sun. Jamie locked her car and kept the keys in hand, her purse tucked underneath one arm as she proceeded toward the elevator. Almost there, she noticed that a couple of the ceiling lights had blown and made a mental note to tell the manager.

She punched the call button, distracted by a scuffling sound behind her. Turning, startled, she had time to recognize a human hand before it clamped across her face, a damp cloth covering her nose and mouth. Its mate was locked behind her head, strong fingers tangled in her hair, when Jamie recognized the stench of chloroform.

She struggled, but a second pair of hands had pinned her arms against her sides. Her heel caught someone's shin, eliciting a muffled curse before the fingers in her hair began to twist, applying painful pressure.

Jamie tried to hold her breath, but the exertion had already robbed her blood of oxygen. Survival instincts took control as colored specks began to dance before her eyes. She drew a halting breath, her throat and lungs on fire, tears welling in her eyes. Her legs were rubber now, ignoring the commands from Jamie's brain.

She felt the world revolving, tipping upside down. Her final conscious thoughts were focused on a silent scream.

*   *   *

Fitzpatrick was fed up with playing games. If Jamie had herself a lover—a *Korean* lover—he could live with that. The choice was hers, and they were both adults. Before he gave it up, however, she would hear him out and realize precisely what she was about to throw away.

It might not be the best idea, all things considered. He had never been adept at confrontations, least of all where raw emotions were involved, but he was sick to death of standing on the sidelines, waiting for a break that never came. So far, the casual approach had failed across the board.

He had checked out an hour early, knowing he would not be missed around the office, beating heavy traffic on the drive to Jamie's flat. Arriving well before the neighbors got off work, he parked across the street and settled down to wait, rehearsing in his mind precisely what he ought to say.

Surprise would offer him a small advantage. Jamie would not be expecting him to call, and while she put him off with plastic smiles, there would be time enough for him to speak his mind, his heart. If she was still unmoved, at least Fitzpatrick would have done his best. He could request a transfer to another duty station, start from scratch, forget her face in time.

A sudden pang of apprehension pierced his cool resolve. Suppose that Jamie did not come directly home from work. What then? Fitzpatrick smiled at his reflection in the rearview mirror. He would wait. He had all night.

And if, like last night, she was not alone?

His knuckles whitened as he clutched the steering wheel. He pictured Jamie, naked, the Korean riding her, their bodies slick with perspiration, and his stomach churned.

Fitzpatrick was not prejudiced against Koreans, though he sometimes found them difficult to understand. The thought of *any* other man with Jamie drove him to distraction, sparking jumbled feelings of arousal and disgust. He tried to blot the image out by picturing himself in Jamie's bed, but it was hopeless. Painfully erect at first, he wilted under Jamie's scrutiny, recoiling from her touch. The echo of her laughter drove a spike of pain between his eyes.

Imagination. Ghosts and shadows.

He was glancing at his watch when Jamie's car rolled into view. Fitzpatrick slouched behind the wheel, refused to duck completely out of sight before he verified that Jamie was alone. No passenger, no second car behind her. This time, he would have her to himself.

Her small Toyota vanished down the gullet of the subterranean garage. He could surprise her there, but Ray had no desire to frighten Jamie. Showing up outside her door, *sans* invitation, was the limit of his daring. It would be surprise enough.

Five minutes. He could see her in the elevator now, a quick stop in the lobby for her mail, and then the ride to her apartment on the seventh floor. Another five, and he would make the trip himself.

A dark sedan pulled up across the street, its driver studying the entrance to the underground garage. Fitzpatrick scanned the Asian face in profile, wishing he would get the hell away from there before Ray's arbitrary deadline came and went. His entrance would be difficult enough without an audience.

Two men emerged from the garage, supporting a life-sized rag doll between them. With her head down, face concealed, their captive might have passed for any other woman on the street, but Fitz had made a point of memorizing every outfit Jamie owned. He recognized the blouse and slacks on sight, struck dumb as he sized up the situation at a glance.

Unarmed, without a second thought, he left his car and raced across the street to help. The men were strangers, so he shouted Jamie's name, demanding that the captors stop, release her, and identify themselves. He was prepared to fight, but death had never crossed his mind.

Until he saw the pistol.

They were nearly at the waiting car when one of Jamie's captors drew and fired his weapon in a single fluid motion. Its report was dissipated in the open street, a *crack* like someone clapping wooden blocks together, and Fitzpatrick stumbled, nearly fell.

No pain at first, although the impact took his breath away. He staggered, reeling, one hand pressed against the warmth and wetness of his abdomen. Another bullet struck him in the chest and knocked him off his feet, the pavement rushing up to meet him. Dazed, Fitzpatrick realized his ears had never registered the second shot.

You never hear the shot that kills you.

Something he had heard a soldier say, but where? The movies? Television?

Jamie.

Struggling to rise, he heard a screech of rubber, turned in time to see the juggernaut approaching.

"Jamie?"

The sedan dragged Fitzpatrick for half a block before it dropped him in the middle of the street. He lay with arms outstretched, as if in death he was preparing to embrace the sky. A line of bloody Rorschach patterns marked his trail along the pavement.

Jamie and her captors were a mile away before a neighbor drew his curtains back, examined Ray Fitzpatrick from a bird's-eye view, and ran to call police.

"Once more. What is your business with Chin Sung?"

Kim braced himself, eyes closed, and felt the shock baton's electrodes prod his stomach, perspiration offering a better ground. On contact, every muscle in his abdomen convulsed, his body twisting like a bait fish on a hook. His lungs refused to function while the spasm lasted, and he learned the pains of drowning while suspended in mid-air.

He had discovered electricity.

Each application of the shock baton disrupted concentration, scrambling orders from the brain, defeating his attempts to block out physical sensation. It was not the pain, so much as lack of self-control, that left him feeling helpless for the first time since his childhood.

"Still no answer?" Yee did not seem weary of the game. "Then we must try again."

The twin electrodes kissed his scrotum, arced before he had a chance to clench his thighs, and he was twisting, straining at the cuffs that held his wrists and ankles fast. He did not recognize the sound of ragged screaming as his own.

A failure. Years of training, concentration—wasted. He was putty now, in the interrogator's hands, unable to resist. It was a simple thing his captors sought, no more than words.

Kim steeled himself against the pain, refusing to submit. His lower body felt like broken glass, but it was something he could deal with, a sensation he could master, given time.

The colonel stood before him, an inverted giant, still the fashion plate with every hair in place. The prod was cocked across one shoulder, resting.

"I commend your stamina," the giant said, his voice distorted by the pulse that throbbed inside Kim's skull. "A pity that your courage should be wasted so. Inevitably, you will speak."

Kim did not waste his fading energy on a reply.

The prod reached out to tease him, tickling his ribs, but Yee refrained from squeezing off another charge. He toyed with Kim and set him swinging on his perch, a human pendulum.

"Chin Sung has told us everything. He lacks your courage, and his wound...ah, well." The colonel shrugged, dismissing Chin. "We simply need your confirmation now, and we are finished. I will have you driven back to your hotel. Tomorrow or the next day, when you feel a little stronger, you can go in peace."

Yee used the shock baton to halt Kim's swinging.

"Tell me what you spoke about this afternoon, confirm Chin's story, and you're free to leave."

Kim's lips were swollen, cracked and dry. He scarcely had the energy to speak.

"What's that?" The colonel knelt before him eagerly, their faces separated by an inch or less. "What did you talk about?"

Kim got it right this time, and even managed to approximate a smile.

"Your mother."

In his rage, the colonel swung his shock baton against Kim's ribs, forgetting the electrodes, a demented batter warming up on deck. He landed half a dozen solid blows before the goons restrained him, warning that it might be rash to kill the prisoner before he broke. Yee shook his flunkies off and charged the prod, approaching from the flank to drive it deep between Kim's thighs.

He clenched his teeth around the rising scream, unable to contain it as his muscles knotted, jerking in response to voltage. It might have lasted for a second or an hour; time had lost its meaning in a world where pain and its relief were everything. His life was measured out in micro-units of endurance, his every conscious thought committed to surviving for another heartbeat, and another, and . . .

The colonel stepped away, cheeks mottled with the residue of fury, to survey his handiwork. His tie was pulled off-center and a button on his dress shirt had come open, half way down. A sheen of perspiration glistened on his forehead.

"You enjoy your little joke?" he rasped. "I hope so. Now, we must begin again."

A rapping on the outer door distracted Yee, and he dispatched one of his goons to deal with the intrusion. Muttered conversation, and the hulk returned, another figure on his heels. Kim thought the new arrival looked familiar, but his vision was obscured by sweat and tears of pain.

"I am not finished here," Yee snapped. "The questioning—"

"You're finished. It's official."

An American. A voice he ought to recognize.

"I should have been consulted."

"Maybe next time." The American produced a sheaf of papers, handed them to Yee. "I'm taking him. If that's a problem, you can talk it over with your deputy director."

Fuming, Yee snapped orders at his two subordinates and left the chamber in a huff. The winch began to whine a moment later, lowering Kim's perch until his body rested on the concrete floor. Without the manacles, his hands and feet felt numb.

"He'll need a shower."

One of the interrogators grumbled in response and lingered in the doorway, waiting, while his partner disappeared.

"Come on," said Barrett Ross. "You're going home."

Chapter 16

The shower gradually relaxed Kim's knotted muscles, stinging when the soap encountered open wounds. They had avoided working on his face, but tender bruises made a patchwork of his abdomen. No broken ribs, but it was not for lack of trying.

It had taken him a quarter of an hour to negotiate the narrow hall and stairs connecting the interrogation chambers with the locker room and showers. Kim refused to lean on Ross, and they made the halting trek in silence, moving like an old man and his escort through the empty corridors. Ross waited on a wooden bench, around the corner, while Kim occupied an open shower stall.

"You nearly blew it," he declared, voice raised to reach Kim's ears above the drumming of the shower. "If we didn't have a man inside, I never would've known they had you in the bag."

Kim turned the water off and wrapped a towel around his waist, returning to the locker room.

"They had me set up going in."

"Set up?" Ross frowned. "Who's 'they'?"

"My money's on the NSP."

"No good. I'll buy them sponsoring the fracas at the demonstration. It's their style. The rest of it..."

Kim finished toweling off and stepped into his briefs, pulling them snug in spite of the pain.

"What are you talking about?"

"Your handler. Someone bagged her an hour ago, at her place. Wasted my number three in the process. Very messy, lots of paperwork and questions."

193

Kim felt sick. He sat down on the bench opposite Ross, his slacks in hand. If Jamie had been hurt—or worse—because of him . . .

"You've had no word?"

"Not yet. It's early I suppose, but normally we'd have some bunch of assholes claiming credit for the job by now."

"What happened?"

"What's the difference? You've done your job, after a fashion. You're out of it."

"Let's say I'm curious."

Ross shrugged. "Why not? But get your clothes on, will you? I don't like to hang around this place."

He dressed as Ross continued, stoically ignoring protests from his battered limbs and torso.

"As we reconstruct the action, they were waiting for her in the underground garage. The locals found her purse and keys down there, outside the elevator. Anyway, they dropped the net and probably sedated her somehow. They've got wheels waiting on the street, and they're about to move it out when Fitz shows up and tries to play James Bond."

"Who's Fitz?"

"My number three. At least, he *was*. Fitzpatrick, Raymond T. Don't ask me how he came to be there at the time. For all I know, they had some kind of thing together, if you get my drift. A little hide-the-salami after hours. Fine with me, unless it interferes with business."

"You were saying?"

"Right. The way it looks, Fitzpatrick tried to stage a rescue. Someone shot him twice and then ran over him to make it stick. He's dead and Jamie's gone. No witnesses, no leads, no nothing."

"The police?"

Ross smiled and shook his head. "They go through all the motions, make a lot of noise, but they're notorious for getting nowhere fast. A case involving foreigners is likely to remain unsolved, unless we crack it on our own."

Kim finished buttoning his shirt.

"I'm ready."

"Not a chance. When I say 'we,' I mean the Company."

"I'm still on payroll."

"Guess again. We brought you over here to find Chin Sung. You found him. End of story. You're retired again."

"The rest of it is my fault."

"Probably. You'll have to live with that the best you can. You're going home."

"Suppose I told you I can get her back?"

"I'd say you're crazy, but it doesn't matter, either way. The only thing that got you off that parrot's perch was my assurance that you're on your way to the United States, ASAP. These people don't appreciate it when you kill their men, and you're on tap for three. If they weren't tickled pink about Chin Sung right now, I couldn't get you out of here at any price."

"You wouldn't have to tell them."

"I'm supposed to play some kind of guessing game, so you can run around and be a hero? Thanks, but no thanks. You've got reservations on the first flight out tomorrow, nine-fifteen a.m. to Honolulu."

"What about Chin Sung?"

"He's history."

"I didn't make the tag."

"Who cares? We wanted him for Holland, and the NSP just wants him, period. It all comes out the same."

"What happens to him now?"

"Past tense. It seems he had a little accident while trying to escape."

"That's crap. He wasn't going anywhere in his condition."

"What's your point? We brought you over here to tag the guy, remember? So, he's tagged. Dead's dead."

"You're writing Jamie off?"

"I'm doing what I can," Ross snapped. "The fact is, I'm prepared to cut my losses if I have to. Life goes on."

"For some."

"That's right. I'd say it's just a little late for you to get religion."

Ross displayed credentials to a pair of sentries at the exit, leading Kim through double doors that overlooked a parking lot. The night was soft and warm, in contrast to the steady chill of air-conditioning.

Two suits were waiting at the car. One slid behind the wheel as Ross and Kim appeared; the other held their door and took the shotgun seat when they were settled. Kim allowed Remonclo to recede without a backward glance.

"Remember, nine-fifteen," the chief of section said again.

"I heard you."

"Right. I'm making Curt and Roger your official chaperones until you fly. Who knows? Your playmates back at NSP might have a change of heart."

"I'm touched by your concern."

"Don't mention it."

Kim knew the truth: Ross would not run the risk of leaving him at large in Seoul, unsupervised. The suits were baby-sitters, plain and simple, under orders to remain with Kim that night and put him on an airplane in the morning, bright and early. In the meantime, he was their responsibility, and they would recognize the consequences of allowing him to slip away.

How far were they prepared to go in stopping him? They carried sidearms—Kim had seen that much before he climbed inside the car—but guns were merely tools, their usefulness dependent on a craftsman's skill. If they were slow or sloppy, weapons would be worse than useless.

"Jamie didn't know what she was getting into," he informed the chief of section.

"She's a trained professional. She knew the odds before she left the Farm."

"It's not her fight."

Ross turned to study Kim in profile. "Why the great concern?"

"Let's say I don't believe in needless waste."

"Humanitarian concerns? It's getting deep in here."

"I don't think Ramsey's going to appreciate your next report."

"I'll manage. History is written by the winners."

"You don't have a winner, yet."

"I'm close enough. Besides, who's going to contradict me? You?"

"It never crossed my mind."

"Good thinking. You could use a boost yourself."

"I didn't take this job for rave reviews."

"Whatever. It's a sloppy wrap-up, letting NSP do all the

dirty work and bag you in the bargain. Some might say you've lost your touch."

"Is that what you think?"

"I don't give a damn. You're out of here at nine-fifteen tomorrow. I don't expect we'll meet again."

"Small favors."

They pulled up outside the embassy, and the Marines saluted Ross. He hesitated on the sidewalk, held the door and leaned back in.

"Be smart," he said. "Don't push your luck."

"One question, Ross: How do you sleep at night?"

"My left side, mostly."

"Don't forget to say your prayers."

Ross closed the door, and they were back in traffic by the time he cleared the gate. Kim spent a moment studying his escorts, then dismissed them, concentrating on the problem of retrieving Jamie Constable. She might be dead already, but he had to find out for himself, and he was not prepared to kiss Seoul off before he had an answer, one way or the other.

Ross had learned to live with disappointment in his time; one more would matter little in the cosmic scheme of things.

Kim had a flight to miss, but first, he had to deal with Curt and Roger.

Ross slouched behind his desk and eyed the scrambler telephone as if it were an enemy, caught lurking in his office after hours. A small lamp framed the instrument within a pool of light, but he had left the office dark deliberately, in deference to his mood.

The call was necessary—overdue, in fact—but given any choice he would have put it off another day, until he knew that Kim was safely back in San Francisco. While he lingered on in Seoul there was a chance, however slim, that he would try some kind of grandstand play and ruin everything.

Ross poured himself a shot of Chivas Regal, drank it down to calm himself. Kim's baby-sitters were the best available: professionals, well armed, with black belts in tae kwon do. They would put him on the plane tomorrow morning, see him off, and that would be the end of it.

Except for Ramsey.

Theoretically, the Texan should be happy. Chin was

neutralized without perceptible involvement from the West, and Company relations with the NSP—while strained—were still intact. The job had not come cheap, with two men down and Jamie Constable as good as dead, but Ross was satisfied with the results. If he could sell his point of view to Langley, fine. If Ramsey was dissatisfied . . .

Ross brightened. He could always blame the latest rash of deaths on Kim Sunim, and using Kim was Ramsey's brainstorm from the start. Ross had performed his duties by the book, allowing Jamie room to run in her position as the project officer. He would be forced to shoulder some of the responsibility, by virtue of his rank, but Ross was not about to take another beating like he had in Bangkok.

Inexperience had nearly cost him everything in that fiasco. Ross was older now, and vastly wiser. He had learned to spread the blame around.

A hefty share would fall on Jamie, now that she was not in a position to defend herself. It would not be the first time that a handler's negligence had led to near disaster. Ross could write himself a few back-dated memos if he had to, warning Jamie in absentia of the risks involved in handling an operative like Kim.

The wild card was undoubtedly his best defense, across the board. Emotionally involved, unstable, eleven years out of harness, Kim had been the world's worst choice for any kind of payback mission. Ross had placed his own objections in the record, thankful now for spite that stood in place of foresight. If the job was kicked upstairs for an executive *post mortem*, he should come out smelling like a rose.

Experience and preparation. They were ninety-five percent of what it took to stay alive inside the Company.

The other five percent was luck.

Not feeling lucky, even with the odds behind him, Ross threw down another shot of Chivas, waiting for its warmth to reach his fingertips and toes. He was not drunk, by any means, but he could feel himself beginning to relax in preparation for the call that he would have to put through any moment now.

It would be two a.m. in Langley. Wednesday morning. Ramsey would be home, asleep, tucked up in bed beside his wife. The sun would not rise over Washington for hours.

Reaching for the telephone, Ross saw it as a time machine. By punching numbered buttons, he would drag the Texan forward, spanning eighteen hours in a heartbeat, forcing Ramsey to confront the facts of life and death on Wednesday evening, half a world away.

The prospect made him smile.

Ross keyed the scrambler, double-checked that it was set for Wednesday's code, and tapped a thirteen-digit number out from memory.

The nicest thing about bad news was passing it along and spoiling someone else's day.

"I want a full report, eyes only, on my desk in twenty-four."

The deputy director registered a confirmation of his order, scowling as he dropped the telephone receiver in its cradle. Glancing at the bedside clock, he found that it was half-past two and muttered to himself, disgusted. He was wide awake now, and they would not be expecting him at Langley prior to nine.

A perfect way to start the morning.

Ramsey donned his robe and made his way downstairs to start the coffee. Years of working nights and taking early wake-up calls had taught him how to move around the house without disturbing Carol or the kids. The "kids" were all long gone, of course, enrolled in liberal universities and learning God-knows-what about the "crimes" of the United States, but Carol still liked her sleep and Ramsey saw no reason she should keep his crazy hours.

He was troubled by the call from Barrett Ross in Seoul, concerned as much by what his chief of station left unsaid as by the grim report itself. Chin Sung was dead, eliminated by the South Koreans, but there had been trouble with the NSP. Unspecified, so far, but Ramsey gathered Kim Sunim had trashed a couple of their agents in the field. Worse yet, Ross had a second agent down and one abducted; that made three, with Domino, and Ramsey did not like the odds.

He thought of calling Bragg, decided it could wait. No point in stirring up a hornet's nest before he had the facts in hand. A summary would do until he had a chance to scrutinize the paperwork from Ross, assess his chief of station's damage estimate.

Mathematics was the problem. If it cost him three to cancel one, the one had better be a damned important target. In Korean politics, Chin Sung had been a wild card, dangerous perhaps, his real strength open to debate. His rumored link with North Korea made him worth investigating, and the death of Domino had marked him automatically for payback. Up to that point, it was more or less routine. Since then . . .

His choice of Kim to make the tag had raised some eyebrows in the Company. It was unorthodox, to say the least, but he had pushed it through by stressing how the use of a retiree minimized potential risks. If Kim succeeded, fine; if something happened to him, it was no real loss. The whole thing sounded great on paper, but reality could be a bitch sometimes.

For openers, it hurt that Chin had been eliminated by the NSP. Inevitably, Ramsey would be called to answer for their own man's failure to produce results. It could be argued that the mission was unnecessary, since the South Koreans had Chin in their sights. And if the mission was a waste of time, the loss of two more agents was a bona-fide disaster.

Whipping up a plate of scrambled eggs and bacon, Ramsey wondered if the fault might lie with Kim Sunim. Eleven years was ample time for any man to lose his edge, and Kim had left the Company determined to erase the memories of wet work executed on his government's behalf. It never entered Ramsey's mind that Kim would throw the mission—Holland's death provided all the motivation he would need—but times and people change. An expert sniper, eleven years out of practice, might not score a bull's-eye, either.

Ramsey had exhausted the debate before he made his choice and sought approval for the operation. There appeared to be no downside; live or die, Kim seemed the best choice for a relatively simple job.

But Ramsey had been wrong about the downside. Two dead agents—three, if Ross was right about his number two—and Kim was still alive. His target had been taken down by someone else, outside the Company, and that scrubbed any hope of balancing the scales. His "simple" project had become a nightmare, and the deputy director still had no clear picture of the problem.

Memories of Bangkok left a sour taste in Ramsey's

mouth. The failure, that time, had belonged to Barrett Ross; he let himself be suckered, fingering a target based on worthless information. Ramsey had been quick to double-check the facts on Chin, confirming his alleged involvement with the communists, attempting to insure that history did not repeat itself.

Seoul was not Bangkok.

It was worse.

The first fiasco was embarrassing, but all the dead were Asian nationals. The Company had learned to live with its mistakes, providing always that deniability could be maintained. In Seoul, the body-count included two Americans—more likely three—and Ramsey had no credits on his balance sheet.

He wolfed the eggs and bacon, scarcely tasting anything, and burned his tongue with scalding coffee. Perfect. Now his lunch would taste like tinfoil, if he found the time to eat at all.

Three-thirty.

Ramsey lit his first cigar of the day, considering the preliminary report he would file with Bragg. Lead with the good news, such as it was, playing down friendly casualties until all the facts were available. He still did not know all the players in Seoul, their alignment, and Ramsey would not let himself be provoked into speaking from ignorance.

He remembered the Old Days, under LBJ and Nixon, flying by the seat of his pants with operations in Cuba, Santo Domingo, Guatemala, El Salvador. Things had been simpler then; the very threat of creeping socialism was enough to put clandestine agents in the field, recruiting allies in the mob, ex-Nazis, anybody who could do the side some good. It was a rougher game, with fewer rules of play, but Ramsey sometimes thought that it had been a cleaner game, in spite of everything.

Today, with Congress breathing down his neck and OMB examining expenditures, the deputy director often felt that he was living in a fishbowl. Ever since the Church committee started airing dirty laundry on the network news, his job had been a hundred times more difficult. The Company was ordered to produce results, without infringing on the precious civil liberties of aliens and traitors, terrorists and tyrants. Wet work was a dying specialty, no pun intended, and innumerable sources had been lost through liberal insistence that America's clandestine warriors all "play fair."

A few more years, and Ramsey would be looking at his pension, a secure position in the ranks of private industry. At one time, he had cherished hopes of rising to the apex of the Company, becoming the director of intelligence, but he had long since pushed those hopes aside. Above his present rank, the supergrades were hopelessly mired down in office politics, and Ramsey had enough of that already. He had found his niche, if only circumstance did not conspire to force him out before his time.

If there was any way to put a happy face on the events in Seoul, he had to find it quickly. Bragg would not be handing out awards for failure, and the last thing Ramsey needed now was any kind of scandal. Ross would bear a portion of the heat, but as the brains behind the operation, Ramsey was prepared to take his share.

He cleared the dirty dishes off and rinsed them, put them in the washer. One more cup of coffee, cooler now, but tasteless on his scalded tongue.

Perhaps if he could get in touch with Kim himself, obtain another view of what had happened, what went wrong. Ross had a vested interest in allowing Kim to take the blame, and he would gladly toss the hot potato back to Ramsey. His report would be a masterpiece of logic, carefully avoiding any accusations, letting "facts" and personal impressions point the way for anyone with eyes to see. Kim blew it; Ramsey had selected Kim, despite objections from his station chief. Case closed, next case.

His stomach warned him to forget about the coffee, and he poured it down the sink. Upstairs, his wife was fast asleep, and Ramsey wondered if she dreamed—about the children, their vacation coming up in August, anything at all. He felt a sudden urge to wake her, knew it would not earn him any points, and let it go.

His day was shot, and Ramsey thought he might as well inflict his dour mood on someone at the office. He would leave a note for Carol and drive the Buick in himself, alert his driver later, at an hour when he would not have to wake the dead.

The extra time would let him draft a suitable report for Bragg, relating the events from Seoul while playing down the damage. In a day or two, when he had all the facts in hand, there would be time to count the cost, assess the blame.

The deputy director took a final drag on his cigar and stubbed it out, remembering to take his time and keep it quiet on the stairs. His suit had been laid out the night before, an ancient habit. Ramsey was retreating toward the dressing room when Carol turned over, called to him from bed.

"Is everything all right?"

"I couldn't sleep. I'm going in a little early."

Carol found the clock and studied its illuminated face. "At four-fifteen?"

"I didn't mean to wake you." It was no response, but he could think of nothing else to say.

"Are they expecting you right now?"

He shook his head, then realized she could not see him in the darkness.

"No."

"Then, what's your hurry?"

"Carol—"

"Come here," she told him. "That's an order, mister."

Ramsey swore that he could hear her smiling.

"Ma'am," he said, "we aim to please."

Chapter 17

Upon arrival at the Metro, Curt and Roger spent a quarter-hour checking out Kim's suite, "securing" the premises. They poked through drawers and closets, seeming vaguely disappointed when they found no weapons. Satisfied that Kim was not about to spring an ambush or escape by leaping from the balcony, his watchdogs settled in the living area with television to amuse them, leaving Kim his bedroom and the bath.

Discarding clothes that smelled of pain and perspiration, Kim began his preparations with a second shower. Emerging, he was stiff and sore from head to foot, but he could function on command; his injuries were not debilitating. Under other circumstances, he would have preferred to work the soreness out with t'ai chi exercises, but he had no time to spare.

How many hours since the enemy had taken Jamie? Ross had been deliberately obscure, but an abduction from her building meant that she had finished work and driven home before the trap was sprung. Three hours, then—or less, if she had put in over time.

He had a chance. If she was still alive...

It made no sense to kidnap Jamie if the goal was simply murder. Her abductors had no qualms about a public execution; they had proved that when they killed a second agent at the scene. A pickup meant they needed Jamie—for a trade, a lure, whatever—and it served their interest to preserve her, more or less intact, while she had value to their cause.

When she had served her purpose, she would be eliminated. Simple.

It would be Kim's task to find her first, before that

happened. Ross would shit a cinder block, and Kim anticipated further trouble from the NSP if he remained in Seoul, but he had more immediate concerns. Before he could begin the hunt, he had to lose his "chaperones."

They would expect him to be near exhaustion, following his ordeal at Remonclo. Under different circumstances, Kim would gladly have retired to sleep around the clock, but he had work to do and urgency had banished his fatigue.

He dressed in silence, picked out a long-sleeved turtleneck and jeans in basic black. He slipped the dagger-belt around his waist and laced his Nike runners, also black, before he checked his outfit in the bathroom's full-length mirror. With a mask, Kim thought he would have made a classic thief. The pea coat from his closet would complete the transformation and divert suspicion, making him a simple merchant seaman home on leave.

He laid the coat aside and worked his way through several t'ai chi postures, concentrating on the high kicks, doggedly ignoring angry protests from his ribs and groin, the muscles in his legs. When he was satisfied, Kim practiced with the buckle-dagger, drawing several times before his mind and hand were synchronized in perfect rhythm.

Done.

Two men with pistols waited on the far side of his bedroom door. In theory, they were not supposed to kill him, but if he should have an "accident" while trying to escape, Kim doubted whether Barrett Ross would lose a moment's sleep.

Potential killers, then. The enemy.

Kim had no wish to kill his baby-sitters, but he was prepared to do so if they left him no alternative. They seemed professional enough, despite a certain arrogance that might be turned to Kim's advantage, and he took for granted that they must possess some skills in unarmed combat. Ross would not be fool enough to trust in guns alone.

His watchdogs were American of military bearing. That meant veterans, maybe mercenaries, and their training would include at least the basics of karate, with some judo or jujitsu added for variety. American servicemen spent less time on hand-to-hand combat than their Asian counterparts—in the ROK Special Forces, for example, every solider held a black belt in some form of martial arts—but they were capable, for all of that.

And sometimes deadly.

Kim would have to watch his step, remembering that Curt and Roger had not spent the afternoon with Park Han Yee and his associates. They would be rested, fresh, anticipating trouble. They would stop him from assisting Jamie, maybe kill him, if he gave them half a chance.

The trick, he finally decided, was to steal their edge.

He would not give them any chance at all.

The job had sounded like a milk run, which was fine with Curt. He knew that Roger had been getting restless lately, checking out the classifieds in half a dozen monthlies catering to mercenaries, but they still had six more weeks to run on contract with the CIA, and easy work paid off the same as humping through the jungle with a mortar on your back.

Curt wondered, sometimes, if he might be getting old. It had not shown up in the mirror yet, but he was less excited by the prospect of a mission now than in the past. Their last full-scale engagement had been eighteen months ago, in Africa, and while he still enjoyed the killing, Curt could do without the rigors of the hunt.

Old age.

He caught himself before the frown could add new worry lines around his eyes. If twenty-nine was old, then Father Time could kiss his ass. Curt knew a lot of mercs—well, some; a few—who kept on humping through their forties. Baradet was fifty-one last month, and he was going strong, still leading Contra raids against the Sandinistas.

Curt decided that his problem had to be the easy life, hotels and cushy jobs like baby-sitting for the Company. What kind of work was that, for Christ's sake, putting some Korean on an airplane? It was kid stuff.

Sure, their contact at the embassy had emphasized the "dangers" of their "mission." Mr. Moto was supposed to be some kind of slick karate-ka, a slant-eyed Superman, which all meant shit to Curt. Their man had come out losers in the main event before they took delivery from the NSP; if he had any fight left in him, Curt was ready to administer the *coup de grace*.

Or, better still, let Roger do it.

Glancing over at his partner, catching Roger's profile as he watched an ancient episode of "Happy Days," Curt felt the warm, familiar stirring of desire. If they had been alone, he thought, they could have managed better than a stupid sit-com for their evening's entertainment. Picturing his lover's cock, imagining its texture in his hand, Curt felt his own responding and he shifted his position on the couch, accommodating his erection.

In the past five years, no one of any consequence had tumbled to the fact that Curt and Roger might be more than "buddies," drawn together by their mutual affinity for arms and combat. Curt had not been sure, himself, until the afternoon their Black Hawk helicopter took a solid hit from Cuban ground fire at Calvigny Barracks, in Grenada. Out of twenty Rangers on the flight, there had been six uninjured when the chopper made its sloppy landing; one of those was subdivided by a spinning rotor blade and snipers nailed two more before they cleared the helipad. It had been Curt and Roger, on their own, who stormed the nest with M-16s and frag grenades to root the bastards out and win themselves a matching set of silver stars.

He still remembered standing in the ruins, smeared with war paint, smelling blood and cordite, an erection straining at the crotch of his fatigues. Before he had a chance to be embarrassed, Roger lent a hand and brought him home with short, swift strokes that left Curt trembling, weak inside. He wasted several days before he found the courage to return the favor. They had been together ever since.

Another year in service, keeping up the macho front and killing time with women who repulsed him, holding images of Roger in his mind to keep it up and make the bitches think that he was really fucking them. Three years since discharge, chasing wars and revolutions from Honduras to the Horn. Addicted to the blood and Roger's touch. Uncertain, sometimes, which was more important in his life.

The past ten months, on contract with the CIA, had been a cakewalk. Simple jobs in Hong Kong, Tokyo and Seoul, demanding patience more than courage. He had am-

ple time with Roger, but it had not been the same, somehow.
Without the added element of risk, the spice of danger, Curt
could feel their passion growing stale.

Six weeks. It didn't sound that long, but he wondered
whether they could last. If Roger had begun to check the
trades, it meant he must be feeling something, too. It was a
risky business, skipping out on contracts with the CIA, but if
he had to make a quick decision . . .

Richie Cunningham was standing up to Fonzie on the
tube and calling him "Me bucko." With the stupid laugh track
cackling, Curt nearly missed the whisper of the bedroom
door.

He turned to find their pigeon standing in the doorway,
watching. He was all in black, a change of clothes, and
carrying a jacket. Punching Roger's arm, Curt rose and
moved around the couch, remembering to keep it casual.

"You going somewhere?"

And the little guy was smiling as he answered.

"Out."

The baby-sitters glanced at one another, weighing his
remark.

"That isn't such a good idea," said Curt.

"Why not?"

"I don't think Mr. Ross would like it," Roger answered
for him, smirking.

"I won't tell if you don't."

"Sorry pal, that's not the way it works. We've got a job to
do, you know?"

"I understand," Kim told him, shifting one step closer to
the door and watching Curt begin to drift in that direction,
on an intercepting course. "I have responsibilities, myself."

"The way I heard it, you're retired."

Another step, and Roger shifted to his left, a classic
pincers.

"Circumstances change," Kim said. "I've caused some
problems here. I'd like to clean them up before I leave."

"We've got our orders. Sorry."

"So am I."

Kim dropped his pea coat in a chair. His watchdogs
registered the move and passed a silent signal. Both men had

their jackets open, making hardware more accessible, but neither made a move to draw his weapon. Rather, watching Kim ease toward the door, they struck defensive postures from tae kwon do. Kim saw Roger grinning; Curt was solemn as an undertaker.

"Think about it, man," his nearest adversary cautioned. "We don't get a dime for trashing you, okay? I'd like to keep this nice and peaceful."

"Perfect. All you have to do is step aside."

"No way."

"In that case . . ."

Kim heard Roger coming on his flank, a fairly smooth approach betrayed by eagerness for contact. Pivoting and crouching in a single move, relying on the fact that students of tae kwon do use their feet in roughly eighty-five percent of their attacks, he ducked beneath the snap-kick and responded with a squatting whip, *tan pien hsia shih*. His heel clipped Roger's ankle, sweeping it from under him, and dropped him on his back.

The big man saved it with a roll-out, using the momentum of his fall to gain some distance from his enemy and scramble to his feet, but Kim was on the move by then and carrying the war to Curt.

The scowling mercenary stood his ground, prepared for anything—except what happened next. Kim feinted left, then right, avoiding Curt's defensive kick, and struck him with a solid blow across the face. Curt staggered, anger bringing color to his cheeks that emphasized the pallid point of impact. With a snarl, he sprang at Kim, unleashing half a dozen kicks in swift succession.

Kim absorbed one with his shoulder, felt another graze his hip, but fury made his adversary careless, sapping some of his potential strength. Kim caught his ankle, twisted, and his own high kick struck Curt behind the ear as gravity and leverage brought him down. It should have rendered him unconscious, but the mercenary's head was hard and he had taken beatings in the past. Kim saw him struggling to rise, blood smeared across one cheek, before he turned to deal with Roger.

There were no more smiles as Roger circled, waiting for an opportunity to strike. Kim gave him one, relaxing his defenses, standing with his arms against his sides. The escort hesitated, smelling trouble, but his pride was smarting and he could not let it go. Another heartbeat and he lunged, a simple forward kick preceding the assault of flying fists.

Kim ducked and weaved, avoiding contact, drawing Roger forward. When a meaty fist snapped past his face, Kim took advantage of the opening and hammered Roger's ribs, evading swift retaliation with a bobbing backstep. Roger staggered, cursing, but he found his fighting stance again and pressed home the offensive.

Concentrating on the words of Master Rhee, Kim waited like a sacrificial victim, picturing the move before he made it. Roger might be mad enough to kill him, but he had not fallen back on firearms yet, and Kim was bent on wrapping up their contest soon, before it came to that.

His own kick seemed to come from nowhere, landing square in Roger's face. Kim felt the nose implode, incisors snapped off at the gum life, and his opposition vaulted backward, landing on a coffee table that collapsed beneath his weight.

He did not rise, and that left Curt to guard the door alone.

"You're history," the tall man rasped, and now he had one hand inside his jacket, digging for the gun.

Kim had no choice. He rushed the mercenary, veering to the left as Curt produced the automatic. He could see the muzzle rising, tracking toward his face, Curt's thumb upon the hammer.

It was going to be close.

He seized the tall man's wrist and twisted, putting all his weight behind a blow that snapped Curt's elbow. Shock preceded pain, and spastic fingers let the pistol fall between Kim's feet. Ignoring it, he cranked the broken arm around with force enough to separate Curt's shoulder, letting go in time to land a stunning blow behind the mercenary's ear.

Curt staggered, fell to hands and knees, the right arm buckling beneath his weight. Kim might have killed him then, in any one of half a dozen ways, but Curt had merely tried to earn his pay. His death would serve no purpose. It would be a waste.

He dropped the mercenary with a rabbit punch delivered

to the juncture of his skull and spine, deliberately stopping short of lethal force. Curt folded like a rag doll, broken arm tucked in against his side, and Kim retrieved his pistol from the floor. It was a Browning Hi-Power, chambered in 9mm parabellum, with thirteen rounds in the magazine and one in the chamber. He took an identical weapon from Roger, pulling the clip before leaving the gun on the couch.

Kim remembered that Curt had been driving the embassy car, parked downstairs in the self-service lot, and he rifled the fallen merc's pockets until he discovered the keys. It would not take him far, but the NSP still had his rental, and government wheels would provide him a running head start. He could ditch the car somewhere and pick up another before he got on with his task.

Slipping into the pea coat, securing the pistol and spare magazine in a pocket, he paused on the threshold, surveying the room. When his escorts revived, they would telephone Ross and report Kim's escape. If his luck held, he might have an hour before Ross was warned. After that...

The response would depend on available strength and the heat Ross was willing to bear. He would have other soldiers on tap, but it should take the strike force some time to respond. An alert to the NSP brass would save time, but it came with a price tag attached. Ross would have to confess his mistake, losing face in the process, and Kim thought the station chief's ego might prompt him to stick with the in-house approach. It was risky, a gamble, but Kim was committed, unable to fold.

He dismissed Curt and Roger as soon as the door closed behind him, intent on the problem of locating Jamie. He needed a handle, some clue to the motive behind her abduction, before he could finger a target. So far, he had nothing to go on, no way of determining who he must deal with.

Or who he must punish.

If Jamie was safe, Kim would do what he could to affect her release. If she wasn't...

Enough.

He would find her, one way or another. Defeatism poisoned the mind and the spirit, distorting one's vision and granting the enemy time to prepare.

Kim would have all the time he required for reflection

once Jamie was free. Until then, he was running on instinct, his mission defined by his enemies.

Search and destroy.

In private moments of reflection, Sun Min Wha looked back upon his life with feelings of accomplishment. He would be sixty-two years old next month, but if he never saw another birthday he would still have reason to be proud.

How many men could honestly proclaim themselves the architects and rulers of a modern empire?

He had traveled far, a child of peasant stock, to occupy a guarded palace in the suburbs east of Seoul. In 1934, when Sun Min Wha was eight years old, his parents had been executed by the Japanese as partisans. By age fourteen, their orphaned son was known as a resistance fighter in his own right, youthful innocence providing perfect cover as he moved among the hated occupation troops, selecting those he would destroy. He favored knives, and by the age of seventeen he had dispatched one soldier of Nippon for every year that he had been alive.

Arrested as a vagrant in the spring of 1944, Sun was deported to the homeland of his enemies, compelled to work with thousands of his kinsmen, freeing younger Japanese for combat with the British and Americans. He huddled in their stinking shelters during air raids, and by night he stalked their wives and daughters through the dark streets of Osaka, taking his revenge where he could find it, relishing their pain.

Repatriated after the surrender, Sun Min Wha discovered he had little taste for school or honest labor. He had grown up on the streets and they were still his home, a rough-and-tumble world where strength and courage were the minimum requirements for success. Possessed of both, by 1948 Sun was the ruling warlord of a fighting gang in Seoul, dubbed tosei-kai: the Voice of the East. Beginning as a rag-tag band of thieves and vandals, tosei-kai was driven under Sun Wha's leadership to earn a growing measure of respect in the Korean underworld. Its members fought for domination of illegal gambling, prostitution, and the entertainment industry in Seoul, establishing a foothold on the ground floor of the brand-new traffic in amphetamines.

Along the way, Sun Wha picked up a dozen felony arrests from 1949 to 1958, on charges of assault, extortion, robbery, attempted murder. Three convictions brought him little prison time; the warlord was already making friends with the Americans, the Syngman Rhee regime, and ranking officers of the Korean CIA. If payoffs were required, he made them gladly, adding healthy bonuses to demonstrate the measure of his friendship. As a patriot and anticommunist, Sun also served his friends in other ways, suppressing radical dissent and breaking strikes by force of arms, unleashing goon squads on command while the police took pains to look the other way.

By 1960, Sun could field 2,000 soldiers on an hour's notice, but his power was selectively applied. His ancient enemies, the Japanese, were allies now, and delegations from the Yakuza were welcomed lavishly in Seoul, cementing ties that kept the rich narcotics traffic flowing smoothly. In 1965, Sun was instrumental in promoting the Korea-Japan Normalization Treaty, opening new trade routes for his runners, recruiting thousands of prostitutes to service the influx of Japanese tourists. By 1970, when Sun acquired control of the main ferry line between Pusan and Shimanoseki, Japan—the shortest, most heavily traveled route between nations—his dominance of the Korean underworld was a recognized fact of life.

In politics, his touch was sometimes subtle, sometimes crude and brutal. Having failed to stem the tide of radical dissent in 1960, Sun threw his support behind the military coup in May of 1961. He was not strong enough to fight the army, but its leaders might be purchased one by one, and Sun was serious enough about his anticommunism to believe that martial law might save Korea from herself. American congressmen would be charged with accepting Korean bribes during 1977 and '78, but Sun's name did not appear in the indictments; he was perfectly content for Tongsun Park and others of his ilk to bear the heat alone.

There had been cautious speculation—never published—over Sun's involvement in the October 1979 assassination of President Park Chung Hee by KCIA leader Kim Jae Kyu, but nothing could be proven. If the warlord was involved—and even his most trusted confidantes could never say, with certainty—the sudden change of leadership had been a grievous error. Park's successor, Choi Kyu Hah, released imprisoned dissidents and thereby sparked a wave of rioting in Seoul that forced Choi's resignation during August 1980. His replacement, Chun Doo Wha, had learned to deal with rebels as a leader of the military Special Committee for National Security Measures, and imposition of martial law was Chun's first step toward the restoration of order in 1981.

Korea and the tosei-kai had prospered under Chun, and Sun Min Wha had shown his gratitude with generous political donations. On the side, his troops were still available whenever agents of the NSP were spread too thin in the eternal war against subversion.

Still, it should not be supposed that Sun stubbornly opposed change. He had been moved when spokesmen for the governments of North and South Korea issued declarations of their mutual intent to work toward peaceful reunification of the peninsula. If north and south could bind their wounds, if Sun Min Wha could trade in peace with members of the Yakuza, was anything impossible? Someday, somehow, he might be able to forgive the communists.

In fact, he had already made a start.

In secret, he had launched negotiations with an agent from the North, a man whose link with Sun Min Wha would certainly have raised some eyebrows at Remonclo. Not enough to threaten Sun's established empire—he had fought too long and paid too well for that—but there were members of the NSP who might have questioned Sun's commitment to the cause of national defense.

No matter. They would never know unless he chose to spread the news himself, and in the meantime, there was money to be made. New markets opening above the parallel. New sources of supply. It all came down to business in the end, and money made the world go 'round.

Before much longer, with the final obstacles removed, their bargain would be sealed.

He was distracted by the telephone, his train of thought disrupted. Sun made no attempt to answer it, although he could have reached the instrument without arising from the soft reclining chair he favored over sitting on the floor. It was a servant's job to screen his calls, no matter what the hour.

Moments passed before a muffled rapping on the study door distracted him again. Sun bade the servant enter, nodded as the caller was identified, and waited for the servant to depart before he lifted the receiver.

"Yes?"

Sun listened, frowning, for a minute and a half before he spoke.

"I understand. Yes. Thank-you."

Moments later, Sun picked up the telephone again and punched a number out from memory. His call was answered on the second ring.

"Hello?" A soft, familiar voice.

The frown was carving furrows in Sun's face.

"We have a problem."

Chapter 18

Kim dropped the stolen car at the Plaza Hotel, catching the subway from there to Seoul Station. He chose a rental agency, displayed a back-up set of false I.D., and fifteen minutes later he was rolling north on Taepyong-ro in a brand-new Honda sedan.

The Company would need some time to trace the car, since he had not employed the "Kim Chung" cover name, but it could still be done. The timing was a giveaway, and photographs would clinch it, but he only needed hours. Possibly a day.

If he could not find Jamie safe and sound within that time, Kim knew that it was hopeless. Nothing would remain, in that case, but revenge.

He drove direct to Jamie's building, circled twice around the block to check for watchers, and went on to find himself a parking space in back. It was a risk—he could be trapped inside the tiny lot reserved for visitors—but Kim preferred that risk to parking blocks away and walking back.

The lobby was deserted, and he rode the elevator up alone. On seven, he surveyed the empty corridor before he knelt to pick the lock on Jamie's door. The landlord might be charging extra on the basis of "security," but he had not invested any major sums in hardware. Thirty seconds with the pick, and Kim was safe inside.

The place still smelled of Jamie, but he caught another fragrance, too: an after-shave he did not recognize. Not fresh, but clinging to the air as if its user had a habit of applying far too much.

They would be gone by now, but Kim checked out the

several rooms to satisfy his paranoia. No one lurking in the
shower. No one in the closet. No one underneath the bed.
He did not check the balcony, since he would have to draw
the curtains back and thus betray his presence in the flat. If
anyone approached from that direction, they would make
sufficient noise to put him on alert.

Kim did not use the lights, relying on a pencil flash to
find his way around the small apartment. Jamie kept a tidy
house, as he recalled, but everything was perfect now,
confirming his immediate suspicion.

Ross had sanitized the flat, most probably within an hour
of the time that Jamie disappeared. His clean-up crew had no
doubt been extremely thorough, bagging each and every item
that pertained—however indirectly—to the Company. Kim
knew before he looked that nothing would be left behind in
terms of notes or correspondence, personal I.D., or home-
work from the office. Address books and shopping lists would
go, along with any but the most innocuous of periodicals and
publications. Kim saw empty spaces in the little bookcase,
where selected novels had been lifted from the shelves. In
Jamie's bathroom, they had stripped the medicine cabinet,
leaving only her toothbrush behind.

Kim drifted through the empty rooms, disgusted, checking
out the freezer and the toilet tank from force of habit,
knowing in advance that he would come up empty. Jamie left
her secrets at the office, and it was ridiculous for him to look
for notes of any kind. If Ross had laid out the scenario
correctly, her abductors had been waiting in the underground
garage. She never got this far, before they had her in the bag.

The bedroom bore her scent most strongly, overpowering
the tacky after-shave. He *felt* her there, remembering, and
almost blamed himself for bringing this upon her.

Almost.

But the game had not been his selection; he had not
devised the rules. Kim was not even certain that he knew the
players yet, but he would have to learn their names and
quickly. He was running out of time.

Ross would have dusted everything for fingerprints, of
course, before he had the place swept clean. That meant the
chief of station knew about his night with Jamie. Some of it,
at least. He would surmise the rest and draw his own

conclusions, writing off her loss to negligence in his report. A handler losing her perspective, spending leisure time with agents in her charge and taking them to bed. When Ross had finished polishing the innuendos, Langley would assume that Jamie brought destruction on herself. It was a simple out that left Ross free and clear. Again.

Kim made a silent promise to himself. If there was time, if he survived that long, he would devise a way to pay Ross back. For Bangkok. And for Jamie.

He had not begun to think in terms of leaving Seoul, returning to the States. Once Curt and Roger pulled themselves together, raising the alarm, the Company's reaction would be by-the-book. A watch on railroad stations and the airport, even though Ross knew that he would not be leaving town. A doctored auto theft report to the authorities, thereby recruiting several thousand extra men to seek the missing car. Covertly, Ross would have his people scouring hotels and rental agencies, attempting to determine whether Kim had found himself a bolt-hole.

In a pinch, Ross might invite the NSP to join the hunt, but Kim still thought that it would be a last resort. They might have other ways of finding out, however, and he knew that he would have to stay alert, trust no one but himself.

And Syngman Chiul.

The dealer had no part in Kim's pursuit of Jamie, but he would not turn a friend away. If anyone could listen to the streets, decipher what had happened here and why, that man was Syngman Chiul. He also carried certain hardware items Kim might need to prosecute his search.

The game was heating up, and he would have to be prepared for fighting fire with fire. The Browning automatic in his pocket was a start, but Ross could field an army and he had to count on stiff resistance from the men who had abducted Jamie. Either way, a pistol and an extra magazine would barely get him started.

Chiul would have the answers and the hardware, but his shop would not be open at this hour of the night. No matter. As the dealer had been doing business in the same location over twenty years, so he had occupied the same address. Kim knew the number, but he double-checked his memory against the listing in a phone book Ross's cleanup crew had left behind.

It would not do to place the call from Jamie's flat. If Ross was on his toes, he would have tapped the line to trace in-coming calls, and Kim did not intend to tip his hand just yet. Downstairs, he scanned the parking lot before he made his move, still half expecting footsteps or a bullet from the darkness as he slid behind the Honda's steering wheel. Surviving, he was curious to know why Ross had missed so obvious a move as staking out the flat.

Perhaps, because he thought that Kim was safely tucked in bed and would be airborne in the morning, back to San Francisco and a life that smacked of self-indulgence. Ross was banking on a free hand in negotiating Jamie's freedom or allowing her to die.

With any luck, it might be hours yet before he knew that Kim had changed the rules.

It was unusual for Syngman Chiul to get a call at home. He had installed a telephone in 1963, for the convenience of his "special" customers, but in the actual event they used it rarely. In the past twelve months, he had received three calls, including two wrong numbers.

It was an event, therefore, when Chiul picked up the phone at half-past nine on Thursday night and recognized the caller's voice.

"Is this line clean?"

"Of course."

"I need some information. And some merchandise."

"How long?"

"I can be there in fifteen minutes."

"Make it twenty-five."

It was within Chiul's power to refuse, but such a course of action never crossed his mind. He knew that Kim Sunim would take precautions to avoid a tail, and he would not have called unless the line at his end was secure. Whatever peril Kim might bring upon himself, he still took pains to keep his contacts safe.

This time, however, might be different.

Syngman Chiul was fairly certain what Kim wanted in the line of information and equipment. He was looking for the woman, and he thought—correctly—that he might need arms to win her back. In fact, Chiul would have given odds that she was dead by now, but he could not be certain. Knowing Kim, it would have made no difference to the end result.

Chiul did not know the woman's whereabouts, although he had a fair idea of who had taken her, and why. The information would be little use to Kim, unless he had his heart set on a ritual of self-destruction, but the odds would not intimidate him, either. He would try because he felt it was his duty. He would waste his life because he had no hope of coming out alive.

Chiul's *other* information might yet make a difference. It had come into his hands by sheer coincidence—or karma—and he could not keep it to himself. The timing was significant, perhaps a sign.

He had intended to dispatch a messenger tomorrow and discretely summon Kim, but it would not be necessary now. The fates had lent a hand, confirming Chiul's belief in destiny. Despite the things that he had witnessed in his life, the crimes in which he played the role of an accessory, Chiul stubbornly maintained his personal belief in Good and Evil. Neither side could triumph on its own, but with a helping hand from dedicated men . . .

Before he left the house, Chiul called his eldest son aside and issued terse instructions, waiting while they were repeated back to him, verbatim. It was a familiar ritual, though practiced less compulsively in recent years. The young man knew his part and memorized instructions automatically, unquestioning. He was his father's son.

Chiul did not own a car, though he had access to a wide variety of vehicles at need. Tonight, he used the Vespa scooter, covering the seven blocks between his residence and Sinmum-ro in something under fifteen minutes. Time to spare, and he would have a sampling of merchandise prepared when Kim arrived.

He disconnected the alarm and entered through the rear, disarming secondary systems as he sorted through his inventory. The alarm would startle burglars and alert police if he were being robbed; the backup systems would destroy his "special" inventory—and the prowlers—if selected items were disturbed. Chiul was prepared to lose the shop and blame it on a gas leak, rather than submit to lengthy questioning about the presence of assorted military weapons and explosives on the premises.

He kept no more than samples in the shop, prepared to deal in quantity upon demand, but samples would be adequate for Kim Sunim. One man was not an army, after all; regardless of his best intentions, he could only do so much.

Chiul left the storeroom, moving through the darkened shop to reach the entrance facing Sinmum-ro. He slipped the latch, deactivated the alarm, turned back to face a stranger's smile.

"Good evening."

Oozing courtesy, a slender man around Kim's height, but somewhat older. Syngman Chiul suppressed an urge to break and run.

"You are . . . ?"

"A friend, perhaps."

"How may I help you."

Smiling, moving closer with a serpent's grace.

"I hope that we can help each other."

Sinmum-ro is not a street for tourists. Most shops close there by nightfall and the prostitutes work elsewhere, trolling the expensive restaurants and great hotels. Approaching ten o'clock on Thursday night, the sidewalks were deserted and the traffic had begun to fade.

Kim knew that Syngman Chiul would not betray him, but he drove around the block from force of habit, checking doorways, alleys, stairwells. He had not been followed on the crosstown drive, but there was still a chance—however slim— that someone might have tapped Chiul's line without the dealer's knowledge. Anything was possible, and Kim could not afford to let his guard down for an instant.

Before he left the car, he double-checked the Browning automatic, making sure he had a live round in the firing chamber. Heavy in his pocket, it provided him a measure of security against the enemies who recognized no code of honor. Syngman Chiul could fit him out with other weapons, but he also needed names, a place to start.

The dealer was his last, best hope.

He tried the door and found it open, stepped inside. A pale light spilling from the storeroom framed the register, a portion of the showcase where selected jewelry items were displayed, and left the rest of the establishment in darkness. Piles of luggage, racks of cast-off clothing, crates of sundry merchandise surrounded Kim with shadow-shapes that made him think of sleeping dragons. One false step, and they might wake to eat him up alive.

A human silhouette this time, the office doorway, and he tensed involuntarily before he recognized the form of Syngman Chiul. The dealer beckoned Kim to follow him and Kim obeyed, one hand inside the weighted pocket of his pea coat. It was warm inside the shop, and still he felt a chill.

Shadows filled the storeroom, crowding close around the pool of light provided by a single desk lamp. Chiul invited Kim to sit, and he obliged.

"The merchandise?"

"A mini-Uzi, if you have it. Otherwise, an Ingram—any caliber—with extra magazines and a suppressor."

"It will have to be the Ingram, I'm afraid. I'm having trouble with the Uzis, lately."

"Fine."

Chiul spent a moment on the combination lock securing a stand-up metal cabinet. It was hardly maximum security, but Kim saw blocks of putty-like *plastique* attached inside the door when it was opened, primed and ready to disintegrate the cache—along with any would-be thief who tripped the hidden trigger. Automatic rifles, submachine guns and assorted other weapons filled the cabinet, long guns standing upright, smaller weapons dangling from hooks or stacked on shelves.

The dealer's inventory was impressive, but Kim realized that these were only samples, kept on hand for show and the occasional emergency. Bulk orders would require more time to fill, and weapons would not pass directly through the pawn shop.

Chiul returned and placed two items on the desk. "MAC-10," he said. "Nine-millimeter."

Kim picked up the stubby Ingram, worked its bolt and dry-fired several times, letting himself get the feel of the weapon. Measuring eleven inches overall, it was the second smallest submachine gun in the world. With a thirty-round magazine in place, it weighed less than nine pounds, firing at a cyclic rate of nearly 1,200 rounds per minute. The suppressor added twelve more inches to the package and reduced the Ingram's chatter to a sound like ripping canvas.

"Magazines?"

"How many do you have?"

Chiul counted swiftly. "Twelve."

"All loaded?"

"Certainly."

"I'll take them all."

It might be overkill, but at the Ingram's normal rate of fire, one magazine would empty in a second and a half. He might not stop an army with 360 rounds, but at the very least he ought to capture their attention.

Chiul produced a leather satchel, like an outsized doctor's bag, and stowed the magazines with the suppressor. Kim placed the Ingram in on top of everything and snapped the satchel shut.

"You mentioned information?"

"I am looking for a woman."

"Yes."

Despite himself, Kim felt a ripple of surprise. "You know?"

"Why else would you be here?"

"I mean to see her safely home, if possible."

"At any cost?"

The silence hung between them, giving Chiul his answer. There was something—sadness?—in the dealer's face as he leaned back, retreating from the pool of light.

"I listen to the street," Chiul said. "Sometimes she tells me lies."

"At least a lie breaks silence."

"You are searching for a man of power. He has many friends in the republic, in Japan . . . some say in the United States. An army guards his interests, but they wear no uniforms."

"His name?"

"Think twice, my friend."

"I'm waiting."

Slowly, with reluctance. "Sun Min Wha."

Kim's face remained impassive, but his mind was racing,

churning through the substance of his recent conversation with the late Chin Sung. He pictured Holland, lying dead on Eulji-ro, the image fading into one of Jamie. Still alive? He could not say.

"Why should the woman interest such a man?"

"A piece of merchandise for bargaining, perhaps. In case his friends prove faithless, or his enemies grow too aggressive."

"Friends within the Company?"

Chiul shrugged. "Who knows? They come to me for help, from time to time, but they do not reciprocate. If there are vermin in the house . . ."

He left the comment hanging, but his point was made. Chin Sung had spoken of a syndicate connection with the NSP, implying some equivalent relationship between the Company and Sun Min Wha. It would not be the first time elements within the CIA had bargained with the underworld for politics or profit—and it might explain the breaking of his cover—but he still resisted blind acceptance of the notion, looking cautiously for holes.

"How much?" he said at last. "For everything?"

"Forty thousand *won* for this." He nudged the leather satchel with his toe. "The information may be worthless. Take it as a gift."

Kim counted out the money, adding several thousand *won* despite Chiul's protest. Picking up the heavy satchel, he retreated through the darkened shop, Chiul watching from his office door.

"Take every care," the dealer called, as Kim stood on the threshold. "Nothing may be as it seems."

Kim nodded, closed the door behind him, moving toward his rental car. Chiul's final warning was superfluous; he was inured to deceit, betrayal, unexpected challenges. If he was looking at a war, so be it. If he had to die for honor's sake, it was a price he could afford.

"An adequate performance."

Dae Li Chong, emerging from the shadows, favored Syngman Chiul with an ironic smile. He slipped the automatic pistol back into its holster, moving closer.

"I could feel your urge to warn him. You were wise to hold your tongue."

"He lives to fight another day," the dealer said.

"My fondest wish. Unfortunately, you will not be there to see it."

Chiul did not appear surprised by the announcement of his death. Instead, he gave Dae Chong a look of absolute contempt. "You are a traitor to your race," he spat.

"But ever loyal to myself. One final bit of information . . ."

"Nothing more."

"You underestimate my powers of persuasion."

With a snarl, the dealer bolted, breaking for the door and Sunmim-ro beyond. Chong closed the gap between them easily and tripped him up, the old man plowing headlong through a standing rack of suits and dresses.

Scrambling to his feet, Chiul spun to face the enemy.

"It will be easier if you cooperate."

"Then do your worst."

Before the words had left his lips, Chiul turned and picked a wrench up from an open box of tools, and pitched it overhand at Dae Li Chong. His target sidestepped, grinning as the wrench spun past his face.

"Too slow, old man."

Chiul rummaged in the box, produced a hammer, hanging on to it this time, as he began to circle Chong.

"A contest?" Smiling ruefully, the younger man refused to take up a defensive posture. "I'm afraid I really don't have time for games."

"Then die!"

Chiul's rush was perfectly predictable, and Dae Li Chong was ready when it came. He kept his eye upon the hammer, stepping out of range and darting back again to take the dealer's wrist before he could attempt a second blow. The bones felt fragile in his hand as pressure was applied—a simple twist, some basic leverage—and Chiul was on his knees, the hammer long forgotten, mangled arm clutched tight against his chest.

"Stand up, old man."

The dealer staggered to his feet.

"How do you like the game so far?"

"Is this your worst?"

"Not half."

He stepped in close to launch the kick, remembering to

pull its killing force before his heel made contact with the dealer's face. Chiul vaulted backward, shattering a glass display case, rolling in the sharp debris and picking up a myriad of superficial cuts before he got his bearings, struggled free.

The old man's face was pale and streaked with blood. Inside his chest, Dae Chong imagined he could hear the frail heart working overtime. If he did not extract the necessary answers soon...

"Enough of games," he snapped. "I need one final piece of information. You will give it to me, and your generosity will find its own reward in swift release. If you resist me further..."

He did not elaborate the threat. Anticipation was the most persuasive form of mental torture.

"I have not yet seen your worst," the dealer said, a failing whisper.

"As you wish."

Chiul tried to flinch away, but he did not possess the necessary speed. Dae Chong applied a snap-kick, shattering the old man's kneecap, dropping him as if a snare had yanked him off his feet. The dealer did not scream until his other knee was twisted, broken like a turkey drumstick.

Chong knelt down beside him, careful to remain outside the old man's reach. "Must we continue?"

Chiul struggled to respond, chest heaving as he tried to catch his breath. Another moment, and his one good hand was beckoning Dae Chong a little closer. Cautiously, the younger man leaned forward—and received a wad of spittle on his cheek.

He left it there, a smile appearing in defiance of the crimson rage that filled his brain.

"You win," he said.

And showed his prey the very worst that he could do.

Chapter 19

Driving south on Taepyong-ro, Kim turned off near the southside railroad yards and found himself an isolated stretch of road near Hyochang Stadium. He trusted Syngman Chiul, but this was business and his life was riding on the line. He had to check the Ingram out and get its feel, make sure the piece would function on command.

The narrow road was dark, deserted, warehouses pressing close to the tracks on one side, with empty waste ground on the other. It was perfect.

Kim removed the Ingram MAC-10 from its satchel, reaching back inside to find the "silencer." The submachine gun's muzzle had been threaded to facilitate attachment of the tube, a bonus that eliminated any need for alterations, and he coupled them with practiced movements to produce a weapon roughly two feet long. A magazine inserted in the pistol grip completed the ensemble, and he drew the bolt back, chambering a parabellum round.

His chosen target was a garbage dumpster, squatting in the shadow of a nearby warehouse. Moving into range, he held the Ingram in his right hand, gripped the long suppressor in his left. He did not bother with the weapon's folding stock or try to aim it like a rifle; with the Ingram's rate of fire, precision work was difficult, if not impossible. The weapon was designed for sweeping snipers out of occupied apartments and the like, in situations where firepower took precedence over pinpoint accuracy.

Kim had qualified with Ingrams at the Farm, but that was long ago, and he had never used one on a mission. The

refresher course would take perhaps ten seconds, if he daw-
dled, and the extra time might save his life.

He scanned the empty street once more and took his
stance, the Ingram level at his waist. The first squeeze fired
off half his magazine, the fat suppressor stuttering as fifteen
holes were drilled across the dumpster, left to right. Before
the magazine was empty, Kim had found the touch required
for shorter bursts, and he was reasonably certain that he
would not rattle off a magazine each time he squeezed the
trigger.

Back inside his car, Kim stripped the empty clip and
snapped a fresh one into place, unscrewing the suppressor as
he stowed his hardware in the bag. The piece would serve his
purposes, if he was called upon to wage a full-scale war, but
Kim still hoped that he could find another way around his
problem. Fireworks would increase the risk to Jamie, and his
goal was still her rescue, not her execution.

Rolling through Yeouido, past the KBS building and the
Korean National Assembly, Kim was conscious of the affluence around him. Stately homes were planted on this island
in the middle of the Han, and he was an intruder, plotting to
disrupt the measured pace of life among the rich and power-
ful. Whatever happened next, the fat cats of Yeouido would
be traumatized, but Kim was not concerned about their
peace of mind.

The island's northern tip was subdivided into rambling
estates, the more expensive boasting river frontage and a
view of Seoul across the water. Sun Min Wha owned one of
these, the great house crouching on a fifteen-acre tract with
trees and sculpted shrubbery, the full perimeter surrounded
by an eight-foot wrought-iron fence.

Kim doused his lights and followed the perimeter as far
as possible, examining the fence and grounds within before
the narrow track dead-ended into trees. He doubled back and
found a place to park the Honda out of sight, concealed from
prying eyes.

He would be forced to scale the fence and cross two
hundred yards of wooded ground to reach Sun's house, but
the alternative—a more direct approach, past sentries on the
gate—was tantamount to suicide. If Sun Min Wha had not
installed the kind of infrared or seismic gear employed at

Langley, Kim would have a decent chance of getting to the house alive.

He paused outside the fence and listened to the night, alert to any sounds of gunmen working the perimeter. If there were dogs on duty, they had managed to ignore him so far, and Kim knew that he would have to take the chance.

It was a calculated gamble, dropping in on Sun this way, but Kim had weighed the risks ahead of time. He knew that Jamie probably would not be held on Sun's estate, but once he had the information on her whereabouts, once he had neutralized the threat of premature alerts, he would be free to take the final step and set her free. If Jamie *was* inside, so much the better; he could liberate her and extract his pound of flesh from Sun Min Wha together, in a single stroke.

But first, he had to reach the house.

Alive.

The Ingram had a sling of military webbing, which he slipped around his neck, the extra magazines divided up between his pockets, tucked inside his belt. He tossed a fallen branch against the fence, confirming that the bars were not electrified, then scrambled nimbly over, touching down inside.

From this point on, he would be vulnerable to attack from every side, cut off from swift retreat. The Ingram hung beneath his arm, accessible at need, but Kim was hoping to avoid that kind of confrontation with the enemy. A running battle on the grounds would only warn his prey, allowing Sun to hide himself or flee. If Kim could not invade the house by stealth, his weapons would be useless.

Scudding clouds obscured a quarter moon as Kim began to make his way across the grounds. The midnight shadows offered cover as he slipped between the trees, a gliding wraith dressed all in black, alert to any sign of opposition.

Kim was halfway to the house before he met the sentry. Huddled in the shadow of a sculpted hedge, he heard the lookout coming, footsteps whispering across the lawn. With luck, he might lie still and go unnoticed, but he did not fancy leaving gunmen at his back. If he could take the sentry down without commotion and conceal his body well enough to pass

a cursory inspection, Kim would buy himself some time and
cheap insurance.

He would have to kill, but he had come prepared.

The sentry was a small man, even by Korean standards,
thin and wiry. Kim remained immobile as the enemy passed
by, emerging from his cover with the silence of a shadow,
falling into step behind. He matched the gunner's pace and
spent a moment planning out his move before he struck.

It was essential that the kill be swift and silent, cutting
short the struggle that would give his enemy a chance to call
for help. A simple thing, but not so simply executed with a
moving target.

Springing forward, Kim brought one foot down behind
the sentry's knee, the left leg buckling beneath his weight.
One hand clasped tight across the target's nose and mouth,
he used the other as a fulcrum, twisting sharply, separating
vertebrae and finishing the movement with a muffled *crack*.

The sentry trembled for a moment, stiffened, and became a dead weight in his arms. Kim grasped his ankles,
dragged the body under cover of a hedge and left it there, in
shadow. A determined search with lights would turn the body
up, of course, but he did not intend to linger on the grounds
that long. Once Kim had found his way inside the house, he
hoped his business could be finished quickly, with a minimum of fuss.

And if he failed?

In that case, it would scarcely matter when they found
the sentry. Kim would be long dead, and nothing else would
matter, anyway.

The final fifty yards were open ground, without a trace of
cover in between the tree line and the house. He scanned for
lookouts, left and right, without detecting anyone. There was
a chance they might be hidden, even watching from the
house, but up to now security had not been tight. Sun Wha
had obviously grown secure in his position, trusting half a
dozen sentries and his own fierce reputation to protect his
privacy.

So much the better.

Kim braced himself, the Ingram clutched beneath his
arm. Once he began the move, abandoned cover, there could
be no turning back. If he was spotted on the way, he would

be forced to kill as many of the enemy as possible before they cut him down, and there would be no hope for Jamie.

None.

He left the shelter of the tree line, running in a crouch, expecting lights and claxons any moment, with converging streams of automatic fire. He was a helpless insect in the open, scuttling for safety, with a giant boot descending from the heavens, bound to crush him if he faltered on the way. Another moment, just a few more yards, and then—

He reached the house, collapsing in its shadow as the moon broke through a veil of clouds. No lights or sirens, nothing to betray the presence of an enemy. If they were watching, they had missed their chance to kill him easily, without a fight.

Kim spent a moment on himself, recuperating from his dash across the open lawn. When he felt steady on his feet again, he circled toward the rear, encroaching on a patio where workmen had installed a hot tub and a barbecue constructed out of bricks, Sun Wha's concessions to the Western style of luxury. Kim noted that the barbecue was spotless, and he wondered whether Sun had ever cared enough to try it out.

The sliding plate glass doors were locked, but they were not secure. Kim used the short blade of a pocket knife to trip the latch, his finger on the Ingram's trigger as he slid the door back far enough to step inside. The instant chill of air-conditioning raised goose bumps underneath the perspiration on his skin.

The sliding doors gave access to a semi-formal dining room, deserted now and dark. Kim made his way across the room by moonlight, listening with one ear pressed against the door before he pulled it open wide enough to scrutinize the corridor beyond.

A pudgy thug was seated on the floor directly opposite, his back against the wall. Kim had his finger on the Ingram's trigger when he realized the man was dead already, mottled color in his face betraying signs of swift asphyxiation. Crouching at his side, Kim slipped a hand beneath the gunner's chin and felt the crumpled larynx with his fingertips.

One down, and someone had been there ahead of him. Kim felt a tension now that was completely unrelated to the risk of meeting Sun Wha's soldiers in a free-for-all. His intuition told him he had come too late for Sun—for Jamie— but he had to see it through, in any case.

Upstairs, two more. One lay spread-eagle in the middle of the corridor, eyes wide and gaping at the ceiling. In the middle of his forehead, leaking crimson, was a wound too small for any bullet known to man. Kim recognized the trademark of a *shuriken*, the razor-pointed throwing stars employed by many martial artists and a few assassins. Impact on the forehead was enough to stun, but it was rarely fatal; other means would be employed at leisure, once the target had been incapacitated.

Further down, the dead man's partner lay against the wall, his knees drawn up in something like a fetal curl. This one was breathing, but he would not last much longer. Broken ribs had pierced his lungs, the evidence apparent in a bloody froth around his nose and mouth, while crush-ing blows had cracked his skull and left him bleeding from the ears. Oblivion was all that he could hope for in his final moments, and from what Kim saw, the man was there already.

Kim moved along the hallway, checking out each room in turn, secure in the knowledge that Sun's bodyguards had been disposed of. There was still a risk that someone from the yard might duck inside and find the bodies, but his first concern was finding Sun Min Wha, alive or otherwise.

The study was a shambles. Sun had not gone quietly, but neither had he reached the gun that would have automatical-ly alerted those outside. The gangster's home had been constructed with an emphasis on privacy and it had served him well; his outer guards had never realized their boss was being murdered one flight up, above the patio.

Seoul's leading pimp and pusher was a short man, broad across the chest and stout around the middle, bullet-headed with his stringy hair gone thin on top. Kim vaguely recog-nized the face, from ancient photos in the press, but it was different now. Sun's jaw was twisted, canted to one side, the mottled bruising on his cheek mute evidence to the destruc-tive impact of a roundhouse kick. One eye was swollen shut, and blood was crusted on his flattened nostrils.

None of that had killed Sun Wha. The fatal blow had

been delivered as he lay stretched out across his desk, legs dangling, like a sacrificial victim on an altar. Someone strong enough and skilled enough to do it right the first time had administered a killing blow above the sternum, freezing up Sun's heartbeat in a single stroke. The rumpled shirt and pulpy indentation of his chest spoke clearly of the executioner's technique.

No answers here, but Kim already knew that he would not find Jamie on the premises. He doubted, now, that Sun Min Wha had even been involved in her abduction. That meant Syngman Chiul had lied, or he had been deceived himself. But why? Deceived by whom?

Kim had been aimed at Sun Min Wha the way a weapon might be aimed. The way his handlers in the Company had used him, years ago. He had been primed to kill the mobster, but another hand had done his work ahead of him. It made no sense, unless . . .

The sirens, fast approaching, told Kim everything he had to know about the setup. Sun and his attendants had been executed, using martial arts, and now a martial artist was about to be arrested at the scene. It was a simple-minded frame, but executed with precision. It could still succeed, if Kim remained on hand to welcome the police.

His plans did not include a murder charge, and he was halfway down the stairs when one of Sun Wha's lookouts tumbled through the door, all breathless, babbling about police outside. It took the sentry several heartbeats to discover he was talking to a stranger. Worse, the stranger had a weapon in his hand.

"Don't try it."

Digging underneath his jacket for a hidden pistol, he ignored Kim's warning. It was suicide, but he was young and reckless, almost fast enough to make it work.

Almost.

The Ingram stuttered, spewing death and raking Kim's opponent with a dozen parabellum rounds. The impact lifted him completely off his feet and hurled him backward, hammering his skull against the plaster wall. Wet traces of himself were left behind as gravity took over and he slithered to the floor.

Kim left the same way he had entered, through the

dining room, across the patio. Outside, the sirens sounded close enough to touch. He knew they must be at the gate, demanding entry. In another moment they would be inside, lights flashing as they sped along the curving drive.

He struck off for the trees, was nearly there when one of Sun Wha's roving sentries suddenly emerged and barked a challenge. This one had his gun in hand, but something made him hesitate and it was all the edge Kim needed. Firing from a range of thirty feet, he saw the gunner's dress shirt ripple, crimson flowers opening their shiny petals as he fell.

Too late. The pistol in his adversary's hand went off, a reflex action, with the muzzle canted skyward. Wasted effort, but the shot would bring pursuers down upon him in another moment, leaving Kim without a moment left to spare.

He cleared the tree line, crashing through the smaller undergrowth, ignoring thorny limbs that snagged his clothes and tried to bring him down. Another one-hundred fifty yards to reach the fence, if no one intercepted him along the way. It would be simple, then, to scale the fence, retrieve his car and put Sun's house of death behind him.

Simple, right.

Unless police were watching the perimeter. Unless they had already found his car and staked it out.

The trees were thicker now, and while Kim thought he heard the sounds of a pursuit, he could not accurately judge the distance. Never mind. They were *behind* him. It would have to do.

He reached the fence and scrambled over, winded by his run. Outside, he dropped and landed on all fours, alert to any sign of lookouts posted on the road, relieved to find himself alone. Kim had a fleeting glimpse of flashlights, stabbing through the trees, as he retreated to his car.

Kim left his lights off as he shifted through the Honda's gears, accelerating through the darkness. He was half a mile from Sun Wha's house and running free before he turned the headlights on. If anyone was chasing him, he should have picked them out by then.

It had been close, but he had managed to evade the trap. Sun Wha had paid the tab for sins beyond remembering, and half a dozen of his goons had also been removed from circulation. At another time, he might have called the evening a success, but now it tasted bitterly of failure.

He was still no closer to delivery of Jamie from her captors than he had been when he spoke to Syngman Chiul. Kim frowned, his face forbidding in the dashboard's feeble light.

He did not wish to think the dealer had betrayed him. Such behavior called for punishment, and Syngman Chiul had been a friend for fifteen years. Kim would take no pleasure in his death, but neither could betrayal be allowed to pass.

He checked the dashboard clock. Too late to call on Chiul at home, but in the morning they would have another talk. If he did not receive a satisfactory response...

Kim tried the Honda's radio, found something mindless, waiting for the sounds to carry him away. His thoughts were dark and troubled as he made his way across Yeouido, toward Weonhyo Bridge.

Park Han Yee was furious, and Ross could hardly blame him. Hanging on the line, he listened dutifully while Yee reminded him that Kim had been in custody, secure, before Ross bailed him out. If not for meddling by the CIA, there would have been no problem. Kim was CIA's responsibility; the NSP could hardly be expected to repair the damage now.

Ross made the necessary sounds of understanding, taking full responsibility for the mistake. There would be time enough to crucify his chosen escorts later, when the medics finished patching up their injuries. For now, if Ross was going to obtain the help he needed, he would have to play the humble idiot and eat his share of crow.

The NSP colonel spent a few more moments dwelling on the lunacy of choosing feebleminded amateurs to escort Kim Sunim. Ross ground his teeth and took it, livid, drawing satisfaction from the knowledge that his own subordinates would be available for payback in due course. As Yee ran out of steam, Ross worked his way around to offering the proposition.

Yee feigned surprise, then anger, finally amusement. When he finished gloating, the Korean made a counteroffer. Ross accepted, grudgingly, and so their pact was sealed.

"We have a deal?"

"A deal," Yee said, and beat him to the punch by hanging up.

"Smart bastard."

Calling on the NSP for help had been humiliating—and it had been unavoidable. Ross had no more than half a dozen contract agents at his beck and call, with two of them already stricken off the list by Kim Sunim. A dragnet needed troops, and he could not afford to wait for Langley to approve the reinforcements. Ramsey would be asking pointed questions soon enough, but Ross could salvage something from the situation, yet, if he put Kim away before the deputy director started making waves.

Eliminating Kim would solve a number of his problems—or, at least, prevent them from becoming more severe. While Kim was running free in Seoul, he stood a chance of making matters worse, disrupting all that Ross had worked for in his tenure as the station chief. There were connections to be guarded, operations to be salvaged.

Kim would have to die.

The choice had been an easy one to make, but Ross had been in no position to effect the tag, with four young mercenaries on his payroll. He could always pull his scattering of agents from the field, but that would cause more problems than it solved, and none of them were manhunters. Killers such as Kim took special handling, and Park Han Yee had bagged him once already, thereby proving he was equal to the task.

Ross had another reason for involving NSP, distinct and separate from his own shorthanded forces. If the South Koreans dealt with Kim, Ross could preserve deniability. He had already rescued Kim, attempted to provide him with an escort out of Seoul, but Kim had gone berserk and trashed his baby-sitters, placed himself in mortal jeopardy. No matter how he tried, Ross could not save the wild card from himself.

It was a perfect cover. Ramsey would attempt to break him down, of course, but Ross had learned to stand his ground since Bangkok. This time, all he had to do was tell the plain, unvarnished truth . . . omitting any portions of the tale that did not suit his purposes.

But in the meantime, there was work to do. He still had people on the street, and there was still an outside chance that one of them might make the tag before Yee's troops could run Kim down. In that case, Kim would simply disappear, affording Ross the opportunity to cancel his agreement with the NSP.

He punched a private number up and heard it answered on the second ring.

"We're on," he told the other party, smiling. "Shoot on sight."

Chapter 20

The safe house had not come with a garage, and Kim drove two blocks farther on to find a parking space, for safety's sake. If Ross or anybody else ran down the rental agency within the next few hours, they would have to sweep the neighborhood at large before they found him, thereby granting Kim a momentary edge.

He needed rest and time to put his thoughts in order, sorting out the scrambled pieces of a puzzle that eluded him. The urgency of finding Jamie drove him on, but now exhaustion was competing strongly, and he had nowhere to turn.

Sun Wha's assassination had been obviously timed and executed as a setup. Members of the Yakuza might carry swords on ceremonial occasions, posing as a kind of modern samurai, but they would not rely on martial arts techniques to ice a ranking mobster and his bodyguards. A raid on Sun's estate would normally have taken on the aspect of a military operation, but the goal this time was clearly different. Sun's demise was secondary in importance to the fingering of a selected suspect.

Knowing he had been selected as the scapegoat, Kim was still no closer to an answer on the basic questions. Why? By whom?

It had required a healthy dose of nerve—and skill—to enter Sun's estate and penetrate the house, drop three of his gorillas with a *shuriken* and empty hands before proceeding to the main event, then exit past the sentries guarding the perimeter. Whoever took the trouble to conceive that plan and execute it flawlessly was obviously serious in their desire to see Kim locked away or killed.

He ran the mental list of enemies again, beginning with the NSP and working through the local hoodlums he had managed to offend while working for the Company in Seoul. The NSP had means and opportunity, but they were known to favor the direct approach. A sniper's bullet or a bomb attached to the ignition of his rental car would be their style, without the intricate concoction of a frame.

Besides, he thought, if Chin Sung's information was correct, the NSP would sacrifice a major source of revenue by liquidating Sun. Remonclo needed no excuse to hunt Kim down. They made the rules, and they would not have thrown away a major contact for the benefit of some scenario designed to fool the press.

Sun's nominal competitors, the lesser pimps and pushers, made an even more unlikely cast of suspects. Living in the great man's shadow, feeding off his crumbs, they doubtless wished him dead, but wishing for a miracle and bringing down the wrath of God upon one's head through overt action were entirely different things. It would be suicide for any single operator—or for any combination of them—to attack Sun Wha directly. While a few might have the self-destructive nerve, none had the strength to pull it off or the finesse to execute the contract with an eye toward framing Kim Sunim. A few might know that he was back in Seoul, but none would recognize his link with Jamie Constable or make the necessary jump to using her as bait.

He had stripped the Ingram for a cleaning and was swabbing out the barrel when he heard a noise outside. Too late for neighbors to be stirring, but he recognized the sound of footsteps on the stairs, ascending.

They were on the landing now, outside his door. He grimaced at the Ingram's disassembled parts and took the Browning automatic with him as he crossed the living room. Without the benefit of a suppressor, any fireworks would be sure to rouse the neighborhood and bring police, but he was running out of options.

Peering through a peephole in the door, he saw a young Korean on his doorstep. Shifting left to right and back again, he used the fish-eye lens to search the landing and the upper stairs for reinforcements. They might still be hiding, farther down, but Kim was cornered either way, and he was curious to know how anyone had traced him.

Opening the door a crack, he left the chain in place, his automatic aimed directly through the flimsy panel at the young man's heart. Whatever happened next, Kim would not go alone.

"Who are you?"

"Wongsin Chiul. My father bids me speak with Kim Su Chung."

Another trick? There was a family resemblance, certainly, but it was not conclusive. Syngman Chiul must know, by now, that Kim had wriggled through the net at Sun's estate. If he was working for the enemy—whoever they might be—it would be easier for him to give the NSP or the police Kim's address than to send his son. Assuming that it *was* his son.

Kim weighed the odds and knew he had to take the chance.

"Come in."

He slipped the chain, then locked the door and fastened it again behind his uninvited guest. He did not bother trying to conceal the pistol.

"You are Kim Su Chung?"

"I am. The message?"

"I must first be certain."

"As must I."

They swapped I.D.s, Kim covering the young man as he dipped a hand inside his jacket, coming out with nothing more offensive than a billfold. It was possible, in theory, that the unknown enemy had manufactured an identity for Wongsin Chiul, but Kim knew he would have to draw the line on paranoia somewhere. This would be as good a place as any.

Handing back the boy's I.D., Kim pocketed the California driver's license that had been provided for him by the Company. He said, "I meant to call upon your father in the morning."

"That will not be possible."

Kim raised an eyebrow, waiting for an explanation, realizing it would do no good to ask.

"My father has been killed," the young man said. "I am instructed to deliver certain information, as an act of friendship."

"Tell me how he died."

"There was a struggle at the shop, perhaps a prowler. He was badly beaten. There were injuries... inside."

"A robbery, perhaps?"

Kim knew the answer going in, but still he had to ask.

The young man shrugged. "My brothers are examining the inventory. It appears that nothing has been taken."

As assassination, then, to silence Syngman Chiul. Despite a sense of loss, Kim felt himself relax a bit, inside. It helped to know the dealer had not turned against him at the end.

"The message?"

"I was asked to warn you that the North Korean has another name. The man you know as Dae Li Chong was once called Tonsung Yun. Does this have meaning for you?"

"Yes, it does."

Kim palmed a wad of currency, uncounted, but the dealer's son ignored it. He was studying the disassembled Ingram and its extra magazines.

"The man who killed my father... will you punish him?"

"I will."

He waved the cash away. "It is enough."

Kim saw him to the door and watched the young man disappear before he set the chain, returning to the dining table and the Ingram. Working automatically, he had the weapon reassembled in a moment, even though his thoughts were elsewhere.

Tonsung Yun.

The name had drawn him miles and years away, to Songgwang Sa and childhood. He could see his enemy before him, but the face was still an adolescent's. Kim found that he could not imagine Tonsung Yun as an adult.

The jigsaw pieces tumbled into place now, of their own volition. Yun—as Dae Li Chong—had found a way of playing both ends off against the middle. As a North Korean agent, he could offer valuable services to Chin Kyu Sung; an opportunist, totally devoid of scruples, he could likewise deal with Sun Min Wha—or cut him off, at need, to serve some higher purpose.

Tonsung Yun undoubtedly possessed the nerve and skill to murder Sun, the devious intelligence required to set Kim up and let him take the fall. Reese Holland's death would merely be coincidental, the removal of a minor irritation, which, ironically and unexpectedly, had brought Kim back to Seoul.

The traitor's motive was a riddle. Did he lust for money? Power? The respect of those he considered his inferiors? Or was he merely evil, running true to character as always?

In the last analysis, it made no difference. Kim had spent the better part of adolescence hating Tonsung Yun and wishing for the opportunity to pay him back for his betrayal of the brotherhood at Songgwang Sa. Kim's journey to America, the war and years of service to the Company had dampened the desire for vengeance, pushed it back into his dark subconscious, but the simple mention of a name had stripped those years away.

If he could only find the bastard now, repay his treachery in blood . . .

The tab had grown since Kim was driven from the monastery by a lie. He owed a debt to Master Rhee, to Holland, and to Jamie Constable. His enemy had shamed the first and killed the second, but there still might be a chance to save the third.

If not, at least he could devote himself to tracking Yun, however long it took. The exercise would give him purpose, something that his life had lacked for . . . what? How long? Since Vietnam?

No matter.

He was focused now, on Jamie and the enemy. If he could not save one, he would destroy the other with his dying breath.

It was his karma.

Jamie strained against her bonds and cursed the darkness. It had frightened her at first, when she was giddy from the chloroform and thought she might be blind, but she was angry now.

And frightened, yes. That, too.

She had awakened on the floor, with musty-smelling carpet pressed against her face. It took a moment to discover that the darkness was a physical phenomenon, outside herself, but Jamie's eyes had found a razor line of light beneath a door, perhaps ten feet away. Perspective was a tricky thing in darkness, but the distance did not matter. She was satisfied to know that she could see.

Correction: Could have seen.

The tiny slit of light permitted her to count the bristles on the carpet near the door, and after half an hour Jamie thought she saw the outline of her own bare legs. Her skirt had ridden up around her hips, and Jamie felt the carpet rough against her thigh, but when she kicked her feet—a test—the ghost-legs seemed to move in opposite directions, taunting her with their refusal to conform.

Disheartened, Jamie closed her useless eyes and made a private inventory, starting from the top. The skin felt tight and raw around her nose and mouth, a minor burn resulting from the chloroform, but she could breathe and whisper to herself without obstruction, meaning she had not been gagged. Bad news. Her captors felt secure enough to let her scream, if she was so inclined, which told her screaming was a waste of time.

She noted minor bruises on her arms, no doubt from grappling with her abductors, and her wrists were tightly bound. She could not reach the knots, but from its oily feel against her skin she finally decided that the rope was made of nylon.

Jamie's back and shoulders ached from lying on the floor, immobile. Time was meaningless, but muscle cramps and creaky joints assured her she had held the same position for a period of hours. Christ, could it be *days*?

She struggled to recall the information her instructors had dispensed on tranquilizers at the Farm. Unless her memory was failing, chloroform had limited effectiveness, depending on the dose. Repeated applications were required to put a subject down for days on end, and Jamie had no fragmentary memories of fighting back to consciousness and being gassed again.

A period of hours, then, and much of that spent lying on her side exactly where she was. And what had happened in the meantime?

Jamie went on with her inventory. She was fully clothed, the disarrangement of her skirt no doubt attributable to the fact that she was carried from her captors' car. She felt a momentary tremor of anxiety and pressed her thighs together, instantly confirming that her panties were in place. She had not been molested, then, for what it might be worth.

Her keepers might intend to kill her, but at least they seemed to have no interest in her body.

Wonderful.

Her ankles were secured with rope, and while her stockings insulated her from contact with the bindings, she assumed the nylon rope had been employed again. Her shoes were missing, and a cool draft played across the soles of Jamie's feet.

She found the wall behind her, tracing angles with her feet until she understood that she was lying in a corner. If the room had any furnishings, they were beyond her reach, invisible in darkness. From the claustrophobic air, her distance from the door, she judged her cell to be a smallish room, perhaps no larger than a walk-in closet.

Jamie had a sudden thought of spiders, spinning in the darkness, and she shrugged it off before her mind could take the brush of hair against her cheek and turn it into creeping legs. Her danger lay outside the door, and she would have to keep her wits about her if she wanted to survive.

The spiders vanished as she thought of Kim. Would he be looking for her? Did he even know that she was missing? Would he care? If Ross commanded him to concentrate on Chin, ignoring her disappearance, would he follow orders?

Jamie tried to straighten up, her muscles groaning, and she found that it was difficult without the use of hands or feet. She made it on her third attempt, convulsive movements planting pins and needles in her spine. She wriggled backward, feeling for the corner with her fingertips and shoulders, wedging in to keep herself from tipping either way.

She still felt dizzy, from the chloroform and the exertion, but she drove the shadows back. Above all else, she needed clarity of mind to solve her problem and devise a method of escape. If she sat back to wait for Ross or Kim, they might not come in time.

They might not come at all.

She started with a list of suspects and potential motives. In the latter area, she had no shortage: she was an American, a government employee, and an agent of the CIA. The latter fact, presumably, was not a topic of discussion with the

general public, but her function would be recognized by
agents of the NSP and KGB, selected North Koreans, plus a
scattering of politicians and police in Seoul.

A random terrorist abduction might have targeted the
embassy or picked her off the street, but Jamie's captors had
been waiting at her home address, inside the subterranean
garage. That indicated research, the selection of a special
target, and she did not like the sound of that at all.

Things could be worse, she told herself. If they had
meant to kill her, she would certainly be dead by now.
Abduction meant she had some value to her captors, either
for the information in her mind or as a game piece, to be
traded off for something else.

Her mind retreated to the Farm again, the simulated
"enemy interrogation" she had undergone in training. Her
instructors did their best to pose as foreign agents, shouting,
flashing bright lights in her face and muttering about the
possibility of torture, but the exercise had never come within
a country mile of realism. From the outset, Jamie knew that
she would not be beaten, raped, or wired for voltage. It was
all a game.

Reality was something else, entirely. In a darkened room
where strangers weren't afraid to let you scream.

A shadow passed outside the door, and Jamie flinched
involuntarily. The carpet muffled footsteps and the shadow
moved on past her cell without a second thought.

Had they forgotten her already? Was it worse to be
remembered?

Jamie concentrated on the notion of a trade, refusing to
consider the varieties of torture commonly attributed to
Soviet and North Korean agents. An exchange meant freedom, if the Company agreed—but what would they be asked
to trade?

She racked her brain for recent seizures or defections,
and she came up empty. Seoul had problems with the North,
persistent difficulties with the student radicals, but all the
great arrests were made in Europe. If the Company had
anyone in custody, it would be news to Jamie. And her
captors would be out of luck in setting up a trade. The White
House had been standing firm on its refusal to negotiate for

Middle Eastern hostages; one agent, more or less, would scarcely make a ripple in the pond of Southeast Asia.

It was hopeless, then, unless she managed to escape. If nothing else, negotiations with the Company could buy some time, permit her to devise a plan. The odds were stacked against her, but she had to try.

She thought of Kim again, encouraged by the knowledge that his mission would proceed without her.

"Watch yourself," she whispered in the silent dark. "And give the bastards one for me."

For Tonsung Yun, the past three days had been a time of bitter memories and sweet anticipation. Word of Kim Sunim's arrival had initially produced a tremor of uneasiness, before Yun recognized his golden opportunity and started laying plans.

How often is a man in middle age permitted to review his childhood, cleaning up mistakes, correcting oversights? It would be madness to ignore the possibilities.

Yun's memories of Kim had galled him through a lifetime otherwise distinguished by success. Across the years, he had been haunted by the image of a timeless face, forever frozen in the mold of adolescence, dark eyes staring through him to discover the corruption in his soul. He should have closed those eyes forever when he had the chance, at Songgwang Sa, instead of framing Kim and driving him away, but there had been no second chance.

Until today.

He had attempted to keep track of Kim, without success. The boy had gone to Seoul, directly from the monastery, but his trail was lost from there until the early 1970s, when Tonsung Yun discovered that his enemy was working for the CIA in Asia. Yun enjoyed the irony that placed them, once again, in opposition, but he had no opportunity to lay a snare for Kim. The Company had kept his target moving, and a premature retirement cheated Yun of satisfaction at the last.

That should have been the end, but Fate had intervened. A nosy agent, sniffing after Chin Kyu Sung, had come to Yun's attention ten days earlier. Yun took the wet work on himself, as much from boredom as a wish to see the job done properly. From out of nowhere, Kim was suddenly recalled to pick up where the dead man's trail had ended.

Fate was sometimes kind.

Yun did not know or care about Kim's personal connection with the dead man. He was willing to accept a second chance on any terms, regardless of the cost or risks involved. The woman was his bait, and Yun was confident that she would be enough.

Once Kim knew his opponent, nothing short of death would keep him from their final confrontation. Tonsung Yun decided they were much alike in that respect.

Kim hated him because he had betrayed the nest of pious fools at Songgwang Sa. It was a small thing, given all that he had done in later years, but it would be sufficient.

Small things, nurtured over time, became the stuff of nightmares.

Yun's betrayal of the brotherhood had started out with money, changing rapidly to something else. The boy had seen an opportunity to exercise his power, teach the moral idiots a lesson they would not forget. Their gods could not protect them from a simple child, and all their meditation finally produced was callused knees. Their vaunted wisdom was as nothing when arrayed against his will.

The old man, Master Rhee, had taught him well . . . but only to a point. The introduction to t'ai chi had been a crucial turning point for Tonsung Yun, permitting him to maximize the hidden strength within himself, but he had cared no more for the religious teachings of the order than he did for childhood fairy tales. A man possessed of power, who refused to use it out of reverence for weaker life forms, was himself a waste of life.

Kim had become the master's pet, his timid style epitomizing everything that Yun despised about the brotherhood. Only through his skill in martial arts had he revealed a trace of strength, and Yun had been superior in that regard as well, until the master favored Kim with personal instruction, giving him a treacherous advantage. Slowly, Kim had risen to become Yun's equal, finally surpassing him with tricks the old man saved for "special" students.

Yun remembered how the others crowed with laughter on the day Kim knocked him down, and he could feel the anger burning in his cheeks. A quarter-century had not been long enough to damp the fire.

But Tonsung Yun had learned a few tricks of his own. He had disposed of Kim and then destroyed the brotherhood itself. His triumph was complete . . . except that Kim Sunim was still alive.

So far.

From Songgwang Sa, he went to Seoul, but Kim had slipped beyond his reach. Yun quickly tired of living on the streets, accepting minor jobs for the Korean CIA, and he began to look around for something more. Across the parallel, an alternate regime dismissed the hoary trappings of religion, bargaining from military strength. Its leaders seemed to have no scruples. They were men he could admire.

Yun traveled north and settled in Pyongyang. The streets were no more comfortable there, but now he had a goal, a master plan. He brought himself to the attention of authorities, initially denouncing malcontents and later taking on the kind of muscle jobs he had performed for members of the other side, in Seoul. The communists were quick to recognize his talent, and they seemed to value his initiative—within the limits of the party line.

A year of service to the Northern government, and he had been selected as a special candidate for special training at Patrice Lumumba Friendship University in Moscow. Founded by Nikita Khruschev in 1960 to train Third World "intelligentsia cadres," the university is staffed and supervised by agents of the KGB, devoted to the political education of foreign radicals. Lumumba U's most infamous alumnus is Venezuela's Ilyich Ramirez Sanchez—a.k.a. "Carlos the Jackal"—but countless revolutionaries have been trained and then sent home to countries as diverse as Chile and Iran, Angola and Morocco, Mozambique and Mexico, the Arab states and South America.

For three years, Tonsung Yun immersed himself in Russian language classes and the Marxist scriptures, dutifully absorbing dogma, killing time off-campus with the girls who found his Asian background fascinating and a little dangerous. He screwed them all, the Lenin groupies and his dour instructors, telling each precisely what they longed to hear and scoring well across the board. His final year in Moscow had been more instructive, with subversive training at the Lenin Institute, preparing Yun for his return to South Korea.

He came home as Dae Li Chong, a North Korean agent rich in cash and contacts. Wooing dissidents in Seoul had been a relatively simple job; their various complaints about the system had been drowned by water cannons, while America continued massive foreign aid to the establishment. Chin Sung and others like him were becoming desperate for money, leadership, a shoulder they could cry on. Yun—as Dae Li Chong—provided all of that, and more.

Along the way, he also made a profit and established secret contacts with "the enemy." In truth, he held no grudge against the NSP, the homegrown Yakuza, or any of their kind. He recognized an opportunist when he saw one, and he trusted them to act from positive self-interest every time. It was a system he could live with, prosper with, and his "superiors" above the parallel need never know that he had gone in business for himself.

The meddling CIA had changed all that—or, more precisely, one of its employees had. The agent code-named Domino had been a bulldog, stubbornly ignoring all diversions once he smelled corruption, following the trail to its inevitable end. If Yun had known the agent's death would bring him Kim Sunim, he would have acted sooner, risking anything and everything to see his enemy once more.

He had Kim now, and this time there would be no mercy. Kim was vulnerable, primed to self-destruct.

The woman was his weakness.

She would be his death.

Chapter 21

Her hands were going numb, and Jamie shifted her position slightly, careful not to topple over on her side once more. She flexed her fingers, straining with her wrists in an attempt to loosen up her bonds, but it was hopeless.

Jamie thought that she could stand, with difficulty, propped against the wall . . . and then, what? If she tried to hop in the direction of the door, she would be guaranteed to lose her balance, plunging face-first to the floor. There seemed to be no obstacles—she had observed that much by shifting her position carefully and noting that the narrow slit of light beneath the door remained unbroken—but she could not travel with her ankles bound. The thought of plummeting through darkness made her toes curl, and she shuddered, cursing silently at her timidity.

It was not just the prospect of a broken nose, she told herself. Suppose she reached the door and managed not to knock herself unconscious in the process. How would she manipulate the latch? And if she found it locked, her effort wasted, would she simply hop back to her corner? Could she even find it in the dark?

Goddamn it! Why had she allowed herself to be surprised?

Instructors at the Farm had stressed preparedness, the need to be alert at every moment on a foreign station, even in the States. She had believed their line at first and spent her first few weeks in Seoul convinced that she was being followed by the North Koreans, possibly the KGB, but Ross had finally put her mind at ease.

"Forget about that cloak-and-dagger stuff," he had advised her. "Langley gives us covers, but the opposition knows

250

exactly who we are. You're not a threat to them, per se, because you're not conducting operations in the field. They think of us—and no offense—as secretaries. Picking off a station chief or his exec would raise a shit storm, Jamie. It's a luxury they can't afford."

So much for theory.

Someone obviously did not know the rules, or else they had decided it was time to change the nature of the game. They were prepared to risk the shit storm if they got results, but *what* results? Again, she drew a blank, the darkness smothering her efforts at cohesive thought. If only . . .

Footsteps.

Jamie stiffened as the narrow slit of light was blotted out. This time, the footsteps did not pass her by. There was a jingling of keys, the sound of tumblers falling, and she smiled. It would have been a waste. The door *was* locked.

At first, the light was painful, nearly blinding Jamie. She made out a silhouette, average height, slender. A man. Jamie winced as he reached for the light switch and lit up her prison.

A closet, with shelves on the two facing walls where her skull might have cracked them in falling. The lock on the door was a new one, with no inside latch. Whatever its designer had in mind, the closet had been simply altered to become a cell.

Her jailer was a slim Korean, somewhere in the range of thirty-five to forty-five, his age obscured by race and physical conditioning. His slacks and jacket had a tailored look; his pastel shirt was open at the neck.

"Who are you?" Jamie was embarrassed by the croaking sound that emanated from her throat.

He smiled and crouched before her, working on her ankle bonds, releasing them in something like a second and a half. Some kind of slip knot, she decided. If her hands were free . . .

She thought of kicking him—the smooth face made a most inviting target—but impulsive violence now, before she knew the nature of the game, would gain her nothing. It might even get her killed.

His eyes were dangerous. They mocked the artificial smile, and Jamie knew that she was dealing with a killer. This one would be capable of anything, a man without remorse or conscience. A machine.

Like Kim?

She winced at the comparison and knew that she was wrong. There *was* a difference. There had to be.

"Stand up."

He slid a hand beneath her arm, the fingers grazing Jamie's breast, and helped her rise. Her feet were tingling with the swift return of circulation and she tottered, nearly falling, but the Asian held her upright. He was average height for a Korean, slightly taller than his prisoner. Around Kim's size, she thought.

"This way."

He led her from the closet, killed the light and closed the door behind her, saw her seated in a straight-backed chair. Her wrists, still bound behind her back, prevented Jamie from relaxing, and she sat at stiff attention, studying her captor.

Try again, she thought.

"Who are you?"

"Langley would not recognize my name."

There was a trace of accent in his speech, but in comparison with most Koreans speaking English, he could pass for Harvard. Dangerous *and* educated. Things were looking worse, and she was getting nowhere fast.

"In answer to your next two questions," he advised her, "you are still in Seoul. A safe house. I require your temporary presence for completion of a game, which has become . . . involved."

"Why me?"

"Because of who and what you are."

"I'm just—"

"The U.S. cultural attache's personal assistant. Certainly." His smile cut through the flimsy lie. "I hope we can dispose of pretense for the moment. It would make things so much easier, for all concerned."

"I don't know what you want from me, but I can tell you that the embassy won't bargain."

"I desire no bargain with your embassy. A brief intrusion on your time, a journey. It is nothing in the cosmic scheme of things."

A journey. Jamie felt her skin begin to crawl. Pyongyang? Moscow? Were they desperate enough for information to abduct a member of the staff and take her out of the country? On its face, the notion seemed preposterous, unless her captor represented private interests—terrorists or some such— who were not intimidated by the threat of diplomatic protest or covert retaliation.

What would a Korean terrorist demand from the United States? Continued military presence was a sore point with the North, as well as certain ultra-nationalists in the South. There might be something in the field of foreign aid, or . . .

Jamie stopped herself, aware that she was veering off the track. The risk involved in her abduction, its specific timing, spoke of more immediate concerns. Her captors had a mission to perform—or one to foil. Specifically, a mission where her presence as a hostage might be useful.

Kim.

The Asian studied her with all the concentration of a psychic, trying to invade her thoughts. It was ridiculous, but Jamie tried to make her mind a blank, imagining a snowstorm in Vermont. A blizzard. Icy crystals forming on her brain.

He seemed to understand what she was doing, and his smile grew wider, still without a trace of warmth. "You are concerned about interrogation." It was not a question. "Please, dismiss the prospect from your mind. I have no need of information."

"What, then?"

"You will be my bait," he said. "A lure to entice my prey. An offer he cannot refuse. But first, we ought to let him know that you are safe and sound."

The last thing Kim anticipated was a phone call. He had never used the safe house telephone, and he did not expect to. Paying extra for the service was a safety measure, taken as a backup for emergencies. Aside from Syngman Chiul, Kim's landlord was the only person left in Seoul who had the number.

Therefore, when the telephone began to ring at midnight, he was startled. Rising from his chair, he almost took the Ingram with him, but he reconsidered and replaced it on the dining table. No one could attack him through the telephone, unless...

He visualized the enemy nearby, perhaps downstairs. A member of the team assigned to call and see if he was in before they made their move. A signal flashed to others, waiting just below, when he responded. Thunder on the stairs as half a dozen gunmen rushed his door and crashed through, firing.

Kim allowed himself a smile. The whole scenario was something lifted from *Miami Vice*. If he was truly facing Tongsun Yun, the killing team would be a last resort. His enemy would opt for a more personal approach, an intimate reunion to resolve their differences and finally, irrevocably choose the better man.

He lifted the receiver on the seventh ring and listened, silent as a dead man.

"Kim."

He knew the voice immediately, would have recognized it anywhere. Despite the years, the changes every man experiences as he moves toward middle age, he would have known *that* voice in any circumstances.

"What, no greeting for a long lost friend?"

"Not long or lost enough."

"He speaks! We're making progress."

"You have made a serious mistake."

"I recognized my error when you left the monastery. There is time, I think, to make amends."

"I want the woman."

"Yes, I thought you might."

"If you have harmed her..."

"Threats? I'm disappointed, Kim. What's happened to your fabled self-control?"

"The woman," he repeated, knuckles blanching as he clenched the telephone receiver.

"She is safe, for now. She may remain so, if you do precisely as I say."

"You did not have to kill the dealer."

"He resisted me. Resistance must be punished. Have you learned so little since I saw you last?"

"Enough."

"Perhaps. The woman's life is in your hands."

Kim understood the basic nature of the game before he spoke. "I'm listening."

"I could destroy you with another phone call," Yun informed him. "Your employers have released a kill-on-sight directive; likewise with the NSP. Your hours are numbered, Kim."

"We still have time."

"I hope so. It would be a shame to waste our golden opportunity."

He thought of Jamie, wondered if she was, in fact, alive.

"I need a guarantee."

"You have my word."

Kim laughed out loud. "I'm interested in something more substantial."

"Very well." If Tonsung Yun was irritated, he concealed it perfectly. "A moment."

Muffled sounds, as Yun laid down the telephone receiver. Moments later he was back, his voice still distant as he issued orders.

"Speak."

"Hello?"

He heard the fear in Jamie's voice and knew that she was covering. "Are you all right?"

"Oh, Kim." She hesitated, drawing breath. "Don't listen to him! Don't do anything! He wants—"

A wet, explosive sound of impact cleared the line. Yun's voice replaced the woman, and he was not even breathing hard from his exertion.

"These Americans are so excitable. No discipline."

Kim swallowed bitter rage. "I've dealt with worse."

"Perhaps the quality arouses you? I must admit, I sometimes find their women . . . stimulating."

Kim refused to take the bait. His stomach churned, but there was only caution in his voice. "Your offer?"

"A reunion. I will bring the woman; you may come alone."

Of course, he had no choice. As Yun had noted, it was open season now, in Seoul. A call to Ross, regardless of the message, would be tantamount to suicide.

"The time and place?"

His enemy pretended to consider options. "Songgwang Sa, this afternoon. Shall we say one o'clock?"

"I'll be there."

"On your own."

"Of course."

"If you should change your mind . . ."

"I said—"

The scream cut through his soul and left a ragged scar.

"—I'll be there."

"Excellent. We understand each other, then."

"We always have."

He lowered the receiver on a humming dial tone, stricken with a sudden urge to hurl the instrument across the room. It would accomplish nothing, and he let it rest, internalizing rage, preserving it for later, when it might be useful.

Jamie was the bait, Yun's ace, though he must realize that Kim would readily agree to meet him anywhere, at any time, without coercion. Nothing short of death itself would halt that confrontation, but his enemy had felt the need for some insurance. Just in case.

Kim knew the game and realized that bait, by definition, was expendable. If Jamie lived to see the monastery one more time, it would be Tonsung Yun's decision. He would spare her for a reason—probably to watch Kim die—but he could not afford to let her walk away. A living witness might spell trouble for a man whose life was founded on deception, false identities and double-crosses.

Mentally, he braced himself for Jamie's death, imagining the worst that Yun could do. If he arrived at Songgwang Sa to find the woman dead, there must be no time spared for mourning, nothing in the way of hesitation that would give his enemy an edge. He would rely on instinct and the training he received in childhood, honed by grim experience as an adult.

And this time, given half a chance, he was prepared to kill.

Kim hesitated, breathing deeply, waiting for the anger to subside. He needed clarity of mind, above all else, and there were preparations to be made. He would be facing Yun alone, but he would not be blinded and disarmed by rage.

This time, the game would be for life and death, instead

of praise from Master Rhee. Kim wondered if the stakes had always been the same, concealed from childish eyes but lurking in the background, waiting. Had the *go-jang* recognized the conflict set in motion more than thirty years before, as two boys grappled in the dust?

No matter.

He would stand and fight, this time, as an adult. If he was destined to survive, so be it. If his karma called for sacrifice, there still might be a chance for Kim to drop his enemy, save Jamie or avenge her murder.

Perfectly at peace, Kim went to pack his satchel for the drive to Songgwang Sa.

The conversation had been entertaining, to a point. It would have been more pleasant if his enemy had groveled, pleaded for the woman's life, but he could not expect such histrionics from a man like Kim Sunim. Like Tonsung Yun, Kim was an expert at concealing his emotions, channeling his pain and anger into more constructive—or *de*structive—outlets.

Kim would go to Songgwang Sa because he had no choice. He cared about the woman—or enough, at any rate, to ask about her on the telephone—but Yun did not believe that she would be his driving motivation. Kim would go to Songgwang Sa because he hated Tonsung Yun and meant to kill him. Enemies they might have been, but they were much alike in that respect.

The difference lay in honor, or in Kim's naive perception of the concept. He would come alone, because a promise had been made, and more importantly because he did not wish to share the kill. He might be armed, of course, but it would make no difference in the end. His bid to save the woman would be futile. He would pay the price of failure with his life.

Tonsung Yun had early learned the truth: that "honor" and its correspondent—"duty"—were devised as tools for subjugating foolish men, compelling them to follow self-destructive paths on the behalf of others. "Honor" called for sacrifice in hopeless causes, sublimation of desires, a life cut short by martyrdom. If he had been a man of "honor," Tonsung Yun would never have abducted Jamie Constable, but he was a devotee of the practical and recognized the

value of a lure. There was an outside chance that Kim might
hesitate to act on hate alone, and so the woman had been
necessary to his plan.

Yun studied her, a cringing, frightened animal, and
pondered whether he should let her live a little longer. It
would be expedient to kill her now, eliminating any threat of
accidents in transit and avoiding any risk, however marginal,
that she might somehow rise to Kim's defense at Songgwang
Sa. She would be safer dead, and yet . . .

Kim's tender feelings for the woman were a weakness
that would get him killed. Her presence at the monastery was
desirable, but it was not an absolute necessity. Yun's final
choice was based on personal, subjective reasoning, and
while he recognized the fact it made no difference to his
ultimate decision.

He would spare the woman's life until tomorrow, when
she might be useful as a tool in the annihilation of his enemy.
Kim's nerve was strong, his concentration nearly perfect, but
the woman held a measure of his interest now. A threat to her
well-being might distract him, giving Yun the necessary edge
to make his kill.

The seeds were sown, already. Kim would try to put his
mind at rest, but he could not escape subconscious fears
about the woman and her treatment in captivity. He would
imagine torments Yun could never think of on his own,
inflicting them upon the woman in his mind's eye, wasting
precious energy and concentration on the game. With any
luck, the cycle of his *chi* would be disrupted, with a
corresponding loss of strength.

It was a start, but Yun had studied human nature in his
dealings with the sycophants and zealots of Korea, Moscow,
other places. Fear and grief could shake a man, but they
could also *motivate* him, touching off displays of fury that
were almost supernatural. If Kim believed the woman had
been sacrificed, regardless of his pain, he would redouble
efforts to destroy his enemy. He must be kept in doubt, then
shaken by her presence at the killing ground, his concentration forcibly divided as he tried to cope with both her danger
and his own.

It was a plan, the best available, and all it needed were a
few refinements. Studying the woman's face, her body, Tonsung

Yun could feel himself responding, slow arousal burning in his loins.

"Your friend is very much concerned about your health."

"He'll kill you."

"He will try. I'm trusting you to slow him down."

"You must be joking."

"Not at all." Yun's smile was sinister, rapacious. "If, as I suspect, he is infatuated, his concern for you will slow him down, disrupt his concentration. I will kill him while he ponders ways to save your life."

"You bastard!"

"As a point of fact, my parents were legitimately married, but the matter is irrelevant to our discussion. You will join me, shortly, on the drive to Songgwang Sa."

"I've been there."

"This time shall be different, I assure you. I've arranged for you to witness an event, which I must say, with all due modesty, should be unique in living memory."

"A duel?" She sneered at him, disdainfully.

"Of sorts. A contest, if you will, between old adversaries. Karma shall decide the outcome, with a little help from you."

A light of recognition dawned behind her eyes, some memory recalled.

"*You* sold the monastery out. When was it? Twenty years ago?"

"Nineteen."

His smile remained in place. If Kim had taken her to Songgwang Sa, it stood to reason that he would have bared his soul, relating ancient history as he remembered the events. More proof of his attraction to the woman, weakness that could be exploited on the killing field.

"You were a traitor, even then."

"A realist," he countered, "choosing sides before the choice was forced upon me. In the end, I chose myself. It's a decision I can live with."

"If you live."

"I've managed nicely, up to now. Kim represents a challenge, nothing more. With your assistance, he will be eliminated."

"Go to hell. I'd rather die."

"In time. But first, you have a function to perform."

"I won't do anything to help you."

"You already have. By warning Kim to stay away, you have ensured that he will follow my instructions. He will try to save your life, and thereby sacrifice his own."

Bright tears of anger glistened on her cheeks. "And if he doesn't?"

"Have no fear. Your knight in shining armor will perform on cue. It should be quite a spectacle."

"Why are you doing this?"

The question took Yun by surprise.

"Because I must."

"You have no right!"

She twisted in her chair, revealing just a flash of creamy thigh. Without a second thought, Yun knew precisely what was needed to destroy Kim's concentration, subjugate his will to anger. There was ample time, before they had to leave for Songgwang Sa.

She saw it in his eyes and bolted from her seat, but Tonsung Yun was faster, stretching out his leg to bring her down. Unable to protect herself, she cracked her head against the floor, the carpet sparing her from a concussion. Even so, the impact left her dazed; she offered no resistance as he rolled her over, pushed her skirt above her waist, and tore her flimsy undergarments off.

Yun wedged himself between her thighs, blood singing as he entered her without preliminaries. Jamie's body struggled to expel him, but resistance only heightened his excitement, driving him toward climax. Ripping at her blouse and bra, he freed one breast, his mouth descending on the nipple with a starving predator's finesse. She found her voice, a ragged cry of pain, and that was all it took to put him over, muscles going rigid as he spilled his semen deep inside.

He left her on the floor and stood to rearrange his clothing, breathing heavily. The woman held no interest for him now, but he might change his mind again once they had reached their destination. It amused him to believe that he could hurt Kim in absentia, foul his nest in such a way that he would never feel another urge to touch the woman.

Not that he would have the chance.

He reached the telephone in three long strides and dialed a private number, heard it answered on the second ring. He spoke a name and waited, briefly, for his contact to respond.

"Get ready," he commanded. "Bring two others you can trust. We leave within the hour."

He hung up before the orders were acknowledged. There would be no argument, no effort to evade responsibility. He owned these men, and they would answer when he called.

They would be hours early for the rendezvous, as Tonsung Yun intended. Ample time for preparation at the scene . . . and, possibly, some more diversion with the woman. If she failed to please him, he might give her to the others as incentive on the eve of combat. All the better to humiliate his enemy and prod Kim into ill-considered action.

This time, only one of them would walk away from Songgwang Sa, and it would not be Kim Sunim.

The dark man swore it to himself, and guaranteed the promise with his life.

Chapter 22

Kim drove south through early morning darkness, watching pale dawn break behind the rugged mountains on his right. He made good time, all things considered, and had reached Suncheon by half-past nine.

The enemy would be ahead of him, he had no doubt of that, but it could not be helped. Reactive measures presupposed surrender of initiative, but there were ways that he could change the game plan, even now. It would be risky, even suicidal, but he had no options left. If Jamie was alive, he had to help her; if she wasn't, then he had a double score to settle.

It occurred to Kim that Tonsung Yun might have surveillance mounted in Suncheon, but it would be precisely that: surveillance. Yun would not deny himself the pleasure of a final confrontation by dispatching goons to murder Kim in town. It would defeat the purpose of his exercise, deprive him of his sport.

Kim's empty stomach had been rumbling for miles. He found an open restaurant and ordered simple fare: a steaming bowl of rice, some fish, and strong, dark tea. He ate enough to keep his body quiet, pushing back the rest before he started feeling over-stuffed and sluggish. Through it all, his thoughts were never far from Jamie and his strategy for bringing her alive from Songgwang Sa.

Kim knew he might already be too late, but it was not a thought he cared to dwell on. Jamie had already served her purpose as a lure, and her performance on the telephone might easily have been the last time he would ever hear her voice. It was a bitter thought, but Kim had come to terms with loss and loneliness in childhood, subsequently watching other friends cut down in Vietnam and in the service of the Company. He would not write her off until he knew for certain she was dead. His mourning, if it came to that, would be expressed in terms that Tonsung Yun could understand.

From his position near the window, Kim surveyed the street outside. If he was being watched, the lookouts had themselves well-hidden. They would probably report to Yun by radio, and final preparations would be made for his arrival at the monastery. They would be expecting him to turn up early. They would also be expecting him to use the road—the *only* road—that linked Suncheon with Songgwang Sa.

On that point, Kim would have to disappoint his adversaries. He had other plans in mind.

The day was warm already, but it would be cooler in the mountains. Kim was looking forward to the change, old memories of adolescence vying with his concentration on the task at hand. He thought again of Brother Kee and Jung Kaesong, his fellow orphan Monsin Dok. Above all else, he thought of Master Rhee, the frowning, ageless face, with eyes that plumbed the secrets of the soul.

At last, he had an opportunity to strike a blow on Rhee's behalf, avenging Tonsung Yun's betrayal of the brotherhood. He understood that Master Rhee had never countenanced revenge, but Kim was not a holy man. He thought in concrete terms, of wrongs avenged and debts repaid. If that prevented him from finding true enlightenment, he was prepared to make the sacrifice.

T'ai chi had been his life, but there were facets of the discipline's philosophy that failed, in his opinion, to allow for the irrational response of a selected adversary. Master Rhee had taught him that enlightened men proceed from understanding of their own self-interest, recognizing strength, and shaping their response accordingly. It was an adequate perspective in the normal world of business dealings, social interaction, even confrontations with an enemy whose mind was clear and rational. Unfortunately, it could have no bearing on the thought processes of a psychopath.

He found the road to Songgwang Sa and motored out of town. If there were lookouts, they would radio his progress, putting Tonsung Yun and any members of his backup team on full alert. The watchers would expect him to proceed along the only route available to vehicles, arriving at the monastery in approximately half an hour.

They were going to be disappointed.

Fifteen minutes out, he found a narrow track that left the road and lost itself among the trees, a dead end going nowhere, nearly overgrown. It suited him ideally and he parked the rental there, allowing several minutes to elapse before he satisfied himself that he had not been followed.

He had showered at the safe house, and he wore the same black outfit that had seen him in and out of Sun Min Wha's estate, a sport coat serving as his sole concession to the daylight world. He shed the jacket now, retrieved his satchel from the trunk and double-checked the Ingram, picking out four extra magazines to fill his pockets. He felt heavy with the hardware, but he tucked the Browning automatic through his belt, in back, as extra life insurance. Just in case.

He did not plan on shooting Tonsung Yun, but neither could he count on entering the monastery unopposed. The fact that he had come alone, on orders, would mean nothing to the enemy's defensive preparations. Yun would almost certainly have backup at the scene, to close the trap if nothing else.

Kim left the Ingram's other magazines behind, unwilling to proceed on the assumption he would have to fight an army. Yun was cautious and deceptive, but he also wanted *personal* revenge on Kim for ancient insults. Ultimately, he would have to make the kill himself, or all his preparations were a waste of time.

Kim slipped the Ingram's strap around his neck and left the rental car unlocked, his keys in the ignition. It would still be there when he returned. *If* he returned.

Without a backward glance, he started climbing through the trees.

"He's on his way."

The woman glared at Tonsung Yun with hatred in her eyes, apparently unmoved by the announcement from his lookout in Suncheon. She knew that Kim was coming to his death, that hers must follow, and she would have murdered Yun without a second thought if it had been within her power.

Tonsung Yun admired the focus of her anger: raw emotion channeled toward a goal, regardless of the fact that goal could never be obtained. Determination was the key to focus, and it told him something of the woman's strength that she had not surrendered to despair.

Not yet.

Yun had deposited his hostage in the master's quarters of the upper compound, moving easily through space where Master Rhee had once held court, commanding the obedience of those who served him. Tonsung Yun had been a rebel, even then, but no one had suspected him, so perfect was his mask. No one, perhaps, except the master.

Rhee had never treated him the same once Kim was gone, disgraced for his supposed betrayal of the brotherhood. The old man made it clear, in subtle ways, that Tonsung Yun would never stand beside him as his strong right hand. Instead, he had been put on hold, inheriting the dead-end jobs more commonly reserved for neophytes and humble refugees. The master answered his complaints with parables about humility and sacrifice, but Yun had recognized the truth.

His guilt was known, and he was being punished.

There was nothing in the way of solid evidence against him, nothing to support an accusation. By his very silence, Kim had strengthened Yun's position, but the old man had no need of proof. His intuition was enough, and Tonsung Yun would suffer for his crime without the privilege of mounting a defense. He would be driven out in time, unless he acted first.

Destruction of the order had been relatively simple, selling information to the government and simultaneously spreading discontent among the refugees at Songgwang Sa. Their inbred paranoia made it easy, factional disputes providing him with leverage as Yun applied the pressure with a whisper here, a rumor there. He drove his wedges deep and settled back to watch the whole thing fall apart, as tensions led to violence, violence to murder. Agents of the state had been required to act, in the defense of national security, and Tonsung Yun's reward had been the impotence of Master Rhee, his inability to save the day.

If only Kim had been around to see the old man broken by a child he despised. It would have been the final triumph, icing on the cake.

Instead, Kim would be treated to a rather different

punishment. The woman would be part of it, but in the end the climax would be just between themselves.

He caught the woman straining at her bonds and smiled. The nylon ropes had been replaced with handcuffs, anchored by a slender chain to one of the support beams in the master's quarters. She was free to move about within a six-foot radius, but Jamie was not going anywhere.

"You should feel privileged," he informed her. "You will have a ringside seat for the conclusion of our ceremony."

"I'll be watching when he kills you," she replied, pure venom in her tone.

"Such confidence. I hope you have the strength to live with disappointment."

"Go to hell."

He crouched beside her, thrust a hand beneath her skirt and touched her intimately, smiling as she stiffened, stubbornly refusing to respond. She still had courage, even in the face of death.

"You will discover, I believe, that hell is relative."

He clenched his fingers, twisting, making Jamie whimper. Tighter, and the sound became a sob. He drew his hand away before she escalated to a scream.

"All relative," he said again.

Her eyes were downcast, livid color rising in her cheeks. He chuckled, turned away and stepped outside before he raised the compact walkie-talkie.

"Anything?"

"Not yet."

"He's overdue. Be sure your people are alert."

"They know their job."

"I hope so."

Park Han Yee released the compact radio's transmitter button, scowling at the handset as he muttered, "Bastard."

He was sick and tired of being treated like an amateur, as if his years of service with the NSP and KCIA stood for nothing. He had been within an hour or two of breaking Kim Sunim, before the damned Americans had interfered, and then, before the night was out, the Company came crawling back to him for help.

In truth, he had been looking forward to the hunt, before he got his summons from the man he knew as Dae Li

Chong. It was a summons Park Han Yee could not refuse, considering the debts he owed to Chong, but he was tempted all the same. There was a chance that Chong might not expose him, after all.

There was a chance he might do worse.

Exposure could have ruined Park in the republic, but at least there would have been a chance for him to run, escape with all the payoff money he had been afraid to bank for fear of leaving paper trails. If Chong decided on a more direct and physical response, the money would be useless. Dead men could not take their hidden riches with them to the grave.

He knew Chong's reputation as a killer, having checked a number of the stories for himself, through channels. They were true; worse yet, they had been understated in the telling, leaving out a number of the graphic details he had managed to obtain from first-hand sources. Colonel Park was not a coward, but he knew when he was dealing with a madman. He did not intend to press the issue, not when he could follow orders, draw his pay, and still go home at night alive.

It had been relatively simple, signing off two men to join him on the trip to Songgwang Sa. There were reports to file, but he had covered private use of personnel with paperwork before. He was conducting sensitive surveillance of a dissident who saw himself as Chin Kyu Sung's replacement in the underground. If word of the impending action leaked somehow, it would be covered with a clever blend of truth and lies. The CIA would back him, anxious to avoid another scandal of their own.

The colonel sat down on a weathered bench, surrounded by the leafy riot of a garden gone to seed, his submachine gun resting on his knees. He raised the walkie-talkie, keyed its red transmitter button once again, and spoke a single word.

"Report."

The word came back from Number One, his lookout on the southern face of the perimeter. "All clear."

He waited, drumming nervous fingers on the barrel of his weapon, waiting for the final confirmation.

"Number Two, report!"

Dead air. He counted off five seconds, cursing underneath his breath.

"Report as ordered, Number Two!"

Again, no answer. On his feet, he quickly checked the safety on his submachine gun, making certain it was off, a live round in the chamber.

"Number One, report!"

His only answer was a hiss of static, severed by a blade of silence after something like a second and a half. Uneasy now, he slipped the walkie-talkie back inside its simulated leather holster, freeing both hands for his weapon.

Kim Sunim was overdue, Dae Chong had said as much. But what if he was actually on time, inside the monastery even now? If he had found a secret entrance to the compound, crept inside without the lookouts spotting him, he might be anywhere. The sentries were—had been?—a pair of tough professionals, and yet...

The colonel felt a sudden chill, ignoring it. He had to move at once, prevent himself from being taken as a stationary target. He considered warning Dae Li Chong and instantly dismissed the notion. If the North Korean had his radio turned on, he must be conscious of their problem. On the other hand, if Kim *had* taken out the sentries, *had* retrieved a walkie-talkie for himself, there was no point in keeping him advised of their defensive moves.

A lifetime of deception and intrigue had taught the colonel to mistrust coincidence. There was a chance two radios might fail on cue, but it defied the laws of probability. And what about the static, quickly silenced, as if Number One had been about to answer when...

Colonel Park began to circle eastward, counterclockwise, following the monastery's outer wall. He took his time, alert to shadows where an enemy might crouch in hiding, listening for telltale sounds of flight or close pursuit. Their target was a man of flesh and blood, the worse for wear since his interrogation at Remonclo. He could still be hunted, killed, like any other man.

The North Korean wanted Kim alive, but Colonel Park was not concerned about that now. He had been called to back Chong's play, but he was not required to stand and die on order. Nothing Chong had paid him heretofore would cancel Park's survival instinct. Given any chance at all, he would destroy their common enemy and make his explanations afterward.

Ahead of him, an outstretched leg protruded from the shrubbery. The boot was regulation issue and he recognized the slacks before he closed the distance, moving cautiously, his weapon poised for an immediate response to any threat.

He had discovered Number One, a slim lieutenant who had once aspired to higher rank inside the NSP. His aspirations had not saved him from the enemy who took him unaware.

Park knelt beside the dead man, feeling for a pulse, aware that he was wasting precious time. The sentry had been executed quietly, efficiently, without a telltale mark to indicate the cause of death. The coroner might find a ruptured spleen or torn aorta, possibly a hairline fracture to the skull or separation of the vertebrae. It held no interest for the colonel as he marked the dead man's weapon, on the ground beside his body.

Either Kim was armed already, or he felt no need for weapons. In his arrogance, perhaps he meant to kill them all bare-handed, as a gesture of contempt.

So much the better. Let him try his hand against an officer with combat training and experience, prepared to slaughter anything that moved. Kim might be fast and quiet, but he was not bullet-proof.

The silent, haunted monastery had become a killing ground, from which one victor might emerge alive. The colonel meant to be that victor, if he had to take out Kim Sunim and Dae Li Chong together. Yes, he thought, that might not be a bad idea.

Park thrust his dead lieutenant out of mind and went in search of Number Two.

Kim had observed the monastery for an hour before he chose a point of entry on the east perimeter. The forest crowded close against the walls on that side, and it was a simple matter to select a tree, conceal himself within its foliage, use an overhanging limb to make the drop when it was clear.

One sentry had been visible, but he was talking on the radio, which meant at least one more. It came as no surprise to Kim that Tonsung Yun would hedge his bets. In fact, he would have been surprised if Yun had come alone.

At least two sentries, then. The one Kim spotted wore a

submachine gun casually slung across his shoulder, like a martial fashion statement. He would give up precious seconds fumbling with the weapon in a sudden confrontation, time enough for Kim to take him down.

He would have liked to know the sentry's orders, whether Yun had primed his men to shoot on sight or simply cover the perimeter and keep their eyes peeled. Either way, the end result would be the same. He could not leave armed men behind him when he made his move on Tonsung Yun. The sentries had to die.

The first one never heard him coming. Kim was touching-close before the gunman recognized his danger, and by that time it was much too late. One hand across his nose and mouth, the other braced behind his skull for leverage, a simple twist to separate the vertebrae. Kim brought it back the other way—insurance—and the man was limp before he hit the ground.

Kim checked his pulse to guarantee a job well done. At one time it had bothered him, the ease with which a life was severed at the root, but he had learned to shut those feelings off and go about his business. Now, he hoped the others would be just as easy, knowing all the while that one of them, at least, would put up more resistance.

It was eerie, hunting on the grounds of Songgwang Sa, where he had passed his childhood and a major part of adolescence. There were ghosts here, lurking in the shadows, but they meant no harm. If anything, their presence gave him strength.

He found the second sentry moments later, simply following the wall until it brought him near the gates. A younger man this time, his mode of dress more casual, but the civilian clothes could not disguise his military bearing. This one kept his submachine gun in his hands, presenting the appearance of a man alert for trouble. Still, Kim noticed that he did not have his finger on the trigger. There was still a chance.

Kim used the shadow of the Buddha hall for cover, feeling totally exposed as he began the final stalk. No more than fifty feet, an easy stroll, but if the gunman's concentration drifted from the wall, if he should turn . . .

Kim did not want to use the Ingram. Even with the fat

suppressor it was far from silent, and he had to know the number of his enemies before he risked engaging them in open combat. There was Jamie to consider. And his date with Tonsung Yun.

Kim's target wore a walkie-talkie on his belt, and he had closed the gap to twenty feet before it crackled into life.

"Report."

At least one other sentry, then. A man in charge.

The gunner raised his handset, keyed the button, and replied, "All clear."

The caller spent no time on small talk.

"Number Two, report!"

Kim's target listened to the steady hiss of static, frowning as his counterpart made no response. He had no way of knowing Number Two had made his last transmission.

Anger tinged the disembodied voice. "Report as ordered, Number Two!"

He crept in closer, poised to strike immediately if the lookout turned around. Kim placed his footsteps carefully, avoiding any careless sound, but he need not have bothered. The intended target's full attention had been captured by the drama on his walkie-talkie.

"Number One, report!"

Kim launched a kick that clipped his adversary's skull, behind one ear, and pitched him forward on his face. The submachine gun slithered from his fingers, clattering across the paving stones and out of reach. Before he had a chance to scramble after it, Kim landed on the gunman's shoulders, slipping one hand underneath his chin to lock his jaws, the other adding lift and tension as he brought the head around to face him.

Weak convulsions rippled through the dying body, gone in seconds. Kim dismounted, scooping up the radio and waiting for the next command, rewarded only with a steady silence. No one tried to check on numbers three or four, which told him they did not exist. The sergeant of the guard was on his own.

Kim thought the voice had been familiar, but distortion through transmission made it difficult to recognize. It had not been the voice of Tonsung Yun, he knew that much, so there was one more sentry to eliminate before the main event. Kim

found himself a sheltered cubbyhole and settled down to
wait.

It took a little longer than expected, but he recognized
the figure scuttling across the courtyard. Colonel Park Han
Yee had shed his uniform for the occasion, and a measure of
his artificial dignity was lost in the translation. In civilian
clothes, without his weapon, Park might easily have passed
for an accountant or a salesman. Stocky, slightly overweight,
the change of clothes and strange surroundings had deprived
him of the menace he projected at Remonclo, in the torture
cells. But he was lethal, all the same.

Kim watched as Park knelt down beside the body, feeling
for a pulse. In profile, he could see the colonel sweating,
heard his muffled curse. Kim held the Ingram in his fist as he
emerged from cover.

"Park."

The colonel froze. A moment passed before he cranked
his head around to stare at Kim.

"The weapon."

Park laid down his submachine gun, lurching to his feet.
The knowledge of his own impending death was written on
his face.

"I should have killed you when I had the chance."

"You tried."

"Dae Chong is waiting for you, there." Park cocked his
head in the direction of the upper compound. "Will you kill
him?"

"Yes."

"I'm glad. If not for him, I might still be alive."

Kim stroked the Ingram's trigger, holding steady as the
colonel vaulted backward, blood exploding from his throat
and chest. He lay with arms outflung, embracing death.

Kim stooped to claim the radio and raised it to his face,
depressing the transmitter button.

"We're alone now, Yun. I'm on my way."

For nearly half an hour, since he warned his gunmen
Kim was late, Jamie's captor had been pacing like a panther
in a cage. The business with his missing sentries, on the
radio, had made him pause, but then he scowled and muttered
"Idiots!" before he went back to his pacing.

Jamie sat against the upright post where she was anchored by the chain connected to her handcuffs. She had been too long without a shower; the aroma of her body and the memory of rape combined to make her feel unclean, disgusted with herself, but she was focused on her enemy just now.

He meant to kill her, that was certain. Jamie was surprised that he had let her live this long, when he could easily have dumped her body anywhere along the road from Seoul. He had devised some plan, a means of using her to get at Kim. It was the only explanation for her own survival.

Kim was getting closer. She could almost feel his presence, and it pleased her to believe that he had killed the sentries—maybe all of them, by now. Three down, and one to go.

She tried her handcuffs one more time, relenting when she felt fresh blood upon her wrists. Houdini might have found a way to shake them off, but she would have to find another way of striking at her enemy, distracting him.

Her body would not do. He had already taken her by force, and any obvious seductive overtures would be rejected, putting him on guard. The sole alternative was conversation, and she cleared her throat, aware that one wrong word could mean her death.

"You didn't bring enough support," she said.

He turned to face her, frowning.

"What?"

"Your backup. Ten or fifteen men might do it, but with three? No way. They never had a chance."

"Such confidence."

"Where are they, if I'm wrong? You think they all decided it was nap time?"

"Park will find the others. They are all expendable, in any case."

"More bait?"

"Insurance. They were never meant to deal with Kim, unless he flaunts my orders."

"Reinforcements?" Jamie sneered. "He doesn't need them."

"More precisely, he would have some difficulty finding anyone to help him. At the moment, he is being hunted by the CIA and NSP together, not to mention the assorted comrades of my late associate, Sun Wha."

"We'll get that straightened out once he's disposed of you."

Her captor smiled. "The arrogance of an American. I hope you won't be disappointed in the death I have selected for you. If you're very lucky, we may have some private time together, first."

She felt a giddy rush of nausea and hoped it did not show. Demented by his passion for revenge, the man was grinning at her, chuckling to himself. His smug expression was immediately canceled as his walkie-talkie crackled into life, emitting a familiar voice.

"We're alone now, Yun. I'm coming."

Kim!

Her captor's face was frozen for an instant, then the cunning smile crept back. "You should be ready for your hero."

Jamie struggled to her feet, but he was faster, tripping her in such a fashion that she landed on her face. Before she had a chance to wriggle free, he grasped the collar of her blouse and ripped it backward, off her shoulders, down her arms, the few remaining buttons torn away. Another tug, and she could hear the fabric shredding, ragged cuffs remaining at her wrists as he discarded the remainder.

Kneeling in the small of Jamie's back, he drew a knife and slit her bra in back, again across the shoulder straps, and jerked it out from under her with force enough to scorch her nipples. Jamie felt the cold blade slip inside the waistband of her skirt, retreating with a whisper through the soft material, and then the weight was lifted from her spine. He caught the hem and whipped the final garment off her legs, twirling it like a matador's cape before he cast it aside.

She huddled on the earthen floor, knees drawn up to her chest, and prayed that he would not have time to rape her now.

"Much better," he announced, retreating toward the open doorway. "Let Kim see what he is fighting for."

His silhouette was blurred by tears, but Jamie saw him fold his knife and slip it in a pocket of his slacks. He kicked his shoes off, hesitated on the threshold, glancing back across one shoulder.

"If you care to watch," he said, "your chain should

almost let you reach the door. Don't be embarrassed. Kim may benefit from the incentive."

Smiling to himself, he stepped beyond her line of sight and vanished.

Tonsung Yun was waiting on the practice field when Kim arrived. He had dressed casually for the occasion, in a loose pullover shirt with denim jeans, and he was barefoot. Recognizing Kim, he cracked a smile that brought back memories of fear and anger.

"Do you plan on using that?"

He pointed toward the Ingram. Smiling.

Kim was tempted. More than thirty years of hate were bottled up inside him, rushing toward the surface now, and he could vent it all by simply shooting Yun, right here, right now. It would be simple, quick, efficient.

And it would accomplish nothing.

He set the Ingram's safety, laid the weapon down, and emptied out his bulging pockets of the extra magazines. The Browning automatic joined his other weapons on the ground. Still kneeling, Kim unlaced his shoes and slipped them off, together with his stockings. He enjoyed the feel of stone and earth beneath his feet.

"It's too bad that the old man couldn't be here." Yun removed his shirt and flexed his shoulders. "Don't you think he would have been amused? His students meeting after all these years, at Songgwang Sa? It's like a class reunion."

Kim shed his turtleneck and left it with the guns. "I think he would have been disgusted with us both."

Yun barked a bitter, grating laugh. "Not you," he said. "You were his favorite from the moment you arrived."

"Have you forgotten I was sent away?"

"To save your life. The old man must have known that I would kill you, given time. It made things simple when you offered no defense."

"The woman?"

"She is here."

Yun glanced in the direction of the master's quarters, where a pale form huddled on the floor, inside the open doorway. Naked. Kim remembered Master Rhee and used his will, his breathing, to control the sudden rage.

"You have another chance," Kim said. "To kill me."

"And I mean to take it."

In a single fluid motion, Yun attained a fighting stance. Kim followed suit and they began to circle one another on the practice field.

"I've followed your career, when possible," Yun said. "You've earned yourself a reputation."

"So have you, as Dae Li Chong."

"Was I your target?"

"No."

"Too bad. It would have been appropriate."

Without a flicker of his eyes to telegraph the move, Yun launched a kick that might have crushed Kim's jaw. Kim parried with a forearm, lunged to counterpunch, but Tonsung Yun had scuttled out of range.

Kim followed, circling, wary of a trap, ignoring signs of movement in the master's quarters. Jamie was alive, but he could not concern himself with her condition at the moment. If he was defeated, Kim knew Tonsung Yun would kill them both and relish every moment of it.

He felt the rush, this time, before it came, and he was braced for Yun's attack. The snap-kick missed him by a foot or more, and he responded with a squatting whip that dumped Yun on his backside. Rolling out of it, his enemy was flushed with anger and exertion, fighting to maintain the death's-head smile.

The stones were warm beneath Kim's feet; a cool breeze dried the perspiration on his chest and left him with a pleasant chill. He kept his guard up as he circled Tonsung Yun, but shied away from any rigid posture that would leave him open to an obvious attack. His loose, disjointed movements seemed to frustrate Yun. The cocky smile was more a grimace now.

Kim weighed his move before he made it, measuring Yun's steps, allowing for his reach. They had been circling counterclockwise, but he suddenly reversed directions, pivoting to meet his adversary with a looping kick that should have crushed his nose and cheekbones. Yun was quick enough to block it, but the effort cost him in his balance, and he staggered backward, momentarily off guard.

Kim followed through, a human whirlwind, throwing out

a second kick, a third. Yun parried both, and he was waiting for a fourth when Kim surprised him, sliding forward to engage him with a rapid double-punch.

Yun blocked the first and flinched away to stop the second blow from knocking him unconscious, but it left an angry mark upon his cheek. The impact rocked him, left him open for the kick that Kim directed toward his chest.

Instinctively, Yun caught his foot, began the twist that would have brought Kim down or snapped his ankle. Gambling on leverage and his adversary's strength, Kim rolled in the direction of the twist and kicked off with his other foot, to catch Yun in the face.

Kim landed on his hands and knees, recovered just as Yun was struggling to his feet. Yun shook his head, the movement flinging crimson droplets from his swollen, lacerated lips.

The dark man found relief from his embarrassment in action, pressing the attack with kicks and blows that drove Kim back, across the practice field. None landed with destructive force, but they prevented him from launching an offensive of his own, maintaining the initiative for Tonsung Yun. Kim knew that, given time, the pounding on his arms and thighs would wear him down, provide his adversary with the lethal opening he needed.

Risking everything, Kim dropped his guard for something like a second and a half, allowing Yun to feel the rush of triumph, act upon it in the heat of combat. Stepping close, Yun aimed a crushing blow directly at Kim's face . . . and it was all the edge Kim needed to complete his move.

He drove an elbow hard against the other's ribs, his forearm snapping up to strike Yun's cheek with hammer force. Yun staggered, flailing with his arms to ward off further blows, and Kim lashed out to catch him with a kick beneath one arm. The impact lifted Yun completely off his feet and dropped him on his side.

Kim could have killed him, then, but he delayed the finish, giving Yun another chance to rise. It took a moment, but he made it to his feet, the mocking smile forgotten in his pain.

"You learned your lessons well."

"We haven't finished yet."

"I think, perhaps, we have."

Yun palmed the *shuriken* and threw it in a single practiced motion, grimacing in pain as he put all of his remaining
strength behind the pitch. Kim saw it coming, whirling
toward his face, and brought his left hand up, reflexively, as
he began to dodge away. His palm was suddenly on fire, the
star imbedded in his flesh, one inch-long blade sunk deep
between his thumb and index finger.

Tonsung Yun retreated toward the master's quarters in
an awkward, lurching run. Kim pulled the dripping star out
of his palm and followed, missed his opportunity as Yun got
there ahead of him and ducked inside. A startled cry from
Jamie urged him on to greater speed.

He cleared the threshold in a fighting crouch and found
his adversary waiting, holding Jamie close in front of him, a
human shield. One hand was tangled in her hair, the other
held a slim stiletto at her throat. She stood on tiptoes, with
her back arched slightly, in a pose that might have been
erotic under different circumstances. The position of her
hands told Kim that they were bound behind her back.

"Come in."

Kim held his breath a moment, tried to modulate his
voice.

"You don't need her."

Across her naked shoulder, Tonsung Yun displayed a
crimson grin.

"I think *you* need her, Kim. That makes it all the
sweeter."

"And suppose you're wrong?"

A moment of prospective doubt cost Yun his smile.

"You came for her."

"I came for you."

"It doesn't matter if I kill her, then?" He gestured with
the knife, expansively, and Kim's attention focused on the
glinting blade.

"Your fight's with me. Are you reduced to killing women
now?"

"I kill my enemies, regardless of their sex."

"The Company will hunt you down."

"They're busy hunting you, as I recall. Besides, we have
an understanding."

"Oh?"

"Are you surprised? Have you forgotten why you left?"

The knife described another circle, well removed from Jamie's throat, and she was clearly conscious of the difference. Her eyes met Kim's and locked there.

"I don't think you've got the balls."

On cue, she slumped enough to reach her captor's groin, her shackled hands on target as the fingers closed and twisted. Bellowing in pain, the knife forgotten, Yun responded with a heavy blow between her shoulders, driving Jamie to her knees.

Kim used his one and only opening to hurl the *shuriken* with deadly force. It struck Yun in the chest and burrowed deep, blood spouting from the wound. In agony, Yun dropped his knife and turned away from Kim, his fingers groping for the metal star that pierced his flesh.

Kim cleared the intervening space in three long strides, and he was airborne when the snarl erupted from his lips. Both heels struck Tonsung Yun between the shoulder blades and flattened him against the wall, his impact burying the *shuriken* between his ribs.

Kim rolled away and vaulted to his feet in time to see the dark man fall, blood streaming through the fingers pressed against his chest. The *shuriken* had pierced a lung, as evidenced by bloody foam around Yun's lips.

"Remember Bangkok!"

With a final tremor, he was gone. Kim turned the dead man's pockets inside-out to find the handcuff key, releasing Jamie's wrists before he took her in his arms. She clutched him tightly, trembling as if with fever.

"Is he . . . ?"

"Yes."

"He knew you'd come."

"I'm here," Kim said. "It's almost finished, now."

Chapter 23

The problem with a Sunday, Barrett Ross decided, was that everybody went to church. That was not strictly true, of course—especially in Korea—but officials in the Land of Morning Calm had learned to emulate Americans by closing down their offices and putting life on hold, as if the real world paid attention to a calendar.

Some Sundays, Ross sought refuge in his office at the embassy, escaping from the dreary round of social obligations that were forced upon him in his role as cultural attache. Other times—this Sunday morning, for example—his attempts to do his job were sorely hampered by the trappings of religiosity. And there was something else . . .

He *knew* that Colonel Park Han Yee had not set foot inside a church for twenty years, except when he was busting ministers on charges of subversion. Park enjoyed his work, devoted countless hours of overtime to the pursuit of communists, and he invariably left a number where he could be reached in an emergency.

Except today.

Ross had been leaving messages since noon on Saturday, at the colonel's office and his home, but Park did not return his calls. The NSP had "no idea" where Park had gone or where he spent his weekends. Any vital questions could be answered by his second in command.

Ross passed on that, preferring not to brief some flunky on the details of the hunt for Kim Sunim. His bargain had been struck with Colonel Park, and he would deal with Park directly, if the bastard ever got around to picking up his messages.

There should have been some word on Kim by now, and Ross was growing more uneasy by the hour. Kim at large meant Kim pursuing questions that were better left unanswered, stirring up a hornet's nest of problems for the Company, the NSP, and all concerned. Police in Seoul already wanted him for killing Sun Min Wha and half a dozen of the mobster's bodyguards, but they were having no more luck in flushing Kim from cover than the mercenaries Ross had paid to join the hunt.

It was a risky business, issuing the orders for an execution on his own authority, when Langley had not been informed. His time was running out in that regard, as well, and Ross knew he would have to make the call that afternoon, regardless of his progress on the hunt.

He had a solid case for Ramsey, with the NSP prepared to back him up on major details, but he needed Park to put it over, and the idiot was nowhere to be found. Without supporting testimony from the locals, there might still be questions on the need to shoot Kim down on sight. Park's testimony would describe their quarry as a turncoat, fighting for the dissidents and communists in Seoul.

Kim's motives—bitterness against the South Korean government that dated from the murder of his parents, paranoid conviction that the NSP had killed Reese Holland—were believable within the context of his recent actions. Sent to tag Chin Sung, he had been captured in the act of helping Chin evade arrest. Released from custody by Ross, his mission scrubbed, Kim had refused to leave the country, roughing up a pair of contract agents in the process and embarking on a one-man war against imaginary enemies. He was a traitor and a murderer, whose trial in open court would give the Company its worst black eye in fifteen years. Elimination was the only way to go.

Ross smiled and nodded as he passed the uniformed Marines on duty at the gate. It hung together, but he could not sell the package by himself. They knew about his personal dislike for Kim at Langley; Ramsey might suspect a frame. Ross needed Park, or someone in authority at NSP, to put the frosting on the cake.

He passed another guard and raised a hand in greeting to the information officer who manned a lobby desk, directing visitors to their appointed destinations. There were seldom any visitors on Sunday, and the girl on duty—was it Sharon? Susan?—read a steamy paperback to help her pass the time. It bothered Ross that he could not recall her name, but he could always check with personnel. When he had solved his latest crisis, maybe she could help him celebrate.

His secretary did not work on Sundays, meaning Ross would have the office to himself. He crossed the waiting room and used his key for access to his private office. Ross had closed the door behind him, turned the lights on, and was moving toward his desk before he realized that he was not alone.

A subtle movement in the corner, on his blind side, and he turned to challenge the intruder. Kim Sunim had risen from the couch and shifted toward the doorway, blocking his retreat. He seemed to be unarmed, his left hand swathed in bandages.

"What are you doing here? The guards—"

"It's what I do," Kim said. "We've got some business to discuss. Sit down."

"You've hurt your hand."

"It's nothing. Just a scratch."

Ross moved around his desk and settled in the swivel chair. He cleared his throat and said, "I'm glad you've come. I've had my people looking for you."

"So I understand. The word was shoot on sight."

Ross stiffened. "You've been misinformed."

"Convince me."

"There was nothing I could do about the NSP. They want your head for helping Chin, but I believe we can negotiate with the police about Sun Wha. It's not like he was any kind of sterling citizen."

"I didn't kill Sun Wha."

"How's that?"

"I was supposed to take the fall for someone else . . . but then, you know that, don't you, Ross?"

"I beg your pardon?"

"That's a start. How long have you been dealing on the side?"

It took a moment for the chief of station to respond. "You must be cracking up." He slipped one hand beneath his desk.

"Don't bother," Kim advised him. "The alarm's been disconnected."

"Listen, Kim, I don't know where you got this wild idea—"

"The confirmation came from Tonsung Yun."

Ross seemed confused. "Who's that?"

"You called him Dae Li Chong."

The color drained from Ross's face as if someone had pulled a plug below his belt. His lips worked silently for several seconds, and he had to clear his throat again before he found his voice.

"You spoke with Chong?"

Kim took a seat directly opposite the station chief, with only Ross's desk between them. He could clear it in a single move, if necessary.

"His name was Tonsung Yun. It won't be in your files, but I became acquainted with him years before I moved to the United States. We talked about old times. He had some fascinating things to say about the Company, before I killed him."

"Ah. He's dead, then. All we have is your report of what he said."

"My word . . . and Jamie's."

"She's alive?"

"And well," he lied, remembering the way that he had found her. "Is that a disappointment, or surprise?"

A flush of angry color had returned to Ross's cheeks. "I was prepared to write her off, I'll grant you. No communique from her abductors, no demand for ransom. I had every reason to believe we'd find her dead."

"Or not at all? Whichever way you planned it with your cronies, it's a washout. Yun died talking. Jamie heard it all."

Ross snorted, a derisive sound.

"So, what? A North Korean agent fighting for his life throws out some cryptic 'revelations' naming Company officials as his co-conspirators? I'm sorry, Kim. It won't be good enough."

"It was for Ramsey."

"*What?*"

"I spoke with him this morning. He got back to the ambassador. They've canceled your alert."

"The guards downstairs?"

"They have their orders. Ramsey thought that we should have a little chat before you catch the next flight home."

"I see."

"Remember Bangkok."

"Come again?"

"It was the last thing Yun had time to say before he died. 'Remember Bangkok.' Can you, Ross?"

"I don't see any point to this discussion."

"Humor me. I'm asking you if you remember Bangkok."

"Certainly." Ross heaved a weary sigh. "I didn't check my sources thoroughly enough. I've paid for that mistake. Case closed."

"It seems to me your punishment turned out to be promotion. Others paid the tab in blood. I barely walked away, myself."

"Is that what this is all about? You nurse a grudge for thirteen years, and now you try to ruin my career? For Christ's sake, Kim, the Company reviewed that operation. You were part of the investigation. If it's slipped your mind, why don't you have your buddy Ramsey pull the files?"

"We're not discussing negligence."

"What, then?"

"Collusion and conspiracy."

"You've lost your mind."

Kim faced his adversary squarely, frowning. "I was dumb enough to write you off as one more Company incompetent. By that time, I was looking for an out, and you were handy. If I'd had my head on straight, I would have realized I hit the targets you intended all along."

His memory regurgitated grainy images of twisted bodies, lying on the thread-bare carpet in a Bangkok flat. Dead eyes, locked open, had already lost their focus on the ceiling.

". . . reason would I have?"

Kim did not need to hear his enemy repeat the question.

"Competition," he replied, without a beat of hesitation. "You were dealing, even then, but on a smaller scale. Your contact wanted to eliminate his chief competitors, and you were willing to oblige. Whip up a couple of informant interviews, conduct your own 'investigation' of the targets, and you suckered Langley for a rubber-stamp approval. When the smoke cleared, you were looking at a charge of negligence. You're lucky that it wasn't Murder One."

"You can't expect to make that stick."

"I'm not a prosecutor, Ross. I'd simply like to know what pushed you over."

"What's the difference? Greed, ambition—take your pick. How were your grades in history?"

"I passed."

"Remember Samuel Gompers? Used to run the AFL, from eighteen-something through the early 1920s."

"What's your point?"

"He was aggressive, hungry all the time. An interviewer asked him, once, to spell out what he wanted for his union. Gompers summed it up in one word: 'More.' That's all. I wanted more."

"It has a price."

"Are you collecting?"

Casually, Kim flexed his hands, the stitches in his left palm tugging at his flesh. "I'm here to get some answers," he replied.

"*He* sent you, didn't he? That cowboy bastard."

"Ramsey knows I'm here. He didn't send me."

"No, he wouldn't have to. You're a volunteer."

"Did you expect to walk?"

"Of course. Who doesn't? No one ever *really* thinks they're riding for a fall."

"Why drugs?"

"Why not? The Company has dealt with criminals before. I'm not the first, and I feel safe in saying that I will not be the last. Remember Cuba? Air America in Vietnam? The Company's been holding hands with warlords in the Golden Triangle for decades. Surely, I don't have to tell you that."

"I've heard it all. I don't believe you came in through the back door on a case."

Ross frowned. "All right. Let's say it was the easy way to get ahead. You must have some idea. I mean, the profits are obscene."

"The whole damned business is obscene."

"Semantic quibbling. Have you tried to chart the progress in our country's 'war on drugs'? The President wants pushers on death row, so naturally he slashes funding for the DEA. I mean, who's really kidding whom?"

"How much?"

Ross looked confused, his dark eyes narrowed.

"Money," Kim continued. "How much money? Was it worth it?"

"Who's to say? I have... that is, I *would* have had... enough to make retirement very comfortable. Basically, I still want more."

"For that, you sold yourself?"

"We all have prices, Kim. At least I never hurt the Company."

"Does Holland ring a bell? Or Jamie's aide—what was his name? Fitzpatrick. You were primed to burn your number two, and now you're looking at a trial that's bound to generate publicity around the world. I'd say you've done your best to trash the Company. You still may get your wish."

Ross shifted in his chair, his right hand sliding toward the top desk drawer.

"A trial? You must be joking. Ramsey won't allow it. Do you think I'm so naive that I don't know precisely why you're here?"

Ross cleared the last few inches in a lunge, his fingers wrapped around a satin-finish stainless automatic. Kim sat back and raised his eyebrows.

"You surprise me." Ross looked vaguely disappointed. "I expected something more dramatic in the way of a reaction. I suppose you plan to catch the bullets with your teeth."

"My pocket," Kim corrected.

"Ah, of course."

Kim dipped his right hand in the pocket of his sport coat, palmed the seven cartridges and rattled them in front of Ross.

"I took the liberty of emptying the magazine."

Ross squeezed the double-action trigger, rewarded by successive sharp, metallic snapping sounds.

Kim rose, his adversary shrinking back until his swivel chair collided with the wall.

"I don't intend to kill you Ross. In your position, it would be a favor, and you haven't got one coming."

"Ramsey won't allow a trial. He can't."

"That's not my problem." Kim considered it and smiled. "He might send Curt and Roger. Wouldn't that be fun?"

"I didn't put the contract out on Holland, if it matters."

"Not at all."

Ross shrugged. "Whatever. It was Chong, or. . . what was that you called him?"

"Tonsung Yun."

"He found out Holland had been digging into Sun Wha's operation, running down informants. Taking Holland down was strictly business. If you think about it, it makes sense."

"And Jamie?"

"That was out of my control. Your buddy didn't tell me what he had in mind. Somehow, I guess he figured you might try to get her back."

"He figured right."

"I'm glad," Ross said. "I know it won't make any difference, but I'm glad that she came through all right."

But had she? Kim remembered Jamie, dressed in clothes that he had stripped from one of Park's subordinates, a frightened rabbit huddled in her seat throughout the drive from Songgwang Sa to Seoul. He took a slow, deep breath and somehow managed not to leap across the desk at Barrett Ross.

The telephone began to ring. Ross jumped, was reaching for it when he caught himself.

Kim checked his watch and said, "That's Langley. Tell them how you never hurt the Company."

He turned to leave, thought better of it, and returned to drop a single cartridge on the desk.

"Your move."

He felt Ross watching as he crossed the office, closed the door behind him. Kim was on the threshold of the waiting room before he heard the muffled shot. The telephone's incessant ringing followed him downstairs.

Epilogue

Langley, Virginia

The gate man did not recognize their faces, and he left the guard house, pointedly unfastening his holster as he crossed the fifteen feet of asphalt.

"May I help you, sir?"

Kim didn't bother putting on a smile. "We have a one o'clock appointment with the D.D.O." He gave their names and saw them checked against a yellow piece of paper on the gate man's clipboard.

"I'll be needing some I.D."

Kim handed over driver's licenses and waited while the man in uniform compared their living faces with the photographs.

"All right, sir. These will be returned to you upon departure."

"Thank-you."

Fastening their I.D. to the clipboard, he retreated to his guard house, stepped inside, and flipped a switch to activate the gate. Kim drove the rented Chevy through and turned left past the guard house, rolling on until the complex loomed behind its wall of trees.

"I'm nervous," Jamie told him.

"Don't be. If he wanted anything but conversation, we'd be meeting in some cheap motel."

"You're trusting Ramsey, then?"

He smiled and said, "Not quite."

They went in black, at Ramsey's own suggestion. Jamie was concerned about another double-cross, but Kim had made it clear to Ramsey on the telephone that any "accidents" or sudden disappearances would trigger the delivery of tape cassettes to well-known hostile journalists in Washington, New York, Los Angeles, and San Francisco. The alternative—a simple cease-fire—would insure the tapes remained secure.

It was a gamble, leading with a threat, and Kim did not believe that Alex Ramsey was his enemy, but he had learned enough about the Company's duplicity to know he had to deal from strength. If Ramsey wanted peace, so much the better... but he had to understand the costs of war.

They motored past the auditorium, the "public" entrance, past the looming cliff of stone and tinted glass. Kim found a place to park, and Jamie, visibly reluctant, followed him inside.

Two men in uniform were waiting, one behind the checkpoint's desk, another standing rigid at his side. Their names were checked against another flimsy printout, faces checked against a set of Polaroids extracted from their files. The sentry satisfied himself before producing plastic badges, waiting while the new arrivals clipped them to lapels.

"Your escort will deliver you to Mr. Ramsey's office and return you when you're finished."

"If you'll follow me," the second uniform instructed, tacking on a "please" that clearly did not fit his normal disposition. On his hip, a new Beretta had replaced the standard Army-issue .45, a sign of changing times.

They did not speak inside the elevator as it took them to the seventh floor. Their escort muttered something to the guard on duty in the corridor, and they were passed along to Ramsey's office with a cursory inspection. Kim stayed close to Jamie as they reached the waiting room and were deposited inside.

Before they had a chance to state their business, Ramsey's secretary flashed a smile and told them, "You can go right in."

She buzzed them through, and Ramsey met them just inside the door, to pump their hands in greeting. "Please, sit down," he said, his attitude a careful mixture of concern and pleasure at their company. "You must be tired. I could have had some people meet your flight."

"It wasn't necessary."

As a matter of security, they had flown out of Seoul on

different airlines, Jamie stopping over briefly in Hawaii, Kim on KAL direct to San Francisco. Ramsey could have tracked them, even so, but he had sense enough to let it slide.

They settled into chairs that Kim remembered from his other visit . . . could it really be eight days ago? So much had happened that he might have been away for weeks, and yet the office had not changed.

"You both look well," the deputy director said, relaxing in his leather chair. "I half expected you to look like death warmed over, after . . . everything that's happened."

Kim resisted an instinctive urge to glance at Jamie, checking her for signs of strain. She had been alternately silent and deliberately cheerful since they met in San Francisco, passing one day there before they started East, again on separate flights.

"We're fine," she answered simply, with a reassuring note of confidence.

"I'm glad to hear it." Ramsey spent a moment frowning at his desk top. "Something comes along like this, who knows exactly what to say. I owe you one for Ross. The Company is grateful for your help. We frankly didn't have a clue."

Kim met the deputy director's gaze. "That's reassuring."

"Hey, it happens. Ross was under scrutiny for Bangkok, but it looked like he was overzealous, wet behind the ears. We didn't make him at the time, and later . . . well, I have to give the bastard credit. He was slicker than I thought."

"He had a little help."

"Your buddy from the old days?"

Nodding, Kim said, "Ross was riding for a fall whichever way it went. In time, Yun would have found himself another playmate. We just forced the issue, brought it to a head."

"You did all right. I grant you, when we sent you over there, I wasn't counting on the whole damned section being wiped." He turned to Jamie. "Are you sure I can't persuade you to remain in Seoul? We've never had a female chief of station. I suspect it's overdue."

"No thanks. I'm hanging up my cloak and dagger."

"That's a goddamned shame, if you'll excuse my language. You have more experience than anybody else I've got on tap. You understand I'm talking rank, not tokenism."

"I appreciate the offer, but I really can't accept."

"There is the matter of your clearance, the material you've handled over time."

Kim had prepared her for the Company's technique of using guilt to sway employees toward extension of their contracts. Ramsey was prepared to trot out figures on expense, the hardship he would suffer in the search for a replacement, the potential risk to national security.

"I understand the problems, sir, and I'm aware that I would still be bound by oaths of confidentiality. If you have affidavits drawn to that effect, I'll gladly sign."

"They're in the works," he answered gruffly. "Still, I hate to see you go." The deputy director turned to Kim, considering a smile and thinking better of it. "I suppose you've got your mind made up, as well? You're leaving us again?"

"You sound surprised."

The Texan shrugged. "I thought you might've felt the old excitement, just a little. Hell, we need you. Plain enough? You saved our bacon, and the DCI is well aware it's not the first time. I've been authorized to say that you can name your price, within reason."

"No sale."

"That's what I told my boss, but still, I had to try."

"I understand."

"So tell me, why'd you bother coming in? You could have told me 'no sale' on the phone."

"We have another piece of business to discuss," Kim said. "Security."

The deputy director frowned. "I think you may be getting just a little paranoid. You did us one tremendous favor, and we're grateful. We don't hunt our friends. If something changes, somewhere down the line, and one of you breaks silence, all we have to do is dust your affidavits off and throw your ass in Leavenworth for twenty years."

"It's like you said: things change. A year from now, *five* years from now, this office may be occupied by someone who considers us as liabilities. I know the charter bans domestic operations, and I also know it isn't worth the paper that it's printed on."

Kim glanced at Jamie as he spoke, and found her watching him.

"We plan to keep in touch," he said. "It's very simple.

I've already given you the gist of what we've got on tape. If either of us has an accident or turns up missing, copies will be automatically delivered to the *New York Times*, the L.A. *Times*, the *Post*, the *San Francisco Chronicle*, and two more major dailies we've decided not to name."

"You know, if we decide to kill a story, there are ways to do the job."

"The editors and writers we've selected wouldn't play. You'd have to make your case in court, and you remember how Marchetti jerked your chain."

The Texan scowled at mention of the senior Company official who had bailed out after fourteen years and gone to press with details of the CIA's covert activities. The CIA had gone to federal court in an attempt to scuttle publication, but their partial victory had been a hollow one. Publicity insured the book would be an overnight best-seller, and 168 deletions from the text were clearly marked in boldface type, allowing readers to complete the puzzle with their own imaginations.

"This really isn't necessary."

"Did I mention that we've got a line on European contacts."

Ramsey raised an open hand to signal his surrender. "What's the deal?"

"I told you. We get left alone, and no one hears the tapes."

"We're living in a violent country, Kim. We've got a murder every half an hour. Accidents are killing people off like flies. You can't blame me for everything that happens to you in the next—what? Forty years?"

"Are you religious, Ramsey?"

"Mmm?" The deputy director looked confused. "Not so you'd notice."

"That's a pity. You should really give some thought to prayer."

"I'll think about it. Are we finished?"

"I believe I have a week's pay coming."

Ramsey slid an envelope across the desk. "You'll find a little something extra in there, for the tag on Ross."

"He tagged himself."

"Whatever. We consider it a job well done."

Kim pocketed the envelope, unopened. "Now we're finished."

Ramsey walked them to the door. "I hope you'll take some time and reconsider your decision, both of you. I promise no hard feelings, if and when you change your minds."

Kim hesitated on the threshold of the deputy director's inner sanctum.

"Sorry, I can't say the same."

The duty officer retrieved their badges at the exit, and the gate man handed Kim their driver's licenses without the slightest hint of an expression on his face.

"You're doing super work," Kim told him, deadpan. "I've discussed your efforts with the seventh floor."

A cautious smile lit up the sentry's face. "Why, thank-you, sir."

"Don't mention it."

He pulled the Chevy over just before they reached the highway, opened Ramsey's envelope and pocketed his standard-issue check before he started counting thousand-dollar bills. It was a decent bonus, he decided, and he handed it to Jamie.

"Keep it."

"I don't need it," he replied. "I got my payoff at the monastery."

"I don't need it, either."

"It'll tide you over while you're looking for a job."

"What's San Francisco like this time of year?"

Kim swiveled in his seat to face her, thinking fast.

"The nights get chilly."

"Well," she said, "I guess you'll have to find some way to keep me warm."

If you enjoyed KOREA KILL, Book 1 in
THE ASIA TRILOGY by Michael Newton
You won't want to miss Book 2 in this explosive
series:

CHINA WHITE
by
Michael Newton

Turn the page for an exciting preview of CHINA
WHITE, Book 2 in
THE ASIA TRILOGY
On sale Spring 1990 wherever Bantam Books are sold.

Chapter 1

San Francisco, August 1995

The night he almost bought it, Joey Lee was sitting in the fog and waiting for a dealer known as One-nut Ma to take delivery on a load of China white.

The dealer's parents didn't name him One-nut. They had called him Thomas, and they died together in a freeway accident when he was nine years old, before they ever saw the kind of sleazy shit their only son turned out to be. An uncle on his mother's side adopted Tommy Ma and did his best to raise the boy with a respect for family, but there was nothing he could do about the wild streak that produced erratic and rebellious conduct, first at school and later on the streets.

The "One-nut" tag resulted from a bungled teenage B and E in North Beach. Tommy Ma was crawling out a window with his bag of goodies when a uniformed patrolman took him by surprise. The kid was packing heat, but he was nervous, and his shot went wild. The officer took time to aim—for Tommy's leg, he later testified, but he would only grin if anybody asked which one—and the physician at emergency receiving said he couldn't have performed a cleaner nip-and-tuck, himself. The court suspended Tommy's sentence in consideration of his loss, and One-nut started working overtime to cultivate a reputation as a cocksman, but the nickname was too colorful to die. He could have had a transplant, grafted on a Brahma bull's equipment, and he would have still been One-nut Ma.

One thing he learned along the way, aside from how to

cross his legs and keep from pulling sutures, was the mortal risk involved in burglary. It could have been some trigger-happy bastard with a twelve-gauge, just as easy, and he wouldn't have to think about the nicknames. You could call a headless body anything you want.

It was about that time, three years ago, that Tommy One-nut went for a career change and began to deal in pharmaceuticals. Less risk involved, if you observed the rules, and there was money out the ass.

"You think he called it off?"

Lee's partner, Eddie Hovis, was behind the wheel, an open package of Doritos and a thermos full of luke-warm coffee in between them, on the seat.

"He'll be here."

Eddie checked his watch, a bargain digital. "It's getting late. Somebody shoulda made a pass by now."

"Relax. No reason to believe we made their action, they don't need to make a pass. It's cool."

"You hope."

Their undercover rent-a-wreck was parked on Mission, facing the Embarcadero and a giant smudge that should have been the World Trade Center. Everything beyond the looming hulk was *terra incognita*, lost in fog. Lee figured that it had to be a righteous deal, for One-nut Ma to venture out of Chinatown, a night like this.

"It's gonna be a fucking miracle if we can even *see* his ass."

"We'll see him fine."

"I need a smoke," said Hovis, but he made no move to light the cigarette that would have given them away.

"You smoke too much."

"It's something oral." Eddie grinned, another handful of Doritos going down. "Like I was telling Meg, this afternoon, I said—"

"He's here."

They scrunched down in their seats, on instinct, even knowing Tommy One-nut couldn't see them in the dark and fog. Lee recognized the dealer by his walk—a cocky swagger—and the wide-brimmed hat he always wore, like something from the movies. He was carrying a gym bag, and it seemed to weight him down. Two hundred thousand dollars, give or take. He checked the street and ducked into the shadowed doorway of a shop, a half-block down.

They weren't concerned with busting Tommy Ma tonight. In fact, they could have hauled him in a dozen times within the past three months, but all their work so far was leading up to this. Ideally, they would watch and wait, identify the dealer's contact, trail him home. Another link toward the completion of a chain.

"They think we're jerking off, downtown."

Lee pinned his partner with a glare.

"Somebody tell you that?"

"Nobody had to tell me. You can see the way they look at you, you memtion Bobby Chan."

"We make him, I don't give a shit how anybody looks. He'll still be ours."

"What's this?"

A dark sedan was turning left, off Steuart, southbound onto Mission, headlights blinding in the fog before the driver cut them off and pulled in to the curb across from Tommy Ma, his parking lights like yellow eyes.

"It's showtime."

Tommy One-nut swaggered into view and checked the street each way before he crossed, just like they taught the kids in school. He made it to the center stripe, half way, before the muzzle flash of semiautomatic fire erupted from the driver's side of the sedan, like strobe lights in the fog. From where they sat, the narcs could see him jerking, spinning like a poor man's Michael Jackson to the music of the guns.

And they were stunned, both groping for their weapons in the darkness, Eddie with his left hand on the latch and spitting out Doritos as he muttered, "Holy shit." They never saw the second car approaching from behind them, running dark, until it pulled abreast.

By that time, Eddie had his door wide open, nothing in the way to save him when the gunners opened fire. Two submachine guns, they decided later. Maybe Uzis, maybe not. They raked the car in tandem, punching abstract patterns in one side and out the other, Eddie taking most of it and screaming in a voice that didn't sound like his, at all.

Lee's holster must have worked around behind him,

somehow, but he had the automatic now, and he was thumbing off the safety when a bullet drilled his shoulder with the impact of a hammer stroke. It drove him backward, and he lost the pistol down between his knees, his good hand clawing at the inside handle. Anything to get away from there, as someone kicked him in the ribs, and once more at the hip.

Some kind of moisture on his face—had it been raining? —and he registered that some of it was Eddy, some of it his own, before he found the latch and threw his weight against the door.

Dead weight.

Another solid blow, beneath one arm, and there was still no pain. Incredible. He should have been on fire.

The door gave way and spilled him out, a flaccid, dying thing.

He seemed to fall forever, into darkness streaked by blood-red shooting stars.